SOME MEN ARE B

Hellbent on arranging a pardon for her exiled cousin, Madolyn Carver will stop at nothing to achieve her aim, even if it means seducing the mysterious Earl of Swafford. So what if he's known as "The Beast" and is immensely powerful? Plucky Maddie isn't frightened off easily.

Returned home after too long abroad, The Beast also has a mission. He must remove his younger brother and heir to the vast Swafford estate from the clutches of a most unsuitable woman. When a misunderstanding leads him to mistake Maddie for his brother's cunning mistress, he takes her captive under the guise of The Beast's manservant. Now she can no longer be a threat to his misguided brother's future, or so he thinks. And surely, The Beast's infamous iron will can resist the charms of one particularly disobedient, witty, intriguingly stubborn young woman.

But there is a far greater danger. A deadly assassin has come to the Swafford estate, and The Beast's fear of falling in love might just be his downfall. Maddie, the woman he won't trust, is the one innocent soul who can save his life--and his heart.

A Lyrical Press Historical Romance | Lyrical Press Vintage

Seducing the Beast

Jayne Fresina

Lyrical Press, Inc.
New Jersey

Lyrical Press, Incorporated

Seducing the Beast
ISBN: 9781616504342
Copyright © 2011, Jayne Fresina
Edited by Tiffany Maxwell
Book design by Lyrical Press, Inc.
Cover Art by Renee Rocco
Line: Vintage

Lyrical Press, Incorporated
http://www.lyricalpress.com

All Rights Are Reserved. No part of this book may be used or reproduced in any manner whatsoever without written permission, except in the case of brief quotations embodied in critical articles and reviews. The unauthorized reproduction or distribution of this copyrighted work is illegal. No part of this book may be scanned, uploaded or distributed via the Internet or any other means, electronic or print, without the publisher's permission.

PUBLISHER'S NOTE:

This book is a work of fiction. The names, characters, places, and incidents are products of the writer's imagination or have been used fictitiously and are not to be construed as real. Any resemblance to persons, living or dead, actual events, locale or organizations is entirely coincidental.

The publisher does not have any control over and does not assume any responsibility for author or third-party Web sites or their content.

Published in the United States of America by Lyrical Press, Incorporated
First Lyrical Press, Inc digital publication: August 2011
First Lyrical Press, Inc print publication: January 2013

Dedication

To our mum.

Acknowledgements

I would like to thank Renee and the folks at Lyrical Press for being brave enough to take me on as an author, and my terrific editor Tiffany Maxwell, for keeping me sane throughout the process. I would also like to thank my husband for his patient support; my sisters for occasionally slapping me down to size, and the good friends who volunteered to be my very first readers -- Nancy, Stephen, Annie, Jill and Cate. Without all of you I would never have persevered. Thank you.

To Lisa
Best wishes
Jayne Keanu

Chapter 1
London 1563

Madolyn Carver had decided God must be female. Although shocking, subversive ideas were not uncommon in her head, this one she kept to herself, for once. And the reason for her outrageous conclusion? Breasts.

Clearly, a man would have given himself breasts, since he was so fond of the objects and spent most of his life--from infancy to dotage--in their pursuit. However, not only was this habit predictable among the male species, it was most propitious for Madolyn, who had a certain fellow to seduce today, and a bosom to assist her. Indeed she had an excess, about to be put to good use, if only it would temporarily behave itself.

Hands gripping the bedpost in a murderous throttle, she groaned. "Make haste, for the love of Saint Pete. How much longer will it take?"

"Patience, Maddie!" her sister exclaimed, tugging on the laces of a bodice several inches too small. "I go as fast as I can. Breathe in!"

Apparently her sister thought her lungs were in her bosom. "Grace, there is no more '*in*' to be had."

"There must be."

Madolyn replied, with as much solemnity as the scant wisps of air at her disposal might allow, "Sorry, sister. The more you squeeze one part of me, another falls out." It seemed an awful lot to go through when she fully expected to be undressed again quite soon. Not that she could tell her sister.

"Just a half inch to go."

"Oh, farewell cruel life! It may have been tragically short, and I'll die a maid, but don't weep for me, Grace. Bring flowers to my grave and take comfort knowing I died in the worthy pursuit of a narrow body."

Her sister shook her head. "With your flare for the dramaticals Maddie, 'tis a pity women cannot act in plays. There, now I think 'tis in-- or as much of it as possible. I suggest you accept no more of Cousin

Eustacia's cast-off gowns. There is much less of her than there is of you."

Releasing the much-abused bedpost, Madolyn whirled around, impatient to examine her reflection in the looking-glass.

Over her left shoulder, her sister's countenance tightened with reproof. "I sincerely hope, Maddie, you're not thinking of wearing that gown in public."

With every stunted breath, a little more plump flesh popped out under the strain, and the overall effect wouldn't look out of place in a Southwark bawdy house.

"Why ever not?"

"Because you'll take someone's eyes out with...all that."

She snorted with laughter, ruthlessly disposing of her sister's warnings, for while Grace was the dutiful sibling, the epitome of goodness, Madolyn, having barely survived an unruly childhood, was dedicated in the pursuit of an equally mutinous adulthood. People expected it of her and she hated to disappoint.

Long, soot-black curls swept back over her shoulders, she thoughtfully considered that bosom, now directly under her chin, like two squabbling, precocious, bald-headed babes, and returned to her previous holy musings, concluding that if God was a man he would also have given himself a womb and left no need for woman at all. No, no, God was definitely female and man simply an afterthought when She suddenly realized there was no challenging entertainment for women without them.

"This burden," Grace proclaimed crisply of her sister's wayward appendage, "is the Good Lord's way of punishing you for an ill-spent youth." Patting down her own demure shape, discreetly hidden by a lace partlet and ruff, she added with a sniff, "All those hours spent in our barn, stabbing a carving knife at a hanging sack of straw..."

"Cousin Nathaniel's lessons on how to defend myself."

"Were an utter waste of time. Lessons with needle and thread would have served you better. You favored so many unladylike pursuits, I daresay the Almighty had to do something to remind you of your place and purpose in life."

Nothing provoked Madolyn's temper with as much frequency as her elder sister's lectures, but today she found no retort suitably satisfying and supposed, with her lungs so severely constricted, she was too stupid to think of a witty retort. It was effort enough to roll her eyes.

This, however, was no time to fret over a little thing like breathing. If all went as planned, she would soon have those laces undone again in any case.

Or the Earl of Swafford would.

Hopefully he liked the look of her. She'd done her best to arrange her finest feature to its advantage, front and center, but she was not blind to her many imperfections.

Regretfully eyeing her reflection, she remembered what their Cousin Eustacia, previous inhabitant of this fine damask gown, often said. *A silk purse cannot be made from a sow's ear.* Here was proof. She wondered if she was truly so short, or if it was simply a cruel trick of the mirror. Until they'd come to stay with their cousin, she never saw her full reflection.

It was disheartening to say the least.

"Papa would never let you out of the house in that gown," her sister cautioned. "It's indecent. I fear Cousin Eustacia's lifestyle is a bad influence on you."

"As long as you pray for me, dear sister, I'm sure I'll be safe from the temptations thrust upon me in this wicked town," Maddie coyly assured her. "Besides, do trials like these not make us stronger?" She paused. "Don't purse your lips, Grace, it makes little pin-tucks around your mouth and Eustacia says frowning encourages wrinkles. We can't have you getting old and haggard, since you're the family's greatest hope of a good match."

Grace began smoothing her forehead with one hand, before apparently remembering how she always insisted she was neither vain, nor concerned at being twenty-five and unwed. "Watching you fall head first into yet another jar of pickles, Maddie Carver, 'tis no wonder I begin to look frayed."

Disapproving of adventure, especially her younger sister's brand of diablerie, Grace claimed to get all the excitement she required from poetry and needlework, but she had lately caught the eye of a very fine gentleman who professed himself ardently in love and had courted her for almost a month. She was unusually jittery because of it, and Madolyn was delighted at least one of her missions in London--the getting of a husband for Grace--progressed smoothly. All that remained was to secure a pardon for their exiled cousin Nathaniel. This mission she embarked upon now.

The mysterious Earl of Swafford, by all accounts a very powerful man and the only soul who might save Nathaniel, was about to be seduced. Thoroughly. Maddie would devote every scrap of her energy to the cause.

Possessing no valuable trinket with which to bribe the earl, no silver cup or cameo ring to slip into his hands, instead she made do with what God gave her. Despicable as the means might be, the ends would surely justify them and, as Cousin Nathaniel himself would say, grand principles and scruples were for those who could afford them.

Grace would be appalled, lecturing her on the sainted virtue which must be saved, but Madolyn saw no cause for it in her case. She'd lost her childhood sweetheart two years ago and deeply regretted not giving herself to him when she'd had the chance. Furthermore, she was unlikely to make a good marriage now, for with her uncurbed tongue and penchant for doing exactly as she pleased, no other man--sober--considered her wifely material. All considered, maidenhood was, in her opinion, a vastly overrated commodity. Better use it now, than throw it away out of sheer desperation for excitement at the hands of some sweaty youth, or the village carpenter, a lusty, eager fellow who, whenever in his cups, declared himself in love with her.

Scrumpy cider, she mused wryly, the great beautifier. If only she had a jug to aid her seduction today.

Usually, she depended on her tongue to argue a cause, but Grace assured her she would get herself arrested if she dashed around London expressing opinions, thus she resorted to these desperate measures of negotiation. No one was ever arrested for "feminine wiles". Or were they? Now an itch began, somewhere under her corset. Running to the carved bedpost, she wriggled her back against it, cursing under her breath, while Grace looked on in bemusement, exclaiming she must have fleas.

"Or else you're up to no good," she added. "That nervous itch is always a sign."

Maddie protested her innocence, while frantically rubbing a new shine into the ridges of the old bedpost.

New to her, seduction sat awkwardly on her shoulders, but her course was set, nothing would stand in her way. Her family didn't call her "Maddie the Merciless" for naught.

And so what if folk referred to the Earl of Swafford as "The Beast"?

It could be a term of endearment.

* * * *

Portsmouth--two days earlier

Huddled within the glowing embrace of an inglenook hearth, the two men spoke rarely, but their silence was not the awkward discomfort of strangers. They were good friends, their relationship forged recently in genuine respect and admiration, despite a shared reticence to make new acquaintances. One being a generation older than the other, anyone looking on might mistake them for father and son, yet they came from two different worlds, and the fact they shared anything in common would surprise a great many folk who knew either man.

The younger of the two was absorbed in deep, dismal thoughts. He felt his companion waiting patiently, poised to give comfort and advice whenever needed, but Griff, as he called himself today, couldn't find the words to share this problem, even with his friend. It was customary to swallow his troubles and deal with them alone; a hard habit to break.

Captain Carver, a sun-browned fellow with whitened hair and a few weathered scars, peered at him with piercing blue eyes above a second mug of ale. "Bad tidings?" He nodded at the folded missive on the table between them. Its contents, once read at speed, had been angrily set aside, the parchment reduced to lowly service under the younger man's mug of ale. "Anything I can do to help, Griff?"

He managed a slight grimace. "'Tis my duty, Captain. I'm never done with it."

"I hear your master the Earl of Swafford is a notoriously ill-tempered fellow, a hard man to please. What's his latest trouble?"

Griff hesitated. He slowly rubbed the bristles of his chin with one hand, his focus trained on the streaks of amber firelight gilding his pewter tankard. "The earl's brother is embroiled in an affair with yet another unsuitable wench."

"Ah. The earl does not approve?"

Nodding curtly, Griff held his lips taut. Like a heavy threat of thunder in the air, his formidable size and aura of barely-stifled discontent filled that small tavern. Overt physical strength, conspicuous with every gesture, was so potent and volatile that the sudden, innocent motion of reaching for his ale pricked several men nearby into a twitch. "Gabriel Mallory falls in love and out again, four times annually," he growled. "Consequently, with each change of season he rediscovers the pain of a broken heart. The earl tries to save him from it. Sometimes I wonder if 'tis worth the trouble."

"Perhaps young Mallory doesn't want to be saved."

"Or else he deliberately causes his brother anguish," Griff snapped. "He certainly chose a woman of scarlet hue this time." Aware of the captain's cool gaze searching his face, he struggled to smooth the frown he knew lurked there, but it was too deeply ingrained. Anxious to escape his companion's steady, keen perusal, he raised his tankard, closed his eyes and drank. Cheap ale tasted remarkably good, he mused, when one was thirsty and in a foul temper. "I leave for London at once," he said, the idea bringing him as much joy as a wasp down his breeches.

"'Tis a pity. If you might delay another day or two, until I conclude my business here, we could travel together. I'm to collect my daughters there and bring them home to Norfolk."

Staring gloomily into the distance, he barely heard the captain. Whenever his friend talked proudly of those little girls, Griff adopted the least surly expression he could muster, while his mind slipped sideways to ponder more important matters. His only interest in women of any shape, size, or age, was to know where they skulked in wait, so they might be avoided.

"I bring gifts for them both, but my youngest daughter, Madolyn, is a difficult wench," the captain rambled on. "Never know what she might like. Now, Grace, the eldest--she's a good girl--easily content with a bolt of fine cloth or a pretty bauble. Not Maddie though. She asked me to bring her a Spanish rose, but 'tis not the sort of thing I can bring her over the sea is it? I try to explain to her--they'd be dead before I got home." He stopped, looking at Griff, realizing the young man's mind floated elsewhere. "A penny for your thoughts, lad."

"I muse, captain, on how otherwise sane men let their codpiece rule their head." He gestured with a nod toward the stained letter on the table between them. "I'd rather keep a mangy hound dog than a wench for company."

The captain laughed. Reaching over, he laid a hand on his shoulder. "Many years ago, I might have said the same. Then I met my wife and she put paid to that."

Glancing down again at the stained parchment, Griff's eyelids flickered wearily, for the great, lumbering weight of those burdens pressing on his shoulders felt far heavier than the comforting reassurance of the captain's work-scored hand. "I'll never let any woman get the better of me."

"One day, some mischievous wench will come alongside in a sinking vessel, adrift in her own jiggery pokery, and you'll feel obliged to save her, as I once did."

"I think not."

"And when the day comes, we'll share another ale together."

Adamant he was above the folly of chasing females, Griff stated firmly, "Women are like pomegranates--too many pips and not nearly enough sweetness to recompense. If ever I'm tempted by such troublesome fruit, I'll gladly lay down coin for all the ale you can drink, captain."

The two men shook upon it.

He entertained no fear of losing his wager. He was, after all, Lord Griffyn Mallory, Earl of Swafford, The Beast. Always right, and accustomed to getting his own way.

CHAPTER 2

"Move your rancid, worm-holed head out of my view, you pustulous, stinking wretch!"

In the ruckus no one heard her. The fellow to whom she addressed this tirade kept his back turned, refusing to apologize for having trampled her like muck under his feet. Now, shoving her ruthlessly aside, he won a coveted spot at the very front of the throng and, smug in this victory, stoically ignored her pokes.

Despite all attempts to remember ladylike manners, Maddie lost her temper so far she wouldn't recognize it again if it ran up to bite her. Time was of the essence and she was in a desperate mood. Temporarily under the lax guardianship of her widowed cousin Eustacia, and with her father away at sea, she made the most of her unusual freedom and these last days in London. Their father could arrive any day and hurry his daughters home to Norfolk, in which case, this would be her last chance to see the Earl.

Very soon Queen Elizabeth and her courtiers would pass en route to Whitehall, and all these humble folk lining the street, crammed in around leaning houses and shop fronts, hoped to win a glimpse of her, perhaps even catch her eye in return. It was every man and woman for themselves. As the writhing mass of sweating humanity seethed and swelled, Madolyn covered her nose with the letter of petition in her hands, momentarily overcome by the stench. Jostled from side to side like the runt of the litter, almost knocked off her feet, she cursed again at the man blocking her view, before resuming her assault against the glowing red flaps on either side of his head.

A guard at the edge of the crowd looked over his shoulder and studied her for a moment. Dismissive, he turned away again.

* * * *

The Earl of Swafford ploughed swiftly through the scrum with excessive use of elbow. Having no patience for the obsequious fawning of courtiers, rather than join the noble procession, he chose this anonymous route among the rough and rowdy, sparing no one more than the briefest of glances. Until he heard her.

"Odious, maggoty villain! Look what you did to my gown with your jiggery pokery. This is very costly, branched damask, you rotten, poxy cur!"

Astonished, Griff watched the short, dark haired creature, as she leapt up to slap her victim's ear between each curse. No one seemed in control of her and he had no tolerance for unguarded wenches. They were, in his opinion, a danger to themselves and everyone around them.

Caught up in their own business, the crowd paid her no more heed than they would a minor irritant in the corner of their eye, but for some inconvenient and inexplicable reason, he found his own gaze rooted upon that small, noisy, bouncing disturbance. The long black curls, uncovered and left loose, suggested she was a young, unwed maid. The gaudy scarlet gown and brazen attitude suggested otherwise. Whatever she was, she displayed a surplus of dangerous energy, not to mention a reckless disregard for her own safety.

While he weighed the option of not getting involved, the crowd surged to one side; the woman lost her footing and, with another ribald curse, disappeared from view. A creature that size could be trampled by the mob, and even the Earl of Swafford was occasionally obliged to be gallant--though he'd never admit it to a living soul. Thrusting his way forward, he came to where she knelt in her crumpled, foot-printed skirt and offered one hand, fluttering his fingers in an impatient gesture, showing how he put himself out for her.

She looked up, surly, frustrated, not in the least thankful. Her eyes were hot and blue as an unspoiled August sky, her lips still complaining. The gown about which she'd expressed such pride, stretched beyond capacity by a bountiful bosom, expanded further with each indignant breath.

Incredibly, it seemed she would refuse the assistance he deigned to offer, so before she crawled away, he leaned down, swept his hands under her arms and scooped her upright in one swift motion. No one interfered as he apprehended her, no one claimed ownership of the mouthy, voluptuous wench. A lofty, cumbersome fellow with shoulders that did credit to any Tudor doorframe worth its wood grain, his sheer size warned off potential rivals.

"God's Teeth! Who gave you the right to manhandle me? Poxy, presumptuous..." She shot him full of arrows in the form of fulsome oaths one might expect from the mouth of a drunken sailor.

Impervious to insult--accustomed to it--he held her a good distance off the ground, wanting a closer look at this anomaly, wondering at her untended state. Why did no man step forward to keep her in order?

Suddenly ceasing her complaints, she took advantage of his considerable height, using his frame like a mounting block to press herself higher still, consequently kneeing him in the belly. Struggling to maintain his footing, Griff's protests met the warm, sweet-scented curves of her plump bosom and were immediately muffled, both in execution and thought. As for the folk around them, they ignored this unseemly behavior. Simply because he now held her in his arms, he supposed they considered her in his charge, therefore his to reprimand. Burdened with the sudden responsibility, Griff wasn't sure what to do with her; he'd never known anything quite like this, but his mind was open and curious when it came to new discoveries in flora and fauna. At least, this was the excuse he gave for his inertia.

Now with a good view of the approaching procession, the resourceful wench writhed and wriggled, holding on by his ears and alternately, his nose. "I seek the Earl of Swafford. Do you see him?"

Startled out of his drowsy thoughts, he almost dropped her. He felt the excitement trembling through her, could even hear her heartbeat leaping like a spring coney as she draped herself around his shoulders. Aware he should be enraged by her behavior, instead he struggled for several breaths, fighting the rare urge to laugh.

Finally he managed a hoarse, "Yes, there he is--the Earl of Swafford. Did you not see?"

"Where?"

"The ancient fellow with the ear trumpet," he grunted, shifting his shoulder under her weight. "There--with the hump and the limp. And the magnificent wart. Ah, he dropped his wooden teeth and it seems a dog ran off with them, poor, bent old wretch. You missed him. What a pity."

With a frustrated gasp, she fought her way back down the length of his body, until he felt considerably molested, slightly breathless, and perversely intrigued. "What business could a little thing like you have with the old Earl of Swafford?"

"Something most important."

"Hmm?"

Trying to get around him now, his rangy form blocking her view and her progress, she muttered a resentful explanation. "Seduction."

He must have misheard, surely.

Someone knocked against her and she stumbled again. He granted the clumsy intruder a fierce, contemptuous scowl over her curly head. No need for words, one solitary glare of Swafford wrath was enough to wring a stammered apology from the other man, and then at last a space cleared around them. Not that she thanked him for it. "Unhand me at once, man," the ungrateful chit commanded breathlessly.

He hadn't realized he still had her in his arms, precisely where she shouldn't be.

Tempting, very; trouble, definitely.

"Excuse me, madam," he grumbled. "I thought you a lady in need of rescue, now I see I was mistaken. You are, in fact, a strumpet in need of a scold's bridle."

Her eyes widened, brows arched high. Now he counted three freckles on the bridge of her nose--a rarity, since many women painted their faces with a thick white concoction, often to mask the scars of smallpox. Her complexion was colored only by the air itself, and her emotions. He stared at her lips. They were maidenly pink, full, and now damp as she passed the tip of her tongue over the lower and then the upper in a quick, irritable fashion. A deceptively innocent-looking mouth. He suspected it could also be deadly, especially in proximity to such a pretty bosom. The eyes were stunning. Thickly lashed, wide and an utterly beguiling blue, they drew him in until he thought he might do something scandalous and wicked. And he suspected she would not object. Neither would he regret it.

Despite the inherent danger, he stared into those stormy, sea-blue whorls, determined to issue a warning. She did not blink. There was no retreat.

Slowly relinquishing his grip, he muttered, "*Mais vous etes tres beau et si je n'etais pas un camarade prudent, je vous prendais a la maison avec moi.*" She would be ignorant of what he said, of course, and having got the idea off his chest, he moved away with his customary trampling.

He had never looked twice at any woman. It took every ounce of his willpower not to look again at that one.

* * * *

Good thing he took himself out of her reach before she could kick him in the kneecaps. So he thought her lovely, and if he were not such a prudent fellow, he would take her home with him. Would he indeed? His assumption that she wouldn't understand French annoyed her more than the suggestive words themselves. Of course, he couldn't know about their rather unconventional upbringing, how their mother believed in a well-rounded education, providing her daughters with every opportunity to learn--at least, as much as could be afforded. Their last tutor, sadly, fell in love with Grace, obliging Maddie to chase him off with the wood axe because he was too old, had sausage fingers and stank of onions. Thus ended their formal education. After that, she'd taught herself with the books her father and cousin brought home from their travels. None of this could her lonely-eyed stranger be expected to know.

Although busy with an important mission, she spared a few moments to watch the tall, scruffy, vexing fellow sail away through the crowd. Who the devil did he think he was, the blasted Earl of Swafford? Part of her wanted him to look back again, part of her wanted him to fall on his conceited face. Her head spun, and wicked pixies raced up and down her spine in little wooden clogs. Perhaps she could blame it on the tantalizing promise in his strong hands, protective yet gentle, guarding her from the surging crowd. Not conventionally handsome, he exuded a powerful maleness, unapologetic, unadorned, unperfumed. Definitely untamed.

When he stared into her eyes as if he meant to frighten her, Maddie saw a warm glimmer of gold, tentatively sparking through the darkness. Little secrets buried. Treasure, she sensed, he didn't want anyone to see.

Now he walked away, she suddenly hungered for a marchpane tart, which along with her other sweet favorites, she'd sadly given up for Lent. *Concentrate Maddie, you're here for one reason only, remember?*

Letter of petition clutched in one hand, she dropped to her knees again, praying no other foolish windbag puffed up with his own importance would try to "rescue" her, and crawled through the swaying forest of legs and skirts. She'd been in barns and pigsties that smelled sweeter, but Madolyn was no meek, fading lily. Desperate measures were required, and she, accustomed to fighting for good causes, understood the necessary sacrifice.

Her sister would lecture her, "Maddie, you cannot cure the world of every ill and injustice. You cannot save every injured soul." Madolyn, however, couldn't rest if she thought she left anything undone which might be fixed and, although folk seldom appreciated her efforts on their behalf, she fought for the downtrodden and abused as if her life depended on it. And she would do anything for her cousin.

Nathaniel was a major constellation in her sky, a bright, glorious figure formed from a cluster of stars, against whom all other men, except her father, paled in comparison. Abandoned by his own, unwed parents, he was raised in their home, as dear as any son and brother. Unable to bear the thought of never seeing him again, Maddie wouldn't let propriety stand in the way of delivering this petition for his pardon.

The crowd fell respectfully silent, so she knew the queen must be near. Aha! Just a few inches more. She almost made it to the edge of the crowd, when a foot stepped back unexpectedly, the heel pressing down hard on her knuckles. Maddie's subsequent howl caught the attention of a courtier walking behind the queen. Seizing her chance, she scrambled to her feet, only to be blocked in by two guards with crossed pikes. The royal procession moved on, but the courtier remained, signaling for the guards to release her.

"Please, sir." She kept her lashes meekly lowered. "'Tis a petition for the pardon of Captain Nathaniel Downing, falsely accused of piracy. I'm told the Earl of Swafford has her majesty's ear in this matter."

Perhaps, she thought eagerly, another courtier might take her petition to the earl, since she'd missed her chance. Alas, nothing would go as planned today. Under the guise of leaning down and taking her letter, the courtier's gloved finger brushed her wrist and he pressed a soft, sly suggestion to her ear. Lifting her gaze, she recognized Lord Henry Jessop, who recently paid court to her sister. Although preceded by a somewhat hasty romance, his proposal was expected any day--at least, Madolyn had decided it should be--and all that remained was to get their father's approval when he returned from sea. But the words Lord Jessop now whispered in her ear were not arranged in the fancy poetry he used to court her sister; they formed a suggestion, in base language, of the sort he might use to any sixpenny whore in a dockside bawdy house. He looked at her face only briefly, then at her bosom and lastly at the letter. His gaze returned almost immediately to the second item, where it stayed.

"We'll discuss this matter of yours, wench." His nostrils flared. "You may convince me of your case in defense of Captain Downing. Although I'm a *rigid* fellow, a persuasive tongue and a comely pair of lips working efficiently together may win me over."

She replied in outrage. "Sir, I believe you would not want my sharp teeth in such close proximity to the meager, dangly collection of sundry objects between your legs."

He blanched. "Very well," he said, swinging his mantle with as much hauteur as he could scrabble into place. "Find another to take your petition. Though if the Earl of Swafford has her majesty's ear on the matter, I advise you to abandon your case. The Beast is never swayed."

Her heart sank. Another bubble of hope popped. Now she had more to fret over--her pure-hearted sister wasted her love on that blackguard Jessop, who apparently didn't think of her unless she was immediately in his sights. Instead, he looked to prey upon any other woman for a casual tumble. How could she possibly tell Grace without breaking her tender heart?

Fuming, Maddie declared, "I heartily despise London. And all the men in it. Especially 'noble' men." As the crowd dispersed and no one paid her any attention, she added loudly, "The next one who encounters me will bear the full brunt of my wrath, make no mistake."

Noticing the lowering angle of the sun, she realized it was getting late. She would have to find a bargeman to take her down river back to Cousin Eustacia's house, before her sister sent someone to find her. She doubted other great adventurers on important missions suffered so many obstacles and setbacks. Clearly she was being tested. Good. She was in the mood for a scrap.

* * * *

Entering the queen's privy chamber, Griff managed a low bow, showing only a little stiffness and perhaps slight irritability at being summoned when burdened with so many other things on his mind. The herald was still announcing his name, when he began the upward swing of his rusty bow and took a brisk, disdainful glance around the chamber. He'd been told before that his gaze, at its kindest, was forbidding. At its cruelest, it might be called damning. Since this assessment had come from his brother, he paid it little heed. He had no time to waste worrying what people thought of his looks. Now, however, he was reminded of his brother's comment, when the courtiers present shrank into a tighter knot, like a bunch of grapes left out too long in frosty weather.

A horse, somewhere below in the stables, stamped and whinnied in its stall. In the distance, a dog howled.

Someone dropped a pin and it was heard.

He approached the queen, lowering to one knee.

"Swafford, you are late! We began to think you found some other lady on which to dance attendance." She offered her hand for his kiss, which was cold, hard, and quick.

"I came as soon as I could. The journey home was long and I have, this very hour, arrived in London, Majesty."

She only teased him about being late. He was actually very prompt, as always. "If only you smiled a little more, Swafford," she muttered. "Grim as you are, you terrify our ladies. We think one of them behind us now suffers palpitations that will shortly send her to the floor in a dead faint."

He raised an eyebrow. "Thank you, majesty."

"It was not a compliment, Swafford! You frighten our maids to such a degree and quarrel with our gentlemen so often, it is better simply to send you off abroad to terrify foreigners, instead of keep you here at court."

That odd little thing he'd just encountered, who'd proclaimed, quite unabashedly, that she meant to seduce him...was that usual behavior for a seductress? Did they often run wild, declaring their intentions to anyone they met?

Was that one of her curls on his sleeve?

"Swafford! Are you ill?"

"No, majesty." But he felt feverish. The stray wench may have slipped poison in his ear. With far more enemies than friends, he was no stranger to attacks against his life. It was one of the reasons why he always traveled incognito, dressing plainly.

"Swafford?"

Seduce him indeed! Ha! He looked up. "Majesty?"

Her eyes narrowed. "We said it is best to send you abroad to terrify foreigners, instead of keep you here at court."

"I'm glad to go wherever I'm bid, Majesty."

She gestured impatiently and he rose from his knee. "The point being, Swafford, you are our dear old friend and we would much rather keep you here. We have missed you these past two years."

He frowned. "Ah."

"So please, do make an effort to smile."

Instead he winced. "Majesty, I fear this is the unfortunate shape of my face. Any great change requires more strength than a man my age possesses."

She shook her head, seemingly bemused. "We are glad to have you back, Swafford, dour face not withstanding. You must be delighted to see home again after so long away. You will have many affairs to put in order."

"Indeed, there are always matters of the estate to tend."

"And of your brother."

Of course, news of his brother's latest escapade with Lady Eustacia Shelton, also known as the notorious "Scarlet Widow", probably festered all over London by now. No matter, he'd put a stop to the affair, now he'd returned.

"Swafford! You're scowling again!"

"Forgive me, majesty." In his peripheral vision, a fashionable cluster of gentlemen watched and whispered, among them Robert Dudley, a favorite of the queen's and a great braggart, but apparently a "charming" fellow whose laughing presence she could not do without. "I cannot smile without due cause," he said sharply. "When *I* smile, majesty, you might trust it's genuine."

"We must be grateful for your stern face then, that dull countenance you wear."

"Indeed, majesty. I will always serve you with honesty and devotion. A merry expression is only skin deep." As he and the queen passed that small group of favored courtiers, he caught their sly whispers.

"What the Beast requires is a good tumble in the hay."

"I hear he's incapable."

"It's why his wife left him. She says he never could…"

"She enjoys the wealth and title, if not his bed."

The laughter slithered from their mouths with the hiss of a serpent's tongue. No one watching his face would suspect he heard the insults, but out of their sight, deep inside, in that dark, cold vault where he remained a gawky, stammering seventeen year-old boy forced into a marriage of duty, he withered away a little more. In private. The soaring humiliation of his marriage was a matter he discussed with no one. To others it might be a tale of beauty and the beast, him being the latter, of course. They didn't know the cruel and spiteful woman behind that perfect mask.

The queen slid her hand under his rigid arm. "Walk with us in the garden. What news from Phillip of Spain?"

"He sends his warm regards and adoration, majesty," he replied. "Make of that what you choose."

"Yes. He adores us so much, he thinks every day of our demise. And hopes we shall name Cousin Mary as our successor!"

"I hear parliament continues to push you in this matter of marriage and succession, majesty."

"And now you return they will enlist you in their harangue against us, Swafford."

"They may try, majesty." Again Griff's thoughts returned to his self-proclaimed seductress. One could never be too careful in this court, where ambitious men seethed and plotted, desperate for preferment and favor. Was she sent to him as some sort of inducement, a bribe? Clever. He glowered across the walled garden, singeing the spring growth of a short, round topiary with the white-hot flame of his fury. Very clever indeed. She'd somehow got inside his mind and clambered over it.

The queen, he realized abruptly, still talked of her problems with parliament. "They would like us to be a weak and feeble woman, but we have the upper hand here. As they shall discover, as will our sweet coz in Scotland. They think they have weight against us."

"The people of England are loyal to you," he assured her. "They hope you will marry and produce heirs of your own--in time. You are yet in your prime, majesty. There is no haste."

"Dear Swafford, you may be awkward, crotchety and seldom have a humorous tale to tell, but you always know the dutiful thing to say." She paused. "Now, what do you truly advise us, as your queen, not as a woman."

"As my sovereign, I counsel you to marry for duty. Make your choice solely politick."

"Is there no room for love in this dutiful binding, Swafford?"

He barely restrained his eyes from rolling in the royal presence.

"There is no such thing as love, majesty."

"How can this be, when our poets write of it daily, and our minstrels sing of it nightly?"

"It is a lie," he replied. "A fantasy, a myth, like dragons, unicorns, faeries and mermaids." He shot her a look, his eyelids lowered slyly. "Your minstrels and your poets tell you what you want to hear, Majesty. Whatever you pay them to tell you. Any fantasy might be bought for the right price. Hence the existence of brothels."

"How cynical you are, Swafford! One of these days you'll admit love exists. We should place a wager on it."

"Don't waste your coin, majesty. Save it for your minstrels." He paused, fighting a tremor of amusement. "You'll never hear that tune from my lips."

She must have caught the sudden twitch in his jaw. "Swafford, do I see the precursor to a smile?"

Griff carefully made his face grave again as a stone vault in Westminster Abbey.

She resumed her teasing. "We think we saw it once, the Swafford smile, and were unexpectedly swept off our feet by it. It happened so long ago, of course, it could simply be in our imagination."

He kept his lips tight, his countenance unmoved.

"But indeed," she added softly, "we should be sorry never to have the pleasure again."

Seduce *him*? Who would put the little wench up to such an ill-advised scheme? She shouldn't be wandering the streets unguarded. She could get herself arrested. Or worse.

He shook his head. No time to think of that now. One duty over, his next was a meeting with his foolish brother. He must find a barge for hire and make his way up the river.

He raised his fingers to his lips and tasted the lingering hint of chalky sweetness. Lavender and honey--a little rosemary perhaps.

Seduce *him*? Let her try. Let her do her worst.

CHAPTER 3

Madolyn didn't know, until they were already out on the river, that someone in the crowd had stolen her purse, leaving her no coin to pay the bargeman. Now he stoically refused to take her any further, oblivious to alternate pleas and threats. Desperate and in a foul mood, she decided to take the oars herself.

"Oy!" the bargeman bellowed, as she scrambled gracelessly to her feet, "Look out! You'll tip the boat."

She tripped on the hastily-pinned hem of her borrowed gown and with a solitary, surprised cry, went over the edge of the barge, landing in the river with a loud splash. Bobbing there, held afloat by Eustacia's voluminous skirt, she was far too angry for tears. She struggled, spitting out a mouthful of filthy water, kicking against her skirt as it took on water and grew heavier, threatening to pull her under.

Suddenly another rocking boat drew alongside. One hand reached down, long fingers clawing for her sleeve. As the man hauled her to the side of his vessel, she heard an impatient sigh, suggesting this put her rescuer out far more than it did her, then, in one heave, he pulled her up, over the side of his barge and across his lap. Exhausted, she would gladly have laid there like a dead thing, but he poked her in the ribs and made her sit up.

"Astonishing what one finds polluting the river these days. All manner of flotsam and jetsam."

The sun no longer in her eyes, she now recognized the interfering fool who'd earlier lifted her--a woman who, despite her size, was never rendered helpless in her life--clean off her feet. This time she made a longer study of the man before her, knowing she might have to rely on his help to row her back to her cousin's house, and free of charge.

His hair, a dark, rich shade of chestnut, seemed almost deliberately limp and unkempt, discouraging anyone from running their fingers through it, but Maddie was not fooled. It might have been quite lovely hair for a man, if washed and brushed. Several days' growth of beard darkened his chin, so while she usually prided herself on reading a man's character by the shape and firmness of his jaw, today she looked for other clues. Under considerable time constraint, with little in his favor already, she made a speedy assessment. He sported neither the looks nor manners of a gentleman, and his hands were already proven dangerously presumptive, however, his was the only offer of rescue and sometimes one must make the best of a bad situation.

Resolved to thank him, she opened her mouth.

"I've already heard enough from you. Kindly shut that vast hole in your face and keep it thus."

Just her luck, she thought, to be rescued by the rudest man in England.

Struggling to escape his lap, she was subjected to another rancorous bark, "Stay where you are and be still, unless you want another ducking." A threat, rather than concern for her safety, and with one of his arms laid heavily across her knees, the other around her waist, holding her trapped, it was also redundant. He squinted at her warily, somewhat resentfully. Like tiny minnows in a fisherman's net, sun beams reflected off the water became trapped under his dark lashes, and a wry bulge in his cheek where he tucked his tongue suggested he kept some words to himself, afraid they might misbehave when mixed with the fertile spring air.

She gathered her half-drowned courage. "Will you take me home? I suppose you may convey me the rest of the way, although you are, obviously, not the sort of escort to which I'm accustomed."

His mouth twitched, his eyebrow quirked. "Did I not tell you to be silent? Women should be seen and not heard. Has no man ever taught you that?"

"None who lived to tell the tale!"

He stared.

"Will you take me or not? I'm an excessively busy person and have no time to waste. I need..."

"A damned good spanking. Bend over me again and I'll deliver it."

After the many disappointments of her day, this was the final straw.

"Impertinent knave! You ever lay a violent hand on me, it *will* be retaliated. Make haste and do as I say. Pick up your oars."

Disregarding her threats, he transferred both hands to her waist. Iron-hard, inflexible, bronzed fingers gripped her too tightly.

"Do you mean to sit there gaping, or will you take me down the river?" she demanded. "If not, row me to the bank side at once, you great, witless oaf." Writhing in his lap, she plucked at his immoveable fingers, looking for escape.

He kept his hands on her waist, seemingly oblivious to her pinches. "You want a favor from me, you must give me payment in return, madam."

Suddenly he leaned forward until his lips were almost upon hers, poised a hair's breadth from possession. Blood rushed through her ears like a violent stream over rocky terrain, bringing with it a strange, exultant giddiness. Perhaps it was spring in the air, or some other villainous sorcery, but in that moment of confusion she tipped her head to the left, felt his breath on her mouth and then...

When it began, she put her hands to his shoulders, ready to wield them as weapons, but somehow she forgot their purpose, and after the initial testing, a measuring of danger, he proceeded to take her mouth as if it and she were spoils of war. His tongue, verging on brutal, pressed between her lips, invading, plundering and forceful.

Men generally asked permission before they kissed her, and most often they were denied. Today she closed her eyes against the sun's brilliant rays, setting all protests aside.

One arm drew her up against his chest, and she felt conscious suddenly of her overflowing bosom where it rubbed against the dried mud spattered across the sun-warmed leather of his doublet. Underneath, he was all male strength. The hard, thick muscle of his torso was separated from her bare skin by only a flimsy bit of linen and some worn leather. It was almost as if she lay naked in the arms of a warrior fully clothed and rapacious, a conqueror fresh from battle, seeking a pleasure hard-earned. His tongue flicked over hers, drew it into his mouth and delved again. Never had she allowed this much invasion, not even with her lost sweetheart back home, whose genial willingness to let her boss him about once served her unmaidenly curiosity to some degree.

When she thought him done, his tongue thrust again, a rapier wielded to subdue, claim, and harvest. She could blame it on her near drowning, on the sun in her eyes, on anything, but as the first shock subsided, her captive tongue swept over his in a manner that might almost be construed as welcoming.

Mortified by the lapse, she quickly blamed underhand trickery. When he released her lips, they were already in motion, "Knaves, rogues, and cutpurses! This rotten place is full of them. Has no man in this town any goodness or honesty? Are you all villains out to take advantage of poor, innocent ..."

He was glaring at her lips, now surely bruised and swollen, branded by that potent kiss.

Gathering the tattered shreds of her dignity, she exclaimed, "That was supposed to tame me, was it? Put me in my place? A silly little kiss? I've known better."

His eyes quickly narrowed. "Ought to put you back where I found you, ungrateful wench." The deepening lines across his brow suggested he thought he'd earned some right to take that kiss. Afraid he might decide further rights were likewise his to take, realizing she was trapped there on his boat, she began to itch again, fingers groping for the spitefully elusive irritant thriving under her corset, making itself felt at the worst possible moment.

"You have your payment in advance," she said, "now pick up your oars and start rowing...you..." Breathlessly searching for a suitable insult, she soon found one, "...ugly, ill-mannered beast!"

Then, because words were not enough to mollify her temper after the day she'd already endured, she paused her scratching long enough to slap his face.

Silence, except for the tip-tapping of little waves against the side of the rowboat. His eyes were aflame, his lips a thin, trembling line.

Turning the boat, he rowed swiftly to a set of mossy stone steps leading up from the water. "This aggravation, I can do without today." The barge bumped to a halt and he shouted at her to get out. "Good riddance, mouthy wench," he spat. "And good luck with your seduction!"

* * * *

Now he was definitely feverish. Was he poisoned? It wouldn't be the first time someone tried to do away with him. He'd long since concluded some feature of his face made people hate him on sight.

He couldn't remember the last time a woman raised his blood heat to such a degree, if ever, but then there was never a surfeit of women in his life. And what she stirred within held only temporary resemblance to anger, for a certain slumbering part of his anatomy woke from a lengthy hibernation, stuck its head up and looked around with interest. How inconvenient it rose now for a strumpet he should've thrown back into the river, if not for this shockingly tolerant and apparently lusty mood. Yet it pulsed there, no diminutive sensation after so many years of famine.

When she'd bounced mercilessly in his lap, her hair, black as a tinker's pot, had sprawled over her shoulders in long wet strands, wound around his sleeve and curled like the tentacles of a sea creature. He imagined those sinuous tresses spread out over his pillow, surrounding him. He saw her in his bed, tasted her in his mouth, felt warm silk embrace naked marble as her arms held him, her body sheathed him.

It was as if he'd been waiting for her.

Chapter 4

Now forced to embark on the longer route to her cousin's house, Madolyn walked with her head down, carefully dodging piles of steaming horse muck. She was only vaguely aware of a litter drawing alongside, until she heard, "You there! Wench!"

Lord Jessop stepped out of a litter, narrowly missing a puddle, out of breath as he accosted her. "Where do you go, my dear?" His smile stretched, cracking across the lower half of his face, having no effect on his cool, gray eyes. "Let's walk together. I'll be your escort. 'Tis not safe, you know, for a young lady to walk alone on these streets."

"Why? Because some man might proposition me for a quick tumble?"

His eyes gleamed, his smile stiffened. "You wanted to discuss your petition. Did you expect a favor of that magnitude for nothing? You're no fool, neither are you a child. Dressed in such a fashion, I can only conclude you meant to be admired."

She pursed her lips. It was truly no one's fault but her own for wearing this damned gown. Seeking attention, she got it, unfortunately from the wrong folk, and having missed her target entirely. Grace would say she learned a lesson.

"I've seen you before somewhere, have I not?"

He didn't remember her as Grace's sister. Apparently his attention wandered as much as his eyes. "Possibly."

"Let me see, the Pickled Parrot? In Southwark? You must be one of the new girls."

Dryly amused, she replied, "Aye, sir. The Pickled Parrot. I'm flattered you remember me."

"My dear girl, you're soaked to the skin!" Now overly solicitous, he offered to dry her off with an ineffective, lace-trimmed kerchief. "What have you been up to? You'll catch a deathly cold."

"I never caught a cold in my life," she said peevishly, for she would quite like, occasionally, to be the one over whom others fussed and fretted. Alas she was born with the unromantic constitution of an ox.

He offered his arm. "I may be able to get you an audience with the Earl of Swafford, if you still desire it?" He licked his lips. "Walk with me, eh? We'll discuss the favors we might do one another."

Of course this gilded, strutting cockerel didn't baste his words in mead for her. Why would he? He spoke to her in plain terms because she was a plain girl, and squashed into Eustacia's old gown, she apparently bore resemblance to a plain whore.

"We'll help one another, you and I. We both have what the other needs, do we not?"

She kept her face bland, holding her temper at bay.

"Trade is the way of the world you know, and in your occupation, you're surely aware of that," he added. "We have much to offer one another...goods to barter." His eyes strayed over her damp gown. "There's no harm in a simple give and take."

"What do you suggest, my lord?" She sighed deeply. "If you can help me to an audience with the Earl, I should be most grateful of course."

He smiled slowly.

* * * *

As Griff crossed the tavern yard, still mulling over the odd little strumpet on the river, he heard a familiar, merry shout, "At last! You are returned!" Gabriel suddenly appeared at his side, a jovial spring in his step.

"Not a moment too soon, it seems."

Ignoring the sharp-edged remark, Gabriel embraced his brother's stiff shoulders. "Journey was good I trust?"

"Fair enough."

"You look....well, brother. The Spanish sun was good for you."

"Hmph. It took the aches out of my bones, if that's what you mean. I daresay the English rain will put them back again."

His brother laughed, trying for another embrace like a lanky pup attempting play. "Come share an ale with me. We've much to catch up on."

Although Gabriel Mallory inherited the family height, his shoulders were not so broad as Griff's. His coloring was lighter, his features refined, even boyish, in marked contrast to those of his brother. Griff knew he could not, by any stretch of the imagination, be called handsome. In fact, he had little in common physically with Gabriel, and saw even fewer similarities in character. Where Gabriel had a frustrating, easy-going nature, content to drift along with the tide, Griff believed in swimming against it, never one to placate or stand down from a fight. But despite their differences, they shared one bond - a lonely childhood of privilege, devoid of parental affection. Griff remembered their mother as a distant woman, uncomfortable with motherhood. Their father was an unforgiving man, who never rewarded accomplishments, but quickly and severely punished mistakes. Often, Griff had taken the beatings on his younger brother's behalf and he was grateful now for the toughened skin.

Gabriel stood aside to let his brother enter the tavern first, both men stooping to fit under the low lintel.

"We might have met at my apartments," said Griff, looking around with an eye ready to disapprove.

"Ah, but here in public you'll be obliged to keep a level head and not beat me to a pulp." Said in a joking manner, it fooled neither brother. Gabriel's laugh was strained, a frenzied twitter. "But before we speak of solemn matters, can we not share an ale first? I've yet to offer you felicitations on the anniversary of your birth!"

He'd forgotten his birthday completely, and suspected his brother made so much of it now simply to avoid other subjects. "I confess my day has been a full and tiring one. The fact I've survived thirty five years of life seems scant cause for celebration. I've not yet even returned to my chambers for a change of clothes, so I've no fancy to delay here longer than necessary."

Gabriel's merry countenance fell quickly to a sad pout. "We might stay a while and talk. Brothers who've been apart two years surely have much news to share."

Disgruntled, Griff agreed to stay for one drink. After his encounter on the river with that stray wench, he suffered a fierce thirst and surely there could be no harm in one quick sup.

He gestured irritably to a corner table. It was already occupied, which meant nothing to him. He'd chosen it and therefore he would have it. As he strode to the table, the men seated there broke off their conversation, scattering hastily from his view. The brothers sat facing one another across the pitted table, and Gabriel looked for the serving wench.

Assessing his brother quickly and thoroughly, Griff decided he looked a little fatter than before, his face fleshier, the result, no doubt, of a lazy, indolent lifestyle at court. The boy never enjoyed riding, hunting, swimming, or any of those physical pursuits his brother favored for retaining strength, discipline and endurance. Gabriel's only two sports were gambling and women. The latter might keep him in some level of vitality, but he put little effort into it. Women flocked around Gabriel and, in all likelihood, initiated the sport. He never broke a healthy sweat.

Griff cleared his throat. "Now what do you mean to do about that woman?"

"Ah. It seems we have no other subject after all."

"It is the most important matter."

This latest affair with a scandalous woman must be brought to a quick end, like all the others before it. Reputedly an ambitious concubine, Eustacia Shelton was thrice conveniently widowed and entirely unacceptable companionship for Gabriel.

"You should go home to Starling's Roost," said Griff. "Get some fresh air in your lungs. The stench of the city is rife this year."

"Why?" his brother replied facetiously. "To get me away from her?"

"In part."

"I can see she is much on your mind, and you'll not be at ease until you've said your piece and insulted her. So have at it." Gabriel raised a languid hand to the tippler for more ale. "Say what you will, if it makes you content."

Griff ascertained his brother was half-way to cupshotten already--

eyes glazed, gestures sloppy. However, the new sharpness in the boy's tone caused greater concern. He looked almost sly and rather cocky, which he never was before. Instantly Griff blamed this unpleasant change on the influence of that woman currently holding his poor brother enthralled.

"You will quit her and London. Neither has done you any good whatsoever. That much is plain."

Gabriel blinked, eyes foggy. "I know what you think, but you haven't even met her. I intend to marry Lady Shelton, Eustacia."

"*Marry her?*" A near ungovernable fury choked out of him. "The heir to my estate, marry that woman, the Scarlet Widow? Never! I forbid it!"

"I'm in love," said Gabriel. "I don't expect you to understand."

"*Love?*" He lowered his voice and hissed. "Love is for fools. Have I not told you this many times?"

"Because you've never known it."

"Because I have a brain and use it, unlike most apparently."

Gabriel's head swung like a pendulum from his stooped shoulders. "Then I pity you, brother."

"Spare your pity!" he spat. "Save it for that woman. She'll need it when I'm done with her."

"I love her!"

Griff struggled to control his wrath. His brother's love affairs were mercurial, seldom outlasting a season, so he shouldn't be so perturbed by this one. Indeed, he wouldn't be, if not for that worrisome tone in the boy's voice. Eyes fixed on Gabriel's face, he said slowly and carefully, "Marry her and I will disinherit you."

"How can you? What will you do? Suddenly produce a child of your own?"

The words sat between them, the rumor of Griff's unfortunate incapability laid out with a conjurer's flourish.

Gabriel wilted. He reached across for his brother's clenched fist. "I should not have--"

Griff stood, leaving his drink untouched. On his way out he slipped on some spilled ale and smashed his hand through the leaded glass window. No one dared offer help and he sought none, striding out of the tavern, trailing blood in his wake.

* * * *

Eustacia lived in a grand house along the river, but her tenancy there was in dispute. Her stepchildren contested their late father's will, embroiling her in a lawsuit likely to be held up in chancery court for months, even years. Meanwhile, she refused to leave her dead husband's house and until her stepchildren and their solicitors found legal means to remove her, or until she found another protector, remained in residence, making the most of a life to which many thought her ill-deserving. And sneaking pieces of furniture out to sell on the sly.

Madolyn and Grace were never close to their cousin, but that winter, much to their surprise, she'd written to Grace, inviting her to visit. Their mother had insisted both girls go to "broaden their horizons", also to look out for one another. Primarily, Madolyn believed she was there to stand guard over her sweet-natured, elder sister, a mission she undertook with great solemnity.

When she entered the house that afternoon, wet and bedraggled, Grace was mortified. "Maddie! Where have you been?"

"Out walking."

"London is not Sydney Dovedale. You shouldn't go wandering alone here as you do at home. And in that gown? If papa ever knew..."

"There's no cause to fret, Grace. I can look after myself." She gave her sister a quick kiss and ran to warm her hands by the fire.

"You're soaking wet! What have you been up to?"

"An argument with a man on the river."

"Anything might have happened to you. The place is filled with knaves and cutpurses!"

Yes, she thought dourly, *and one such knave currently pays court to you, my sister.* Grace lectured her on the pitfalls of life in the great city, yet failed to heed her own warnings, sadly the victim of a romantic soul, vulnerable to poetry, especially when it came from the lips of a deceptively smooth and distinguished gentleman, but Madolyn decided it would serve no purpose to upset her now. Only if Lord Jessop did propose marriage to Grace would there be cause to tell her. Besides, they would return to Norfolk once their father's ship made anchor and he arrived in London to collect them.

Home. It would be a bittersweet departure. On one hand she looked forward to going home again, back to their mother and the familiar routine. She even missed their naughty little brother, John Sydney Carver. At five years of age, he was the most dreadful accident that ever befell a family and neither she nor Grace could understand why their parents saw need for another child when they were already long past the age when they should think of such matters. Yet, she even remembered little John with a degree of fondness now. Indeed, she acknowledged much to be thankful for in the safe return of their father and in going home, but now it seemed she would return defeated, no husband found for her sister, and failing in her mission to save Nathaniel.

"Cousin Eustacia expects guests again this evening," said Grace, squinting over her embroidery. "You must promise to behave and hold your tongue, or else she says you can stay in our room and not come down."

Turning her back to the fire, Maddie lifted her skirt to warm her posterior. "My behavior is always most decorous."

Grace looked up, brows arched.

"Indeed it is!" Maddie insisted. "How is it my fault, if her guests can't abide a woman with opinions?"

"You may have your opinions, but keep them to yourself."

"Bugger that! I'm not mute."

"Much is the pity." Grace put down her sewing. "You'll get yourself in trouble one day with your wretched tongue."

"Somebody has to speak up for what is right and fair."

"Must it always be you, Maddie?"

She rolled her eyes. "Hey ho!"

"You're a hothead like Cousin Nathaniel, and see what trouble it got him into."

Dropping the hem of her skirt, Maddie walked over to admire her sister's neat stitch. "Nathaniel is innocent," she said, leaning over Grace's shoulder. "And I intend to bring him safely home."

At this moment Eustacia swept in, catching their conversation by the tail. "Don't put yourself to any trouble for that witless bastard," she exclaimed. "He causes his own trouble and can get himself out of it the same way."

Maddie protested. "He is your brother!"

"Half-brother, and illegitimate," Eustacia corrected tartly. She nurtured few tender feelings in her body, and all were spent on herself. "Have you grown *fatter* since you came here?" she demanded. "Your appetites should be restrained, cousin. The stitches will soon give out completely." Then she discovered the puddle around Maddie's feet. "What, pray tell, happened to you?"

"I went for a swim. Unexpectedly."

"You'll never get a straight answer from her," Grace explained wearily, her delicate features assuming the customary apology. "'Tis as well not to ask and usually best not to know."

Eustacia winced, one hand to her slender throat. "I suggest you change before my guests arrive. There's a distinct odor of the Thames clinging to your person."

"Am I permitted to join your guests this evening?" Maddie smiled pleasantly. "My sister thought I might not be welcome."

"Can you be trusted to behave?"

"I'll try my damnedest." Tongue tucked into her cheek, she returned to the admiration of her sister's embroidery, the sharp pins of Eustacia's angry scrutiny pricking at her.

"Gabriel Mallory comes again this evening," said her cousin. "Do not embarrass me, as you did yesterday."

"How did I embarrass you?"

"You spoke to him of horse...breeding."

"He spoke of it first, when he talked of his brother's stables and fine stud horses."

Eustacia wouldn't listen to excuses. "Do not talk at all in future, unless remarking on the weather. That is surely a safe subject, even for you. And please refrain from guzzling the wine," she added. "And leave some of the food to my other guests."

Repressing her laughter, Maddie agreed to follow her cousin's orders. Eustacia turned to look out the window, watching, no doubt, for her lover. Suddenly remembering her failed mission, Maddie thoughtfully considered her cousin's potential usefulness. Eustacia entertained a great many gentlemen in the evenings and she might have access to important people. At least, she liked to act as if she had her finger on the very pulse of court life.

"What do you know of the Earl of Swafford, cousin?" Maddie asked. "Is it very difficult to get an audience with him?"

Eustacia's face never warmed with any color. It was often painted white to hide her freckles, and now even her green eyes faded to a moldy hue. "The Earl of Swafford is a vile, vicious monster. He is vengeful, cruel and heartless. He will do all in his power to separate me from the man I love. Why seek an audience with that ogre?"

"The Earl of Swafford is Master Gabriel Mallory's elder brother," Grace whispered.

Ah, now she understood their cousin's venom. Gabriel Mallory was the latest prey for whom their cousin primed her marital trap, and although he walked blithely into it, his elder brother, as Eustacia now angrily exclaimed, formed one, large, hairy obstacle in her path. Disapproving of the relationship, he swore to put an end to it.

With three dead husbands to her credit, folk disdainfully called their cousin the "Scarlet Widow", which Maddie considered an injustice. By making three wealthy marriages to old, possibly senile gentlemen, Eustacia had kept her scapegrace father solvent for the last few years, herself well-fed and clothed, but why should she be slandered for taking matters into her own hands, assuring her own survival? Certainly, with a mother dead, a half-brother exiled and a father in debtor's prison, no one else would do it for her.

Young Gabriel Mallory, potential husband number four, was a rare prize, the complete opposite of Eustacia's last unfortunate spouse, if the gruesome portrait hanging in the gallery was a true likeness. Handsome and even-tempered, Gabriel was also good-hearted to a fault, but Maddie now discovered the young man scarcely dared move a hair on his fine head without his elder brother's approval, and it was possible their cousin's affair had only outlasted the winter because the Earl stayed abroad. News of his imminent return to England had put Eustacia in a nervous temper, for although she'd never met the man, she'd heard enough tales of his legendary rages to fear for her own scrawny neck.

"If you thought to tempt him into a pardon for Nathaniel," she said, casting another scornful glance at Maddie's snug bodice, "think again. I hear he is incapable."

"Incapable of what?"

Eustacia's plucked brows wrinkled like pulled stitches. "You know very well."

She looked at her sister for explanation, but Grace, blushing prettily, bent even further over her embroidery.

Her cousin continued. "It is impossible to get an audience with him. When at court he keeps himself shut away in his apartments."

"Why? Is he so wretchedly ugly? I heard he limps and has a hunched back. And a wart."

"He has all those things...and worse," Eustacia assured her, with enough vinegar and salt to season further dark ideas in her cousin's overactive imagination.

Suddenly Maddie understood. Striding around her sister's chair, she cried, "Incapable! Of course, I see! You mean he cannot get his cock erect." Remarkably pleased with herself for figuring it out, she retrieved the embroidery that fell at her feet and used it to cool her sister's scorched cheeks. "I don't know why no one ever speaks plainly about these matters.

It is only rumpy pumpy and we all know it exists."

"Ladies," Eustacia sternly reminded her, "do not use words of that nature in public."

"None of us would be here without it, would we?" Maddie replied. But her mind already moved on. So much for seduction. Still, there was always an alternative. She could try talking to the man. As her father often said, when there was a favor she wanted badly enough, she could talk the wax out of a man's ears.

Later, when Gabriel Mallory arrived at the house, Madolyn asked if he might arrange an audience for her with his brother.

His slurred reply was thus: "My dear Mistress Madolyn, he'll eat you alive. I could not, in all conscience, put you in his way, for he has a temper like the very devil when roused. If you catch him on a bad day he is likely to hunt you down, and your family, to see you hoisted on the gibbet and left for scavengers to pick out your eyes."

Although he laughed, she was not entirely sure he teased. Luckily she kept a contingency plan already in place. Cousin Nathaniel must be saved and she would put his case before the Beast, one way or another.

It was not in her nature to give up on a good cause, and peril only made her goal that much more alluring.

CHAPTER 5

The day, which began so fine, now returned to its usual mood. A bone-cold wind blew through the arches of the gallery, and the first fat drops of rain spattered Griff's boots. Looking up, he saw a lit candle fluttering wildly in the open window of his apartments, where the rain would eventually put it out. His new manservant, Wickes, was either airing out the room or too slow to shut the window.

Entering his chambers, he swept off his cloak, yelling for Wickes and kicking the door shut with his foot. There was no refreshment left out, nothing to wet his dry mouth, and he was in no state to survive a visit from his wife without wine to dull the senses. But there was no reply to his gruff summons.

At least the fire was lit.

He sincerely hoped Wickes wouldn't turn unpredictable or brain-addled, like Matthew, the last good man he was forced to dismiss. Wickes was possibly the most unprepossessing fellow he'd ever hired, but he'd learned his lesson with handsome, spirited, talkative Matthew, who'd had the sheer audacity to fall in "love" and choose a woman over his duty to the earl. Wickes, with his lank, greasy hair, limp demeanor and perpetually moist nose, the contents of which were often smeared along his sleeve, was a welcome change. He, at least, wasn't likely to run off with a giggling female.

Flinging his drenched cloak across the nearest chair, he cursed the English weather. He'd almost forgotten how quickly the sky could fall.

"Wickes!" he bellowed again.

Striding to the door, he swung it open and looked out into the hall. There was no guard outside his door, an odd fact he was in too bad a mood to consider long. Slamming the door shut, he turned, suddenly catching some slight movement in the shadows.

It was too late for wine. His wife was already there, sitting primly in the corner by the open window, her large, full-lipped mouth curled in disgust and disappointment. Perhaps she'd hoped he wouldn't return to

England, at least not in one piece. The fluttering candle drew sinister shadows across her face, accentuating the elegant slope of her broad brow, the slender line of her nose and the sharp angle of her high cheekbones.

"I sent your man out so we could talk alone," she said in a dispassionate, clipped voice, each word granted with apathy, as if he bought her conversation by the syllable. Perhaps, he mused, that was how she calculated her annual allowance.

Eighteen years may have slunk by since their wedding night, still, each time he saw her, he relived the humiliating ordeal. He was barely seventeen then, his experience limited to brief, hasty encounters with girls on his father's estate. The future generation of Swaffords didn't depend on his performance with them. There was no pressure, merely uncomplicated, quickly-known and speedily-forgotten pleasure. In the case of a wife, especially one hand-picked by his father, it was different. Her only purpose was to beget an heir. Although she'd made it clear from the beginning she found him unattractive and took an aversion to his bed, she was glad enough to revel in his wealth and the privileges she knew as his wife.

She lived in Leicestershire now, in a house she'd brought to the marriage as part of her dowry. She wanted nothing from her husband beyond his name and wealth, certainly wanted no more of "that" as she called it. And by Christ was he grateful she'd taken an immediate distaste to conjugal relations.

On their wedding night, she'd lain there, this infamous beauty, indifferent and pristine. He'd been almost afraid to touch her in case he got her dirty. He'd tried closing his eyes, thinking of anything else, but she'd been lifeless under him, a reluctant vessel impatient to get it over with. Lady Isabelle Blanchard had been considered prime stock for the Swafford stables, and he a mere boy eager for approval, desperate to prove himself worthy. Five years his senior, a spoiled, cosseted only child with a mean, spiteful temper, she'd ridiculed him for his failure to perform in the marriage bed. He was little better, so she said, than a young bull, sweating over her. She was repulsed by it. The more he'd tried, the more she hated it; the more she'd railed at him and mocked him, the more he'd shrunk away inside, until he shut out the world as far as he could.

When the first few months passed and there was no child in her womb, his father berated him for it, reminding him of his Swafford duty.

"I might have known," he'd ranted. "I suppose you'll undo everything ten generations of Swaffords have achieved. Are we to be brought down by a fool boy who cannot perform the most basic of duties?" The marriage, however, was binding. In his father's mind, an annulment or divorce was a modern-day outrage, an admission of failure, not to mention the scandal it would cause, the besmirching of the honorable Swafford crest. He'd chosen Isabelle for his son and he was always right. It was almost as if he thought Griff had failed deliberately to embarrass him, therefore he must not be permitted to get away with it. He would produce a child with Isabelle. His father, even on his deathbed, still insisted, and his father's word was law.

Now here she sat, the untouchable fortress, bringing the horror back again.

Always precise and scrupulous in her movements, she slid her elegant hands from a large ermine muff, set it to one side, smoothed down her sleeves, checked her neck ruff, and then slowly lifted the lace veil of her bonnet. Apparently she meant to stay a while, but the quicker he got her out of his sight the better.

"What do you want?" he asked. He could have said, "How *much* do you want?" She always attacked him in the purse, because she knew where it hurt him most. She was cruelly skilled at summing a person up at first sight, finding how best to cause them pain.

"I want an additional two hundred a month," she said in her brittle, emotionless voice. This was excessive, even for her. Until she added, "To come back and live as your wife."

A sudden gust blew rain in at the window, ruffling the veil of her headdress, toying with the feathers. For a brief moment, they regained the life they'd known before being plucked from a hapless pheasant and requisitioned for the frivolous decoration of a velvet bonnet.

"I fail to understand."

"It's surely time we came to a better arrangement."

After eighteen years? He thought perhaps he'd walked through the wrong door into some nightmarish, supernatural world, where everything was inside out and upside down.

"I'll keep Blanchard House as my own retreat, and we'll share a bed no more than once a month." She spoke with confidence. No flush of shame colored her face, no nuance of doubt marred her speech. It seemed she thought he pined for her, and would eagerly take her back, arms outstretched. Admired throughout her life as a great beauty, she assumed no man would refuse whatever scraps she threw his way.

"For the discomfort of doing your duty as my wife, you want two hundred additional pounds a month?" he clarified slowly.

Her eyes, previously vacant, shimmered with spite-formed crystals, like frost on a window. "Reasonable compensation for the inconvenience."

"What happened to your other lovers?" He knew she'd found pleasure with other men since their wedding, and now she assumed the fault for their abysmal coupling lay with him. "Did you grow bored, or did they?"

Gliding silently across his floor, she leaned down, pushing her white, powdered face so close to his that he saw the little cracks forming. "I came here to offer a truce. Do you really want to discuss my lovers and how they pleased me as you never could?"

He was bemused by her apparent desire to see him jealous, when he could hardly care less what she did, or who she did it with. She wanted to prick him with her witch's needles. It was a female need to make a man jealous, he supposed, any man, even one they hated.

"Why? After eighteen years?" he asked, genuinely confused.

"You need an heir."

"I have one--my brother."

"Are you truly content to leave the estate in Gabriel's tender hands, knowing his choice of female companion? Rumor is he plans to marry Lady Shelton."

His hands clasped tightly around the arms of his chair, his eyes focused on her narrow, veiny throat. "My brother's choices continue to disappoint, but he's young yet. His tastes will mature."

"Apparently he's in love with her. Men will do strange things for love."

Love? Even this viper of a woman believed in that nonsense? Apparently he was the only sane soul in the country.

She straightened up, palms pressed together. "Will you let her offspring sully the Swafford lineage? Can you tolerate the idea of her child inheriting the estate and the earldom?" Now she raised her praying fingers to her chin in a thoughtful pose. "I hear her father languishes in debtor's prison, and her brother is exiled for piracy. Her family is nothing. She has no fortune. She's been passed from man to man, and put three husbands in their graves already. Will Gabriel, your beloved brother, be her fourth victim? Once he's impregnated her with the next Earl of Swafford, of course." She smiled thinly. "Is that what you want?"

"It will never happen."

"Then you must provide another heir."

"How do you propose I do that?" he ground out his words, each one carefully controlled.

She shrugged. "We can try again. We are, sadly, stuck with one another. Rather than let *her* child inherit, I'm willing to share your bed once a month, until the child is conceived. Then it need not continue and you can pay me a lump sum, to be agreed upon later, depending on the sex of the child. Think of it as a pension of sorts."

Oh, she had it all planned. He ought to give her credit for thinking of her future financial status. If Gabriel did marry, she realized her position would slowly be usurped, ultimately her power stripped away. Having provided no heir, she'd be superfluous, and when Griff died, she'd be passed over, her advantages as his wife, gone. There was, of course, a widow's jointure, but she was a woman of expensive tastes. She wanted to be the mother of the next earl as insurance for her future comforts and she knew how devoted he was to Swafford duty.

Alas, these were his sad choices: bed his wife, or rely on his brother's judgment to provide a worthy heir. Not for the first time, he wished he might escape this life and be someone else entirely, even if it was for one day only.

It was sickening, her cold, calm cunning, her willingness to use his bed despite her obvious disgust for him as a man. Accustomed to being used, he knew he'd never been anything more to his wife than the provider of her feathered nest. Why it should suddenly hit him so hard today, he couldn't imagine, but the thought of trading his life in for another became more and more agreeable.

If he was truly as powerful as most folk believed, he could simply have her neck broken and her body thrown down a flight of stairs, as, it was rumored, Robert Dudley dealt with his unwanted wife. Alas, he was obliged to be civilized. Duty and honor came first in the life of a Swafford, and for him, there was no option of annulment or divorce. Such a scandal was not to be borne, and he was, as she said, "stuck" with the woman he married, as many unhappy Swaffords had been before him. He'd promised his dying father that this marriage, like a foul canker, would take one of them to the grave before it was ended, and a Swafford vow, once made, was not to be undone, however tortuous.

She was, he realized, nearing the end of her childbearing years, hence the sudden haste. He actually considered it for a moment. Having another heir to the Swafford estate would certainly solve the problem with Gabriel. The countess was, in the eyes of God and the law, still his wife. Her body was his property.

However, a new spirit flourished inside him today, spinning clumsily, knocking into things. It was nothing to do with Swafford obligation and everything to do with him as a person, as a man. He couldn't understand it, or where it came from, and it made any sensible, dutiful decision quite impossible.

Slowly he drew his fingers across his mouth. "Unfortunately, I have a number of appointments this evening. I must decline the offer, however enticing. Perhaps...another time. We'll talk again later."

Isabelle stared,

uncomprehending.

"In the meantime, I'll give due consideration to your proposal," he added. "I'm flattered by your willingness to suffer degradation on behalf of future heirs to my estate."

She finally understood he mocked her. "Do you think I wanted to come here and throw myself at your feet? I could have anyone."

"As indeed you do, so my spies inform me." He leaned back, stretching out his long legs, ankles crossed. "I think I'll skip my turn today. If you make haste you might catch the crowd exiting the theatre and find someone there to service you."

She swore at him, a vile insult, accusing him of impotency.

"Yes, I heard that rumor," he said calmly, knowing it originated with her spiteful tongue.

"Then disprove it. Give me a child."

Her eyes were eerily opaque like those of a marble caryatid. Rather than delve deeper and explore the evil labyrinth of her mind, he wanted her gone from his chambers. "As I told you, I'll consider it." He gave a quick, sweeping clap of his hands, signaling her dismissal.

Retrieving her ermine muff, she brushed it down as if it might have become sullied in his presence. "Well, I gave you a choice." She stood a moment, glaring down on his head. "Wickes left your wine in the annex."

He wondered why she bothered telling him, but then she was gone. The door closed and he, at last, could breathe.

No one else would ever know it, but good God, even now when he was no longer an awestruck boy, that woman terrified him, shrank his balls to raisins.

Looking down he realized he'd cut his hand. Of course, at the tavern.

Blood dripped to his shirt cuff and his knee. And it hurt.

CHAPTER 6

Cursing, he strode into the annex, and found a jug of hippocras waiting there on a tray. Wickes must have prepared it before going out. He'd better have a damned good excuse for leaving so abruptly, or he'd find himself out on his ear already.

He poured some wine into a goblet, moved back to the fire, dropped into his chair and put his heels up on a tapestry footstool, relishing a rare moment of peace.

Before he could take his first sip, there was a knock at the door. Since he'd forgotten to bolt the latch, and this new arrival was too impatient to wait for any reply, the door opened and they came in, bold as brass. Immediately he was on the alert, fingers tight around the wine goblet.

It was a woman. He knew it from the faint, chalky scent of lavender, the whisper of her skirt against the floor.

"Pardon me, sir," she said, so politely it had to be trouble. "Is the Earl of Swafford here?"

"What do you want?" he grunted, weary and sour.

"I come to speak on behalf of Captain Nathaniel Downing."

"Downing? The pirate?"

"He is no pirate, sir. Captain Downing was commissioned to attack that Spanish galleon. Only when the Spanish ambassador protested did the queen deny knowing anything of it. The distinction between privateer and pirate is too often distorted, depending on whoever the changeable queen decides is her latest enemy."

"Madam, you speak treason," he warned. "Tread with care if you come here for the earl's help."

Behind him, the woman sighed, releasing a shattered breath of frustration. "I did not mean any ill of her majesty. I confess, when I'm nervous or my temper is up, my tongue does run on."

There was a familiar note in her voice. He swiveled around to look, and almost dropped his goblet.

She wore no elaborate headdress, just a simple caul for her midnight black hair. Her gown was rich, crimson damask, the sleeves a little too long, the bodice too tight. He stood swiftly, spilling wine from his goblet.

"Oh." Her eyes were wide and clear blue, the color of a robin's egg. "You? Once again? It must be providential." She was flustered, her cheeks tinted pink

He bit down on his tongue, tasting his own blood. Damn. Where was Wickes? Where was the guard outside his door? He never dealt with women petitioners. Now, left entirely alone and at her mercy, he was tongue-tied, fumbling for the words to chase her out again. She was even lovelier than he remembered from earlier. Who the devil... Someone had put her up to this. It was some sort of scheme to make a fool of him perhaps, to verify the rumors of his "great incapability".

Was it possible one of those devious courtiers, Dudley for instance, sent this creature here out of mischief?

He made a sudden, whimsical decision. "The earl isn't here."

And so it was done. Like that, the burden was shifted. For a while.

Aware of his hand trembling, he set his wine on the stack of books by his chair. "Still hoping to seduce him, eh? No luck yet?"

"The man is elusive as a unicorn." Her lips parted to expel a quick, irritated sigh. "I was assured he'd be here tonight."

"Alas, you find only me."

"And who *are* you exactly?"

He couldn't even be annoyed with her, although he knew he should. "I am, exactly, Griff, his manservant." Pausing, he looked her up and down. "And this is your big plan? You came to seduce him for Downing's pardon?" He chortled with dour amusement, couldn't help it.

"I take offense at your tone, sir." Even her netted hair bristled, as she squared her shoulders.

"It's certainly a different approach, madam. No one has ever tried to sweeten their case before the earl quite so...candidly." He pondered her peevish face, betaken with an unexpected, incandescent desire to claim what she offered. Oddly enough, his wife had just offered him the same thing, but for two hundred pounds a month, a proposition that left him cold. Not the case with this young lady. He cleared his throat. "Why not seduce me instead? Save yourself the trouble of hunting him down again. And he's an old man. You'd enjoy yourself far more with me." The wit spilled out of him suddenly, fluid and easy. Of course, he could talk to her, since she thought he was someone else.

"Is he very old? As old as thirty?"

He winced. "Ancient."

Pressing a finger to her lips, she weighed her choices. "And ugly?"

"Why do you suppose they call him the Beast, madam?"

A curious glint warmed her dangerously blue eyes.

"Why not share my company instead? Suppose I can spare the time, save my master the inconvenience."

A dimple appeared in her cheek. "While I appreciate your sacrifice on the Earl's behalf, I'm saving myself for a good cause. Unfortunately."

The woman must be an unscrupulous strumpet. He ought to send her out of his chambers before another word was said. Yet her polite rejection, delivered with a degree of bold humor, had a mollifying effect on his temper. The twitch of an almost extinct smile pulled at his reluctant mouth.

Good cause? He could think of no better cause than himself.

She read his expression, evidently. "Don't be tiresome, there's a good fellow," she said genially, cheeks tinted pink as the underskirt of a daisy. "I came here on serious business."

He frowned, scratching his nose again. "What makes you think you have anything special to offer him? What makes you different to any other wench?" Perhaps she had some fancy skill, he mused, a trick she thought no other woman could do for the Earl of Swafford.

But she faltered, lashes sweeping her cheeks, teeth nibbling her lower lip. Clearly, she hadn't thought her plan through quite well enough. Watching her fingers tighten around the pleats of her skirt, he noted a few chewed fingernails.

"Give your message to me, wench, and I'll deliver it. I'll save you from the fate worse than death at my master's fumbling, grotesque claws."

"How do I know I can trust you?" She raised her haughty chin. "You have shifty eyes and low set ears, signs of a criminal mind. Not to mention, groping hands and lips that take without asking."

"You have my word on it, madam. As a gentleman." He bowed, one hand to his heart.

"Hmm." She wrinkled her nose. "I know what the word of most men is worth. And I never trust one who feels the need to *tell* me he is a gentleman, because I might not think it from his shabby appearance. And especially after the way he treated me already."

She shouldn't trust him, he mused. Should turn her funny little tail and flee and he, if he possessed any good conscience, would tell her so. He didn't, however.

"I have no letter of petition to leave for the Earl," she was saying. "I lost it today in the river." Her shoulders lifted in a pert shrug, drawing his attention to that overflowing bodice.

He carefully moved his gaze back to her face. "Whatever made you believe the earl might be seduced, madam? Surely you've been advised against it."

She sighed. "Once set on a course, I'm seldom swayed from it. My father says I get my blinkers on like a plow horse." Smiling with self-deprecating humor, she added, "The Beast might not be so awfully bad. Underneath it all, he must be the same as any other man with a heart that beats."

He looked askance. "You're an optimist, madam."

She merely laughed, a gentle, soothing sound, before proceeding on an uninvited tour of his chamber, inspecting his possessions as if she owned the place and he was the one who'd come to beg a boon of *her*.

"Name, wench?" he asked.

"I can't tell you. I have it on good authority the earl may punish my entire family if I meet with his disapproval, instead of his favor." Resuming her nosy progress around the room, she examined a collection of knives stuck in a wooden target, moving on to his table of books and papers, running impertinent hands over his possessions. "When will the earl return? Will he be gone long? I could wait, if you have no objection."

Objection? *Objection?* The word suddenly meant nothing to him.

"He won't be long. Would you like some wine?" He heard the voice, the question, but couldn't be sure it was his own. What was he thinking to encourage her? She was an impertinent little creature; already she upset the important order of his papers. Now, reading the title of a book, she discarded it with a gusty sigh, as if it was the most boring tome ever written.

So she could read. Who was she? What was she? Her gown, like the one she wore earlier that day, was of rich material, even if the fit left much to be desired--or displayed much to be desired, he corrected himself, with an unusual amount of mischievous humor. She spoke with a slight country burr. That afternoon she'd worn her hair loose, like an unmarried maid; this evening she made an attempt for more sophistication. He was amused by it, even charmed by her desire to dress up for him.

He would rather have her undressed for him.

"Usually I would say, yes, please." She tossed a smile over her shoulder, a decidedly devious, sultry gleam in those blue eyes. "However, I *think* I should keep my wits about me." Her lips lingered over the words, drawing them out with an implied suggestion that he might persuade her not to behave.

Yes, please. Did she read his mind? Oh, it was stirring now. After so many years of famine, the Beast was ravenous tonight.

"The wine," she clarified, lashes lowered. "I must decline."

Ah, the damned wine. He lifted his goblet, saw it was half spilled and so poured more, struggling to put his thoughts in order.

"I've been warned," she said, drawing closer, "the earl will eat me alive."

"Yesss." He paused, ready for his first sip of wine, watching her over the goblet rim. "He might."

Averting her gaze, she touched the back of her neck with those chewed fingernails. "Have you worked long in his service?"

"All my life." Returning to his chair, he put some distance between them, still wondering why he didn't throw her out.

"Poor you!" She followed, sinking to the little tapestry footstool before him, the action performed in a casual manner, without his permission. No one--man or woman--ever dared sit in his presence without first being asked. She smiled warmly up at him. "In a city the size of London, three times in one day we find each other. Do you believe in fate?"

His reply choked him. "No."

Undeterred, she rested her chin in one hand, elbow balanced on her knee. "I didn't thank you properly earlier, for saving me from the river. I'm most grateful to you, sir."

Fidgeting in his chair, he reminded her, "Griff. Not sir."

"Then thank *you*, Griff. See how well-mannered I can be? I'm not always a frowning scold."

He waited, one eyebrow raised.

"I was not in a pleasant mood when you met me this afternoon."

"Will you apologize for slapping my face?"

She considered it, briefly. "No. You deserved it for stealing a kiss."

He could have argued he stole nothing, that she'd given it willingly. Disregarding the thought, he hitched forward in his chair, watching her lips. "What if I want another?"

"Another kiss or another slap?"

"Can one be enjoyed without the other?"

"Try it," she said, giving him an arch look, "and find out."

Falling back in a lazy sprawl, arms behind his head, he sighed, "No matter. I changed my mind. Don't want one now."

"Good, because I must save myself for your master."

The implication in that simple phrase caused another jolt of heat through his body.

"He may not be quite so repellent as you tell me," she went on. "I'll make up my own mind. I may decide to seduce him in any case."

For the first time in his life, the Earl of Swafford experienced a sudden, savage awareness of territorial prerogative in the matter of a woman. "What is your relationship to the pirate Downing, wench?"

"Aha!" She shook her finger. "He is no pirate, as I told you already."

He didn't like the sound of it. Criminals consorted with the like-minded. By association, she was tainted.

A restless creature, as she gestured with her arms, the voluminous sleeve of her gown knocked the pile of books by his chair, and the ill-fated goblet of wine tumbled over. The contents splattered across her skirt and the floor. Immediately all apologies, she collected the rolling goblet, pressed it into his hand and fetched the wine jug to pour again. He said nothing, simply let her do it, his defensive instincts muffled.

Even pouring his wine, she kept up her chatter, paying only scant attention to her actions, soon overfilling his goblet. This necessitated a tiny sip from the brim, which she took without asking, her hands clasped around both the goblet and his fingers. The physical contact, apparently unconsciously done, shocked him to the core and, while he watched her lips on the rim of his goblet, the Beast stirred again. The heaviness of raw desire was almost beyond endurance, beyond sanity. And when she licked her lips, he felt that bold tongue caress his skin, warm and wet, insatiable and brazen.

This was primal instinct, the pure, undeniable recognition of a mate preordained, and for the first time in thirty-five years, he believed in fate. It was as if she belonged there with him, as if they sat like this nightly and she poured his wine, chattering about her day.

Suddenly she cried out. "There's blood on your sleeve. You're wounded!"

He'd forgotten the cut. Now, as she made a fuss over it and over him, he mumbled that it did indeed sting very, very badly. Yes it did. She took charge of him at once, rolling up his shirt sleeve, exclaiming over the likelihood of infection. Gazing at her pale hands, so small against his thick, sun-browned arm, he felt larger and more cumbersome than ever.

"Water?" she demanded, taking charge.

He jerked his head toward the bedchamber, where a jug and basin awaited his evening ablutions. Fetching it, she knelt by his chair and washed his wound. He watched, dazed.

"Tell me what the earl is truly like," she asked, gently wiping blood from his arm. "What is he like inside?"

He replied gruffly. "You've heard what they say of him."

"That he has a foul temper? Yes."

"And yet you're not afraid to share his bed?"

"I enjoy a challenge."

He shifted in his seat, hot and restless. "Whoever told you he will eat you alive was wise to warn you."

"I'm not afraid of him," she declared firmly. "Like most men, he's stubborn and stupid. Being a nobleman, he regards the rest of us like dirt beneath his boots. I daresay he believes women should not be educated, they should remain ignorant chattel, good only for bearing children, no better than beasts of burden. He abuses his privilege and hoards his wealth. He is never satisfied and always suspects others of mishandling his affairs, cheating him in some way."

He coughed. "You have him down so accurately already. Are you certain you've never met the man?"

Looking around for a rag to bandage his arm, finding none, she tore a strip of cloth from her petticoat, briefly showing her ankles and lamenting her mud-spattered stockings, while he tried not to look. "I suppose the earl is stern and miserly," she said with a matter-of-fact shrug, "like all men of vast wealth, who need please none but himself."

"Exactly so. You're amazingly clever. Remarkably insightful." He rubbed his chin, feigning amazement.

"Does he have *any* teeth?"

"Not one," he replied somberly, tilting forward again. "I thought you were interested in the inside, not just his appearance?"

"The condition of a person's teeth reveals much about their character and personal cleanliness," she replied primly.

Another low chuckle built in his throat and he struggled to contain it. "What are you doing here, wench? The truth now!"

His arm neatly bandaged, she sat back on her heels, sighing deeply, the eager swell of her bosom caressed by the gentle firelight. "Someone has to fight for justice."

Warily perusing the woman kneeling before him, he wondered if she did this sort of thing often. How many others did she entice like this?

She smiled complacently. "Are you not glad I came to amuse you again, before I leave London?"

Leave London? Oh no, no, no. "Where do you go?"

"Somewhere." She laughed, the lush sound invading his quiet chambers with so much sudden life the dark, staid, paneled walls trembled with indignation. He flexed his fingers, easing the tension, hastily regrouping his thoughts.

Returning to the little tapestry foot stool, she continued her interrogation that would put the Spanish Inquisition to shame. "Why do you serve the earl, if he's so horrid?"

"I have no choice."

"You're an indentured servant?"

He nodded. "Some of us are born with a duty, a responsibility. Mine is to the Swafford name."

"I think it makes you terribly unhappy."

He managed a terse, "I'm no less happy in my life than any other man in his." As he reached for his wine goblet, she leaned forward again at the same moment. Surprised, he fell back in his chair, empty handed.

"You never smile." Her voice was almost musical, the timbre deceptively soft, but resonating deeply in each dark, neglected corner of his being.

He clamped his lips firmly shut.

"Do you not know how?" she persisted, eyes shining. "Shall I teach you?"

There was no escape, he was trapped. "Ridiculous wench. Leave me be."

"It won't hurt." She chuckled. "Try it. One little smile." Sliding forward she put her hands on the arms of his chair and he froze. How long had it been for him? Too long. If she came much closer she would put him over the edge. With narrowed eyes, he quickly scanned the distance to the woven straw rug by the fire. The bed might be more comfortable, with room to spread out, but the closer convenience of that rug would do to start. Very shortly the natural predator within would obscure any last gentlemanly cavil. She would discover the truth about his impotency, first hand.

But she moved first, tipping from the footstool onto her knees, forcing her way between his thighs. "Come, sir, I see the twitch, right…" she pressed a finger to his unshaven cheek "…there."

It was not the only twitch she caused.

Her teasing ended in a startled yelp as he caught her trespassing finger and trapped it within his fist. "Very well then wench, let's to bed. Or do you prefer the floor here, before the fire?"

"I told you--I'm saving myself for your master."

He growled. "If you please me, I'll speak to the earl on your behalf."

She laughed again, a deep, husky, wanton sound connecting instantly with some needy part of his soul. Watching a faint pulse at the side of her neck, he wanted to press his lips to it.

"I think you drank too much wine," she said, mischievous dimple appearing again in her cheek.

No. He hadn't drunk any wine. She kept preventing it.

"'Tis not the wine, 'tis you." The war drums of his heartbeat rumbled another call to advance. Why restrain it when she made no masquerade of her purpose there in his chambers? He sneered. "Lost your gumption?"

She clambered to her feet, brushing down her skirt. "Now you're being silly."

He scowled, outraged, speechless.

The rotten little tease headed for the door, leaving him without his permission. No one ever left his presence until he decreed it.

Especially not her.

CHAPTER 7

He was tempting, devastatingly tempting to an inquisitive, healthy young woman who clung to her virtue with scant enthusiasm, and began to fear she would die a maid. There was also something inherently sad and lonely in his eyes and she wanted to help.

Pity about the Sainted Virtue. If she stayed longer she might succumb, then she would have nothing left of value to barter for her cousin's pardon. "I must go."

He shifted to the edge of his chair, a great lithe cat, ready to pounce. "Have you forgotten Nathaniel Downing's pardon?"

It was late and dark, altogether too enticing to stay there with him, where it was warm and dry. As if to confirm her thoughts, the rain came down full force suddenly, blowing in through the window, knocking that valiant candle from the ledge, killing the flame. The chamber was lit now only by the glow of the fire.

Her hand on the door latch, she looked at him. Once she passed into the candlelit passage, she might never see this man again, yet there was a connection, raw and almost primeval, palpable the moment he'd touched her.

He challenged her with the suggestion of a little smile. It was not much of one, and rather stiff and rusty from lack of use, it seemed to surprise him that he even made the effort. Silky heat flowed down her body to the juncture of her thighs, where it turned into a fluttering beat of tiny wings.

Suddenly he was at the door, reaching for the latch, and she thought he meant to prevent her leaving.

"I can't stay." Then she added, "'Tis not courage I fear may fail me, only ladylike restraint." Oh, but that restraint, no more than a slender thread, stretched to the point of snapping. Goosebumps prickled along her arms, the craving for discovery was alive in every pore. She was ready like she'd never been.

With a little cry, she flung her

arms around his neck and he fell with his back to the door, slamming it shut again. A gasp of air rushed out of him as she stretched, reaching up on tiptoe, straining to press her lips to his. For a pulse beat he seemed too stunned to react. In the next gasp she was crushed between his body and the paneled door, his mouth on hers, covering it, ravenous and arrogant.

Pure desire, white hot and brand new, trickled through her veins, melting her insides. His lips moved wetly from her mouth to her cheek, as she squirmed and complained faintly, unaccustomed to a man taking the upper hand.

"I must leave," she groaned, trembling, sliding down the door until his lips skimmed her brow.

"Like all women--daughters of Eve--you're a menace, deceitful and cruel to lead me on and then leave."

She protested. "My intention was not to tease! Let me go, fool."

"Not yet, madam." He bent his head, his breath tickling the hollow beneath her ear. "I am not of a mind to let you go, until you tell me your name."

"I told you..." When his mouth brushed the side of her neck, she tipped her head back, trying to catch her breath. "...I can't..."

"Why are you here?" He held her wrists between her back and the door, his body pressed to hers. "Tell me the truth and perhaps I'll be merciful. Although my master would not be. Who sent you here? Who put you up to this?" He bent his head again to lick the curve of her ear.

She swallowed an incapacious cry of protest.

"Tell me," he repeated gruffly, holding her hard against the door, the words partly muffled in her hair.

"You know why I came. I told you my purpose."

"There must be more to it. You would give yourself away for so little?"

"So little?" she gasped, as his tongue boldly caressed the pulse at the side of her neck.

"Captain Downing means much to you."

"Yes. Do you have no loyalty, no devotion to anyone except your master?"

His lips ventured lower, traversing the upper curve of her quaking breast. A light touch, little more than a warm, whispering breeze, it still left a mark on her, the tracing of his damp tongue.

"You put yourself in great danger," he said, planting another kiss to the base of her throat. "What if the earl decides to keep you here as his prisoner?"

"I'm far too disagreeable for any man to want for long."

He paused. She thought she heard him laugh. It was an odd, stilted sound she longed to encourage out of hiding. He needed to laugh. She'd sensed that almost from the first.

"My lord?" Someone knocked at the door briskly, breaking through her balmy daydreams. The loosened bolt rattled, but her captor paid no heed to the noise.

He kissed her hot cheek and then reclaimed her lips. Eyelids fluttering shut, she arched toward him, her body yearning. She wanted to put her arms around his neck again, but his fingers were unrelenting iron cuffs around her wrists.

The visitor at the door knocked harder.

With little kisses he brushed one eyelid, then the other, his breath blowing playfully on her lashes.

She wanted to cry out, beg him not to stop. Instead she whimpered pathetically, "Someone comes for your master."

"Ignore. I'm not done putting you in your place for slapping me today."

"You'd best make haste. I haven't all day."

"Are you always so irritating?"

"Irritating?" she muttered wryly, "I thought I was on my best behavior."

"I'd like to see you at your worst."

"Be careful what you wish for." Heat radiated from her belly now; lust held her ransom against the door.

He growled gently in her ear. "What is it you want from my master? Say the word and I'll see that you have it. Anything."

"Captain Downing's pardon. How many times must I say it?"

"There must be more." His tongue swept over her mouth again as if he couldn't resist, yet when she parted her lips, ready for him, he left her waiting this time. "What could he give you? What could he do for you, not for Downing?"

A third, insistent knock rattled the door.

"Is there nothing you want? No fine pearl earrings? No purse of gold? No silk petticoat?"

She'd never thought of anything like that for herself. Earrings she would undoubtedly lose, a petticoat she would tear, and a purse of gold would only make her terrified of robbers. Where did one keep a purse of gold safely? She knew spending it all at once would be quite impossible. Even sixpence caused her palpitations, trying to decide what to spend it on.

"I want nothing else," she mewled, raising her lashes.

His breath was ragged, her own even less steady. In his eyes, pure gold gleamed through layers of dark and shadow, but despite the riches they held, they were the strangest, saddest, neediest two creatures she'd ever seen. She shivered.

His eyelids lowered slowly, shielding his thoughts and likewise that priceless plunder from her captivated gaze--as if it was not too late for modesty. As if her ideas didn't mirror his in that tense moment.

* * * *

Griff contemplated keeping her there. She was, it seemed, conflicted, and he was certainly loath to let her go. The sparks in her wide eyes lured him with promises of bounty he'd never believed in. He should know better. Glancing down at her full bosom, straining against his leather doublet, he expelled a quick groan of frustration. She was temptation incarnate. He was rigid with this torment. His seed surged vigorously with too much life after an extended dormancy.

If he didn't send her out now, he would embarrass himself like a green youth.

"Best leave now, wench," he muttered.

She hesitated.

"Go," he snapped, clawing through his hair.

She opened the door and pushed her way by the man who stood there, waiting impatiently. One hand clutching her breast, she ran as if the devil himself was on her heels.

"Who was that, milord?" asked Wickes, shuffling in.

"Nobody." He strode to the window, retrieving the fallen candle. The wine goblet rolled across the floor, almost causing him to trip. He swore.

"What happened, milord?"

"Naught," he replied tersely. Glancing over, he caught the manservant's expression and realized the combination of "nobody" and "naught" created considerable upheaval in the chamber. Wickes was staring at the deep red wine stain on the floorboards, looking angry and frustrated--more so than might be expected. "And where have you been for so long, Wickes, leaving me to the mercy of stray wenches?"

Wickes flicked a sly glance at the Earl. "I'm sorry, milord, I should've come back sooner. Didn't know the guard was absent from his post."

Griff slammed the window shut, but as he looked down at the torch-lit gallery, he saw her there, running under the arches. She came to a man who waited by a pillar and the two conversed. Thwarted desire ripped through him with long, greedy talons. There was some argument it seemed, but the couple under the arches were too far away for him to hear their words. He recognized Henry Jessop, a notorious lech, one of the infamous reptilia of court, someone he generally avoided.

"Milord, shall I…"

The earl grabbed his cloak from the back of a chair, already on his way out.

* * * *

"You owe me, wench. Now keep to your side of the bargain."

In all the excitement she'd forgotten Lord Jessop and their agreement. "The earl was not there," she said, "only his manservant."

"Not my fault. I brought you to his chambers, as you wanted." He leaned over her, his lips curled, his fingers pinching her skin. "Now yield, wench."

She struggled against his hard grip and rendered three long scratches down his cheek. He released her, his hand raised to strike, but fast approaching footsteps caused Jessop to falter.

"Get your hands off her!"

Madolyn seized her chance, leaping away through the arches with one last warning for the lecherous cad. "Leave Grace Carver alone! Come near her again and you'll be sorry. Though you think your blood is richer than hers, 'tis just as red and I'll gladly spill more of it, should you misuse that girl again."

"Grace Carver?" he wheezed, "What does she have to do with this?"

He still didn't recognize her, she realized. It was a good thing he didn't.

She vanished into the dark.

* * * *

"Who was that woman?" Griff demanded, arriving at Jessop's side.

"She's a damned whore and when I get my hands on her again, she's a dead one."

"Her name?"

"She promised me a night of sport in exchange for bringing her to your apartments. Now she reneges on that promise. She'll be sorry, whatever her name."

Nothing more to be got from the blabbering fool, Griff left him and ran after her into the night. He saw her climb into a hired litter and followed it through the streets on foot, shoving the occasional drunken wretch out of his path. The litter came to a halt before a large house and she ran inside. Strolling to the gate, he encountered two beggars waiting for alms and so he tossed them a handful of coin in exchange for the name of the lady in residence.

"Lady Shelton, sire. You know what they call her? The Scarlet Widow."

It struck him viciously, like her slap across his face. Of course. Why had he not seen it before? He'd heard she was related to that villain Nathaniel Downing. Why else would she come to plead for his pardon?

Now it made sense. That was why she would not give her name.

She was the consummate seductress, the ruin of many, the Scarlet Widow.

She was his brother's lover.

CHAPTER 8

That evening, when Gabriel suggested he make one last attempt to win his brother's blessing, Eustacia's screams echoed around the walls of the house as she berated her tender lover for being weak and afraid of his own choices. Eventually, Maddie heard Gabriel promise her cousin they would elope without his brother's approval, as she wanted, and by the time he left the house Eustacia was at least partway appeased.

At breakfast the following day, there was little conversation. Unless her lover was present, Eustacia was a mere shell, saving her energy for when he came. She stared off into the distance, her bony fingers quickly twisting apart little pieces of bread and scattering crumbs across the table.

The front door bell clanged and Grace sat up in her chair, her face bright. Observing this, Madolyn felt sick; she knew her sister waited for a visit from Lord Jessop, but surely there would be nothing more from him now. A good thing too, although Grace wouldn't know it.

Her sister never wore her emotions where others might see. Instead she held them deep inside. This morning, only the slightly heightened color on her cheeks proved she was in any way excited by the arrival of a letter, or hoped it might be for her. Her expression, for the most part, remained steady. Her gaze, an unusual shade of silver gray, followed the maid across the room as they would watch the progress of a bird, careful not to frighten it away.

But the message was not for Grace. It was for Eustacia

Stealing a glance at her sister, Maddie saw the shadow of sadness in her eyes. It was a brief lapse, for Grace swept her disappointment away like dirty old floor rushes, letting her anger boil inside, releasing only a little steam through the occasional sharp word or two. It was surely not healthy. Maddie often advised her sister to let it out and scream to the Heavens; Grace would only remind her she did enough shouting for the both of them.

Madolyn was also, as Grace would remind her, the one who made all the mistakes thanks to her impulsive nature.

Once she'd purchased mystical powders from a gypsy, who persuaded her that drinking them down in cider would make her invisible. For an entire day she was convinced it worked, and her family gleefully went along with it, pretending not to see her as she got up to various mischief. The pleasant imagining came undone when she decided, since she was invisible, she no longer needed clothes. Her subsequent encounter with the parson while strolling down the lane on a Sunday afternoon quickly overcame that idea.

Alas, mused Maddie, although much older now she was still prone to reckless impulse. As proven by last night's encounter with the earl's man.

Eustacia ripped open her letter and read it. Her lips puckered, opened and puckered again, before they found words. "How dare he? How dare he!" As she flung the letter across the table, they saw the sloping, thick writing scrawled there amid the ink blots, long, brisk strokes, scribbled in a hurry, quite possibly in a rage. At the bottom of the paper there was a single tall letter 'S', pressed so hard the writer must have broken his quill in the process of putting it there. "The Earl of Swafford requests the pleasure of my company," Eustacia exclaimed, her face wan.

"Perhaps he wishes to give his blessing," Grace asserted hopefully.

"Ha! He means to intimidate me, of course. He commands me to attend his chambers at Whitehall so he can put the fear of Beelzebub into me."

Studying the mess on the paper, Madolyn agreed one might imagine his fury as he'd penned those words in a rushed, trembling hand.

Eustacia's eyes were like a winter's morn when the only light came from a dull, dreary sky with no promise of heat. "I know how he disposed of other women in Gabriel's past. The man is ruthless and lives above the law. For sure he would have me murdered to keep me away from his brother."

Maddie looked again at the letter, morbidly curious.

"He can command me in vain," said Eustacia. "I'll not be summoned and dismissed by that ogre."

"Would it not be best to meet him? Reason with him?"

"There is no reasoning with the Beast. Tonight I leave London with Gabriel. He won't even know we've gone until it's too late."

When Eustacia left them alone a few moments later, Grace said, "I wonder why Lord Jessop hasn't sent a note. He hasn't come here since the day before yesterday. I hope he's not ill." Maddie swallowed a lump of bread rather too quickly and choked, and her sister smacked her on the back until the obstruction shot out again onto the table. "Perhaps he's busy and unable to come," Grace added, searching for excuses on her errant lover's behalf, as was her usual habit.

"Yes. That must be so." Madolyn rose from her chair. "Don't worry, Grace. If he never comes again he wasn't worth your affection was he?"

"Not come again? Why wouldn't he?" Grace clutched her sister's sleeve. "What have you done?"

"What have I... Why am I always accused of wrongdoing?"

"Because trouble is generally your fault," Grace replied sharply, having suffered previous suitors held at knife point, shoved and locked into coffers, or chased through the village by an irate sow specially trained for the purpose. "Not one of my suitors has ever escaped unscathed once you declare them unsuitable."

"With Papa away so often, someone must stand guard over the family treasure." Maddie shrugged. "Anything I do, Grace, is for your own good."

Grace repeated, "What have you done?"

"Naught!"

"Maddie?"

"I told him to leave you alone and never come here again."

Grace's mouth opened wide in shock and quick tears formed, shining like diamond chips in her lashes.

"I had good reason," she rushed to explain. "If only you knew... Grace, he's not a good man, not honest or faithful. He would never make you happy. In fact, I doubt his intention ever was marriage." She clasped her hands, wringing them like a wet rag. "I can't tell you what happened, Grace, but you must trust me. It was the right thing to do."

Abruptly, Grace pushed back her chair. "Madolyn Carver, will you never be done interfering in my life?"

"But I--"

"Why do you assume I need your protection? I'm four years your senior, yet you persist in this meddlesome--"

"That man is not what he appears to be! His feelings are not--"

"And what of my feelings?" Her face was tight and pale, a little rash of angry pink on her neck. "You gave no thought to me did you? No, it's always about you and what you think is best."

Never before had she seen her sister in such a mood, and Madolyn fell silent.

"Who gave you the right to take charge of this family?" Grace continued breathlessly. "No one needs your interference. And why would they? What makes you think you know better than me? What man have you ever loved? *Man,* not boy!"

Madolyn looked down at her hands, chapped fingers and tattered nails.

"You think this family would suffer without you, Madolyn, but I daresay, we could manage by ourselves. Better, in fact, without your foolish meddling. Yes, we would survive without you. If you wish to manage someone's life, let it be your own." She ran out in tears, too overcome by those ravenous emotions, previously stifled.

"See," Madolyn muttered sulkily to the empty room, "I always told you it did no good to hold your temper inside."

* * * *

Refusing to speak to Maddie for the remainder of the day, Grace took herself off to bed shortly after sunset once Eustacia and Gabriel were gone. Left alone at dinner, Madolyn relished the chance to refill her goblet without reprimand from either pious sister or spiteful cousin, and raising several toasts to them both in their absence, drank almost an entire flagon of wine without it seeming to have much effect, beyond the subtle blurring of edges and a cozy warmth in her cheeks.

However, even as she convinced herself she was quite sober, she began a wicked game of 'what if' in regard to that great, ugly, sullen fellow who'd thrice spoiled her plans the day before. What if indeed!

Rising dizzily from her chair, she was distantly aware of a bell clanging. It seemed possible someone came to arrest her for being a disobedient woman with shameful desires. Knowing she was ill-prepared in her current state to defend herself against the allegations, she chose to avoid capture instead. Clutching the flagon of wine, she blew out her candle and hid under the table, which is where a maid found her shortly afterward.

"The Earl of Swafford has sent a messenger for Lady Shelton. You'd best come out and see the man."

She hiccupped. "Me? I'm not going out there. Send the blackguard off with a flea in his ear."

"He says he knows she's here and he won't be sent away. He's a great big fellow and if you don't go out, he'll surely break down the door!"

"Oh, pull yourself together. He's not going to eat you, is he?"

The maid scuttled away, muttering under her breath. Maddie waited anxiously and then, hearing nothing more, assumed it safe to exit her hiding place.

Since Grace was sulking, Maddie wouldn't go to their bed tonight, and decided instead to sleep in their cousin's chamber at the far end of the house. Fortunately, the maid had already lit the candelabra in the hall, so she carried this with her to the second floor of the house. None of the other servants appeared, and she supposed Eustacia's impromptu disappearance gave them license for a holiday. They certainly wouldn't wait upon her "little country cousin" now she was gone.

Stumbling along the gallery, she gave the grim portrait of Eustacia's dead husband a wide berth before locating her cousin's chamber. The door was open. The lovers had taken flight in haste that evening, Eustacia leaving behind many of her clothes and less-valued trinkets scattered across her bed, thrown aside as she'd speedily chosen her attire for the journey ahead. Maddie set the candelabra beside the looking-glass and rummaged through the piles of clothing.

A string of pearls, simple and elegant, caught her eye. It was not like Eustacia's other gaudy jewels and no doubt left behind for that reason. It would not suit her tastes. Maddie lifted the pearls reverently and went to the looking glass, holding them up to her neck. She was fascinated by her image, how perfectly the form of one person could be transferred, mimicked by light and color. Eustacia would say it was vanity that kept her standing there looking for so long, but Maddie was just as amazed at the reflection of anything else in the glass as she was of herself. Anything else. Such as that man climbing through the window.

She blinked.

The pearls still clutched in one hand, she exhaled a high squeak of surprise, for it was the earl's manservant, unfolding himself through Eustacia's window, like a long-legged spider. She might have screamed if she thought anyone would come to her aid. Grace, however, would ignore her, thinking she made a fuss about nothing. She often accused Madolyn of excessive "dramaticals". So she looked for a weapon, but he was over the ledge and upon her in the next instant, hauling her back onto the bed, pinning her beneath his weight, her face pressed into the coverlet.

"Make a sound and you'll know my full wrath, Lady Shelton," he hissed. "So you planned a hasty escape, eh?" Finding the pearls in her hand, he wrenched them from her. "The Swafford pearls! This is what became of them? It wasn't Matthew." He threw the necklace and it hit the wall, the thread snapping like a whip, pearls scattering across the floorboards. "Pearls before swine indeed."

Her curses muffled by the coverlet, she writhed beneath him until he rolled aside and she breathed again. Crawling from the bed, she started for the door, and barely made three steps before he caught up with her, his great claw closing hard around her wrist. "Now you've put me in a very foul mood by forcing me to scale that wall and graze my damned knuckles."

"You're mistaken--"

"If you think for one moment you'll ever marry Gabriel Mallory, you're the mistaken one!"

The earl must have sent him to fetch Eustacia and for some reason he assumed... "But I'm not her," she exclaimed. "She's gone."

"Cease your noise! I don't want to hear another word from you."

Head reeling, she stumbled back to the bed and fell upon it.

"Look...my good man..." she tried to sound infinitely sane and sober, "if you take me to your master, I can explain--"

"My master?"

"Take me to him. I'm not afraid. I have a strong constitution and a high tolerance for pain. I've much to discuss with him." This could be her last chance, she realized. At last she would meet the earl and plead Nathaniel's case. If he thought she was Eustacia and he wanted her out of his brother's life, she could negotiate, and need not resort to "feminine wiles".

He hunkered down before her. A familiar scent filled her with joy and she thought of her father. It was one of the sweetest memories from youth, running to greet him on his return, stuffing her face into his shirt for greedy breaths. He smelled of the sea and adventure.

A mist descended. "I'm mind-numbingly tired now. Excuse me. I would rather discuss this in the morn." She yawned as the room began to spin. "Come back tomorrow, there's a good fellow." And like a grounded rowboat, she keeled over on her side.

Suddenly she felt his fingers tickling her, or so she thought, until she realized they worked with haste to remove her gown. Supposing she ought to protest, she rolled over for that very purpose, only to be distracted again by his scent. She reached for his sleeve and pulled it closer to her face. "You smell like the sea."

"Do I?"

"My father is away at sea."

"I suppose that's one way of putting it. Slightly more dignified than debtors prison."

He resumed the rapid disrobing of her limp body, muttering under his breath about faithless lying trollops and, of all things, pomegranates.

Once she was down to her shift and corset, she heard him tossing clothes from the bed, until he found whatever he sought. Then, much to her indignation, she was being dressed again, poked and prodded like a child's doll. He made her stand up and step into the skirt. Of course, it was too long for her.

"I prefer the other gown," she complained sleepily.

"This garment will serve, Lady Shelton. No need to tempt any men where we're going."

"Where are we going?"

"Far away from here and far away from Gabriel Mallory."

"Good!" She tried to clap her hands and missed. "I was weary of this place, but not ready to go home yet."

"You're drunk," he exclaimed, as if only just aware of it.

"Why else would I let you manhandle me in this fashion?"

"I assumed you were accustomed to it."

"Indeed no. I've never been dressed and undressed like this before. You make an interesting ladies maid." And she broke into chuckles, melting back to the bed. He stood over her, hands on hips. "I should hire you," she said, hugging her arms. "I need a new maid."

"You couldn't afford me." He hauled her upright again.

"Why? Are you very expensive?"

"Oh yesss."

"Your master is indecently rich, so I hear."

"Arms out," he commanded. She complied without hesitation, allowing him to pull the sleeves and bodice over her shift, rather enjoying the firm, masterful touch of his hands. Like the skirt, the sleeves were too long and if he expected that bodice to contain all of Maddie Carver, he would be disappointed. Spinning her around, he made a valiant effort with the laces, but the result was the same as squeezing an open and full sack of grain around the middle. Something was going to spill out. Apparently unfamiliar with this principle, he was utterly nonplussed by the effect. Glaring at her as if she deliberately encouraged her misbehaving bosom, he gave up on the laces, turning his attention to the droopy sleeves instead.

"I suppose you're blindly faithful to your master and can't be tempted to work for another." She sighed. "You must be exceedingly loyal, if you go to these great lengths on his behalf."

He crouched before her again, his hands around her face. "Be still, woman!" She made an effort to obey his order, hands resting meekly in her lap, too amused, weary and pickled to put up any fight. If he knew the truth, that she was an inconsequential nobody, he would leave her there to chase after Gabriel and her cousin. She hiccupped.

"And stop making noise," he added. "You begin to give me a headache."

"I've one too, but 'tis the wine, I 'spect."

* * * *

Although tonight she was delightfully compliant, he couldn't trust a curl on her head. Any moment now his brother would arrive at the house. Evidently she'd been arranging her traveling things when he got there. Time, therefore, was of the essence.

As if she read his mind again, a habit of hers it seemed, she laid her palms to his shoulders and urged, "Make haste. We've not a moment to lose, man. Come now. You've a job to do and I won't stop you." Apparently needing his solid frame to keep her upright, she slid her arms around his neck.

"Do not hang on me madam. I'll not be molested by you."

"Make haste. Take me. Wherever you must."

This was wrong. She was too keen to get away before his brother came. On the other hand--he looked at her drowsily fluttering lashes, pink cheeks and yawning lips--she was clearly soused as a herring. He shouldn't take advantage of it. He undertook these extreme measures solely for the Swafford family line. Couldn't have this woman's tainted blood infecting the noble strain, ruining his brother into the bargain. She over-flowed with tempestuous passion and teasing, slippery-tongued wit, evidently knew no limits with things she enjoyed.

In all likelihood, she was the same in bed. That idea found a way in before he could shut it out. Just like her.

"You're altogether too keen, woman," he grumbled, hot and sweating. It was as though he wrestled a large, overly-friendly wolfhound.

"Would you prefer me to fight and make your job harder?"

He unwound her arms from his neck and held one of her hands within his fist. "You could not fight me. See, your hand is too small."

"Small is not weak. I've felled many a brazen fool."

"I doubt not your abilities." For a moment more he crouched there, keeping her warm hand. If he meant to separate her from his brother, he must take her away now, before it was too late. It would be unthinkable for his brother to marry this woman. "As if I couldn't handle the likes of you. What you need is a little stern discipline." Mind made up, he shifted forward, threw her over his shoulder and lifted her easily from the bed. He carried her down the stairs, across the dark hall and out of the house. No one came to her aid.

He tossed her over his horse, leapt up into the saddle and slapped her hard across the rump. "Sit up, wench. The fresh air will do wonders for your aching head."

As they rode out into the night, not a single shout was raised in alarm, hers nor any other.

PART II
Sins of the Flesh

Chapter 9

"Serves you right, Lady Shelton," he lectured. "This is what happens when you have no restraint."

She groaned miserably, head limp, tongue thick. The greasy odor tied her stomach in a knot, while her kidnapper munched blithely away at the roast pheasant, licking his fingers now, deliberately noisy. Maddie shut her eyes tight.

"No more sleeping," he warned. "We've a long way to go yet. Here," he thrust the platter of meat under her chin. "Eat! Keep your strength up."

Sober now, she had tried, several times, to convince him he had kidnapped the wrong woman, but having made up his mind she was the Scarlet Widow, he listened to no argument. Since he was a stubborn fellow with a hot spur temper, it was doubtful he would look kindly on her once he discovered the truth. Once again, she thought unhappily, Maddie Carver would be blamed.

This dreary path brought her thoughts back to Grace. This morning her sister must have woken to find herself abandoned in Eustacia's house, but at least their father would soon arrive in London. And since Grace insisted she didn't need her sister's "interference", let her manage by herself for a change.

Pushing the platter away, she dropped her head to one arm. Her skull ached. The skin around it wrapped too tightly. Every tiny sound reverberated within, echoing like a blacksmith's hammer.

"Sit up," he exclaimed irritably. "If you could bring yourself to obey me, it will make the journey so much more enjoyable--for both of us. Smile at me, *my lady*, as you did last night. Or is it too much of a trial now you're sober?"

Scornful, she eyed him from beneath a tumble of spilled curls. "Is this how the earl treats women? Can he not get them any other way, than by sending his slave to kidnap them?" Having grown up listening to her father's disdain for noblemen, and holding his regard and his opinions on any matter far above anyone else's, her ideas about men like the Earl were long since ingrained. "As your master is so important," she continued sarcastically, "I suppose he converses directly with God. No wonder he knows what's best for his poor brother Gabriel."

Slowly his jaw moved as he chewed the meat in his mouth, that last great lump, torn off with his ruthless, wolfish teeth. Watching his lips move, she gauged how long it would be before he shouted at her again to be silent. As nothing came out, she added, "I hope the earl's involvement in *my* affairs won't keep him from his own business. He must have a great deal of responsibility and I shouldn't like to be blamed for any misfortune he suffers in his own affairs, simply because he takes such prodigious care of mine."

He picked at his teeth with a bone.

"Perhaps the earl has no affairs of his own and that's why he concerns himself with this one. Could it be..." She leaned across the decimated bird carcass to whisper archly, "jealousy?"

"The earl involves himself, *madam*, in this affair because he cares for his brother's welfare. Not yours." He sneered. "When we reach our destination, you'll write to Gabriel, informing him you've found another lover."

"I thought you were taking me to see the earl," she protested. "I have matters to discuss with him."

"Ah yes, the pirate Downing and his supposed innocence." His expression was pained, skeptical. "As if you would know innocence should it give you a damned good rogering." When this produced a gasp of indignation, he added sternly, "Perhaps the Earl might listen to your petition, once you write to Gabriel and put an end to this ill-advised affair. There, one favor for another."

"And if I refuse?"

"Until you agree to these terms, you must tolerate my company." Apparently that was the only threat he kept up his sleeve; he thought it would be enough. "You'll rapidly tire of me," he assured her proudly, the prospect of his company meant to induce timid quakes of fear. "I can be most uncouth and inhospitable."

"Indeed? I might never have guessed."

"Write that letter and you may return to your frivolous little life in London. And the earl might hear your case in defense of Nathaniel Downing. Of course, I make no promises. He might not."

"This is a splendid plan," she said. "Nevertheless, you overlook one thing. What if Gabriel doesn't believe the letter? He loves her...me, I mean."

"Nonsense. There's no such thing as love." His meal devoured, he raised his hand for the tavern-keeper's bill.

He was so sure of himself, as if no one ever proved him wrong. Hey ho! He'd never met Maddie the Merciless before had he?

Catching her eye twice in quick succession, and finding she did not look away as he evidently thought she should, he gruffly demanded. "What?"

"You're most alluring when so determined and cross," she replied.

He shot her a sideways glance. "Don't try to flatter me, madam. I'm wise to your... jiggery pokery."

It was one of her father's sayings and it made her laugh.

He frowned, hands paused in the motion of counting out coin for the bill. "You're young for a woman thrice widowed. How old are you?"

She raised her chin. "That's a very impertinent question to ask a lady."

"I don't ask a lady. I ask you."

"In that case, I'm one-hundred-and-eight."

He considered her thoughtfully. "You look younger."

"A consequence of witchcraft."

Shaking his head, he returned his attention to the coins in his hand.

* * * *

As they rode on, she amused herself by teasing him on the subject of his "master."

"Will you give the earl a full account of how we met, when you mistook me for a woman bereft of virtue and manhandled me?" She leaned back into the broad curve of his shoulder. "Would he approve of your behavior?"

"Madam, I knew exactly who you were," he lied briskly. "You never fooled me."

She laughed. She did a great deal of that and he was nonplussed by it. What could she possibly find so amusing in her predicament? Now recovered from her overindulgence of the previous evening, her mood improved considerably, and although she ought to be angry, demanding he take her back to London, she seemed content to let him drag her across the countryside.

"If I truly manhandled you," he grumbled, blowing one of her curls from his mouth, "you'd know it."

She wriggled in his lap again. The damned woman would drive him to insanity. Once more he felt the stirrings of a desire formerly in deep hibernation.

"Have we much farther to go?" She yawned.

His reply was curt. "Yes. Be still."

"Your lap is too hard, lumpy and uncomfortable."

"So sorry, madam, that my lap fails to meet your standard of luxury."

"I'll be numb soon," she complained.

He only wished he might be the same. Unfortunately he was increasingly sensitive to her restless fidgeting. "Witchcraft indeed," he muttered.

Rolling her head against his shoulder, she hoped aloud that the Earl appreciated his loyalty. "Or do you expect nothing in return for your services except his noble forbearance, his approval and the occasional scraps from his table? What a bitter old tyrant he must be."

"You know nothing about the earl. You have no right to criticize."

"I know exactly what he is--an ill-tempered ogre who cannot tolerate his own brother's happiness, simply because *he* is miserable." She wriggled again, pressing her bottom into his groin, one hand on his thigh to steady herself.

"Enough," he growled. "You can walk." Without ceremony, he pushed her off his horse and rode on, making no attempt to slow his pace. He turned off the road to cross a field sodden from recent rain, determined to punish her. He showed no pity, could not. He prayed for more rain. A blizzard. Anything to cool his blood.

She struggled to keep up, claiming a twisted ankle.

"It will do you good to walk some more," he flung over his shoulder. "May the exertion wear out your tongue, as well as your feet, temptress." And he urged his horse into a brisk trot.

"It seems the earl breeds his servants to be as proud and pompous as himself," she cried. Shortly after this she fell, tripping over a muddy rut, landing on her face. Hearing that startled yelp, he stopped, turning his horse to find her.

"Come, wench," he mocked. "Make haste, or I'll leave you for crow bait."

Cursing, she scrambled to her feet, the front of her gown covered in mud. Two steps later he heard her stumble again. He halted, looking for her. She was wiping her hair back, leaving her brow bloodied. She must have clutched for anything to break her fall and cut her palm on a thorny bramble. The sight caused a pinch in his chest, and he returned for her.

"Had enough?" he demanded.

When she would neither look at him, nor speak, the pinch grew worse. He swung down from his horse, licked his fingers and wiped the blood from her brow, resisting the urge to touch any more than that, but granting himself this one caress disguised as a practical act.

She mumbled weakly. "Don't touch me. Leave me here to die. No one would miss me, I daresay."

He was amused by her; it couldn't be helped. Pity she was his brother's lover. "Not much further now," he said, his voice softened.

"My ankle is all broke."

"Let me see--"

"Get your filthy paws off me! Yes, I suppose you're sorry now and so you should--"

Once more he lifted her off her feet and carried her, slung over his shoulder like rolled carpet, to the waiting horse. From then on he walked and she rode.

It was dark when they arrived at their destination. She would not see much of her surroundings, but it was a windy hillside and as he'd known it would, that fresh peck of sea salt in the air woke her just enough to resume her complaints in regard to his "rough, filthy, lecherous claws" and "villainous manhandling". Heedless, he carried her inside the cottage, dropped her among the floor rushes, and lit a fire in the hearth. Warning her sharply to sit there and stay warm, he went out to his horse.

By the time he came back, she was fast asleep by the fire and snoring.

It was done. He'd saved his brother from immediate danger. Whether Gabriel would see it in quite the same light was another matter.

He must admit, he'd be fairly enraged himself, if someone took her away from him.

CHAPTER 10

Kissed awake by wooly sunlight warming her face, Maddie found herself on a bed of sorts. Feeling around cautiously, she discovered she was still dressed, her headache was gone, her stomach settled.

It was a tiny, narrow space with one window through which gentle morning sun drifted. The only sound was the warbling cry of a gull. Up on her knees, she looked out and discovered a verdant hillside leading gently down to a breeze-ruffled cliff edge overlooking a peaceful bay. The tide was out, having abandoned piles of seaweed-strewn driftwood along an expanse of wet sand. In the distance, the sea glistened, a treasure chest of sapphires and pearls.

How strange, she mused, that this place was supposed to be punishment. She was a prisoner here, until she complied with the Earl of Swafford's wishes, and his servant promised to be a contrary and hostile host until she relented. Unfortunately for them, she was in no hurry to return to real life, where she failed at every task. Now she was here, she would enjoy herself and get as much out of it as she could.

The loft of the cottage was divided by a half wall and he slept on the other side, sprawling messily on his front across a bale of hay, one foot hanging in mid-air. He'd removed his boots and shirt, but nothing else. On his guard, no doubt.

She descended the narrow, rickety staircase to the lower floor of the cottage. There was little furniture: a table and two chairs, some copper cooking pots hanging over the big hearth, an unsteady writing table by the window, a few books and some shelves holding pewter plates and jugs. The pantry was very adequately stocked, as if the house expected guests. She found an apron there, a headscarf and some wooden clogs.

Hair tied back with the linen scarf, she began humming away while cooking bacon over the fire. She slipped outside to gather a bouquet of dog daisies and loosestrife for the table, returning as her captor, woken by the hearty odor of sizzling bacon, clattered down the stairs with one boot on as if he feared someone set fire to the cottage.

When she bade him a polite "Good morning", he exploded at her.

"What the devil are you doing?"

She slammed the pan of bacon down on the table, her good mood now severely tested. "If you want to eat, put your shirt on before you come to the table."

He sank slowly to the step, halfway down. "You cook?"

"I daresay there are many things I can do that would surprise you. Make haste, before it gets cold."

He came all the way down and when she reminded him again about his shirt, he reached for a sleeveless leather jerkin hanging over the back of a chair, throwing it on with a quick shrug of his shoulders. It fit.

"This is your house?" she asked, pouring from a jug of ale she'd found in the pantry.

"It belongs to the earl." He prodded tentatively at the bacon with one finger. "This is his land, his property. I come here sometimes."

She motioned to her apron. "With women?"

His golden eyes were guarded, thoughtful. "That apron belonged to the plowman's wife who lived here." No further explanation.

"Where is she now, then?"

"Dead. When I was a boy, she and her husband looked after me...sometimes." The explanation ground to a halt and he straightened his shoulders. "Why so many questions?"

"Good Lord, I've a right to be curious, surely!"

When she drew up a chair and sat beside him, he looked startled, uncomfortable, as if no one ever sat so close before; he might decide to shift his chair away. Instead, after a brief hesitation, hunger won out and he tucked into his breakfast.

Eager to learn as much as possible about his master, she prodded him. "The earl spends most of his time away?"

"Diplomatic missions abroad."

"Where to?"

"Wherever he's sent." He glared at her and she waited, brows politely arched. "Often to France," he added reluctantly, "most recently as the queen's ambassador to Spain." He paused, shifted awkwardly in his chair. "That's why he's away so oft. Not by choice--by duty." Again, another pause, followed by a dismissive shrug. "You wouldn't understand." Naturally, he thought she couldn't possibly comprehend a man so complicated and superior as his almighty master.

"And you sailed abroad with him?" That explained the sea salt, she thought, and the sun-browned skin. As he reached for more bacon, speared it on his knife, she coyly admired the lean muscle of his long, deeply-tanned arms. His chest too was partially displayed beneath the open jerkin, revealing more than she, a well-raised young woman, should ponder over. Not that it had ever stopped her before.

She propped her elbows on the table, resting her chin in one upturned palm. "Tell me more about your earl."

"Why? What is it to you?"

"You told me yesterday that since I don't know him, I have no right to criticize. So tell me."

He scowled. "The earl is a proud man and keeps a great deal close to his chest. No one knows him truly, although they might think they do. That's why he's misunderstood...by people like you." Point made, he returned his attention to breakfast.

"He's not married?"

He shoveled bacon into his mouth with the greed of a man who'd starved for days, although she'd seen him ravage an entire roasted pheasant the day before.

Only when she repeated her question did he mumble, "He has a wife."

She was surprised, having assumed the Beast's deformities kept him from marriage. Maddie ran her fingertip casually along the table. "Are you married?"

"I'd rather be boiled in oil."

Lips pressed tight, she watched him eat. After a moment she said, "No doubt your master, at his advanced age, suffers from chronic ill health, digestive ailments and rheumatic disorders."

"Particularly of late, since he encountered something that disagreed with him." Reaching for his ale, he added. "You take an interest in medical matters?"

"It is a hobby of mine, the study of cures and remedies."

The gold sprigs in his eyes gleamed bright. "Did your dead husbands benefit much from your study?"

Remembering abruptly who she was supposed to be, she laughed and he did too this time. A pleasant, unexpected sound, it ended suddenly as someone else intruded.

"Beg pardon, young lady, I saw the smoke and..." The old man standing in the open doorway saw Maddie first, before his heavy-lidded eyes found her companion and his careworn face transformed.

Griff leapt to his feet. "Gregory!" He put his arm around the old man's shoulders and led him outside. "The earl has a guest. She expects to be here a day or two." When he began whispering frantically, she, naturally, got up to follow.

Gregory saw her standing in the doorway and respectfully touched his cap, but Griff looked over his shoulder and snapped at her to go inside.

"It is good to have you home, *Master Griff*," she heard Gregory say. "And, if I might say, with a comely young lady. Shall I send Sally up with a bit of supper?" His voice faded and, peeking around the doorframe, she saw the two men walking away down the path, out of earshot.

* * * *

By the time he returned she was perched on the table, swinging her feet.

"The earl's steward," he explained gruffly. "Gregory, a good man. He and his wife live down by the bay." Wondering why he bothered giving any explanation to the irritating wench, he flopped back into his seat and took a long swig of beer directly from the jug.

As she sat on the table, feet dangling just out of his reach, in clogs several inches too big, he wondered why he'd never met her before. How the devil had Gabriel seen her first? Where had she been two years ago when he was last in London? He vaguely remembered hearing her name slandered at court. Lady Shelton was no favorite of the queen's and so would not have been invited there. Even so, had no one ever drawn his attention to her in some crowd? A notorious woman like this he would have remembered.

"Gregory said I am comely," she hedged.

Was she reading his mind again?

He kept his face stern. "His eyesight has failed these last few years, poor chap."

Aha, victory! Those lips, defiantly kissable, for once found no immediate response. Grabbing a corner of her apron to wipe his greasy mouth, he said, "Now you will write that letter to Gabriel."

"But the sun's out. It would be such a shame to waste it, sitting inside, writing a silly letter. We could go for a walk."

"Walk? For what?"

"For pleasure."

He was appalled by the idea. "I never do anything purely for pleasure."

She folded her arms, the portrait of a stubborn, doubting wench.

Standing quickly, he took her by the shoulders and steered her over to the little, crooked desk by the window. "Sit there and write to Gabriel." He broke open the lid of the pewter ink pot.

"What shall I write? Oh, you write it."

"It must be from you--in your hand," he said crossly. He must get this letter written, so he could send her back to London and out of his sight. Somehow he must cope with this and keep his mind uncluttered by her attempts to distract him.

But when he leaned over her, one heavy set of fingers clasped around her delicate hand, poised to guide the first mark on the paper, she protested, "I've never written a letter meant to break someone's heart."

"You will not break Gabriel's heart," he said firmly.

"He loves me."

"Thinks he does, perhaps, but if that boy kept his brain in a walnut shell it would still rattle." He guided her quill to the ink pot. "I'm sure you know what to say, madam."

She looked up at him. He knew he was too close, it couldn't be helped. He tightened his grip around her fingers.

"The earl is a cruel man to want his brother's heart broken," she said. "If it were my brother, I should want him to be happy, even if I disagreed with his choice of bride." Having said this, she faltered suddenly, her blue eyes dimming subtly. "Still, I suppose I too have been blamed for meddling in the romances of others."

He was barely listening, too aware of his quickened heartbeat, the smallness of her hand, the warmth and closeness of her body and the sweet scent of lavender in her hair.

"At least in my case," she added firmly, "I was justified."

What was she babbling on about? "Would you stop your chatter and apply your energy to this letter?"

"If I wrote to you, what would you want me to say?"

If she didn't keep her lips still, he might be obliged to occupy them in some other way.

"What is it?" she demanded. "Are you ill?"

He straightened up abruptly, releasing her hand. "Need some fresh air," he murmured, walking away. As she twisted around to see where he went, her sleeve caught the ink pot and sent it crashing to the stone floor. Ink spilled in a great glossy black blob at her feet.

He glared at her, arms swinging at his sides, tongue tucked into his cheek.

"It was an accident?" she offered timidly. "Truly." Lifting her shoulders, she smiled sweetly, all wretched innocence and dubious concern.

Speechless again, he tried making sense of her and decided she was the most perplexing conundrum of his existence.

"Shall we go for a walk now?" she chirped. "We have nothing else to do."

* * * *

The concept of a stroll was clearly unknown to him and therefore, like her, to be regarded with suspicion. Instead, he groomed his horse while she watched. "Do not cross that threshold," he bellowed rudely when she began to follow him into the sun-bathed yard. "Stay where I can see you."

So she leaned in the doorway, watching him with his horse. His long fingers combed through the gelding's mane with a gentleness that shocked her, especially after his treatment of *her*. Eventually she grew restless again, unaccustomed to staying put, just as he was to walking purely for pleasure. Since his back was turned, she crossed over to the water trough and perched on the edge.

"What do I do if *I* want a bath?" she asked.

"You must wait for your ablutions, Lady Shelton, until you're back in London, surrounded by your luxuries. There, see? You write that letter..." She watched him look for her by the door. Finding her gone from it, he swung further around, apparently in a pique, until he rediscovered his captive there on the trough. She smiled and turned her face to the sun, feet swinging.

"I thought your ankle was broken?" he snapped.

She opened one eye. "It got better."

He shook his head and turned his attention to brushing the horse's tail.

After a pause, she said nonchalantly, "When will you get more ink?"

"I'll send Gregory to the house tonight."

"What house?"

"Starling's Roost."

Ah yes, the earl's manor house. "Is it nearby?"

"Near enough," he answered.

If she was in Dorset, she was a long way from her home in Norfolk. Sliding from the edge of the stone trough, she crossed the yard to where he worked. "Is the earl there now?"

Moving around his horse, brushing its flanks with a firm, steady rhythm. He stopped abruptly as they almost collided. With a loud curse, he tossed his brush into the bucket, put his hands on her shoulders and turned her around. "I've endured as many questions from you today as I mean to answer in an entire lifetime." He propelled her toward the house. "Go! Inside." The moment his hands left her, she spun back to face him.

"Don't you care to talk? Don't you want to know anything about me?"

Regarding her as they would a fallen tree across his path, his eyes smoldered. At any moment they would burst into flame. "I know all about you, Lady Shelton, already."

"Aha!" Gleeful, she held up one finger. "You know only what you hear from vicious slander. You claim the earl is misunderstood by folk who think they know him, yet never will. Can the same not apply to me?"

He pointed at the house. "Woman...for the love of all saints...go...inside!"

"But..."

"Now! Do as I say, damn you." Arms out, feet apart, he towered over that little yard, trying to frighten her.

"Has no one ever argued with you before?" Maddie inquired, genuinely curious.

In answer he pointed again, thrusting his quivering finger over her head.

Lips pursed tight, she turned on her heel and limped back inside. "I'm hot in the sun," she said crisply, "that's why I'm going in, not because of your blessed orders."

Again he swore.

"And I don't care for your language," she added. "It is unbecoming in the presence of a lady."

He stayed outside with his horse for some time and when he came in she sat by the window, pretending to be absorbed in a dull book on fishing and trapping. Knowing he looked her way a few times, she stubbornly kept her eyes down, deeply enthralled in the book's goodly advice.

Pacing up and down, scratching his head, he exclaimed, "I don't know which is worse--your endless chatter or your stubborn silence. Very well, what will you tell me in your defense? What have you to say for yourself?"

Defense? She thought, for one dreadful moment, her secret was out, exposing her as a counterfeit.

"You catch me in a tolerant mood, willing to hear your case. Make the most of it, Lady Shelton, it doesn't happen often."

Relieved she still had him fooled, more than a little surprised to see a nuance of good humor so close on the heels of his anger, she closed her book with a snap. "What would you like to know?"

"Let's observe the salient facts." He drew up a chair, turning it to sit astride, as he would on a horse, his forearms resting along the back. "You've known three husbands, is that not so?"

She nodded.

"All three now dead, all within months of the wedding."

"Yes," she said gravely. "Poor souls. I've been unlucky."

"Unlucky? Is it not a great coincidence?"

"They were elderly and not in the best of health."

"You wore them out, perhaps?" He was smug, eyes gleaming.

"Never heard them complain."

His face fell into another scowl. "And how many lovers have there been? More than five? Less than fifty?"

"Fifty?" She laughed. "Where would I find the time?"

"Between your marriages. And during, no doubt."

She shook her head, still chuckling. Eustacia spent too much time preserving her beauty with strange rituals and it seemed unlikely she would get herself hot and disheveled on a regular basis, neglecting her carefully arranged appearance for too many passionate trysts.

He relaxed his shoulders a fraction. "You deny knowing so many lovers?"

"If Gabriel does not concern himself with the lovers in my past, why should you?"

Resting on the edge of the chair back, his fingers curled under, the knuckles turning white.

"If I was a man," she added, "you would, no doubt, congratulate me on my conquests. Profligacy is a luxury for men only."

Sweat glistened in a fine sheen across his brow. "Where did you first meet Gabriel? There are few people of rank who would invite you to their house, Lady Shelton. Certainly none my...master's brother would know."

"Mayhap your precious master's brother has a life of his own, a life about which your precious master does not know every detail."

"The earl," he said succinctly, "knows everything."

She groaned. "I suppose you have no life of your own either, like Gabriel. The earl rules over people with a stern, unyielding hand."

He crisply pointed out that no one had asked her for them and no one would, so she might keep those opinions to herself.

"Are you done now then?" she demanded.

"I wager 'tis what you say to all your lovers."

With that self-satisfied twitch pulling on his lips, he looked like a man in need of a good slapping and a firm set-down, both of which Maddie decided she would give freely and soon enough.

"Perhaps," he added, "if you knew one who kept you satisfied, you wouldn't require so many."

"I daresay. Would you volunteer for the post?"

That wiped the arrogant smirk off his face. She watched his fingers flex, his shoulders stiffen. The air in that cottage was suddenly oppressive, warm and thick. Her own heart drummed so hard she feared he would hear it.

"So," she said breezily, "it's a good thing you and I will never be lovers, for I don't take kindly to lectures and you can't tolerate a disobedient woman." She stood hastily, fingertips cautiously touching the back of her neck where it was damp with perspiration.

"Sit," he commanded.

"I tire of sitting," she said, striding around the room, aware of the steam virtually coming out of his ears. "Continue with your questions." She waved her hand carelessly, as she'd seen Eustacia do many times to her servants.

Only his gaze followed her back and forth. "So, you do not even remember where you met Gabriel. How soon was it before you realized his brother is the Earl of Swafford?"

"Immediately, of course! I said to myself, 'There now is your next provider, make haste and draw him in with your seductive charms, so you may bleed him and his villainous, foul-tempered brother dry of every penny.'" It seemed as if he believed her for a moment, not knowing she teased, so she laughed. "Fool!"

He showed his teeth in a wolfish sneer. "You wouldn't tell me the truth, would you? I wonder why I bother."

"Because you're intrigued by me." She'd only just realized it. Despite his loyalty to the Beast and even as he tried to act the part of inquisitor, he was rather too interested in the love life of his victim.

He was saved any reply, for Gregory timidly called out from the yard to see if he might enter. Instantly her captor replied that he may, then warned her, "Don't speak to Gregory and remember, you're the prisoner here. If you think to play your games with me, you sorely underestimate your opponent."

In the next instant, the steward was on the doorstep, cap in hand, and Maddie, ignoring her orders, went to the old man and shook his hand. "Gregory, is it not?"

Poor Gregory looked over her head to where Griff stood, swearing under his breath.

"Don't worry about him," she whispered to the old fellow. "He knows nothing of manners."

Gregory's jowls trembled, his mouth forming a round, black hole through which he uttered a tiny querulous squeak.

"Gregory, go to the manor house tonight and fetch ink." Griff strode up to them, separating their hands with unnecessary force. "Before nightfall. Quick as you can."

"Aye, Master Griff."

"Really, there is no haste," Maddie interrupted.

"There is every haste." He glowered down at her with what was supposed to be menace, but only reminded her of John, her little brother, in one of his temper tantrums.

"Are you bored with my company already? What a pity, I was beginning to enjoy myself."

His chest heaved with another exasperated breath. "Is there anything I can do to convince you to behave?"

She said the first thing that came to her. "You know the answer." What she meant was she would never obey him and he should know it by now. As she turned away from him, his hand moved. His fingers found the back of her neck, and in that one intake of breath, as he stood behind her, impulsively touching her in the same way he caressed his horse earlier, she knew the trouble she was in. The gauntlet was thrown down. Now he surely felt the goose bumps along the nape of her neck and knew what his touch did to her.

As she stood there in a strange cloud of euphoria, that single brush of his fingertips awoke a scandalously wanton imp, previously slumbering within, and it stretched now, lithe and limber, waiting for more of his touch.

"Sally baked a rabbit pie for your supper," Gregory mumbled. He waited, but there was no reply. Griff was distracted, looking at Maddie. She felt his licentious gaze inside her, still prying, demanding answers. Her corset was itching intolerably.

"Come in, Sally," Gregory croaked over his shoulder.

His wife entered, beaming, her face pink. She gave an odd movement, part bow and part curtsey. Maddie quickly assured her neither was necessary. The old lady handed her the pie with great reverence and whispered, "For your supper, my lady. 'Tis his favorite."

Maddie thanked her, warmed by the old lady's kindness.

"He's never brought a young lady here before," Sally burst out, only to be silenced with a frown from her husband. Stupidly pleased by that news and also quite dumbfounded as to why she should care, Maddie glanced over at her captor as he ran his fingers across his lips, those same fingers with which he'd touched her. She trembled, almost dropping the pie.

"My lady, are you well?" Sally asked.

Rather than answer, she turned away, setting the pie on the table. Hot and bothered, she was definitely not "well". True, there was a great deal of vitality surging through her, none of it was the sort to which one referred when inquiring into a person's good health.

Griff herded them out in haste, but she found one last burst of courage and ran to the door, shouting. "Don't forget the ink, Gregory."

A large pair of hands hauled her back into the house and the door slammed shut.

Chapter 11

Wedged between his tall body and the door, she blustered, "Do you want some rabbit pie?"

His size, in comparison to hers, made him feel very male. And very powerful. "*Do you want some rabbit pie?*" he mimicked her.

The wench had the audacity to ask, "What ails you now?"

He leaned closer, wedging her in as he did before in his apartments at Whitehall. Tonight they would not be disturbed. His hands rested against the door, palms flat, arms bent. "Now, where were we? Ah yes, I remember… you asked me to volunteer my services, your ladyship."

"Oh, don't start that again!" She turned her head away. Was she laughing? Hard to tell with her sometimes and he had no experience with this. Whatever it was.

Brief warnings flickered through his mind. She was his brother's lover, a woman of dangerous allure. He should back away now. The blue of her eyes was deceptively light, suggesting shallow waters, yet there were treacherous depths, waiting to drag him down with the current.

And her fingers curled around the armholes of his leather jerkin, clinging rather than pushing him away.

She must know his identity, he thought suddenly. She could have made a great deal more fuss than she did when he stole her away in the night, but she went willingly even encouraged it.

Now it made perfect sense and, of course, if she knew who he was, it completely excused his own behavior. His conscience was assuaged. The woman was incapable of fidelity and it was his brotherly duty to save poor Gabriel from her immoral clutches. Griff thought only briefly of his own morals, but decided they were not his first concern today.

* * * *

His scent was all-consuming, villainously distracting. Her hands, pressed to his leather jerkin, were insignificant before his broad shoulders and the hard planes of his chest.

"Aren't you hungry?"

"Not for rabbit pie,"

"Then for what?"

"For you." Little gold flecks pulsed amid the lush brown of his covetous, mutable gaze. His eyes were always more expressive than his tongue, she realized, liquid anticipation rippling through her. He bent his head another inch, his lips brushing the tip of her nose. She felt how hard he breathed, like a man running uphill in a hurry. "I have a curious appetite, Lady Shelton, and only you can satisfy it. I must know what makes an otherwise sane man like Gabriel lose his head."

"He has not lost his head, only his heart."

"The power you hold, madam, is not over a man's heart." His mouth found her top lip and waited, poised above her trembling breath. It was unbearable. Oh, she wanted that kiss. If he denied her, she would simply melt away in a vast puddle on the stone floor of that little cottage. It already felt as if her skin beaded and dripped like wax down a lit candle. She was itching intolerably inside that corset.

Attempting patience, she failed. Her impertinent mouth lifted to his, not because she allowed it, but because having tasted him before, it no longer cared a pip for Maddie Carver's dignity.

"Do you forget Gabriel already?" he murmured, his lips caressing hers with each word, each tersely granted breath.

"Yes," she sighed, helpless.

"Then this is far enough, proof enough of your inconstancy."

"No!" She reached up around his neck, clinging to him. "Kiss me."

He closed his eyes briefly, cursing.

Imperious, bold and fiery passionate, she commanded him again. At last he relented. His mouth covered her impatient lips, making short work of his previous reluctance. It was a spark in a tinder box. Nothing would halt the blaze now. They were lost.

He lifted her and she clung to him, locked her fingers at the nape of his neck and returned his kiss with a frenzied, greedy desire for more. But as his mouth left a damp trail down her neck, his hands shifting her more securely against the door, she whimpered, "There's a matter you should know."

He grunted. "Talk later. Been too long for me. By Christ!" His arm cradled her weight in precarious balance against the door and she marveled at his strength, letting her hands stray across his tensing shoulders. His eyes were shut, his brow damp, one hand reaching between them.

Suddenly, she felt him. Every inch. Dear God! She was shocked speechless.

Here? Like this? She didn't know it was possible.

Groaning, he lifted her higher against the door, her skirts rapidly bunched aside. She was beyond speech, he was beyond listening. Calling her a wicked temptress, he wanted her to look at what she did to him with her witchcraft, urging her admiration of his rampant shaft, dark and erect in juxtaposition to her pale thighs.

"I should disappoint you now," he whispered, "and leave you wanting this."

The shocking sight of his manhood combined with the warm, damp caress of his words, threatening to leave her unsatisfied, turned her into a woman without shame.

"Don't you dare stop," she cried.

She felt laughter shuddering through him as she wound her legs around his waist, tangled her fingers in his hair and peppered his face with pleading kisses.

She'd been told before she was a persuasive wench, although not quite so convincingly as when he cast his doubts aside, hitched her up onto his rock hard erection and entered her at last, like a battering ram, thrusting her back against the door.

Once, when she was young, Maddie was almost killed by lightning. Caught in a storm that came out of nowhere, she had foolishly sought shelter under a tree and her body had hummed for three days after.

Madolyn Carver relived the thrilling, terrifying moment again on that day, in his arms, the arms of a man she barely knew.

There was a moment of pain, sharp and sudden. Her eyes flew open to find him staring at her, confused. Afraid he might withdraw, she buried her face in his neck, hiding her blushes. She could not feel his breath now and thought he must be holding it. He was inside her, filling her sheath, stretching it slowly, igniting her passion, inch by inch. His muscles were tense, damp with sweat. He groaned, a helpless curse or else a plea for mercy.

Holding her to his body, her legs wrapped around him, he carried her swiftly to the table and with one arm, swept it clean. There, he laid her down, his eyes fierce, lit with primordial fire. She made no protest at the roughness of the table or the ruthless treatment of Eustacia's gown; instead she whispered his name as if she'd waited all her life to say it. As he leaned over her, his thrusts increasing rapidly, each one deeper than the one before, she thought of a stallion covering a mare. She slid her legs up his back, desperate and wanton, her hands under his leather jerkin, spread over the taut muscle of his chest and when her exploring fingers touched his hard nipples, he expelled a low, shuddering breath. His pace slowed. Eyes closed, he leaned back, making each stroke of withdrawal so long and teasing she thought he deliberately tormented her. Yet in equal measure came the blissful, forward-thrusting parry she felt along her entire spine. She could almost taste him in the back of her throat. Sliding his hands under her hips, he arched over her again, his loose leather jerkin catching on the beading of Eustacia's bodice, and then he went rigid. It lasted a breath, perhaps two, before he took the last distance at a hard gallop, hot and slick, and she wound her thighs around his back, riding him home.

By the last groaning thrust she was no longer whispering his name, and the birds down in the bay, pecking in the sands, must surely have taken flight at the sound of their joined cries.

* * * *

He swore. Again. Shoulders trembling, he redressed himself with his back to her and strode out, slamming the door in his wake. She couldn't think why he was in such a dudgeon, especially since she was the one with blood on her skirt. But infuriated to this intense degree, he took himself out of her reach.

At least now she wouldn't die a maid. She knew nothing about the man, yet perhaps that was for the best. This was lust, nothing more. A simple need, blissfully unfettered by rules and foolish emotions. Men did this sort of thing all the time; only women made silken bows around it, causing themselves undue pain and torment. So she would be like a man. She was quite convinced her heart needn't be involved. In any case, she thought with a sigh, look what love had done for Grace.

She returned to her chair and the dull book. While it was a relief to sit, for her legs were weak, her mind was too scattered to read, so eventually she set the book aside again. She tried to amuse herself, exploring the pantry and the long shelves of preserves, vinegars, wines, smoked meats and pickles. Cheering herself up to a false sort of giddiness, she pretended they were an old married couple. He worked in the field and would come home to her fine repast. She lit candles as the sun set, and only then did she think to check outside in the yard.

The door was locked. Now she was truly a captive.

She'd given herself to a complete stranger. He might commit some violence against her and no one even knew she was there. She'd let lust and passion run away with her and now she was at his mercy.

Alone at the table, she watched the candles burn down, her belly rumbling in hunger, yet she was too wretched to eat. Finally, she heard hooves. Hands clenched in her lap, she waited. Footsteps. He was unlocking the door. Ha! Now he came back. She would not speak a word. No, indeed. Let him be the first.

The door opened. She leapt to her feet. "Where have you been?"

Closing the door slowly behind him, he looked at the table.

"Supper's ready," she added, faltering. "Your favorite."

He looked rather pale, standing there, scratching his head.

"Rabbit pie--the one the steward's wife brought," she reminded him. He walked to the table and she followed, hands clenched so tightly they were numb.

"So." He paused, took a knife from the table and raised it. "Would you mind telling me now who the hell you are?"

CHAPTER 12

"I think I might know a maid when I encounter one," he said dryly, "not that it happens oft." He cut into the rabbit pie and passed a slice onto her plate as if they discussed the weather, or the state of this year's harvest, or the fate of a lame horse. She stared at him, confused, whereupon he set down his knife, the blade rattling against his platter. "I know now *what* you are," he clarified, "but I know not *who* you are."

"I don't care to tell," she said hotly. Under no circumstances must her family learn the details of this little adventure and when she met the earl--if she ever did--he couldn't know anything about her.

"What you *care* to do no longer matters." Cutting another slice of pie, he shook his head and marveled, "I've never known a maid so ready and willing to abandon herself. What did they pay you?"

"What did who pay me?"

He regarded her sternly. "I won't be made a fool." He stabbed the pie with his knife. "Aren't you hungry? Sally's cooking is excellent." So expertly and speedily he hid his anger, as if he'd suddenly become another man. She looked at his long, sun-bronzed fingers. Wielding that knife they oozed menace, reminding her again of the danger she courted in the company of this stranger.

"Where did you go for so long?" she asked, angry with herself for sounding childish.

"For a long ride to clear my head and try to make sense of this. Of you."

She sank in her chair, feeling naive and stupid. The masquerade tossed aside, her chance of meeting the earl now was slim to say the least. He might have listened to Lady Shelton, who had a bargaining chip. He would never listen to plain Maddie Carver, who had nothing to give now. Disgusted with herself, she could hardly raise enthusiasm for rabbit pie.

Now he lectured her. "You're an astonishingly foolish and reckless woman. Whoever you are."

"I suppose you'll tell the wretched, stinking earl now."

Reaching quickly for his ale, he drank it in one gulp, watching her with wary eyes, as if she might suddenly lunge at him and bite. His fingers drummed against the empty tankard. "Give me a reason not to tell."

"When he finds out, you'll be in trouble too."

"I think I already am."

"He'll have you whipped for taking the wrong woman. He may dismiss you from his service." Resting her hand on his arm, she added anxiously, "I wouldn't want to see you hurt."

He looked down at her fingers. "Why would you care what happens to me?"

"You're ten times the man he is, for sure. He's not fit to lick your boots, I daresay."

"Would you tell him that to his face?"

"Certainly. I'm not afraid of that pompous, arrogant fool."

Apparently in danger of choking again on the pie, he wiped his mouth with one hand. "I doubt he would take kindly to being called such by a scrap of a maid."

"A scrap indeed!" she exclaimed. "And no more a maid, thanks to you."

He looked up sharply. "How old are you? The truth now." She felt his arm tense under her fingers. "I must know."

"One and twenty."

Groaning, he threw his weight back into the hapless chair.

"A great deal old enough to know my own mind!" She leapt up and began to pace. "I suppose you'll accuse me of deliberately deceiving you. Always the fault is laid at my door, when things go wrong."

"I suspect it often *is* your fault." But his frown relented. "Sit down and eat, woman, or I might feel inclined to beat the truth out of you, especially in my current mood."

Incapable of doing either thing he asked, she resumed a restless circuit, chewing her fingernails. When he held out his empty tankard, she exclaimed curtly he could pour his own ale. She had too much else to consider and no time now to wait on him hand and foot. He slammed his tankard down, pushed back his chair and came to stand in her way, halting her progress. She thought he would slap her; instead he picked her up, swung her legs over his arm, and carried her back to the chair, where he sat her like an errant child, tucking her in and returning to his own seat.

"I still don't know what to call you, so unless you prefer me to whistle when I require your presence, I suggest you tell me your name."

"Indeed you may whistle," she replied. "Whether or not I come to it is another matter."

He opened his mouth, but shut it again quickly, once more holding in his anger. With a long sigh he took possession of the entire remaining rabbit pie and calmly devoured it.

* * * *

Moving his chair over to the fire, he sprawled in the comforting glow, stretching out his legs, patting his stomach. He was pleasantly replete, satisfied in more ways than one that night. "Let's discuss the matter of you and I then."

"What matter?"

Raising his arms over his head, he expelled a great contented sigh. "What happened today, between us, and what ought to be done about it." He let his eyelids drift to half-mast, but still watched her intently. Couldn't afford to take his eyes off her too long, there was no predicting what she might do next.

"No one will find out, rest assured. It can be forgotten."

That's what she thought. He was not in the habit of ruining maidens. "Something troubles me. I think it might be...surely not...could it be, after so long, my conscience?"

"For sure your *conscience* will recover."

She was a disheveled creature now, her scarf abandoned, hair tumbling loose and wild in a thick black mane. When he looked at her, his chest tightened as it did when he spied a particularly fine creature at auction. Just as his eager stud horses flared their nostrils and grew restless when they sensed a new filly nearby, tonight he felt a keening, rampant desire obscuring any other thought. She fascinated him like no other woman ever did and he lost control with her in a way that almost frightened him.

A virgin! He was still trying to comprehend it. "I'm a man of honor. Even if you hold your virtue lightly..."

"For the Love of Saint Pete, you're in no danger. I'll take this secret to my grave."

"That's a dangerously long time to keep a secret." He scratched his chin, watching her thoughtfully. Although she'd traded her virginity for this wicked ploy against the Earl of Swafford, she spoke too politely for a common whore. He already knew she could read and write so she was educated and, since she'd cared enough to shout at him for coming to the table without a shirt, someone raised her with manners.

She was certainly an amusing creature and provocation of the worst kind. Even as she sat before him, deceptively innocent, her spine straight, haughty chin lifted and hands wound tight, probably to keep them out of trouble, he envisaged her naked beneath him. It was shocking, but as so much of this was patently absurd, he let his mind go with the image. He recalled her thighs around him, her supple legs sliding up his back. He wouldn't be surprised to find she rode astride with strong thighs like hers. He bit down on his tongue, his mind drawing licentious images of the sporting pleasure to be enjoyed between those thighs.

"What happens now?" she demanded. "Now you know I'm not Lady Shelton, I suppose you'll throw me into a ditch somewhere, or over the cliff in an old sack and leave me to drown."

He nodded somberly, his voice scraping out at an oddly high pitch. "All good choices."

She stuck out her saucy tongue.

"Can't keep you here indefinitely, can I? And you won't tell me your name so I can't take you home to your family. I won't take you back to London."

"Why?"

"Because you once protested at the number of villains, rogues and knaves you encountered there and I wouldn't want any harm to come to you. In truth, I feel protective toward you now. Almost," he paused, "possessive."

It was a new idea for him, when it came to women, and he wasn't pleased. "Go to bed," he snapped suddenly, not sure where to direct his anger.

"It's early," she protested, pouting.

But he needed as much distance between them as he could make. For her sake, not just his. "Go," he yelled at her, making her jump.

Scowling, swinging her linen headscarf, she traipsed up the stairs, each footstep banging loudly. He stayed below, listening to the gentle waves now covering the bay. Finally he lay down on a fleece before the fire and made some attempt at sleep.

CHAPTER 13

While he plotted to keep her at arms length from now on, Maddie sketched a plan for his undoing. Forged in a mostly sleepless night, her ideas were still fresh the following morning and she keen to embark upon them. This was it then; her long-awaited adventure. She couldn't let it pass her by. They didn't have forever, so she ought to make the most of it.

She asked if she could go down to the bay today, now he knew she was not likely to run off.

"I don't know what you'll do," he replied, grumpily. "I haven't yet ascertained the length and breadth of your capabilities in that regard."

She emerged from the pantry, jar of treacle in one hand, sticky knife in the other. "Am I still your prisoner?"

"Until I decide what to do with you."

The gray shadows under his eyes proved he slept little the night before, but he'd shaved that morning, before she was up. It made him appear younger. His lips she daren't consider for too long. His nose was long and thin, and his eyes, of course, were that luscious combination of spring grass, warm earth and afternoon sun. His jaw was strong and square. He must have a steady hand today, she mused, for there was not a single cut from his razor blade, yet he was not calm the night before. It gave her a little thrill to know she possessed the power to unsettle his hands.

His gaze slid over her, a slow caress almost stopping her heartbeat. "You'll cut your tongue."

She licked the blade again and although he shook his head, his eyes were too warm. "You should pay heed to me," he said huskily. "One of these days you shall."

"If you mean to train me in obedience, sir, think again. I follow no man's orders."

"You," he murmured, "are a dangerous woman."

"Never fear. I only bite when roused."

"I worry not what you could do to me, but what I could do to you." He reached out one long finger and wiped it across her cheek, collecting a stray blob of treacle.

"What keeps you?"

"My gentlemanly restraint."

She laughed. "Hey ho! Like yesterday?"

He shook his head, still holding out his finger with the treacle on it, so she leaned over and licked the sticky treat from the tip of his finger. That loosened his disapproving lips enough to reprimand her again. "'Tis rude to take before you're asked, young woman." In answer to that, she swept her tongue out again, this time capturing his sun-browned finger in her mouth and sucking the last traces of treacle from it. His expression changed rapidly again, from annoyed to shocked, to an emotion for which she had no name. Releasing his finger, she licked her lips slowly. "Like I said before," he croaked. "You're a disobedient, foolhardy woman and you ought to pay heed to your betters."

"Where are they then, my betters?"

"Right," he leaned toward her and almost bit off her nose, "here!"

She swung away, humming, licking her lips.

"You have a sweet tooth," he said, "and now you're sticky."

"I'll go to the bay and wash it off."

"You go nowhere without my permission."

She paused in the doorway, licking the knife's blade again. "I'll go where I please."

"Come...here!"

Her gaze locked with his, horns likewise.

She turned and ran for the bay.

Moments later he caught up with her, but she pleaded, "My ankle. The salt water will do it good."

"If I concede this one thing to you, do I have your word to stop testing my patience?"

"Of course," she said sweetly.

When his long fingers curled gently around her arm, Maddie's heart skipped and danced. A little victory.

The air was cooler today and as they neared the bay, she felt a damp sprinkle that could be rain or a light mist from the water. He mumbled under his breath about her bad behavior, expressing self-righteous surprise that her wayward, wanton temperament didn't get her in trouble with men before now. Talkative today, he wanted to know a great many things, none of which she could tell him.

"Can we not enjoy our time here together?" she said simply, stopping on the path.

"Our time together?" He regarded her doubtfully.

"I am minded to stay here with you a while."

His mouth flapped open and a startled, indignant laugh spurted out. "Oh you are minded, are you?"

She nodded.

Hands on his hips, he looked away briefly, his jerkin blowing open in the breeze. "You can't stay with me. I don't want a woman in my life, no matter how beguiling she is."

"Why?" she demanded, pulling on his shirt sleeve.

He glared down at her insistent, sticky fingers. "Because I have enough responsibilities. I don't want any woman hanging on me." One by one, he peeled her fingers from his sleeve, wincing at the treacle mess she left there.

"I must see the earl and persuade him to arrange a pardon for Nathaniel Downing."

He shook his head, exhaling heavily.

"I'll make him see sense. I daresay no one has ever told him the truth before, too afraid of his wrath. But since he doesn't know me, I need have no fear of reprisals. I'll tell him he's an interfering old bugger, jealous of his brother's love affairs. He needs a woman of his own. Since he has none, perhaps that accounts for his ill-temper." She paused. "Your mouth is hanging open," she pointed out.

Lips snapped shut, he walked on, arms swinging, his stride long and loose. She hurried after him, tripping down the path, until he turned and caught her before she fell into him. "Reckless," he admonished her.

Sliding her arms around his waist, she looked up at him, her hair blowing wild in the churning sea breeze. "I won't go yet. I'll stay with you. I'm quite decided and rarely am I swayed from any scheme once my mind is set. My father could tell you that."

* * * *

Her father. Somewhere she had one.

Setting his feet apart to steady them both he put his hands around her face. "I can't keep you here." He brushed her buttery-soft cheek with his knuckles. "Even if I wanted to, no matter how you tempt me."

"This will be our secret. No one else will ever know."

She was surely a wicked demon, he decided. A siren, like those who lured sailors to their death against rocks. She must know who he was, or she wouldn't waste her time on him. Palms to her shoulders, he tried pushing her away, and when she resisted, clinging, he called her a limpet. The fierce wind buffeted her skirt and she clung around his waist to keep from being blown away.

As her hair billowed around them, slapping his face, his heart quickened in a peculiar fashion, leaving him short of breath. "I can give you nothing." He looked down into those wide blue eyes. "I'm not a rich man, merely a servant indentured to the earl." Waiting for a flicker of scorn to give her away, some sign to prove she knew the truth, instead he was surprised when she threw her head back, demanding a kiss.

"At once, man!" she added when he hesitated.

"Oh, no, no, no! For the Love of Christ! Not again." He stepped back, holding her by the elbows. "Listen, wench, I can't keep you here--as much for my sanity as your safety. And wipe that expression from your face this instant. Stop smiling!" Feeling unusually helpless, he blustered churlishly, "I prefer my life as it is. Predictable and...and..."

"Dull!"

"Orderly," he said. "Uncluttered."

"Are you afraid of me?" She appeared vastly amused by the

prospect. "I'm too small--you said yourself--to do you any harm."

"I wager your father is a great deal larger than you and probably keeps a sword or two on hand, along with the odd disemboweling cutlass."

She chuckled, reaching for him again. When he tried to separate himself from her clutches, those determined hands clung to him with the aid of sticky treacle smudges. "We're stuck together," she observed, enjoying the joke.

"We can be unstuck," he replied firmly.

"Let me stay. I'll not be any trouble, I promise."

"Women's promises are ill-kept. And I have first hand knowledge of your wickedness, your refusal to obey and your utter lack of self-command. Why would I keep such a wayward wench?" When she didn't reply, he knew, without even seeing her face, that she was scheming again.

"Oh look," she exclaimed, suddenly releasing him, as if she was never stuck in the first place, "shells!" Pushing him aside, she ran down onto the sand, leaving him no choice but to follow, if he wanted her back. And he did.

* * * *

Rain threatened, and sometimes she felt the kiss of warm drops, but fancied it came from the sea, not the sky. Over one shoulder, she saw Gregory trotting across the sand to converse with *Master Griff,* as he and his wife so reverently called him. She supposed they'd known him since childhood. Griff once mentioned being born on the earl's estate. Since his parents were both dead she supposed Gregory and Sally were like family, and it was plain they doted on him.

When she waved, Gregory lifted his cap, beaming scant-toothed, but Griff merely crossed his arms and leaned against the rock. God forbid he spare her another smile. Few and far between, their rarity made them even more precious. Turning away, she paddled further along the bay, straying out of the boundaries he'd set for her. A series of rock pools dotted the far end of the crescent and she made her way there to hunt for more shells, collecting them in her borrowed apron.

The pools were already quite deep and she sank to her hips in the water. Unaccustomed to this abuse, Eustacia's skirt bubbled up around her, so, rather than be hindered by it, she slipped it off, spreading it over a rock to dry before resuming her hunt for shells. Occasionally she ducked under the water to retrieve one, and in this manner, was busy for some time, inattentive to the advance of the tide. It was above her waist in the rock pool when Griff came to find her.

Bellowing at her, he stood on the rocks, soaking wet from head to toe, wearing only shirt and breeches. At first she couldn't understand a word out of his mouth, but eventually it became clear, as he stood cursing, spitting and upbraiding her for being reckless and thoughtless yet again. Apparently, when Gregory had left him and he'd come in search of her, the first thing he'd seen was Eustacia's discarded skirt floating away on the advancing tide. So he swam out to rescue her.

Maddie laughed as he told the story and this made him angrier, until his words broke down into a series of stammers and accusations. He splashed into the rock pool, flinging seaweed from his shoulders. "I have been forced," he sputtered, "to watch you...showing off in the water for the last hour...skirt up around your knees...deliberately listening to not one..."

"Could you move your foot?"

He did. She took a breath, ducking under the water to collect another shell. When she emerged again he was still complaining as if she'd never left. "And you speak of being no trouble, gazing up at me with those damnable blue eyes, until I almost forget how much trouble you've already caused me."

"Oh calm yourself! You make a considerable tantrum with very little cause." Twisting her hair over one shoulder, she squeezed out the seawater. "Pity about the skirt, as I have no other and you gave no thought to that when you dragged me out of Lady Shelton's house." Turning away, she laid her collection of shells out on the rock. "You'll have to tolerate me in my shift. Will you manage?"

When there was no reply, she looked

over her shoulder, catching him in the motion of drawing his hands up over his face, washing something off. Seawater dripped from his eyelashes and rendered his shirt translucent. The linen molded to every sculpted detail of the glorious body within. Maddie bit her lip, tasting salt. She remembered the rock hard slabs of his chest pressing her to the door and how as he'd laid her on the table, those same broad muscles arched over her...his masterful hands holding her hips, his manhood plundering her maidenly treasure. As he started toward her again, she turned back to her shells and continued counting, although she'd lost her place.

Glancing over at the cliffs, she saw Gregory's cottage on the edge, an idyllic spot overlooking the right side of the bay, opposite the hill on which their haven perched. Like their temporary residence, it was formed of cob walls, with a deep thatch roof invaded by thick moss in a subtle blend of browns and greens, but their cottage was exposed to the sea breezes. Gregory's was surrounded by bushes and flowers, on the verge of overgrowth. Fortunately, the hedges and plants sheltering his cottage from the wind also hid the rock pool from his view.

"This is your scheme is it?" he asked, coming up behind her.

"I know nothing of schemes. I'm merely a victim of fate."

Suddenly, he put his hands on her, under the water, holding her against his taut body. She swallowed a quick mewl of surprise, for he'd unlaced his breeches and now she felt his arousal; only her thin, wet shift came between them. He whispered in her ear. "Anybody might see through this piece of flotsam."

"There's no one here in this bay."

"No one except me."

"Does it bother *you*?"

He moved against her, his hard manhood stroking her soft curves and the cleft between. "This is what it does to me." He was showing off again.

How could she think of sensible matters like "later" or "consequences"?

"I want you," she said. "I want to learn all there is to know." It came out with the same brutal honesty that had so often caused her trouble. She simply couldn't stop it.

* * * *

Another gentle wave lapped against them, pushing her body against his, and it was the last straw. He had not got this out of his system yesterday, as he'd hoped. His fingers wrenched impatiently at the laces of her bodice, and he spun the temptress around to face him. "Why me?" he demanded. "Do I pay for my sins now?"

"Yes," she replied, sliding her hands under his wet shirt, "I'm here to cleanse you, body and soul." Her eyes were bright, full of wit. Yes, he thought, almost angry, she was pleased with her little game.

"Wait!" He laid his hands over hers, the wet linen shirt between them. "You know who I am. Tell me again. Tell me."

"Griff, of course. The earl's indentured servant and lackey." She grinned. "And yes I know you have nothing to offer me. I know you make no promises for the future. I won't ask you for anything else--"

He kissed her, drinking the breath out of her. Through the dampened shift, his palm cupped her warm, round breast, his thumb gently caressing an eagerly thrusting peak. "How can I refuse?" he groaned, arguing again with his distracted conscience. "Anything you want, I feel inclined to give you in this moment, woman."

"Can you meet my demands?" She chuckled playfully.

"What is it you want from me then?"

"This of course! You."

"This is all you want?" He was incredulous.

Under the water, she stroked his length, rousing him further still. "What more could any woman want?" she whispered.

Blood pulsed rapidly from his heart to his cock. He ground his teeth, letting her explore for as long as he could. She seemed intrigued by his length and breadth, how it reacted to her hand, taking on a life of its own. Now her fingers closed around his width and tugged upward again, squeezing. He groaned, a deep, hollow sound. The sea water lapped around his waist, the swell stroking his thighs. Grabbing her under the arms, he pulled her close, trapping that questing hand between them. Then he lifted her, bent his head, and pressed his voracious lips to her nipple. At the sound of her cries, the savage desire mounted. Oh yes, he would play this game with her, but there would only be one victor. Cradling her to his wet, slick body, he dove down into the water, taking her with him.

Chapter 14

They lay across the fleece spread before the fire, and he curled her into his arms, her head on his shoulder. Slowly, painstakingly, he combed his long fingers through her wet hair, gently separating the tangles. She grew sleepy, her limbs pleasantly exhausted, the way it used to be when she was a child, play-weary after a long day in the summer sun. Lying together in the firelight, they listened to rain drumming against the thatch of their little haven. Their clothes--or what was left of them in her case-- were stretched out across the chairs to dry, dripping rain and saltwater onto the flagstones.

For one of the few times in her life, she didn't care to talk. When he shifted, easing her back to the fleece, she complained at the loss of his firm chest and wide, warm shoulder.

Regarding her carefully, his weight propped up on one elbow, he began, "Woman, I..."

Pressing a finger to his lips, fearing he would lecture her, as he'd done before, she said simply, "I wanted you." It was uncomplicated, in her eyes.

He looked away for a moment, then back down at her. His nostrils flared slightly. "I'm not certain I should approve of you. I don't understand this."

She answered with a relaxed sigh, "You try to make sense of a matter for which there is no explanation."

"I'm a contemplative man. I need sense in my life. I need order and answers."

"Some things have no answers. Have you never before acted purely on instinct?"

That idea was scandalous apparently. "No!"

"When I know what I want, why waste time?" She wriggled back into his embrace. "I might never have another opportunity."

"Indeed." He drew his fingers across her brow, brushing back another lock of damp hair. "And is this how you were raised? To take what you want, without heed to propriety and consequences?"

"My single-minded, independent ways have served you well. I heard no complaints in the rock pool," she reminded him with a smile.

"Yes, yes," he mumbled. "I have no complaint." His fingers stroked the side of her breast. "I'm fortunate you never acted on this lust for some other man, before me." His eyelids lowered and a muted, sulky anger pulled on the corners of his mouth. "Clearly no sense of decorum would have stopped you. Your lusty wandering eye might just as easily have landed on anyone." His hand settled over her breast, his palm brushing the nipple which, yet again, rose instantly. "It takes very little for you to be aroused."

She corrected him. "It takes very little for *you* to arouse me." When his hand continued its slow, meandering journey down her body, she squirmed under his stern gaze, wanting to dispel his serious mood. "Am I solely to blame for this temptation?"

His reply was matter-of-fact. "Yes. I was undone the very moment you flashed those tear-stung blue eyes with beguiling innocence, while offering your bosom to me with the subtlety of a sixpenny whore."

She protested this description, while he teased her with his fingertips, tracing patterns along her inner thighs.

"I assumed these were the cunning, much-practiced arts employed by the infamous Lady Shelton to snare her prey. Warned of her notoriety in that regard, I was prepared to resist her."

"Your powers of resistance failed."

"On the contrary," he said, "I would not succumb to her, as I did to you."

"Liar." She sat up, rolling him over on his back. "Only four days after we met, you trapped Lady Shelton up against the door, preparing to show her she could forget Gabriel Mallory."

"It was you I had against the door, not her." He slid his arms around her waist, trying to wrestle her over, but she clamped her legs around his hips and would not surrender.

"You didn't know that."

"I was consumed with lust, 'tis true. You tempt me beyond endurance. You're an artful hussy, whoever you are." Flat on his back he gave up fighting her. Instead, his heavy hands settled on her hips, holding her astride his body. Already he was erect again, much to her delight. "Limpet," he groaned, catching his breath. "From drought to flood you have brought me." He reached up, threading his fingers through her hair, tugging her down. "From famine," he said, arching up, their lips meeting mid-way, "to feast."

She looked down at the man stretched out beneath her, the gentle valleys and hills of his rugged, sun-browned torso gleaming in the firelight. "I'm glad *you* rescued me from the river," she said, feeling it more certainly than ever.

Some mysterious flint within her, she concluded, must have rubbed against the same within him, for the heat of the fire they produced melted the gold nuggets in his eyes and now they dripped, molten, over his lashes. "No more than I," he replied with a grunt of satisfaction. "Fortune smiled on me that day."

* * * *

For the next few days the sun shone, and they went down to the bay as the tide came in. They waded together in the sea, splashing one another and falling in the waves. She wore her shift with his jerkin belted over it, at his stern insistence, however, none of his concern for modesty lasted long, once they made their way to that rock pool.

Guilt might have invaded his thoughts, if not for his certainty that she knew who he was, knew exactly what she did. Oh, she was beguiling, a delicious sweetmeat, and he would make the most of her talents. It couldn't last forever, of course. He would find out what she was truly after and who'd put her up to it, then he would dole out the punishments.

When they ate luncheon on the sands, he pointed out to her the things he'd seen daily in childhood--the strange shape of the rocks at the mouth of the bay, where the tide's relentless wash had carved faces in the ancient stone. He described his first fishing lesson with Gregory, who'd also taught him to swim in the bay. He told her how Sally had said he would find a mermaid one day, and how, as a boy, he'd stood on the rocks, waiting, watching, always disappointed.

"Then you found me," she said proudly.

"Yesss." Never before had he opened up like this to anyone, but she drank in every detail he gave her. Lying on her front, heels in the air, she listened avidly to his stories while telling him none of her own, he realized grimly.

"Gregory won't come down to talk to you today?" she asked.

"He has business at the manor. He expects the earl any day now."

Her eyes widened. "The earl comes so soon?"

"He has a right to come home surely." He lay back, resting his elbows in the sand and laughed. "You've gone white as salt."

"When the earl comes, our time will be over. We will be separated."

If he didn't know better, he would swear she meant it, that she truly thought she spoke of another man. Artful hussy. His gaze traveled over her slowly, admiring her unconventional, improper state of undress. Good thing he'd told Gregory to order her some new clothes.

"I suppose the end must come eventually," he said carefully.

She nodded, tracing patterns in the sand with a fingertip. "Yet so soon," she murmured.

He smiled slowly.

* * * *

With his teeth shining in the sun and a light dusting of golden sand across his face and chest, Madolyn thought him suddenly despicably beautiful, a demigod before her. How odd that she'd thought him ugly before. "I hope the earl will listen to my case for Nathaniel."

He snorted. "I've never encountered such a convincing minx. You must get anything you want, when you set your mind to it. If anyone ever could change his mind, you would."

"Even him?"

"Your powers of persuasion, limpet, are extraordinary. I know to my own cost."

She liked it when he flicked a smile at her, as if he couldn't help himself, his eyes studying her as they would a winning hand of cards.

"Let's go back to the cottage," she said.

He tipped his head to one side, his expression quizzical.

"Now," she commanded. "I need you."

He leapt to his feet, gathering up the remnants of their picnic and whistling a tune, apparently unconcerned with the impending arrival of his lord and master, but vastly amused by her eagerness to get him indoors.

She had no willpower to resist him. He knew it and duly tormented her. She had discovered an insatiable appetite for more than marchpane tarts.

At breakfast, when he reached for her hand, urging her down into his lap, she protested, "That old trick!"

But she went to him because he was irresistible. It was, she thought, a good thing this affair couldn't last forever, because they would exhaust one another. To her surprise, however, he had no ulterior motive in mind, when he pulled her into his lap. He merely held her there, continuing his breakfast and their conversation. Charmed, she fell quiet, listening to him talk, watching him eat. No one in the world, she mused, could summon her presence quite the way he did. He still thought her disobedient and difficult. If only he knew how much sweeter she was to him than anyone else. She stared at his profile, wanting to keep it safe in her memory forever.

He stopped chewing. "Were you listening to a word I said?"

Smiling, she leaned in to kiss his cheek and he caught his breath in surprise. He lowered his gaze, hiding suddenly and shy. She kissed his eyelids too, whispering that his lap was the most comfortable seat ever and she was sorry she'd once insulted it.

He laughed, in that distant way a person might when they seldom knew tenderness. "You go too far, wench."

Wrinkling her nose, she thought what a funny man he was, but folk were seldom grateful for her help and his reluctance didn't dissuade her in the slightest.

One afternoon, Griff was busy with his horse, so she went out to pick new flowers for the table. Lost in the beauty of the countryside, she was unaware how much time had passed until he came looking for her, galloping up the hill in too much haste even to saddle his horse.

He drew the horse to a sharp halt before her. "Where the devil have you been?" he demanded furiously.

Looking up, eyes shielded from the bright sun with one hand, she calmly surveyed the angry barbarian. "I came out to pick flowers." She showed the colorful bunch in her other hand. "What could be wrong with that?"

"I didn't know where you went," he said through gritted teeth, breathing hard, sunlight shimmering across his chest and shoulders. He'd spared no time to put on a shirt when he'd chased after her intent on recapture. "Anything might have happened to you, wandering off like that."

"Oh for pity's sake!" Equal parts frustrated and bemused, she shook her head. "What could possibly happen out here?"

"There are many dangers, young woman!"

"Were you afraid I might be attacked by a flock of seagulls?"

One hand on his thigh, the other holding the reins, he shrugged, his frown fading. "There are traitors and assassins all over this land. The earl himself has been threatened with murder many times."

"Why?"

"Because he's a loyal subject to Her Majesty, Queen Elizabeth, and others are not so." Now he leaned down, offering his hand to help her up onto the horse. "I trust no one."

"Not even me?" she asked.

His eyes darkened. "Especially not you."

Rather than take his hand, she quickened her pace down the slope, leaving him behind.

* * * *

He knew she was angry; he just didn't understand why. So he let her storm off ahead to get it out of her system. It could be that time of the month, of course. He'd heard of such mysterious womanly things.

Entering the cottage several minutes after her, he pursed his lips in a deliberately merry whistle. She was arranging her wild flowers in the clay jug, ignoring him. He strode to the fire to warm the seat of his breeches. Women were emotional creatures, he knew, and could bite like a mad dog when their bristles were up. One moment she was sweet as honey, in the next she wouldn't even look at him. This was why he never kept a mistress.

Now she sat before the fire, reading her book, weary sighs lifting her extravagant bosom, noticeable even under his belted jerkin.

Restless, he came to her chair, leaning over the back of it. "What keeps you so enthralled?"

Sighing again, she turned the page.

He leaned down a few inches, until her wayward curls caught on his stubble. "If you continue to sulk in this silent manner, I must punish you, devious wench."

Snapping out a short laugh, she turned another page. "Your master makes you as mistrustful as himself."

Suddenly he grabbed the book out of her hands and she demanded it back.

"'Tis not yours," he replied. "It belongs to the earl. Like everything else here."

"Except me."

His stomach clenched. It was true. She belonged somewhere, to someone else. It was not an idea that pleased. Half an hour ago, when he couldn't find her, he'd panicked. Spotting her on the hillside, gathering flowers, the relief had been almost too much to absorb.

Theirs was not only a physical connection, this wench touched him inside, found a part of him that was buried deep, protected by years of scar tissue. Whatever happened, he knew this thing between them was too strong to be denied, or broken, or lost. It was forever.

"You're my chattel now," he said with a calmness he didn't feel. "Whether we like it or not."

She leapt out of the chair and ran for the door. He was after her like bowshot, hauling her back. They struggled together and she stamped on his foot.

"You blow too hot and cold, madam," he growled.

She wriggled and writhed. "You're a hateful, twisted man, just like your master."

This, of course, only spurred him on and he suckled hot, wet kisses at the nape of her neck. Already conversant with her weak spots, he knew where to tickle her.

Gasping with laughter, she squirmed free, but since he easily blocked the door, she ran for the stairs. He followed, dragging her down onto the steps, tickling without a care for her screams. In the midst of this new experience--a childish wrestling game--a very adult male part of him grew eager.

"Will you leave none of my clothes intact?" she protested.

"This is mine, not yours," he pointed out, removing the belt from her waist.

"And now you want it back, I suppose."

This was better. He realized he would rather have her fighting him than her sullen silence of disapproval. "You have no need of clothes in my company, *chattel*," he said, possessive and greedy.

"Chattel indeed! Would you keep me naked in a cage, sir?"

Transferring his weight to one knee, he reached down, lifting her shift, sliding it up over her thighs. "Yes. Then you could conceal nothing from me." And, in the next moment, he rolled forward, driving up into her until she was filled again, his desire sheathed deep within. Her lashes trembled and her lips parted in surprise at this sudden taking.

Immediate, primal need assuaged, he looked down at her, searching her eyes for some sign, a knowing flicker to prove she knew his true identity.

She ran a finger over his lips. "If you don't trust me, what do you suspect me of?"

"All manner of wickedness."

She frowned. "I'm going home. Get off me!"

"You're my chattel. You cannot leave. I forbid it."

"I'm leaving you," she said again. "You're a brute. Let me go."

Rigid inside her, he thought he could feel her pulse beating in rhythm with his heart. "Shall I?"

Lips pursed, she gave no answer.

Moving his hips, he pressed up into her again and saw her pupils dilate. She lifted her chin, arching under him. "Should I stop?" he asked again, beginning slowly to withdraw.

"Oh." She sighed, a throaty sound of frustration. "I suppose you may finish."

He stared down at this willful wench, half-naked and sulky, her black tresses spilled across the stairs and over his arm where he held it beneath her. His chattel was exceptionally fortunate he wanted her so badly he could overlook her vexing behavior.

Thrusting again, he locked them together, his free arm lifting under her knee to ensure deeper penetration. Ah yes, that possession she would feel. And that. And *that*. She cried out, head thrown back, exposing her neck to his breath-moistened lips, and he covered it hungrily, needing the taste of her. She pulled on his shirt, almost ripping it in her haste and he laughed. She was hot, her sheath so incredibly tight, her breasts pressing up at him as he took her. He was already close to spilling and the tiny signal in his brain began to sound, but the pleasure of being buried deep inside this challenging, dangerous wench far outweighed the practical necessity of withdrawal. This was rapture, reckless abandonment in any sense of the word.

Again, the warning sounded shrill in his brain, years of Swafford duty too deeply instilled. He was shaking, a roar building within. Eyes closed, lips firm to stifle the cry of despair, he began to withdraw. Until he felt her thighs wrap around him, clamping tight, forcing him to stay.

He opened his eyes. "No," he growled, at war with his own body.

"I want all of you." Her voice fell around him like warm, spiced wine. He was drenched in it. "Please," she gasped. "All of it. Fill me."

There was no way he could stop now, not with those words begging. What else could he do, but oblige the lady?

Kneeling on the step, he brought her astride his lap, letting her ride, letting her feel every impassioned shudder of his need for her. Hands pressing down on her hips, he thrust upward and she cried out again, long hair tumbling down her back, the ends of it stroking his thighs, tiny, silken whips, driving him on.

She offered her breasts to his mouth and he took them greedily, just as he took her, his lovely chattel. On that afternoon he devoured her, his passion relentless as the tide pounding at those cliffs. There was nothing she refused him, no borders. She must have known the risk. Apparently she didn't care about the consequences.

When it was over, he was the one who lamented his loss of control. "What have you done to me?" he groaned.

"So that was my fault too? I daresay if anyone might find a way to blame me for it, the cause of the Black Death could be laid at my door."

She was still astride his lap, her arms around his shoulders.

"It can't happen again," he muttered into her unbound curls.

"But it *was* wonderful." She moved, her body undulating against his, pert nipples teasing his chest, her tongue licking his sweat-dampened brow.

"You must be mad, woman. Why would you want to risk pregnancy?"

"There are potions I can take to prevent it," she said thoughtfully. "I should make one tomorrow, if I can find the necessary herbs."

He wasn't sure how he felt about a woman controlling conception. Surely it was wrong. No good could come of it. It was against the axiom he'd lived with all his life, that man knew better. In all cases.

On the other hand he didn't want a bastard babe, did he? He didn't want any complications in his life, no more burdens than he bore already.

Chapter 15

That evening they were quiet, and on the surface, peaceful, keeping to their own thoughts. She watched him as he bent over his writing desk, composing a letter he wouldn't let her read. Once this was over, would he ever think of her again? Years from now, would he remember? Would he regret their time together was so brief? Or would he forget her completely?

Would he come to find her?

He looked up and their eyes met. Flustered, she sought any subject so he would never guess the folly of her daydreams. "You said the earl's life has been in danger many times?"

He nodded, and returned his gaze to his letter.

"What would anyone gain from his death?"

"There are folk who would gladly be rid of Queen Elizabeth's most trusted friends to leave her vulnerable and better their own cause."

"Their own cause?"

He scowled. "These are treacherous times. Do you know nothing of politics?"

Politics? Ugh. When anyone mentioned the subject she tended to let her mind wander to far pleasanter things, fried figs and jam tarts, for instance. This evening she made an effort to pay attention, for him.

"The queen's cousin, Mary of Scotland, has her own supporters who would put her on the throne of England. Some say she has more right to it than Elizabeth, some want her on the throne to return England to the Catholic faith, some want her on the throne simply to improve their own status."

"The earl is very close to her majesty?"

"Oh yes. He's known her since childhood."

She knew many considered it wrong for an unwed woman to sit upon the throne of England, but Queen Elizabeth remained unmarried, keeping several foreign princes dangling in hope without conceding defeat to any. "My father says she should be married. He says no woman should rule alone."

Griff shrugged. "If the queen married and bore children it would secure the Tudor line, of course, that's why many folk wish she would marry. It would solidify her claim. Then her cousin would be far less of a threat."

"No woman should marry unless for love. It should never be a duty."

"*Love?*" He shook his head. "This is politics, limpet, serious business, not foolish fancies and giddy emotions in which only an addle-brained female might believe. Her majesty was born to a life of duty and service. Like...my master."

"Then I'm glad to be a plain, uncomplicated girl and not poor Queen Bess."

"We may all be glad at that."

"Sakes, you sound like my father."

He laughed and picked up his quill again. "What you must put that poor fellow through. He has my every sympathy."

* * * *

The nosy wench wandered over to his desk, trying to peer over his shoulder again and read his letter. He held it away from her prying eyes, explaining it was business of the earl's to which he must tend. Business was nothing a woman should understand, he warned her. Too many thoughts cluttering their minds was never a good thing.

He blotted his ink and prepared a wax seal.

"Is this the earl's insignia?" she asked, snatching up the ring he took from inside the desk.

He tried retrieving it, but she dodged away, reading the tiny words upon it.

"This is his motto? *Aut Vincere, Aut Mori.* Victory or Death." She rolled her eyes. "I suppose there's no arguing with that."

"*You* know Latin?"

Her eyes flared, a brilliant blue shower of sparks raining down on him. "*I* know many things."

Griff leaned back in his chair and pondered this enigma of a woman, who thought she might get away with her aversive sauciness. "An educated wench is more dangerous than the common variety, so my master says."

"Yes, I daresay the idea terrifies him. How can women be kept in their place if they know as much about the world as he does?"

"Women do not need education. They have men to take care of them."

"Men to own them you mean?"

"Precisely. I'm glad you agree." He stood quickly and wrestled the ring from her fingers. "Any business of the estate must be marked with his seal, anything that goes through his agent's hands."

"I wonder you don't stamp me with your precious master's crest. Nothing has been through his agent's hands so thoroughly as I. Should I not be stamped?" And she turned, bending over to present herself for his stamp.

Again, she made him laugh when he should be angry, reprimanding her behavior. "Mind yourself, limpet, before you knock this ink pot over, like you did the last."

"I suppose I wouldn't meet with his approval, so I can't be stamped."

"Indeed, you're the utter antithesis of anything he might approve."

Having made his smug comment, he suddenly reconsidered it. She had her hands on her waist, still wearing his leather jerkin belted over her shift. He'd grown accustomed to the sight, he realized, and dangerously accustomed to her presence in his life. He turned the ring over in his fingers.

Suddenly she said, "I wonder what the earl will say when he finds they're married."

He went still. "Married? Gabriel and that…that woman?" The fury billowed up like a red mist, obscuring his sight. "Are they married already? How do you know this?"

"I don't know. Not for sure."

He ground his teeth, pushing back his chair with an almighty squeal across the flagstones. "I didn't think he would dare defy--"

"Oh, for the love of Saint Pete, are you so blindly loyal to the old miser you can't let two people be at peace?"

"Miser?" he roared, spitting the word. "Miser? Who said the earl was a miser?"

"*I* did," she yelled back at him, standing her ground as he strode toward her.

"He's the most generous man I know. He would do anything for those in his care, spare no expense."

"Generous indeed!"

He wanted her silenced now, he wanted her to regret the things she said of him, her sharp-tongued insults. "He's a good man. If anything, he spoils his *poor* brother. You know nothing of his struggles to raise his brother in this world. When you're born into a fortune and a title, there are many, many responsibilities that come with it and many," he barked in her face, "many folk who resent you for what you have, so they cheat, slander and steal from you. No one can be trusted. Everyone has a scheme, an agenda, everyone wants a favor from you and they care not who you really are, because all they see when they look at you is gold coin and an opportunity."

"Forgive me if I shed no tears for the almighty, all-knowing Earl of Swafford," she cried. "He meddles in his brother's affairs under the guise of doing it for Gabriel's own good, but truly because he has no affairs of his own."

His hands clenched into fists, hung heavy at his sides. "Gabriel is constantly at risk from kidnappers. The earl has lived most his life with that knowledge. Always he must be on his guard. How can he protect his brother now?"

"Perhaps Gabriel can protect himself. He's a grown man, not a boy."

He glared at her, shoulders flexing. She did not retreat.

"I suppose this sense of duty to the earl will stand between us," she said, arms folded. "You should leave him," she added, her eyes azure. "He doesn't deserve your fealty."

Suddenly his proud, rigid self-assurance faltered, severely stumbled, in fact. He swept one trembling hand over his face. "I couldn't leave him, even if I wanted to. Even if I wanted another life, there's nothing I can do to change it." Abruptly ending the quarrel, he reached for her, pulling her into his arms. Whoever she was, whatever she was, in that moment he needed her there. "If I could walk in another man's boots, I would. Indeed, these last few days with you, limpet, I have done so."

Much to his chagrin, he realized it likely he would let her get away with anything. Again he flirted with the concept of keeping a woman for his pleasure. He'd never before felt the need for a mistress.

That was before he plucked this bossy, impertinent little madam out of the river Thames. In thirty-five years he'd never known a dilemma like this.

* * * *

Unaccustomed to having an argument so swiftly put aside, Maddie would have preferred to rage and scream, thrashing her anger out so it wouldn't fester inside. Now, her temper prevented from taking a natural course, it lay dormant inside. The argument between them was left for now.

CHAPTER 16

Gregory came up to the cottage to collect his correspondence, and Sally came too that night. During the visit, Maddie was banished to the pantry because Griff was adamant she not parade back and forth in her shift before anyone other than him. She heard him ask Gregory about some clothes for her and the old steward said they'd been ordered.

She was relieved not to have to go home in her torn shift and some borrowed men's clothes. There would be no explaining that one, she thought with a smile.

"Underthings too," Griff was saying. "Proper, ladylike things. Frilly whatnots. And a corset."

Now her smile wavered. Having gone the last few blissful days untethered and free, she had no intention of being hoisted up, strapped in and flattened again. He must have heard her gasp of frustration through the pantry door, because then he raised his voice and said, "She'll be dressed like a lady from now on, not a little heathen."

Sally asked, "Is she staying?"

"I don't know. No, she can't stay...'tis nothing permanent...I've yet to decide."

"You'll need somewhere to keep her. If she stays," said Gregory.

"I know little of these things. Never kept one before."

"She'll need feeding. They all do."

"And grooming," Griff added dryly.

"Aye, that she will." Sally giggled.

"She's a highly strung mount and I'm not certain her temperament suits me."

"A strong, spirited filly, Master Griff, would do you a world of good," said Sally.

"She's skittish and flighty...and damned willful," he grumbled. "Let me think on it. I've much on my mind "

He was thinking of keeping her, letting her stay? Excitement ran pitter-pat up and down her veins, like little toddlers escaped from an overworked nurse. But she couldn't stay with him, could she? Unless, of course, he meant to marry her and make her an honest woman, where so many other good men wouldn't dare try.

Once they were gone, she was released from the pantry and immediately complained about being compared to a horse. Not listening, however, he scratched his chin and paced across the flagged floor. Halting behind a chair, he rested his hands on the back of it, bade her sit and then walked around to crouch before her. He laid his hands on her knees, fingers spread. His hands were warm and weighty through the thin material of her shift and, once again, his touch stirred her wicked pixies into a joyful jig.

"I must know," he said, his voice low, "who you are and where you come from."

Crisply, she pointed out, "After the intimacy we shared, it seems a moot point to make polite inquiries now into my background."

"Your family must be trying to find you."

"I doubt it." She sighed, thinking of Grace's accusations.

"Tell me your name, wench." He paused. "The Earl of Swafford wants to know it."

She leaned back, arms folded, disappointment cold and heavy in her heart. "*He* wants to know? Aren't you going to ask me to marry you? You said to Gregory--"

"Marry you?" He sputtered with laughter. "Why would I want a wife? What would I do with her? I've no money, no house. You know that. You know who I am, remember?"

She nodded, her mouth dry.

He frowned suddenly. "You said you would ask me for no promises. Those were your words."

He was right, of course. For a moment she'd let herself get carried away. "Yes," she said, lashes lowered.

His fingertips made little indents in her knees. "Tell me," he demanded huskily, "who sent you here?"

"No one."

"A woman of wit and intelligence, who reads and writes, who cares that a man wears his shirt to the table, a woman who rises early to pick flowers and cook bacon--this is not a woman who leaves her life behind one day to throw herself on the mercy of a complete stranger."

"You are not a stranger to me," she said simply. It was true. Somehow he never had been.

* * * *

With that one comment she breached his defenses, piercing the Swafford armor with a slender blade of truth. He felt her tremble, but not with fear. Her eyes were too sultry, too ripe with desire, and her lips parted as if they burst apart unable to hold in another breath.

He realized, bemused, that he crouched at her feet like a besotted fool. Never had he done this--considered opening his life, even to some partial degree, for a woman. Yet whatever the world thought of him, he did not casually deflower maidens. Neither had he ever felt the rush of pleasure she gave him simply when she sat near.

Standing swiftly, he turned his back, clawing through his hair. He looked at her over his shoulder, exasperated, bewildered. "What am I going to do with you?"

Slowly her lips turned up in a hopeful smile. "My father says that a lot, but when you say it, my heart beats so hard I feel it in my fingertips."

How did she do it?

How did one smiling mouth deceive so effortlessly?

* * * *

The next morning he was gone when she woke. Thinking him outside with his horse, she came downstairs humming, and when there was a tap at the door, she ran to it, wondering why he didn't just come in. Her smile fell hard.

"He says I'm to take you up to the big house," Gregory said, doffing his cap. "My Sally left you a set of clothes." He pointed one gnarled finger over her shoulder.

A folded dove-gray gown waited there on the table. "Clothes?" she mumbled, as if she did not know what they were.

"Aye, my lady," he said patiently. "The others haven't come yet, so that one must do for now. My Sally will come up and dress you." As he turned away, she asked where Griff had gone.

"Up to the big house, my lady."

She didn't understand at first, then she realized he must have gone on ahead to meet the Earl--perhaps try to smooth things over. Or else he'd been summoned there to be punished.

"Don't worry, my lady," said Gregory, seeing her expression. "He left instructions for you to follow."

"Instructions?"

"He wrote them out, my lady. My Sally tucked them inside the gown for you." With a hasty bow, he scuttled off to find his wife.

* * * *

There were only four instructions, as it turned out. She was surprised there were not a great many more.

I. Speak to no servants except Gregory.

II. Do exactly as he says. Lest you not understand, let me repeat; (and this was underscored thickly) Under No Circumstances Will You Defy Gregory or Cause Him Any Trouble.

III. Wear the clothes Sally has provided. All of them.

IV. Use the bath provided.

Indignant, she stared at the last line. "He has some gall," she exclaimed breathlessly to Sally, who rubbed her dry with a large woolen cloth. "As if he even knows what a bath is! I've ridden horses that smell sweeter."

Helping her into a clean, new shift, the old lady sympathized, tut-tutting and cooing, only in the way a mother would to soothe a fractious child--one whose tantrums could be distracted by a fruit sucket.

"And I shan't be told where to go and what to do," Maddie cried.

"He seems to think the only person entitled to their own life, is the..." She gasped for air as the new corset laces tightened another half inch. "Damnable...Earl of...Swafford." It was not an easy name to say with one's breath squeezed out of one's lungs.

"Yes, my lady."

Flinging her wet hair aside, Maddie frowned over her shoulder, but the old lady beamed pleasantly, as if oblivious to her charge's bad mood.

"We must look our best, my lady, for the earl, mustn't we?"

"The earl? As if I care what--" She stopped, losing the will to speak.

This was why Griff wanted her clean and dressed. She was to be taken to the 'big house', where the earl meant to interrogate her about Gabriel and Eustacia's escape. Her heart skipped two or three beats before it slammed hard and hectic in her chest, making up for the pause.

Hands on her waist, she pulled her shoulders back, straightened her spine. Time to face the ogre bravely, as she'd always planned. Someone must speak up for her relatives, in whose lives he so heartlessly meddled. Because of him, Eustacia had been forced to flee with her lover, like a thief in the night, and Nathaniel likely eaten by cannibals in some Hellish wilderness to whence he was exiled. Every misfortune her family suffered was a consequence of the earl's temper, this wretched belief that he was always right.

Sally helped her into the bodice, regretting it was a little small. "You're a healthy young lady, to be sure."

"I wish I was not," Maddie replied, glaring resentfully down at her bosom.

"Now, now, my lady," Sally cooed, "we should be thankful for what God gives us."

"All the good it's done me," she replied.

The last adjustments made, the sleeves tied, Sally exclaimed, "You're from good, strong, healthy stock, my lady. As I said to him," she said as she patted down the sleeves in a motherly way, "that young lady is made for pleasure and no mistake. And do you know what he said? Quiet like and solemn, the way he is, he said to me, *for my pleasure, Sally*--just like that--*for my pleasure, and that's why I mean to keep her.*" She covered her mouth with one hand and whispered. "He never kept a woman before. Oh, there were some on the estate trying to catch his eye, and I daresay he took his pleasure when he fancied--"

"I don't care to hear it," Maddie cried, the mewling cub of jealousy awoken.

"I'm sorry, my lady. Oh dear, I always put my foot in my mouth, I do."

Gregory appeared in the doorway, and seeing their charge flustered and upset, blamed his wife. "Your tongue does run on, Sally. What did I tell you this morn, eh?"

"Do not be angry with your wife," Maddie urged. "She said nothing wrong."

Sally gave her a grateful look, folding her hands together meekly.

"Aye...well..." Gregory still frowned at his wife, who looked at the ground. "If you're ready, my lady, I have the horse and cart harnessed in the yard."

She took one last look around at their little haven, thinking of what Sally said about other women, him taking his pleasure as he fancied it. Yes, no doubt there were many women willing, at the crook of his finger, to tumble in the hay with him.

Perhaps, in his eyes, she was no more significant.

* * * *

Much of the journey passed in silence. Maddie felt too sorry for herself and Gregory was evidently instructed to say as little as possible, but when the sun showed its face through the clouds, the beauty of nature shook her out of the doldrums. They passed through heath land and alongside marshes, under the shadow of broad oaks, then across a bridge over a stream. A slight breeze ruffled the reeds and bulrushes along the bank side. The water meandered along, lapping gently at the emerald-stained arches of the bridge.

"Here we are," said Gregory. "Starling's Roost."

It was a vast square structure of mellow stone, nestled amid gently rounded lawns and oak-clad hills. They drove along a winding lane bordered by tall spruce trees that striped their route with shadows. There was a lake with swans upon it and great, languid willows beside, arching their delicate limbs to the water. Behind the house lay a broad patch of heath land, dotted with lush purple and pink. Industrious birds darted above it, filling the air with song.

It was elegant and tranquil. Nothing could have surprised her more. From the rumors she'd heard and the grim visions her own imagination conjured, she'd anticipated a cold, forbidding fortress with a drawbridge and a viciously spiked portcullis. She'd expected, even, perhaps, *wanted* to find a moat filled with green, stagnant water, a slimy dungeon with blood-stained walls. She'd fully expected severed heads spiked upon his walls, their ghoulish expressions striking terror in the hearts of those who entered.

Instead Gregory drew his cart up before a wide sweep of steps that managed to inspire awe without a solitary bloody skull in sight or one distant scream of horror heard.

He gave Maddie his hand to help her down and shouted, "Jennet, Jennet! Come out here."

A young girl skipped down the steps, bobbed a shy curtsey and addressed Maddie as, "my lady."

"That's not necessary," she said, wondering what excuse they'd heard for her presence there. "And you too." she turned to Gregory. "Stop calling me, *my lady*. I'm no different to any of you. I don't expect to be treated as if I am."

This declaration startled them both and the girl, her pretty face quizzical, looked to Gregory for explanation. "Aye," he murmured, "he did say she runs on with open mouth, but we weren't to mind her any."

Even as she protested, they hurried her up the steps and into the ogre's lair. Bustled along countless corridors, she was escorted to a bedchamber hidden away in a far wing of the house, where mullioned windows looked out onto spacious lawns of serene beauty. In the distance, over beech and oak-lined hills, she saw a sliver of molten silver--the sea. When Gregory asked whether she liked the view, she replied angrily that she did, how could she not, for pity's sake?

Under the window, there was a writing cabinet. Gregory explained the earl thought she might wish to write to her family and let them know she was safe. Immediately she was suspicious. Yes, he wanted her to write to her family, so he'd know who they were and where to find them. No doubt the moment she gave a letter to his servant, it would go directly to him.

"Does the earl know I'm here already?"

Gregory's ruddy, toil-worn face gathered in yet more folds. "Of course he knows."

Yes, she thought darkly, the Beast would know. He knows everything. Poor Griff.

"Oh, aye," Gregory exclaimed, reaching into a little leather pouch hanging from his belt, "I almost forgot. I'm to give you this." He held it out to her-- a little cockleshell, white as a snowdrop, so tiny and perfectly formed. "Went down to the bay this morn, early, before the tide turned. Said he wanted to think. Came back with this, for you...thought you might like it for your collection, he said."

She took it from his hand. It was warm from the sun's rays beating down on the leather purse, but she preferred to imagine it was the heat from Griff's palm. He had thought of her then, before he left the cottage, and not merely to write instructions. Tears rose suddenly, unbidden, unexpected. The earl would punish him, because he'd failed in his mission. Yet it was her fault. Now she must stay and defend her actions, and Griff's, to that odious wretch. Perhaps she might win his mercy, if not for herself, for Griff.

"It was my fault," she would say, "I tricked him into thinking I was Lady Shelton. It wasn't his fault. He's not to blame. I'm a wicked, lusty sinner."

And she loved him.

It struck her in the face like wet linen on a windy washday.

She dropped suddenly to the edge of the bed, her knees giving out.

"Are you all right, my lady?" Head to one side, Gregory peered at her, his silver, caterpillar brows twitching.

Clutching the bedpost, she groaned, not knowing whether to laugh or cry.

He patted her shoulder. "There, there, my good lady. Easy now." Much to her amusement, he petted her as if she was a horse in need of calming.

Suddenly, fiercely aware that she'd not eaten breakfast, Maddie was a little disappointed in herself for having no inclination to pine and waste away. Surely love should cause its victim to reject sustenance until the object of her affections came to rescue her. Therefore, she ought to be weeping and frail, not thinking of food. Disregarding how things should be, however, her uncouth stomach rumbled away, demanding it be fed at once, quickly spoiling any attempt at ladylike pining.

She sat up, recovering her wits.

Ready to face her comeuppance, reconciled to the earl's wrath, it was for Griff she feared most. Living on the whim and mercy of his lord and master, he could not marry, even if he wanted to, without the earl's consent. As her father always said, noblemen used folk in the same way they used their horses. Griff's life and his fealty belonged to his master.

She'd assured him, many times, that she wanted nothing more than those days of adventure, no rules, no expectations attached. How could she now ask for more? It wouldn't be fair.

She hadn't expected this love to come.

Her heart leapt, tripped and leapt again, dipping and diving, like a kite she had when she was ten.Unfortunately that kite had crashed through the pig-sty roof and splintered into pieces. Bits of it were even eaten by the pigs before she could rescue them. She hoped her heart would not meet the same fate.

Chapter 17

Later, when Gregory sent the little maid Jennet to collect her breakfast tray, Madolyn asked if she might be allowed out for some air. With no Gregory at her side, the girl didn't know what to do and, clutching the rattling tray, backed up to the door.

"I must be permitted to answer the call of nature, Jennet."

"There's a chamber pot, madam, under the bed."

"But there's a crack in it." And, indeed, there was. She'd caused it by slamming the pot against the bed post.

"I'm not supposed to let you out until the earl--"

"Where is he then? He drags me here, much to my inconvenience, and now I must wait?"

She had no answer, but her lips trembled.

Madolyn took the unsteady tray from the girl's hands and set it on the bed. "Can we not be friends? It seems I have no other here and I've been very badly treated. I can't tell you the half of it, Jennet. You'd be horrified to learn what's been done to me."

The little maid's brown, cow-like eyes grew big in her small face.

"I'm surprised you--a woman too--would take their side against me," she continued. "You would leave me to be imprisoned when I committed no crime? I might go mad if I cannot stretch my legs further than the width of this room. I might resort to desperate measures." She went to the window and pushed it open. "I may as well end it all, here and now," she said gravely, hitching up her skirt to climb out.

"No, no, madam, you must not."

"Let me go, Jennet. I shall jump to my death. I'm not afraid. It will only take a moment and I daresay it won't hurt much, although," she peered down over the ledge, "if I should not die directly and only crack my head...or break off a limb--"

"No, no, I'll fetch Gregory."

"By the time he comes, I'll be gone. Farewell, cruel, cruel, unjust life." She climbed up, with one knee on the ledge. "I'm sorry, Jennet, if I should leave too much blood upon the stones."

"Oh, do come back in, madam!"

As she leaned out, pretending to consider the fall, she saw a man on a horse, galloping across the lawn toward the house. She wondered who he thought he was to boldly trample the earl's pristine lawn, rather than bother with the gravel path. Was he perhaps one of those daring assassins come to murder the Beast? Jennet still tugged on her skirt, begging her not to jump, but she was too interested in the rider, who now passed under the arches along the west side of the house. Sighting a glimmer of chestnut hair, her heart leapt.

"Griff!"

Horse and rider disappeared from view.

She slid back into the chamber, celebrating because he still had his wonderfully strong limbs attached. Grasping the little maid's hand, she pulled her close and hugged her.

"My lady?"

"Jennet, I am in love."

The maid's eyes popped.

"I am in love with Griff, the earl's loyal servant."

"Griff?"

She paced in a circle. "I must get out of this room and find him."

The maid looked skeptical. On her hands and knees, she searched for the pot under the bed. Drawing it out, she lifted it to the light and discovered it was indeed cracked.

Finally agreeing to show Madolyn the privy, Jennet pulled her along the corridor by one sleeve, little face set stubbornly on the way ahead, in case her troublesome charge might try distracting her from it. Apparently she'd been warned of the danger. "The earl won't be pleased to find you out of your chamber when he left orders to keep you in it, until he was ready to see you."

"What does he think I am, that he can keep me locked up in a cage?"

"Why, his mistress, madam." Jennet flushed scarlet. "That's what you are, his mistress."

Madolyn tripped over her own feet, stumbling to a halt in the corridor. "*Mistress*?" She recoiled. "The earl's *mistress*?"

"'Tis what we were told, madam."

"Told? By whom?"

"By Gregory, madam," Jennet replied, "Do come quick, before you're discovered out of the room."

Madolyn pulled away from her, marching in the other direction. The maid's mousy steps scuttled after her, trying to get her back in her room. Instead she shouted for Gregory, pacing along the maze of corridors, looking to draw blood. He appeared at last, stepping around a corner in their path.

"Please calm yourself, my lady," he pleaded. "The earl merely asked you be kept out of harm's way."

"Out of harm's way, indeed!" she cried. "Why have you told Jennet I'm the earl's mistress?"

Owlish eyes observed her placidly. "Is it not so?"

A dreadful thought came to her: would it be possible for a man like the Beast to keep a woman against her will, as long as it took his fancy?

"My lady, he will treat you with exceptional care. You will want for nothing." Gregory ventured. "It is a post, I think, no woman would dare refuse."

She was appalled, sickened by the thought of it. Once she'd planned to seduce the man, but that was before she knew he was married, and before she met Griff.

"If I'm locked in that room all day, how pleasant do you think I'll be to your precious master when he deigns to see me? And how pleasant will your life be as a consequence?" She resorted to these threats, realizing she might be in a position of some power. "If I'm not kept content, I daresay he won't like what I have to say to his ugly face when I do encounter it. Nor will he like what I have to say about the way I was treated!"

Gregory's eyes widened. She was sorry to threaten him in this dire manner, but desperate means were required.

His lips moved, as if in a silent prayer.

"What are you doing, Gregory?" she demanded, impatient.

"Comparing the danger, my lady. Which of you might cause me the most damage in my old age."

Maddie was amused, despite her situation.

Finally he said, "I concede, my lady, that the measure of locking your chamber door was, perhaps, extreme." He allowed she might walk within the house, as long as she kept Jennet by her side. Dragging a kerchief from his sleeve, he dabbed his brow, where the furrows glistened with perspiration.

"You may have the run of the south tower, my lady," he muttered. "I don't suppose any harm can come to you there."

Any harm? What was there elsewhere in the house? Other women locked up and held hostage? Headless corpses?

If there was danger in that house, as she suspected, Maddie decided she had better sleep with a knife under her pillow from now on.

* * * *

The house was built around a courtyard cornered by four crenellated towers, with a fifth--set with an enormous clock face--rising up from the inner courtyard. Her chamber was in the south tower, which felt sun for a good part of the day. The rooms were designed with both a subtle eye for elegant detail and a practical eye for comfort. She admired several luxurious tapestries, dramatic scenes of battle and war horses mostly, befitting the master of the house. But she also found a few pastoral scenes, depictions of lush harvests, feasting and revelry by a stream.

Bored with the south tower, she went in search of other chambers to explore. Rather than go back to her room, as Jennet wanly suggested, she turned her steps to the north tower, which was used mostly for storage, the rooms full of old coffers and broken furniture. The servants had accommodation here too and although she expected to hear more than one poor soul weeping pitifully about their treatment at the hands of such a master, they seemed remarkably cheerful. There was still no sign of Griff.

Finding her again in one of the corridors, Gregory reminded her of the boundaries she'd been set.

"Have I gone so far?" she asked politely. "It seems but a few steps."

"My lady, you do remember the instructions you were given?"

"Yes."

He regarded her ruefully. "Did you read them, my lady?"

"Indeed I did and thought they must be meant for some naughty child, not for a grown woman, so I did not regard them."

Fatigued, he bowed his head. Rather than quarrel, he said he would let the earl deal with her later. His report on her behavior, she suspected, would be far from glowing.

Gabriel's rooms were in the west tower, where she found a cypress coffer with his name scratched into it, full of boyhood toys: leather balls, wooden skittles, hornbooks and the like. There were other books and items of clothing belonging to a grown man mixed in with these remnants of childhood. It was as if Gabriel never moved, or was allowed to grow, much beyond boyhood. There was a large empty nursery and adjoining chambers with narrow beds, presumably for nursemaids. Children from noble families, so she'd heard, were never raised by their parents. There was no decoration here. The walls were bare and iron bars on the windows--evidently a safety precaution for young children--only served to make the rooms more grim and prison-like. Her natural high spirits in danger of being drained, she hurried out, Jennet trailing fretfully in her wake.

The earl's rooms, she discovered, were in the east tower. She knew they were his at once. They were austere and masculine, nothing kept purely for aesthetic reasons. Fully expecting padlocks on his private apartments, she was shocked when his bedchamber door opened easily, not even the shyest whine of a hinge in protest. Here the walls were darker, the furniture heavier. No extra pillows littered his bed, but piles of books leaned precariously from the table beside it, and an extravagant profusion of fat candles stood poised in wait for him to come back. Thick drips of beeswax hung suspended in time. The entire east tower was quieter, more serene, inspiring a respectful awe for the absent master of the house.

Gregory appeared again, this time with two sturdy fellows in tow. At first she thought they'd come to remove her bodily from the earl's chambers, however, they had more important work at hand. She watched as they moved furniture, swept and dusted, then replaced all the pieces in exactly the same place. Marks on the floor showed where his furniture stood for years and Gregory pointed to them with pride, explaining how this spring cleaning had proceeded in the same unswerving way for generations of earls. "His Lordship dislikes change," he said gravely. "He likes things to be as they were when he left them. As they were, exactly."

They were deadly serious in the task, even measuring with a notched stick if they thought anything was put back at the wrong angle. Madolyn watched in amusement. Old folk like the earl, of course, didn't like change, yet this surely took the idea to extremes.

When she made some suggestions for altering the furniture placement, Gregory looked as if he would like to tap her knuckles with his measuring stick, only restraining himself because of her importance in the house. Enjoying the wicked and unusual sense of power, she concluded she must indeed be a wretched sinner, now lost beyond all hope of saving, as Grace always warned her she would one day become.

"These chambers could be much brighter if that wainscot press didn't block the window," she offered pleasantly. "And his bed faces the wall, when it might face this spectacular view. I wonder no one has thought of it. And these books should be on shelves, not here, cluttering up his little table. I'm surprised they never fall on him when he sleeps. He can't possibly read all these at once. Why are there so many here? He has a library, does he not?"

"My lady," Gregory explained tightly, "his lordship likes his books left where they are in case he cannot sleep. He likes his bed facing the wall because the sunrise in the morning would surely wake him too early if the windows weren't blocked."

"I should think he'd like to wake and see the sunrise over that hill. I would."

"Yes, my lady, but that is *you*, not his lordship."

She shrugged. "I suppose he must have his little foibles. Men have their peculiar ways and I daresay he's worse than most, being pig-headed and spoiled,no one ever daring to say 'no' to the rotten beast. Well, hey ho, he's in for a surprise when he meets me."

Jennet giggled, until she caught Gregory's stony eye and then she looked down at her toes. Maddie laughed too. Gregory shook his head, muttered under his breath that he hoped the earl knew what he was getting himself into, and continued unhooking the bed drapes so they could be brought outside and the dust beaten off.

"Does his wife not live here too?' she asked.

"The countess lives in Leicestershire, my lady," Gregory replied, a low tone of relief shadowing his words.

She lifted a lidded pewter dish to see what was inside, only to have it taken from her immediately and placed, with reverence, back upon the bedside table. "Is this where he keeps his wooden teeth at night?" she asked, causing another snuffle from Jennet.

"Indeed not," Gregory exclaimed. "Wooden teeth, indeed. Please mind yourself now and make way for the chairs."

"Why not set his chairs here, by the window? For the summer."

They all looked at her, annoyed.

"He won't need his fire at night in the summer," she explained. "If his chairs are here, by the window, he might look out at his view and remember how unfairly fortunate he is."

The chairs were put back according to Gregory's measurements on either side of the fireplace.

Since her goodly counsel went unheeded, she decided to go outside in the sun. From the windows of her chamber she'd watched men at work around the grounds and thought they might need her help. As her mother would say, the devil makes work for idle hands. She might get into real mischief if she found no useful employment.

"Where are you going, madam?" Jennet whined.

She hurried on, passing some men trimming yew trees. Almost

falling off their ladders, they responded to her merry greetings with bemused, curious expressions. The appearance of a stray young woman, walking freely around the earl's estate, plainly unprecedented.

"I wish you'd come in," Jennet said, catching up.

"Oh, look." Maddie pointed. "What is that place?" It was a great glass building on the south lawn, directly placed to catch the full heat of the sun.

"'Tis the hothouse. Where the earl keeps the plants he collects on his travels."

Ignoring the maid's plaintive cries for her to go back to the house, Madolyn ran across the lawn to explore the place. She opened the door and entered before Jennet could follow.

Immediately the heat slowed her progress, the heady fragrance filled her until she was almost drunk with it. The air was thick and steamy, the plants reaching their great, glossy, dark green fronds to each other and to the sun, like prisoners missing their home, wanting to know what this place was to which they were brought, like her, out of their natural element. There were flowers of extravagant, brilliant colors, like ruffles of scarlet and apricot petticoats. Other, even stranger looking trees covered in thickly clustered yellow spines, bent their arms to the sky like eager preachers. And between them, fat leaves, taller than she, created an arch of shadow under which she passed.

Suddenly she heard a young man's voice raised in anger.

"It en't right. 'Tis a bloody hypoc...hypoc...you know what I mean...hypocossity. My brother Matthew were the best man he ever had, right loyal he were. Just because he wanted to marry, he got tossed out on his ear. Oh no, we don't want none o' *that* going on--so says his bleedin' lordship. Couldn't stand for my brother to be happy and have another life to go to at night. His lordship didn't want that, in case it might take Matthew away from his duty. But now *he* gets to have his little--" He broke off, catching sight of her striding between the nodding fronds.

At first she thought he was speaking to someone else, until she saw he was alone, addressing the leaves of a plant.

"What are you doing in 'ere, missy? You ain't supposed to be in 'ere!" He was a short, thickset fellow with a shock of pale golden hair. "The earl wouldn't like it."

She smiled. "Never mind that."

He thrust his head forward on that thick neck. "But you--"

"And you mean hypocrisy," she interrupted jovially. "When someone says one thing and does another. What's your name?"

For a moment he simply stared at her, then he answered, "It's Luke." He shook his head rapidly. "But I can't be talkin' to you, missy. Got work to do."

"You have a brother named Matthew?" she pressed. "He used to work here?"

"Beg pardon," he said briskly, "can't hear you, missy."

She raised her voice. "I heard you say he was mistreated by the earl and dismissed from his post."

"Go away. Ain't you got nothin' else to do?"

She felt like a child being sent off to amuse herself so the adults could talk of important matters, but at least now she knew she was not the only one disgusted with the way the earl bullied people.

In Luke, she and Griff might have an ally.

"You ain't supposed to be in here, missy. Get out!"

"No need to be rude."

"Can't hear you, missy."

"I said," she shouted, "there's no need to be rude!"

He shook his head again and smacked his hand to his left ear. "Not a word you're bleedin' saying, missy," he said, promptly turning away.

She left the hothouse and found Jennet waiting outside. When she asked the maid about Luke, she learned that he was the head gardener. He and his brothers had worked on the estate since they were boys. The mysterious Matthew was once the earl's loyal valet, dismissed two years ago because he fell in love with a housemaid, and romance between staff was strictly forbidden. He was also, apparently, accused of stealing some valuable pearls from the Swafford treasury. Madolyn thought this crime was probably entirely made-up to justify the valet's dismissal.

Familiar with injustice, of course, she knew how noblemen treated those they considered inferior.

Suddenly she remembered the night she was abducted from her cousin's house, standing before the looking glass with those beautiful pearls at her throat, and Griff's angry exclamation as he tore them from her hands. *"The Swafford pearls! This is what became of them. It wasn't Matthew!"*

Gabriel must have taken the pearls and given them to Eustacia without telling his brother. Meanwhile, in haste to find a culprit, the beastly Earl found a scapegoat in his valet and poor Matthew was punished unjustly. As Griff would be, if she was not there to defend him.

Chapter 18

In her chamber that evening, she was writing a letter when Jennet returned to help her dress for dinner.

"You write to your family, my lady?" the girl asked.

She didn't look up. "No. I write to the damnable Earl of Swafford."

"Oh."

"I've a tendency to let my temper run away with me and forget what I meant to say, so I'll write it all down, just in case."

"I see, my lady."

A few minutes later, hearing some intriguing sighs and rustling, she looked up from her letter. The maid was lifting clothes from a box, laying them out carefully across the large bed and stroking each garment wistfully. At first determined not to show any interest, curiosity soon got the better of Maddie. She set down her quill and walked to the bed.

There were three new gowns, exquisitely made, finer even than those her cousin Eustacia wore, but youthful and not too fussy. Silk petticoats with lace trim, and stockings embroidered with little flowers, nestled there, waiting for her touch. The final garment was even a bed robe of fine ivory lawn and lace with cascades of ruffles along the hem.

Beside her, the maid ran her hands reverently over this haul of luxury.

"Look away, dear Jennet," Maddie warned. "You're too young, too innocent." These things, she thought angrily, were all his property in the same way he meant her to be. "His lordship thinks I might be tempted, I suppose. As if I might be bought, like any other possession."

Jennet reminded her shyly that the Earl of Swafford was never refused.

"Had he been refused once or twice in his life," she replied curtly, "he might not be such a wretched ogre. Never fear, it will all be in the letter."

The maid nodded solemnly, hands behind her back, resisting the lure of those sinful, lacy garments.

"Remember, Jennet, as I told you earlier, if Swaffords had to work for a living, there might be a pleasanter face among the long line of shriveled, miserable old prunes in the gallery."

It had surprised her, but even with a fortune at their disposal, none of the previous earls bothered to bribe an artist into making them look handsome. The current earl had no portrait yet in the family gallery. She supposed he at least had the good sense not to expose himself to future critics. He was, she'd heard, heinously scarred, dreadful to look upon.

"Think of everything he would buy for you, madam," Jennet whispered, "if you *were* his mistress. There's nothing you could not have."

"Money? If I had a fortune, I wouldn't know what to do with it, I daresay. No. I'm quite content to be poor and happy. It costs naught to make love."

Jennet flushed scarlet.

She clarified. "Unless one must procure one's partner, that is, then I believe it costs sixpence."

Still the little maid was mute.

"Has this wealth bought the Swafford earls much happiness, Jennet?" Maddie continued, getting into her stride. "How can anyone with this much wealth ever be sure the people at his side care for him, rather than his coin? People like my darling Griff and I are far luckier than the earl, you see, because we have each other. We may not have material wealth, but we are rich--far richer than the Earl of Swafford."

Jennet nodded. "If you say so, my lady."

She frowned. "Indeed I do. And stop calling me *my lady*."

"Very good, my lady. Shall I dress you now? The earl waits below."

Her heartbeat rattled and lurched to a halt. "He...he's here? Now?"

"Yes, my lady. And he doesn't like to wait."

Sweating palms clasped tight, she walked to the window for a breath of fresh air. It was almost dark out. Rush torches were lit around the outer walls of the house, casting long flickering shadows like the wings of giant bats.

This was it then. Time to confront the Beast at last.

* * * *

He prowled into the hall, and servants scattered like mice from a tomcat. Things seemed in order, he noted. A comforting fire burned in the great hearth, the table was arrayed with candles and the mouth-watering scent of roast beef drifted through the corridors.

Gregory appeared at his side, gray head respectfully bowed. "Good evening, my lord."

"Hmmph." He removed his riding gloves, passing them along with his hat to a nearby footman. "What of the roan mare? No problem with the pregnancy I hope?"

"No, my lord."

"Good." He turned in a tight circle. "Where is she?"

"The comely young lady, my lord? I...could not say. I find it best to let her do as she will. I daresay she'll come down in good time, when she's ready."

"You...*what*?" he exploded. The idea of any woman being left to do as she would around his precious, beloved estate was completely unacceptable and Gregory, having served him thirty-five years, should know that by now. "Did I or did I not give instructions that she's to remain in the blue chamber, until I want her? I fail to see why keeping one abbreviated wench confined should test our resources."

"I'm sorry, my lord," said Gregory. "But may I say, although of a diminutive size, the young lady is uncommon determined. At my time of life..."

Griff strode up and down before the great hearth, one hand rubbing his neck. "No sign of her accomplices yet, eh?"

"Accomplices, my lord?"

"Of course." He turned on his heel again and started back in the other direction. "She's not in this alone. Someone put her up to it. Now I've let her in, they'll come crawling out of the woodwork to reveal their motives."

"What if there are no accomplices?"

He glared at Gregory, fearing the good man's mind unhinged. "Are you suggesting this woman threw herself at me because it was a dull day and she had naught else to do?" He straightened his shoulders, clasping his hands behind his back. "She's in league with the Scarlet Widow, or that pirate Downing, perhaps both. She was paid to seduce me for their dark ambitions. Oh yes, Gregory, we must watch her every moment of the day. I wouldn't be surprised to find they sent her here to do away with me."

"No doubt you're in the right, my lord," Gregory hastened to agree.

"You surprise me Gregory. Am I ever not?"

"No, my lord. Of course. I've instructed young Jennet to stay close to her."

"May as well leave a kitten to mind a lioness." He paused, head tilted, listening for sounds of her voice, or her footsteps. He never liked it when she was this damned quiet. "Find the wretched woman at once. If you're too afraid of her--as you plainly are--send someone else."

"My lord," Gregory ventured, "you might seek her out yourself."

He puffed out his chest. "I certainly shall not..." he ran a fumbling hand over his black leather doublet, "... demean myself by hunting her down." He looked around and strode across to the sideboard. "Perhaps you're in the right, Gregory. Let her boil in her own juices. If she doesn't wish to join me for supper, let her starve."

"Very good my lord."

Reaching for the wine jug, he paused. "On second thought..." He wouldn't let her make her own rules. She'd come when he wanted her. "Send someone to find her. Tell her I insist."

Gregory swallowed, eyes darting nervously from side to side. "She doesn't take kindly to instructions and commands, my lord."

"For pity's sake! Must I find her and drag her down myself?" However, despite his bluster, he couldn't bring himself to fetch her. Having only recently reconciled himself to the idea of keeping a woman, now he wondered again whether he had the patience for it. "Find her, Gregory. I care not who goes or how 'tis done. Lay mantraps if you must. Send in the hounds, or better yet, the witchfinder."

There was no need, for at that moment she appeared, slowly descending the sweeping staircase to the great hall where he waited.

Negotiating each step cautiously in her new gown, she was half-way down before she looked up at him standing by the fire.

* * * *

Suddenly her feet had wings. She half ran, half fell down the remaining steps to throw her arms around his neck. He grunted in surprise and then she was submerged in his warmth, her senses inundated, her heart's rhythm reckless, throat aching with gladness. He lifted her off her feet and kissed her.

There were no words exchanged for several minutes while she forgot the staff looking on. It was as if they were the only two people in the world. She slid down his body slowly, until her toes felt the floor and she came back to earth.

"Oh Griff!" she cried. "Is the earl with you?"

"Of course he's with me. He's always with me." His eyes shone. He put his hands around her face. "Where else would he be, limpet?"

"Where else?" She inhaled a deep breath of the sun-warmed skin on his hands.

"I'm here, limpet."

And then Gregory cleared his throat and said, "My lord, there are a few matters--."

"Let it wait. Later you may have my attention, Gregory, but this lady demands it now, you see." Griff looked down at her and smiled. "And I suspect she's hungry. She usually is."

The words she'd planned were suddenly erased. The world began to tilt. Losing her balance she tripped backward, away from him. When he held on to her, resisting gently, she felt anger, sharp and painful.

"I don't know you, sir," she breathed, trembling.

His head tipped to one side, brow quizzical. Determined, she fought him, until he gave up trying to hold her. When he glanced over at the others, she knew he only let her go to prevent a scene before them. She waited, conscious of the staff looking on, confused and wondering. But she was aware mostly of her heart being pulled apart. Surprisingly, despite the abuse, it was still beating. Perhaps it was not yet completely broken.

Even so, it was too fast, too wild, and she could not control it.

PART III
Peeled and Plucked

CHAPTER 19

He brusquely dismissed the servants, sending them scattering, leaving them alone.

Her mind spun in circles, making truths out of lies and lies out of truths. "This is what you meant, when you said you wanted to keep me." Attempting a laugh, she made only an odd chirp. "You wanted to *keep* me, as your mistress--a kept woman."

"Was that not your plan when you seduced me?" His tone might have been casual, his eyes were not. They were angry, questioning, as if they had any right to be, when she was the one who should demand answers.

She thought of the things she'd said of him, before she'd known it *was* him. And the things he'd said to her, letting her feel sympathy for him, fooling her into believing he was a humble man, a good man. Making her believe they were equal, two people who'd found one another by some happy coincidence. As if she could help him, care for him, love him.

A thousand thoughts ran through her head, tangled up in a knotted mess, preventing anything sensible coming out of her mouth.

"You needn't continue the act now," he said, his voice low, carefully measured in the same controlled way he'd used before with her. "It was a charming performance, but has served its purpose."

"You thought I knew? You thought I played a game?"

"Of course. No woman is so completely without guile."

He didn't know her any more than she knew him, even after all that had happened.

"It was a delightful, accomplished performance and I'm indebted to you for those days of pleasure. Come," he said to her now, beckoning with his finger.

"You cannot command me." It burst out of her in a rush. "I'm not your servant!"

"The game is over," he said again, stepping toward her.

He must think, in some cold, hard part of his being, that she'd deliberately enticed him. In his mind, she was a despicable, lying, scheming whore. And he was a man with a wife already.

When her lips trembled, she lifted her chin, hoping he wouldn't notice. "I don't want those gowns."

"You need them."

"You thought I might be bought, like a brood mare?"

"Not a brood mare, my sweet," he said. "I've no intention to breed you." His deep voice resonated inside her.

"Please summon my maid. I need her to help me pack my things," she said, although all she had was a leather bag full of shells.

"*Your* maid? I believe this is still my house and my staff. And you'll stay here until I'm done with you."

She looked away, anger coursing through her in waves as irregular as her pulse. "Have it your way."

"I always do. I'm the Earl of Swafford, am I not?" He was showing off, showing he had the power and that her will, however stubborn, was nothing compared to his. How different was this man from the one she knew before, the one who'd lain on that fleece with her in their little cottage by the bay and gently brushed his fingers through her hair.

"I took a great deal of trouble over those clothes," he muttered, gold-grained eyes sweeping her appearance with evident approval. "I never made this many decisions for one damnable woman in my entire life." He was resentful, as if she'd made him do it, when she'd never wanted anything from him. Nothing, she thought miserably, he could give her now. But she banked her tears, determined not to show any weakness in front of him. Later, she would cry enough to flood his damned house.

Chin up, she demanded, "What if they didn't fit?"

"They'd better," he scoffed, suggesting should they not, the poor dressmakers responsible would lose their head.

"I suppose you could keep them for your next paramour, or your wife." She wanted to make him discuss the countess, but he, she discovered quickly, would not.

He spoke sharply, eyes guarded. "Those clothes were made for you. What use would they be to any other woman? They were made to fit you, the way you," he looked at her meaningfully, "were made to fit me." His left brow lifted a fraction. "I believe you enjoyed the fitting as much as I did."

Maddie wished she could block her ears, but his deep voice was a potent brew, slipping inside her, finding a route through her defenses, rendering her temporarily mute.

"I might," he continued, coming closer, "if I were not a gentleman, recall that *you* seduced me. But…" He put his finger under her chin and lifted it, as he bent his head until her clenched lips were barely an inch from his. "…for now, as you're in this fractious mood. I'm hungry and my dinner gets cold, we'll say it was mutual." She couldn't get her breath back, was too enraged by his impudence. "Now, if you would join me for dinner, perhaps we might discuss this arrangement as two sensible adults, rather than rail at one another like foolish adolescents." He gestured to a chair. "Will you sit?"

* * * *

Determined to remain in control and contain his anger, he held the chair out for her, feigning graciousness with a quick bow of his head. It was a duty he'd never before performed, and it showed. Once she was seated, he strode to his chair at the far end of the table and rang a bell for the servants.

After the food was served, the tension in the hall became palpable. The staff hovered nearby, evidently feeling the strain as much as the principles in this farce, so he sent them out again and as the door closed, announced, "Gregory informs me you've been busy today."

She shrugged.

"Did you even read my instructions? I believe I told you to obey Gregory in my absence."

Now she looked up, spearing him with those blue icicles. "Damn your instructions."

Carefully he set down his knife. "You will not try my patience, or defy me in front of the servants again. Do I make myself clear?" Leaning back in his chair, palms flat on the table, he repeated, "Do I make myself clear?"

"I told you, I'm not your servant and I don't follow your orders." She faced him squarely down the length of his table, and he felt a stark jolt of appreciation for her bold, fighting spirit. He'd always appreciated a beautiful animal and she was a tempestuous, high-strung filly. Her eyes were over-bright with the fire burning inside her.

"My instructions will always be for your own good, madam."

"I know what's good for me." Inferring he didn't.

"Can you ever see the day when you might obey?"

"Can you ever see the day when you might learn to trust?"

He said nothing. Apparently she was out to push his temper this evening. How far would she dare go?

"What you said earlier," she began, "about breeding..."

"What of it?"

Her eyes dimmed. The fire inside her was lower now, smoldering. "You don't want children? Don't you need an heir?"

Sitting back in his chair, he brushed down his doublet, hiding his expression. "No, I don't want children. I have an heir already - Gabriel, of course." He reached for his wine, snarling bitterly, "That's why I'd hoped he might make a better choice of wife, for the sake of future earls."

* * * *

Madolyn thought of her mother, who made many sacrifices to raise three surviving children--four including Nathaniel-- mostly alone with their father frequently away at sea. It was never easy. They had few luxuries and were, by most material standards, quite poor, living from harvest to harvest. Their father made a good living, but the cost of raising them, even the basic provision of clothes, shoes and medicines, took its toll. There were disappointments too: shipwrecks with lost cargo, bad harvests and diseased beasts that had to be slaughtered.

"What ails you now?" he demanded.

"You look miles away."

"I was thinking of my own mother and how I would like many--" What she wanted could hardly matter to a man like him. Suddenly she envisaged her old kite, diving too rapidly, head first into the roof of the pigsty, shattered in an instant.

He speared another slice of beef on his knife. "Tell me who sent you to seduce me? I should thank them. You performed the duty admirably." He smiled stiffly, his eyes flinching as if it hurt. "I almost believed...but no. What more is there to come? A knife in my heart one night? Poison in my breakfast ale?"

It was incredible, but, of course, he was a man with a dark, suspicious nature. He almost wallowed in it.

"Was it Lady Shelton who paid for your virtue and sent you to distract me?"

She was silent, stunned by his rambling accusations.

"Did she pay you by the hour or by the lie? I'm curious to know which would cost more--the latter perhaps?"

"And you lied freely."

"I told you no lies." He hesitated. "You knew who I was."

She shook her head slowly.

He fidgeted with his knife, picking it up and putting it down again. "Confess the truth, madam, or else I might be obliged to do away with you. And those gowns can't be returned. I'd hate to waste my coin."

This stiff attempt at humor fell on deaf ears, because she was thinking back to those glorious days by the bay and hating herself for being such a fool. She stared down at her plate, her eyes glassy with trapped tears. Only that morning she'd imagined herself in love with him. Now what? Love and marriage were not what he wanted from her. He had a wife already, a wife, who was never to be mentioned. It burned in her throat, like a splinter of bone stuck there, slowly suffocating her, starving her of sustenance.

"I thought you wanted to discuss this arrangement you planned, my lord."

His eyes narrowed. "Very well. Our arrangement."

"*Your arrangement*," she snapped with a burst of acerbic temper that came out of her just when she thought she was near defeat and likely to shame herself with girly tears. "I never planned for this."

"You set out to seduce me. You told me, within the first few moments we met."

That shot of bitterness was gone. It left her exhausted. "I didn't know it was you." Her words fell like the first flakes of snow, so light she barely heard them, so fragile they melted even as they came into being.

Agitated, he looked for someone to pour more wine, apparently having forgotten he'd already sent them all out. Storming over to fetch the wine jug himself, he flipped the lid open with his thumb and refilled his goblet.

"How long do you expect this arrangement to last?" she asked.

"Until I grow bored," he replied, smug, returning to his chair. He shot her a look but she remained solemn, unblinking.

"And then?"

"Then you may do as you please." Bringing the refilled goblet back to his lips in a hurry, he almost spilled wine. She saw he was drinking too much. It must be unusual for him not to know his own limits, she thought acidly, since he was always prompt and thorough at telling other people theirs.

"Shall I find another lover?" she asked coolly.

Using the kerchief he held crumpled tight in his fist, he dabbed wine from his chin. "Certainly. If you wish."

"It wouldn't matter to you?"

He set down his goblet, fingers splayed around the base. "I've no doubt you'll be ready to leave at the first chance of a better offer."

"You have a deep distrust of women, it seems, your lordship. What happened to make you think this low of us?"

He regarded her thoughtfully, his tongue in his cheek. Suddenly, to her surprise, he began to speak. "My father's first marriage was a match arranged from infancy. There was no love lost betwixt them. The marriage and the children--we were her painful duty." He stopped a moment, his hand clenched around the wine-stained kerchief. "We were left to the care of nurses. Our mother's visits to the nursery or the schoolroom were few and far betwixt. I often had to remind Gabriel who she was. She was not faithful to our father and took no pains to hide her affairs, but flaunted them. When I was sixteen and she lay ill with a fever, she told me she'd tried to abort me, took a potion to be rid of me. Gabriel, she told me that day, was born of passion--a love affair. I was born of hatred and duty."

He leaned back in his chair, long legs stretched out languorously, hands behind his head. But the mercurial gold in his eyes belied the tranquil pose.

"No one knows what she told me, not even Gabriel. But now you know." He gave a short, bewildered laugh, as if he couldn't think why he told her all this. "She died soon after," he went on briskly. "My father's second marriage was brief, to a much younger woman from a noble but impoverished family. He was besotted with her." He curled his lip in disgust. "She used him for his money, of course, and ran off with another man." Sitting up, he shrugged and continued his supper. "Every woman I've ever known has only wanted me for the money and the favors. The minute I turn my back she's in someone else's bed." He laughed abruptly, viciously. "Should be used to it by now."

She could only attribute this speech to a wine-soaked tongue. Under no other circumstances would such a proud man unburden himself with brutal honesty to an inconsequential wench.

"You'll tell me, of course, that you're different," he added.

But she should not have to tell him.

"No? Good. No more lies. We know what to expect from one another and there'll be no disappointment." Cold, dispassionate, his words hung in the brittle air between them. "Whatever your part in this deception perpetrated against me, I find myself loath to give you up. For now you'll stay. You owe me your time a little longer, after the trick you pulled on me in London, pretending to be Lady Shelton. Think of it as a debt to work off."

Even as her anger mounted,

pity kept apace. The fierce struggle threatened to rip her heart asunder and Maddie knew she'd better be far, far away and quickly, before compassion won out and that meddling desire of hers to make things right spoiled any chance of saving herself.

"What happened?" she asked simply. "At the cottage. What happened there, with us? How do you explain it?"

His shoulders slumped and he drew a breath. "You took me off my guard. It won't happen again." So it seemed he considered those days a brief interlude of weakness, a fault to be corrected.

"Now I'm another servant." She wondered if perhaps that was the only way he could deal with it—and with her.

"Your duties will be pleasurable. You can't deny that." He looked at her, waiting. She lifted her shoulders in a half-shrug. "You enjoyed yourself in my company," he exclaimed, his voice catching on the words, as if they hurt. "Or was that a lie too?"

"It's the one thing that was not a lie," she whispered, wistful suddenly.

His eyes regained a little of the old warmth and he swallowed. "I like you in that gown," he choked out. "May I come to you tonight?"

She looked up in wonder that he'd asked, when she'd expected him to command. "Come to me? Would I not come to you?" It seemed unlikely he would put himself out to come to her chamber, but she was not conversant with these "arrangements".

"If I come to you," he explained patiently, "I can leave the moment I'm done. If you came to me, I'd have to ask you to get up and leave."

Her lips parted. He scowled at her and asked if he said something amiss.

Again, the memories stirred, and her heart wept with longing. The change in him was like night from day, but as he told her once, she'd briefly given him the chance to walk in another man's boots.

"Did you like the flowers in your chamber? I don't yet know your favorites." His tone changed. Now he was glib, a courteous lover, but it struck a false note. It was overdone, awkward, and when he came toward her with a slim wooden box, she felt as if they acted parts in a play. Rather than give her the box, he opened it himself, taking out a necklace of blue stones. As he placed it around her neck, he told her it was lapis lazuli, a treasure from the Swafford vault. "It reminded me of your eyes," he said huskily, fixing the little clasp at the nape of her neck. His unsteady fingers brushed against her skin, as if she might be hot to the touch. The surging desire crept in again, the memories too strong.

Standing quickly, she thrust back the chair and it hit him in the thighs. "You shouldn't give me this," she said, fingers scrabbling blindly for the catch. "I don't want your gifts." She was breathing too fast. "And I hate those...those flowers," she gasped, not even knowing their name. "My favorites are daisies--surely too humble and common for you." She pulled on the necklace, while he stood in mute indignation, arms at his sides. "And let me give you a word of advice, your lordship. The next time you play the gallant suitor, at least have the good grace to pretend it's not all about the fucking!"

The throaty word flew out before she even knew it was in her.

He replied icily, "You said it first. You claim not to know me now." His eyes darkened. "And I know nothing about you, because you won't tell me. Therefore, as you sweetly point out, that's the only thing between us that is not a lie. What else can this be about, but the fucking?"

She pulled on the wretched necklace, filling the air with curses aimed at him, his house, his servants, his family, even his horses. Suddenly, his hands were on her waist. He spun her around and unclasped the necklace. "No need to be quite so demonstrative," he said thickly. "You hate everything, I think I grasped that much."

It wasn't true, of course, but she was too angry to speak. While she was losing her heart to him in their cottage by the bay, he'd merely thought her a calculating, mercenary whore.

"Apparently, you no longer desire me," he muttered. "I'm now a monster to you. Perhaps I should've expected it. I was a fool to think..." He dropped the necklace back in its box, but his fingers fumbled and the lid wouldn't close. In a temper he tossed it across the table.

Oh, but she did desire him still.

Contrary to what she knew she should feel for this heartless, arrogant man, lust raised its wicked head the moment he touched her, however slight the caress, however unintentional. Yet to him she was one of those plants to be shut inside the hothouse, carefully tended and kept for his amusement only.

She turned and found him looking at her oddly--why? Ah, her curls were falling loose from their caul. They stroked her shoulders, tickled her warm cheeks. He merely looked at her and she fell apart. If only she could be like Grace and never show her emotion. Instead she gave away every thought in her stupid head. "If you mean to come to me tonight," she snapped, "will it be soon? Because I'm tired and will later have a headache."

He looked askance. "You know in advance when you'll have a headache?"

"I know I shall tonight!"

His lips turned inward.

"Better get on with it," she added, her tone churlish and sing-song, hands on her waist.

"Quite," he muttered. "Best get it over with, as you say."

This was, of course, not what she'd said, but Maddie never bothered to correct it.

With no further delay, he pulled her into an angry kiss. His bristles were rough against her cheek and there was fraught desperation to his passion as he rushed in like a boy with his first fumbling encounter. His damp, forceful lips and wine-stained tongue covered the rapid pulse in her neck, his kisses were almost gasps of anger. His hands fought through her petticoats until they found the silk ribbon garters he'd purchased. Groaning, he slid his fingers across those ribbons and between her thighs. His breeches rubbed against her stockinged legs, his knee nudging hers apart. Then she felt his arrogant, roughened hand seeking, cajoling and demanding the wetness that betrayed her. Now he knew she wanted him. There was no way to hide that.

While his fingers stroked her intimately, exploring the treasured keepsake, his mouth descended to her neck, his rapid, liquid breaths fluttering there in rhythm with her pulse. He nipped her skin, suckling gently but devotedly. He would leave a mark on her, if he was not careful.

Not that she cared. She would give as good as she got, was just in the mood for a scrap.

She gasped, exhaling in a deep shuddering breath. No longer able to remain aloof, she reached for him. It was pitiful. He was the Earl of Swafford, the Beast, a notoriously wicked, unforgiving man, yet she wanted, needed, yearned for him with this pounding carnal desire. Even as her mind and heart railed against the injustice, her body still lusted, ignoring the complexity of this web in which she found herself trapped.

Surprisingly they made it as far as the blue chamber. They didn't quite make it as far as the bed.

* * * *

It was a heated, savage coupling, neither willing to be gentle.

Well matched. The words soared in his mind as he mounted her, unrestrained, forceful and turbulent. She arched to meet him, never still, never submissive, standing her ground. Here, in bed, they quarreled without words, the anger unabated, living side by side with passionate, unceasing, covetous desire.

Once, licking sweat from his chest, she bit his nipple and he felt the tremor cascade down his body, teasing his cock without mercy. The breath ripped out of him, wildly unconstrained. He jerked her head back by the hair. Her eyes, full of sparks, were not afraid of him--she was almost laughing. When her lips parted, he silenced her quickly, his mouth on hers, rapacious, unyielding.

It was bewitchment, he realized, a craving he must surely get out of his system before it killed him. Or both of them.

* * * *

Once he was gone, she lay across the rumpled sheets, his seed warm inside her, and listened to the evensong of nightjars through the open lattice window. Tonight, again, he'd forgotten his blessed self-control, and she'd had no chance to find the herbs she needed. But what did he care?

He could do as he pleased. Nothing would inconvenience him. Perhaps he thought she should be honored to bear his bastard.

Rolling over, she surveyed the wreckage of that moonlit chamber. The exquisite pieces of her gown lay on the floor, crumpled and discarded. There too were the petticoats in another pile and only steps from the bed, her corset. And there, the rose embroidered stockings hung over the arm of a chair where he'd tossed them after removing each with reverent ceremony, reminding her how much they cost. He would probably never reconcile himself to the idea of spending excessive coin on one woman; he marveled over it, as if that too was her fault, part of her cunning plan for his undoing.

A tiny voice reminded her how she had, in fact, set out to seduce him. She'd sold herself in exchange for Cousin Nathaniel's pardon. Griff knew her aim, but not the spirit behind it. She wanted nothing for herself, but he couldn't understand that. In his world, folk were motivated only by greed. He came from a very different world to her own. Ah! Now she made excuses for him too--like his staff.

She thought of the austere nursery in the west wing, the bars on the windows and the lonely, unloved description of his youth. Warm tears pricked under her lashes, but she turned her face into the pillow to dry them, for this was no time for pity. He had none, did he not?

And he already had a wife. He already had a wife. It echoed around her aching head, a cruel taunt by a spiteful bully.

Through her window, the nightjars sang on, a long, loud purr, calling out for a mate in one last frantic burst of enthusiasm before midnight. She knew exactly how they felt.

CHAPTER 20

When she entered the cookhouse the next morning, there was a new face present, a man introduced as Wickes, the earl's valet, freshly arrived from London. None of the other staff knew him, since he was only recently hired. When Gregory introduced them, Wickes was cleaning his fingernails with a knife. He gave no nod, no smile, but with hard, contemptuous eyes looked down his nose at her.

Maddie took a quick dislike to the man and knew instinctively the feeling was mutual.

"There's no need for you to come to the cookhouse, my lady," Gregory reminded her. "Simply pull the bell chord by the fire in your room, and Jennet will come to see to whatever you require."

Aware of that bell, she never used it. Bells were for cattle, not for her or for Jennet.

He shooed her back to the great hall. "Perhaps you might feed the swans on the lake, my lady," he muttered, before scuttling off to his master's library, humming nervously and checking those white strands of hair with anxious hands. She watched him knock upon the library door and enter. A moment later, her ear was pressed to the same door.

Gregory's voice was muted, but *his* was loud, imperious, wanting to know why she wandered around his house again, as if she was a stray piglet trampling the vegetable kitchen.

"Do I need to post a guard outside her room?"

She heard Gregory respectfully reply he didn't think the young lady meant any harm and it wouldn't be kind to keep her confined.

Every person in the house heard what came next, even without their ear pressed to his door. "Has this world gone mad or did she bewitch you too? If we're not careful she'll leave her wretched sticky finger-marks all over the place. I find myself surprised the house still stands!" She heard the piteous, complaining creak of an old, worn-out chair, the low thunder of pacing footsteps. A heavy item slammed hard against the door, making her jump back. "I wouldn't   trust her as far as I can spit. Have you counted the silver lately, Gregory?"

She glared at the door, wishing she could indeed cast a spell upon him--turn him into a toad, or a worm.

"She's certainly clever," he went on. "I almost believed her little performance. Almost. Women, of course, are consummate deceivers. It comes naturally to them as Daughters of Eve."

Gregory sounded confused. "My lord, if I might be so bold, I do think the young lady is genuine."

Dear Gregory! Her heart swelled with gratitude for the poor steward who endangered his life by contradicting the great spoiled baby.

The earl huffed scornfully. "Of course you do. You're easily taken in by a lovely pair of bubbies." Now she heard his big feet rattling the floor boards again. "As was I. Briefly."

"Thank goodness you recovered, my lord."

The pacing continued.

Gregory ventured, "The lady is a caution, my lord. The things she comes out with…"

"A caution?" the Earl muttered dryly. "A cautionary tale perhaps. Women, Gregory, are like pomegranates."

"Pomegranates, my lord?"

"Too many hard little pips and not nearly enough sweetness to recompense."

The door swung open abruptly. Alarmed, Gregory tried to signal with his head, gossamer wisps of hair standing upright, but it was too late--not that she had any intention of retreat. The Beast, directly behind him, didn't look too surprised to see her there.

"Pomegranates?" she demanded.

He muttered some command to Gregory and the old man, heavy eyelids drooping wearily, shuffled off.

"I tend to business in my library each morning," he said. "Duty always comes first, play later. I trust you can find other things to occupy your time until I require your presence?"

"What would you suggest?"

"Whatever little thing it is that treacherous, deceiving wenches do, until their company is required." He blinked and there went the mischievous spark again, the reminder of why she once thought she loved him, when he was another man, of course, not this pompous ogre who might "require" her presence.

"Why can't I sit with you? Perhaps I could..."

"No woman enters my library. Especially," he added, "when she won't even tell me her name or anything else about her."

"Do you truly believe I'm part of a scheme to harm you?"

He grinned, wolfish, one shoulder propped against the door frame. "I've no doubt some villainy is afoot, madam and I will uncover the truth before I let you leave."

"I could walk out of here. I could take one of those fine horses and ride away. I'm not afraid. I'll take my *lovely pair of bubbies* and leave!"

His stark features were calm, but the menace in his tone undeniable. "Try it. See how far you get."

"Oh I'd be far, far away," she said smugly, "before you even knew I was gone."

"I daresay I could still hear your tongue flapping."

She gasped. "You're an uncivil brute with less good manners than a goat."

Like a bonfire on a windy night, the gold in his eyes flickered fitfully. "You do want to persuade me of Captain Downing's innocence do you not?" Still leaning against the door frame, he swept her, head to toe, with another long, steady, appreciative perusal. "You've got your work cut out for you. I suggest you get some rest for now."

Her eyes must have widened, her cheeks colored, because there was the nuance of a smirk, evocative of triumph, before he closed his library door, returning to more important matters.

She marched out of the house, Jennet hurrying in her wake.

"You will stay, my lady, won't you?" the little maid asked.

"Certainly not! When you're a grown, mature woman Jennet, you'll learn there must be more to a relationship than....*that*. A woman needs a man who can love her properly--with his heart." Maddie sighed wistfully. "The Beast has no heart, at least not one he can spare for love. He has one to keep him alive, not to enjoy life."

Jennet chewed on her lower lip. "Can it be fixed? If his heart is ill, can it not be cured?"

"Thanks to my mother, I know many potions and remedies, Jennet, but I know of nothing that can raise the dead."

* * * *

From his library window, he watched her stroll across his lawn. He ought to post a guard to watch her, since Gregory was clearly smitten with the wench and the little maid was no match for her.

He yawned. It was damned tiring keeping up with her.

She had, according to Gregory, a disturbing eagerness to help with housework and gardening, which he concluded was merely part of her act. No doubt she studied his house and his staff, looking for weakness, gaining their confidence for some ulterior motive yet to be revealed. Poor fools. They'd learn.

Of all the women he might have, he chose one with an aversion to instructions and commands. She wouldn't even tell him her name.

Catching his coarse-featured reflection in the window, he scowled deeply. He certainly gave no credence to Gregory's addle-headed assertion that the nameless wench seemed fond of him. How could she be? Not even his own mother could love that face.

No, he couldn't trust her. Only a fool would believe anything she said. Evidently she was sent to distract him until the Scarlet Widow spirited his brother out of London. Now she planned to wheedle a pardon out of him on Nate Downing's behalf. Who knew what else she had up her sleeve, what other demands she might make of him?

He was quite excited already at the mere thought.

Trying to deny it, he shook his head.

Wickes had warned him about her and with his own eyes he'd once seen her fighting off Henry Jessop, who claimed she lied and cheated him.

He also knew she'd taken a knife from the cookhouse. Did she plan to use it on him one night?

More than likely.

But it didn't stop him wanting her.

Chapter 21

She spied Luke's golden head emerging from the cookhouse. Aha! Her potential ally.

Trotting after him, she was soon at his side, lengthening her steps to match his. "Can I help you, Luke? I should like to have useful chores to do." She grew bored with wandering about and being waited on. It was not in her nature to sit lazily by with nothing to do, no one to help. "If I don't have some useful employment, who knows what I might get up to?"

When Luke regarded her in vexation, she added, "I wouldn't want Jennet to be blamed."

Weighing the alternatives, Luke decided to sacrifice his own peace to save the rest of the household, Jennet in particular.

They went into the hothouse together and she asked him about the plants as they walked along. Although he used as few words as possible, uttered in a begrudging manner, he slowly came out of his shell.

"Tell me what happened to your brother Matthew," she said. "I know he was dismissed, Jennet told me."

No reply.

"Be assured the earl is no friend of mine," she urged. "You may speak honestly with no fear of retribution." Still he said nothing and carried on with his pruning. "You may say what you like in my presence," she added hopefully. "I shan't tell Gregory. If you wish to talk of what happened to your brother…"

"Can't hear you, missy. Beg pardon."

"You do hear me, Luke."

He blew out his cheeks, raised his eyebrows and shook his head sadly.

"I know you hear me," she cried.

"Best mind your own business, missy."

Thus she was to be dismissed, once again, as an inconsequential being. Yet she sensed Luke was an independent spirit, like her, and thus she was determined to be his friend. Whether he wanted it or not. "What happened to your brother was a great injustice and I daresay there have been many such injustices in this house. The earl is a tyrant, is he not?"

"He's no tyrant, Missy. He's not a bad man."

She gasped. "You said he was a hypocrite!"

"Aye. He was, missy. And he knows it."

Aha! He forgot his deafness now. "Why doesn't he make amends, if he knows he was wrong?"

He pondered this, scratching his flaxen head. "He's too proud to admit a mistake, missy. He's the Earl o' Swafford, after all."

"Luke!" she exclaimed, "I'm surprised at you for taking his side."

"I ain't taking his side, missy. I said he were wrong. And then I said he knows it."

"I daresay your brother is less understanding of that foul hypocrite."

He looked up in faint surprise. "Matthew bears his lordship no grudge, Missy."

"Even though he was parted from the woman he loves?"

"He were not parted," Luke chuckled benignly. "He and Meg were wed last summer."

"But you..."

"My brother Matthew were the best man his lordship ever had and he lost him over that bit o' foolishness because he were too stubborn to bend his rules." Luke straightened up. "None of us like to see the earl lose a good friend like Matthew. He has few enough he can trust, missy."

Incredible! Apparently the earl skillfully manipulated events, until his poor, brow-beaten servants sympathized with him.

"I'd like to meet Matthew," she said. "I daresay I'd get a truer version of events from him than his brother who remains in the earl's service."

Luke reminded her to water the plants, not his foot. "I don't know where you got your cock-eyed ideas about the master. He's a good man, but sometimes I think even he doesn't believe it."

She remembered what her sister Grace would say. *If you must have opinions, Maddie, keep them to yourself.*

Sulking she observed primly, "Luke, I think I liked you better when you wouldn't talk to me."

"And I liked you better," he said with a grin, "when I couldn't hear a word you said, missy. But someone had to set you right." His expression became serious then. "His lordship doesn't know women, missy. He needs time to get accustomed to having one in his house."

"So he means to make me his prisoner! Like one of these poor plants."

"If you ask me," he said amiably, "you're both too damned stubborn to know what's good for you. You're no better than him."

Of course, she took objection to this. "I'll leave at the first opportunity. He can't hold me captive." She paused, hot and sticky. "What?"

He chuckled. "Go on then. What's stopping you?"

She scowled.

"Perhaps you'd make a difference in his life."

"He's too stuck in his ways," she argued, "too firmly adhered to the tradition of every grim-faced Swafford before him. What can I do?"

"What have you done already?" he answered, golden head cocked to one side.

"Naught apparently! He doesn't believe a word I ever said and thinks me part of some elaborate conspiracy."

His broad face was earnest, his eyes full of warmth, his advice brotherly. "If you leave, he'll think he was right to doubt you, won't he?"

But how could she stay?

Hoping to clear her muddled thoughts and stiffen her resolve, she left the hothouse and took a leisurely stroll through the grounds. Before she saw Griff again, she must somehow get her emotions in concord with reality. If he saw any confusion, any weakness, he would pounce upon it.

She paused by the lake to watch the swans floating in and out of the willow branches that snagged on the water, leisurely drifting in a shower of verdigris and sunlight. Below, among the weeds, minnows dashed and darted frantically. How busy they were, those tiny fish, and here she was, with the luxury to be aimless suddenly. No one called for her to come in, stop daydreaming and tend her chores.

Walking to the summit of a slope, she admired the distant, gleaming, silver sea and the edge of chalk hills. Far below, nestled in the dip, there were villages named Mallory Abbas, Mallory Osborne and Mallory Le Willows, little clusters of stone cottages with thickly thatched rooftops and gardens bursting proudly with wild roses. The narrow lanes winding between the villages were flanked by collars of lush green grasses, embroidered with tall, gold-tinted ferns and sprigged with purple loosestrife. She thought how peaceful and serene the sea appeared from that distance. The tide came in now, but later today, as the sun slipped beyond the horizon, it would pull the sea with it, gathering the quiet waves in silken pleats, dragging them back from the beach where curlews could wade in the muddy sands, pecking for their supper.

She strode across the heath, following the sounds that were now familiar--the scratchy song of the warblers and the distinctive, knocking chortle of the stonechats. Overhead, woodlarks fluttered in a spiral dance accompanied by their clear, mellow, liquid song. She watched as one suddenly dived to the ground, wings folded, targeting insect prey.

She might have come to love this place. How strange she felt at home here in this house she should hate.

Aware suddenly of a cold chill on her shoulders, she spun around to find that unpleasant fellow, Wickes, standing a short distance away. She waited, thinking perhaps his master sent him to find her, but he said nothing, merely stared disrespectfully.

"What is it you want Wickes?" she demanded.

His eyes, pale and watery, narrowed slowly, speculating. "Now that's a question, ain't it?" He smirked in a knowing manner. "What can I get for a shilling?"

As he came toward her, she backed away. "Leave me alone,

Wickes."

"Don't act prim and proper with me, whore. Must have somethin' special under your skirt, eh, to get his lordship tied up in knots? Can't get enough of you can he? Ought to share some with the rest of us."

"Shall I tell the earl what you suggest?"

"He'll be out of the way soon enough. I can wait."

"What do you mean?"

"You'll find out." Sneering, he turned away and walked back toward the house. His low laughter trickled up through her feet, as if the earth vibrated with his scorn.

Despite what the other staff thought of her, no one was ever crude or unpleasant. Perhaps this was why Wickes's nasty comment scored its mark so effectively. It reminded her of the tenuous place she kept in the Beast's life.

* * * *

By late afternoon, done with his neglected business correspondence, he came to find her. She was in the west wing, touring those stark rooms where he spent his childhood.

"What are you doing in here?"

Lost in mournful thoughts, she didn't hear his approach. Now she jumped. He stood framed in the doorway, head bent under the lintel, hands behind his back.

"I was on my way out for a ride," he said. "Will you come?"

When she declined, his eyes grew dark, his face lined with long-ingrained suspicion. "Wickes tells me you've been exploring my woods and the heath. Alone and against my instructions, of course. Now I ask you to come with me, you'll be contrary on purpose."

Sighing deeply, she stared down through the bars of the window.

"I wanted to show you the estate," he grumbled.

"I can see it from here."

Now she heard his steps cross the room toward her. "You cannot see all the estate from here."

"Oh?" The vast size of the place was incomprehensible to her. From that window on the top floor of the west tower, she could see for miles over fields and tree tops. And in the distance, the silver line of ocean, the sun billowing behind it, expiring in a slow sizzle. Was there more still that he owned?

Now, pointing over her shoulder, he described each field and what they grew in it. He knew every tree and hedge, every square inch. She'd never heard this quiet pride in his voice before. When he spoke of the Swafford responsibilities, it was usually with a tone of weary acceptance, as if they were a heavy burden to bear. She stole a quick, sly glance from the corner of her eye as he leaned over her low shoulder, ducking his head to look through the barred window. He seemed younger suddenly, an eager boy, showing off for a guest. Luke had told her the old earl died more than fifteen years ago and Griff was not quite twenty--younger than she was now--when he assumed the title and the responsibilities entailed. Now, when he raised his hand again to point, she noticed his shirt cuff was a little too long. Maddie rarely sewed by choice, but she longed to pick up a needle and mend it for him.

She realized he'd stopped talking and now he stared at her. "Are you even listening?"

His words took her back, instantly, to their little cottage by the bay, when she sat on his knee and kissed him. Dare she take that chance again?

But he frowned, moving away. "I see you have no interest in the estate. Why should you? Excuse me." Bowing hastily, he left her there, heart thundering in her breast, the moment lost.

Of all the men in the world she might have fallen in love with, she mused, it had to be an enigmatic beast who, she suspected, only wanted her because she refused to cower at his feet. And he must win, couldn't stand to lose. He was of the nobility, born to a different world, in which someone like her only existed to serve and obey. For now he was fascinated by her, but the novelty would pass, as Wickes suggested.

Raising fingertips to her cheek, she found tears. Struggling to stop the flow, she had no more leverage against those little drips of water than a piece of driftwood had against the tide. Her emotions were caught up, dragged along by waves of heartbreak pounding at the shore, too wild, too powerful to be restrained. Knocked down, thrown about, she was unable to save herself from the current, had no chance even to catch her breath before she went under. The ferocious sea roared in her ears and then there was silence. She closed her eyes tight.

She floated. The sea was calm, bubbling and clicking leisurely over shells and pebbles at the shoreline where it deposited her exhausted body. And her conscience whispered, in Jennet's small voice, "Is he not worth saving? Is there nothing you can do for him?"

If she ran away without trying to mend that man where he was broken inside, she might always wonder...

She was Maddie the Merciless, for pity's sake, and she didn't give up that easily.

CHAPTER 22

The first item on her agenda at supper was Matthew. Barely had Griff sat to eat, when she announced there were several things she had in mind to discuss and this was the first. Too amused to reply, he let her babble on for several minutes, while she reminded him of the evening he'd found those precious Swafford pearls in Eustacia's London bedchamber, how he now knew he blamed the wrong man. Matthew therefore, she asserted genially, could be reinstated to his post.

She was in a better mood tonight it seemed, on her best behavior. Whether or not this bode favorably for him, he couldn't decide.

Clearing his throat, he said briskly, "The Earl of Swafford never goes back on any decision once made. Matthew was let go for other reasons in addition to the missing pearls."

"Because he had the unmitigated gall to fall in love?"

"Precisely. He will not be rehired." When he saw the dimple in her cheek and thought her preparing an argument, he raised his voice. "And if you had an estate the size of Starling's Roost to run, I'd take your counsel. As a woman who apparently didn't exist until I plucked her out of the Thames, perhaps you'll forgive me when I say your advice is not the wisest I might seek out."

Smug, he returned to his supper and to the letter he'd received that day from his brother. When the mouthy wench declared it rude to read at the table when one had company, he ignored her, signaling to Gregory for the wine jug.

She leapt quickly to her feet, beating the old fellow to it.

"What does the letter say?" she asked, walking toward him with the jug.

He sniffed. "Gabriel expresses his great happiness in marriage. No doubt he waits for an invite to come home with that woman."

"Hey ho!" she exclaimed, as if to jolly along the spirits of a child with a scraped knee. "No point sobbing over spilled milk. You should reconcile yourself to it and be civil to his wife." She snorted. "Oops, what am I saying? Civil? One cannot expect miracles. Or blood from a stone."

He scowled at her, but nothing deterred her merry grin. He almost preferred her in a temper with her claws out, for then he knew how to defend himself. This evening she'd dressed in another of the new gowns and even wore the lapis necklace she'd rejected so violently the night before. Reminded of the Trojan horse, he regarded her stormily as she poured his wine. Why did she insist on acting like a servant?

He threw down his brother's letter. "It won't last. He'll come crying back to me, once she's bled him dry of every penny."

She laughed indulgently. "It is possible for two opposites to come together, by some twist of fate, my lord, and not quite be able to let go again, despite the hopelessness of the situation...*it seems*." She winked. "Is it so hard for you to believe?"

Shocked, he clamped his lips shut, but although he let her win the skirmish, he was only briefly vanquished, not content to let her taste the sweetness of victory too long. "From now on I don't expect to see you working in the garden." His voice echoed around the great hall. "'Tis not a ladylike pursuit."

Safely back in her seat, she replied with a surface giddiness that did not, for one breath, deceive him, "Am I a lady now? I thought I was just your whore."

* * * *

She waited, sensing the air thicken with tension until even her tongue tingled with it.

"You might at least try to act like a lady," he said, "no matter who you are or where you come from, however low and criminal your usual company." The corner of his lip curled upward. "If 'tis not too much trouble, sweetling."

"Nothing is too much trouble for you....*precious*."

"Then I shouldn't have to remind you of what is expected, should I?"

She kept her smile, knowing he sought to push her temper. Apparently he was uneasy when faced with a woman in a good mood and didn't know how to deal with it.

For a while they ate in silence, surreptitiously eyeing one another down the length of the table, on their guard. Plates were removed, sweet dishes offered. Madolyn watched how carefully he moved his food around, cutting it into precise pieces, never letting any one item on his plate touch another. When he ate grapes, he examined each one as if it was a diamond and polished it on his napkin, before it slipped away between his firm lips. Between every mouthful, he dabbled his fingers in the water-bowl by his plate.

"I hope my common ways don't embarrass you, my lord," she said suddenly, having observed this performance for some time and no longer able to stay silent. "I suppose I must be grateful to you--such a man of riches and consequence--willing to tolerate my rustic manners and teach me proper behavior. In exchange for what little I can give you."

"You give me plenty."

There was a moment when his eyes, formerly stern and uncompromising, reached into hers with the needy hands of a child and she forgot everything she meant to say. When he looked away again, she recovered.

"I confess, sir, I'm shocked you chose me, when you might have any other woman--someone you need not train like a disobedient pup." She smiled sweetly. "Wouldn't it be preferable to share your bed with a woman who knows how to behave herself?"

A quick spurt of laughter shot out of him. "Why would I want that? I much prefer a bedmate who doesn't behave herself."

"'Tis not what I meant, as you well know."

He wiped his mouth, still chuckling. "But that, my sweet, is why I chose you. We'll discuss the matter further upstairs, however. I look forward to it." And speaking low, he muttered, *"Vous ete en bonne bouche."*

"Am I indeed? A choice morsel?"

He looked up sharply. Eyes narrowed, he aimed his fiercest sparks down that long table. "You speak French too?"

"*Mais oui.*"

Frozen in his seat, he considered her in a haughty way, as if assessing livestock for purchase. "*Un femme qui sait trop.*"

Of course he would think she knew too much. How unsettling it must be for the stiff-necked ogre. "*A votre avis,*" she replied with an easy shrug.

"Yes indeed--*in my opinion*. My opinion is all that matters."

"Poor *bete*," she teased. "How lonely you must be in your state of perfection."

He brooded over his discovery for a few moments. "I don't suppose you mean to tell me where you acquired this knowledge, or who I should blame for the creation of such a monstrously smug, self-righteous young wench, with a fondness for telling other people how to behave and assuming everyone but herself in the wrong?"

Although he might have been describing himself and she longed to point that out, Maddie held her tongue. Instead she merely smiled and he returned to his letter--either a ridiculously slow reader, or deliberately avoiding conversation.

"If you will not rehire Matthew, simply because he fell in love," she said smoothly, "it proves to me all the bad I ever heard about you!"

He was unmoved by her threat. Sighing, he shook his head, still studying Gabriel's letter.

"But now to my next matter," she added, sitting up straight, businesslike.

"Hmm?" He turned the letter to read on, feigning absorption in its contents.

"Nathaniel Downing...."

"The pirate?"

"...is no pirate. Can you not arrange his pardon with the queen? If you and she are such close friends, can you not--"

"No," he interrupted sharply. Then, to her surprise, he equivocated. "We'll discuss it later."

She licked her lips, hope flaring to life.

He smirked at his letter. "Upstairs."

Her shoulders sagged and she set her pewter goblet down with a hearty bang.

Slowly he wiped his lips on a napkin, hiding his laughter. Arrogant bastard!

"I'm afraid I feel a headache coming on." She paused, perusing the fruit platter offered by Jennet. "Our negotiations may be stymied before they've begun this evening."

That got his attention. "Blackmail now is it?"

After some consideration, she chose a tender peach from that expensive, largely imported bounty.

"Blackmail is what women do best," he added sourly.

"You think you know women, because of a few bad ones you've met."

"And you had a poor opinion of the earls of Swafford before you knew any." He folded his letter, dropping it to the table at last.

"Nathaniel Downing is innocent."

"Of course he is. Any criminal will tell you they're innocent."

"Very well." She fluttered her lashes, leaning back in her chair, bringing the peach to her lips. "I can be just as uncooperative as you, my lord. And similarly fat-headed."

"What exactly does that mean?"

She took a dainty bite of fruit and chewed slowly. "Don't come to me tonight, I definitely feel a headache already."

* * * *

It was blackmail. The little strumpet thought she had him at her mercy. Placing her lips over the bite in her peach, she sucked steadily. He stared, transfixed. Closing her eyes she took another slow bite. A drop of juice dripped to her bosom, where it quivered as she breathed, rapidly joined by another.

Hot and irritated, he exclaimed, "It's the queen's decision, not mine.

And it's not done to quarrel with the queen."

"As it's not done to quarrel with you? Yes, I see how efficiently *that* works and what a good thing it is. How fine and fair you turned out."

"Woman, you try my patience!"

"Hey ho!" She sucked again on the peach, her tongue sneaking out to lick the golden flesh. More droplets fell to her bosom and wobbled there, catching the candlelight as she moved.

Drumming his fingers along the edge of the table, he grumbled, "You know nothing of how these things work--the politics of court."

She slowly wiped the droplets of juice with one finger, feigning complete absorption in the task, then bringing it back to her lips.

The damned woman would be the death of him. He cursed under his breath.

She suckled her finger, eyelids lowered contentedly, lush, dark lashes contrasting with the vivid blue beneath. Shifting too quickly in his chair, his knee hit the table, making the candles tremble in their iron holders.

With a sharp cry of surprise, she dropped the half-eaten peach and it landed on her high cleavage. Swearing low, she retrieved it, in the process managing somehow to wipe more juice across the rounded, pearlescent skin. From where he sat, at the other end of the table, he saw it gleaming with each deep breath she took.

He growled. "They call me the Beast, madam, but I'm not dumb."

"No." She paused. "But stubborn, arrogant and downright uncivil."

"And you are a lying, scheming, underhanded wench who should've been raised with more discipline, before your character was willfully and shamelessly formed, to the detriment of any honest man with the misfortune to pluck you out of the river in a misguided attempt to rescue you." Out of breath, he somehow managed to force the words out, each one sharper than the one before.

Flinty-eyed, she reminded him, "I thought fortune smiled on you the day you rescued me."

Tap, tap, tap went his fingers. If he didn't do something with his hands he might overturn that table, send dishes, cups, flowers and candles crashing to the flagstones in his haste to get to her. He took a breath, waited, stilled.

Then he flexed one eyebrow. He smirked. "Perhaps fortune dropped you in the river that day, but Beelzebub himself made me drag you out again."

It came suddenly. One moment she was enjoying her peach, in the next she was a woman on the attack. The peach hit him on the forehead, the smashed fruit dropping to his lap, leaving a sticky trail of juice down his nose and chin.

She had damned good aim. Once, he recalled in bewilderment, he'd dismissed her as too small to do him any damage.

Apparently she decided she was now too far in to retreat. Standing with a fingerbowl of perfumed water in her hands, she strolled to his end of the table and held it over his head. "Let me wash that off for you, my lord."

"I suggest, madam," he muttered, "you think again before you do anything further you might regret."

"But I'm a woman. I cannot think." She tipped the bowl and water ran through his hair, joining the sticky peach juice in rivulets down his forehead, cascading mint leaves on his head and shoulders. He gripped the table with both hands, slowly licking his lips, his attention riveted on her.

Now she dug both hands into the cream and saffron custard. "Will you, or will you not, listen to my case in defense of Nathaniel Downing?"

His reply was laconic, no doubt anticipated. "I shall not."

Thus she smeared her creamy hands liberally across his face. Smiling with satisfaction at her handiwork, she patted his cheeks, squeezed them lightly, and whispered that he wanted a misbehaving woman, now he had one. Swinging around, she managed two steps before he caught her skirt in his tight grip. Oh no, she was not getting away with that.

He'd indulged her temper too much already.

She resisted, clinging to the table for leverage, but he was far stronger and dragged her back, inch by inch. Grabbing his platters and candlesticks, each one as they came within reach, she threw them to the floor, where they rolled and spun across the stone tiles. The servants made their hasty escape at Gregory's urging, and the door closed with a concise thud behind them, leaving them alone.

Snatching the last candlestick from her hand, he threw it over his shoulder and stood so suddenly she almost toppled backward, her body crushed between his thighs and the table edge. Lifting the hem of her skirt, he slowly wiped his face clean. She was breathing hard, peach-sticky breasts pushing at the boundaries of her embroidered bodice.

"I know you have no taste for pomegranates, my lord," she said, pert and breathless. "Perhaps I might offer you peaches?" He saw the lambent sparks under her lashes, the warning dimple in her cheek.

She was teasing, he realized. It took him a moment to understand, since the teasing he knew was vicious and mean-spirited. No one had ever teased him this way. His anger, which was surprisingly muted anyway, quickly abated. She was too beautiful tonight, and once again easily forgiven as she arched her back, offering her exquisite wares for his tasting.

He ducked his head and let his tongue follow the curve of those firm, full mounds, seeking out the spilled peach juice where it trickled into her deep cleavage. Tonight he would cleanse her with his tongue. The idea brought him quickly to a state of intense arousal. Her skirts gathered up in one fist, he used his free hand to reach down and open his own clothing.

"Wait!" she exclaimed. He raised his head, his lips a few inches from hers, the hunger raging and ravenous. She leaned back and he swayed with her, pressing his body to hers, his hands holding up the skirts and petticoats. "You're too bold and brazen, sir! I offered you peaches and no more of my wares."

"I've a hunger for more. Worry not, I'll pay your price."

"Mayhap you can't afford it."

He laughed low at the idea of anything being beyond his wealth. "Oh, I can afford it."

"My price is high, sir."

In that moment he would give her anything and he was sure she knew it. This was where she wanted him from the first. Now, having teased him to this point, she feigned affront.

"Gracious! I feel your impetuous cock against my bare thighs already, my lord. Is it never restrained by the Swafford rules?"

"It has a mind of its own in your presence."

She stopped him again, fingers splayed against his doublet. "Here and now? In full view of those disapproving Swaffords in the gallery above? This surely is not proper Swafford tradition." But her protest was half-hearted, to say the least. She was smoky-eyed with desire and he watched her bite her lips, almost drawing blood.

She was insatiable, he thought, yet again offering his thanks to whatever brought her into his life--devil or deity. Although a supposed novice, she already knew how to increase his pleasure with countless unexpected caresses. She'd learned how to hasten his climax, and also how to delay, to keep him red hot, trembling, a hair's breadth from imploding. It came to her, as he said, quite naturally. Once buried hilt-deep in her wet, silky heat, he knew he would no longer care about her purpose there, only that she was his. For now he delayed, tantalizing her, as she had done to him. He needed to convince himself he was in control of this. Needed--

"Griff," she whispered, her fingers unhooking his doublet, lifting his shirt. It was the first time she'd called him that since he'd brought her up to the manor house.

He kissed her hungrily, eating at her mouth as if she was another dish set there to tempt his appetite.

"What about the negotiation?" she gasped.

He nuzzled her warm neck. "I told you," he grunted, resettling his feet to keep his balance, "'tis the queen's decision."

* * * *

Maddie fought to keep afloat, her own body betraying her, falling prey to the tidal force of their shared passion.

"But you are a favorite, she'll listen to you." It was running away with her again and she couldn't allow it, or tonight would be like the last, when she was left abandoned in the rumpled sheets, the victory his.

"Your favors for one of mine, eh?"

"If you like, my lord," she purred, resuming the game.

Suddenly he laughed. This time it was neither forced nor full of scorn. Taken by surprise, she waited until he found his breath again. "You needn't act the part. I told you," he sputtered. Wounded, she glared at him and he leaned in to whisper against her lips. "You're a natural, my darling."

She was determined all the sweet "my darlings" in the world wouldn't soothe her feathers, even if it was the first time he ever called her that. And it was.

Rubbing himself on her thigh, it was his turn to tease, letting her feel the extraordinary length she could have. "You need play no role for me," he whispered. "See? I'm ready for you." Bringing her hand to the broad, swollen crest of his manhood, he let her feel the little wet bead trembling there.

"Oh, make haste," she cried, sultry seductress forgotten, her body clamoring for him and that blissful state of completion.

Delaying, he slid his hands over her thighs. "You wear no stockings tonight," he breathed.

"You'd only take them off again."

He laughed huskily against her mouth. "Entirely the purpose, sweetheart."

"Will you make love to me or not?" she gasped, hotly demanding.

In reply, he slid one hand under her knee, lifting her thigh to meet his thrust, but still withholding. Only when she whispered his name again, did he slowly fill her, igniting those little flames one by one.

Desire spinning and spiraling within her, she almost screamed. When he whispered in her ear the promise of what he would shortly do to her, those practical plans she once made--not to be drawn into his web-- were thrown aside, like his plate and his candlesticks. Somehow she dragged herself back from the precipice and found the courage to challenge him further.

"Take me to *your* chamber," she whispered. He shook his head, too enraptured, eyes closed. She repeated the command, louder this time, hands under his shirt, fingers stroking the warm curls of his chest, seeking his nipples. Tonight she was determined to get her own way, to win some ground in this war of wills. *Aut Vincere, Aut Mori*, she mused silently.

"Damn you, wench," he sputtered. "How many more demands will you make of me?"

But he picked her up, her legs wrapped around his waist, their bodies still joined, and carried her down the long corridors to his chamber. The vibration of his heavy steps felt deep within her, causing ripples of pleasure, until he fell with her to his bed--the one reserved only for Swafford earls and where no other woman was ever permitted.

"See?" she whispered, astonished at her own prowess and his concession. "Even you can defy tradition sometimes. The walls still stand, the world does not end." The last word caught in her throat as he withdrew his full length and slickly reentered, barely a pause between. The force pushed her along the bed, his weight crushing her to the noble Swafford crest on his coverlet. She writhed, the silk tapestry caressing her bare bottom, as he thrust again and again, wildly plunging, the bed shaking, the floorboards creaking in shock.

"Did you…find the…herbs you…needed?" he gasped out.

There was no time for her answer.

Low, guttural growls escaped his open mouth as he came the first time that night, not waiting for her, but spilling rapidly, his hands under her, holding her, planting himself deeply and thoroughly, flooding into her body.

As he collapsed over her, she sighed belatedly, "I couldn't find what I needed."

He swore at his own carelessness. "We shouldn't….a child," he murmured, apparently to her right breast, his breath warming her erect nipple.

"If this occurs to you now, my lord," she quipped, as he remained semi-hard within her, "did it not occur to you two minutes ago? Or those many times before?"

"The first time," he reminded her drowsily, "was your idea. I seem to recall you begging me--"

"That's beside the point."

"It is?"

"That was once." She faltered, knowing once was all it took. "And it was your fault."

He didn't argue for once. "It won't happen again."

Rolling her eyes to the tapestry canopy overhead, she was forced to concede the fault lay as much with her, even if she would never admit that aloud.

He lifted his head and planted a kiss on the tip of her nose. "Now 'tis your turn."

"I thought you forgot me," she said coyly. The look he gave her as he slid her legs over his shoulders was more than sufficient for reply.

The Beast was, on this occasion, remarkably pliant to her and her whispered commands. When no one watched, she mused, he forgot duty and tradition, pleasuring her in many new, untraditional, ingenious ways, from head to foot and all places in between.

CHAPTER 23

Propped on one elbow, he watched her sleep, restless, waiting for her to rouse again and play some more. Last night she'd called it "making love" and he wondered if she was even cognizant of the slip. He certainly was.

One hand on the curve of her hip, he considered the possibilities. She twitched like a pup napping. Asleep she looked even younger, her sable hair a tumbled sprawl across his pillows, as he'd once pictured it the first day they'd met. Pity overtook carnal need for a few moments. She was exhausted and he should let her sleep on.

The candles had burned throughout the night until he'd extinguished them a half hour ago. Wax draped over the pewter holders. The black wicks still discharged a drifting, smoky bitterness. On most days, within an hour he would be up and busy, but not this morning. Many things were different now.

He'd never woken with a woman in his bed.

He'd never spent all night with a woman in any bed.

What had she done? Perhaps it was the fault of those three girlish freckles, or that occasional dimple, or the mischievous glimmer in her smile, or those eyes betraying her every mood, amusement and hurt. Or her warm, welcoming body. Most likely it was the combination of these things. She was unique and uniquely his. She was his property now, he decided, and he would take care of her. She should be grateful for that, damn her.

Undoubtedly her presence in his life would cause endless headaches. She'd already tried to rearrange his furniture, according to poor Gregory. And this insistence in arguing her point would eventually give him an apoplexy.

But she was a woman with strongly held convictions and the courage to fight for them. That was admirable, no matter how he wished it might not be.

Looking at her, he felt desire

tighten and then swell inside his chest, as if it might burst out of him.

He slid his hand under her breast, weighing it in his palm. Despite his wealth, he was not an extravagant man, never had much taste for excess, but she was sheer opulent luxury, from the abundant, velvet darkness of her hair, to the vivid changeable blue of her eyes, from those yielding, delectable lips, to those lush, lissome curves. Nestled in his bed, waiting to be roused, she called to him, even as she slept. Sliding toward her on his hip, he bent his head and lifted her full breast to his mouth. His tongue flicked over her nipple, circled the pink blush of areola, and then his lips closed over it. He heard her sigh, felt her stretch languidly as she woke. Still suckling her breast, he stroked down her side to her hip again, long fingers spread. Cupping her bottom, he drew her closer and she moved her leg over his thigh, her hands in his hair, fingers tangled there, stroking his scalp. Holding her nipple in his mouth, he looked up and found her eyes open, watching him.

Fingers entwined in his hair, she drew him closer, nursing him.

On this twilight occasion, he was gentle, unhurried. Both kept their eyes open, as if each feared the other might suddenly vanish.

* * * *

"Let me dress you today," she whispered playfully. "Send Wickes away and let me tend you, my lord."

He shouldn't capitulate and allow her this many liberties, but she wasn't easily refused anything, especially when she said, "my lord" without sarcasm, when she was naked in his arms, one of her incredibly flexible legs stretched casually between both of his. So he conceded a tentative distance. "Perhaps. We'll see."

She laid her cheek to his chest. "Why did you hire Wickes? He's an odd man."

"At least he won't go off *in love* like that damned fool Matthew, who chose a wench over his duty to me."

"Yes," she purred, "I certainly can't see Wickes in love."

"Am I to understand you dislike him?"

"I think I'm a good judge of character. Most of the time."

Low laughter rumbled through his chest and out of his mouth, but there was no inclination to stop it today. Instead, he squeezed her pretty little posterior. "You want me to dismiss him and rehire Matthew, you need a better reason than that."

"He's got shifty eyes," she protested.

"You said the same of me, once."

He was too relaxed this morning to give her worries much credence and when she warned somberly, "You should keep an eye on him", he merely cupped the back of her head and drew her lips closer for a kiss. There was only one thing he wanted to keep an eye on.

"Let me worry about Wickes."

She readjusted her head on his shoulder and he stroked her hair, his fingers combing through her tangled tresses. Sensing she had more on her mind, he waited, patient for once.

"You'll need someone to watch out for you, because I can't stay," she said.

Ah, that. It ripped into him, shattering his contented mood. Grinding his jaw, head pressed back into the pillow, he turned his eyes up to the canopy. "By the bay, you pleaded with me to let you stay. Now you want to leave. What's changed?"

"It was different. *You* were different then."

His hand paused in her hair, velvet curls wrapped around his fingers.

"And I was different too," she added. "I thought, back then, this was enough for me. Now I know I want more." He felt her head raise and he looked down, his gaze meeting hers. "Something you can't give me."

"What do you need?" he demanded, vexed. "I knew you were here for more than Downing's cause! Out with it, wench. How much do you need to stay with me?"

She groaned. "This is not an issue of money, you fool!"

"What then?" Fear and frustration mounted. He couldn't let her leave. It was impossible to contemplate.

With one palm pressed to his heart, she replied, "This."

* * * *

His brow arched, eyes seeking hers and quickly retreating. "I seem to remember it was an item lower down you wanted before. You vowed it was all you wanted from me."

Exasperated, she rolled over, leaving the broad, firm strength of his thigh, astride which she'd lain, drifting in and out of sleep that morning. There, fallen sated across his powerful body, Madolyn felt wonderfully safe and secure--too safe. Time to be practical again. She couldn't explain her needs to him. She could hardly explain them to herself.

"Why would you want that old thing," he whispered to the nape of her neck, sweeping her hair aside with one long, lean hand. "It's twisted and rotten. Never did grow properly."

"It's been ill-tended."

There was a long pause, then, his tone less jovial, he muttered, "I can't marry you."

"No," she said simply. "I know." Even if he was not already married, it would be impossible. With a heart full of emotions requiring reciprocation, she could never fit in his world. With "Griff" she was on a certain level, with the Earl of Swafford she was too far beneath. This was not her own opinion, but it was how the world viewed them and Madolyn now understood no matter how she tried to fight the rules of propriety, however determinedly she ignored them, other folk did not. The world, as Grace would say, was a much bigger place than Sydney Dovedale and she couldn't change it single-handedly. Maddie the Merciless couldn't cure the world's ills, nor save all the poor, sick and slandered. She was a flesh and blood woman. She hurt like any other.

After a still moment of sadness, she added petulantly, "And don't kiss me there. You know what it does to me."

But it was too late.

When Wickes tapped at the door shortly after, ready to help his master dress, he received the harsh, muffled command to go away. The servants would know she spent the night in his chamber, the first and only woman ever to do so.

Chapter 24

He finished his business early to come in search of her, another unprecedented occurrence. For once she was more important than matters of the Swafford estate, but his earlier tenderness was no longer in evidence. Out of breath and patience, he shouted at her for a full ten minutes about the chase she led him on, how she never followed a solitary order and why he now had sympathy for Gregory, even going so far as to feel he might have to apologize to the steward for doubting him before.

"I beg your pardon," she exclaimed. "God forbid I ever cause you to apologize to poor Gregory. I shouldn't want you to strain yourself!"

Snatching the little watering can out of her hands, he set it on the ground. "You're not supposed to be in here."

There was, it seemed, only one place she should ever be. "Why not shackle me to the bedpost?" Flinging her head back, she held out her wrists. "Go ahead, *your lordship*! If that's the only way you can trust me. Chain me to your bed!"

"It's the only time I know you're not lying to me," was the gruff reply. She tried to pass, but he stood in her way. "I see you like at least one of the gowns I bought you."

It was the lightest of the day gowns and yes, she admitted with easy candor, she liked it very much. The design was deceptively simple, but the material costly. "It's more beautiful than anything I've ever owned. Thank you."

A shy pulse in his cheek suggested the beginnings of a nervous smile in response to hers. It hovered there, under the surface, giving her a sign of hope, at least.

Oh, just a little more. Just a little.

Each time he looked at her, she thought she saw a new light struggling to the surface, the soul of a boy forever imprisoned, longing to come out and breathe the glorious fresh air. But how could she help him? She was once a plain, silly girl who'd recently embarked on adventure only to find herself a woman with reckless desires, in over her head, out of her depth. Her heart ached, even when she tried to enclose it in a hard shell for protection. She felt stupid suddenly, and lost.

"It's hot in here," she said tightly.

"'Tis why they call it a hothouse." Leaning toward her, he whispered, "I'm as hot inside, as this house of glass in the midday sun and you are the cause. Wickes claims you use sorcery. Is this true? You told me once before you used witchcraft."

"That, my Lord Doubtful, was a jest." She backed into the trellis and he followed. "Do you not have jests in Dorset?"

"Wickes believes you're up to no good. He sees through your game. Is that why you tried turning me against him this morning?"

She gasped. Bright yellow sun beating down on her face, she squinted up at him. "And you believe him, over me?"

"You're a woman," he pointed out crisply. "Deceit is your middle name."

She shook her head, too irritated to speak.

"Might I remind you," he added, "I hired Wickes to work for me. He's in my life because I put him there. You're here because you forced your way in uninvited. Wickes follows orders. You don't."

"If I'm here to cause you harm, why haven't I succeeded by now? I was alone with you several days in that cottage and you survived. Oh, but you believe whatever Wickes tells you. Far be it for me to spoil your illusions."

He looked down at her, his expression frayed, like that of a frustrated parent, or a weary master. "You won't even tell me your name. I know nothing about you. Every word you say could be a lie."

She clamped her mouth shut.

"Speak, damn you!"

"Why should I?" she replied tartly. "Whether I say yes or no, you're none the wiser. If I say *'yes, every word is a lie'*, wouldn't that also be a lie? If I say *'no'*, I could be lying--as indeed I would, if I were a liar. It seems a hopeless case."

He turned his face away, a bead of sweat running slowly down his temple. She took advantage of his inattention, slipping around him to retrieve the watering can. "You might suddenly have time on your hands, but we can't all be bone idle."

His long stride overtook hers, blocking her path. "Where are you going now?"

"Poor beast," she sighed, "I've disrupted your peaceful existence. Once I'm gone your life can go back to what it was."

"You're not going anywhere."

Head on one side, she watched the ideas simmering beneath his guarded expression. He held his lips tight, keeping more words stifled inside, where they cost him dearly. She saw the neediness in his eyes, the question he daren't ask, the answer he refused to accept.

"Am I another of your exotic captives?" She gestured at the plants around them.

He said nothing, but gave her a meticulous, narrow-eyed appraisal.

"Or are you in love with me?" she asked politely.

Now he blanched. "Love doesn't exist. I told you before..." A fly landed on his cheek, so she slapped it--quite hard, perhaps moreso than necessary. He flinched, rubbing his face with one hand. "Love is for fools."

Laughing, she swung the watering can. "Hey ho!"

Still holding his cheek, he stared at her. "No one ever slapped me before. That's the second time you've raised a hand to me."

Astonished by that, she told him solemnly, "Mine has been slapped many times."

"I can believe it."

With one, overly-solicitous hand she straightened his collar. "What will you do? Send me to bed early with no supper?"

"Your poor family," he groaned. "What you must put them through." He added coyly, "Where is it they reside again?"

"The moon."

"I can believe that too."

Now he looked away, thoughtful, still rubbing his cheek. Never had she ached for him this much, with the memory of their previous, most tender coupling still fresh and warm. But he would never trust her. He said he trusted no one, yet he believed Wickes's word over hers, largely because she was a woman.

She must remind him, and herself, why she was there.

"You will petition the queen for Nathaniel's pardon? You promised last night. Remember?"

"I don't remember promising anything to you. I do, however, remember a great deal of sticky peach juice in my bed. The mess..."

"Will you petition the queen on his behalf, or not?"

"...and now I remember why I never wanted to keep a woman." He shook his head. "Must have suffered a blow to the brain when I met you."

She reached up, pretending to examine his head for bumps and bruises, running her fingertips through his sun-warmed hair. He went still, almost ceased to breathe, and she thought he would tell her she took too many liberties in public, but he was silent.

"Mayhap you did receive a knock to this big head. Or else this is a dream," she teased.

"Then I hope I never wake."

It shocked her when he said it and from the subtle flinch in his eyes, it startled him too.

Sliding his arms around her waist, he held her tight. "You're dark under the eyes this morning," he observed, his cadence softened. "Did I tire you out last night?"

Sometimes he didn't know his own strength. Her breasts ached suddenly, crushed up against his iron-hard chest, but she couldn't complain. He'd never spoken with this much genuine affection before and it was like the first few drops of precious rain falling on parched soil. She didn't want to speak, for fear of saying the wrong thing and being accused again of evil motives.

Slowly he dipped his head and she lifted hers. With the tip of his tongue he tentatively traced the pronounced bow of her upper lip and the shallower curve of the lower. When he teased them apart, his tongue sliding inside to meet hers, she closed her eyes. This kiss was different; it glowed, blooming with much that went unspoken.

He kept his arms around her, his eyelids lowered to shelter her from an ardent, heated gaze, but she felt him tremble. Very slightly.

Somewhere inside the Beast there was a fallible human being, but his secret was safe with her. She wouldn't tell a soul.

And she loved him. Whatever it was he felt for her, she knew now this was deep and everlasting love. But she couldn't tell a soul that either, because she didn't belong in his world and he could never fit in hers.

CHAPTER 25

When he was gone on business of the estate, she helped Jennet polish the plate. This time no one stopped her or suggested she stay in her room. Griff must have relaxed his rules for her. It was a pleasing idea, progress at last.

As she and Jennet worked together, there was suddenly a great ruckus in the hall, a clattering of feet and boxes followed by accusations shrieked out in a pitch of such high dimensions they both covered their ears. Maddie's stomach threw itself into a sideways tumble and she walked into the entrance hall, polishing rag still clutched in one hand.

She hadn't seen her cousin in--how long? The days merged into one another lately.

Eustacia threw off her mantle as if it contained poison ivy. Her hat was dislodged, disturbing the careful arrangement of her hair, which, as she shouted orders at the bewildered staff, began to uncoil, springing out from her head.

"I've been on foot for the last two miles," she cried, flinging her arms out. "I have been rained upon, windblown, spat at, molested by peasants, chased by geese, splattered with God knows what by passing carts--"

Gabriel sneezed, stepping forward to take her elbow. He smiled uncomfortably at the servants. "There, there, dearest, we're home now." His voice was thick with congestion and the flush to his cheeks was plainly the sign of a fever.

Gregory bowed deeply to Gabriel and welcomed him home, followed by rather tardy curtseys and bows from the other staff. Gabriel asked if his brother was returned yet.

"He is, Master Gabriel, but he is presently out and will not return until the morning."

Eustacia groaned again. "Thanks be for small mercies. The last thing I need now is to face that swine."

Poor Gabriel looked mortified. Sneezing again, he tried to regain his wife's arm, but she would have none of it.

"I need a lie down. You know how I am when I'm tired, Gabriel. It was damnably cruel to make me walk. I can't think why you gave up the horses."

"They needed new shoes, my dear. And you didn't want to wait for the blacksmith to be done."

"Surely you did not expect me to sit in that hot, stinking place and *wait?*" She spat the word as if she'd never waited for anything in her life. "The blacksmith was surly and incompetent. I would've struck him if he looked at me once more the way he did. If you had more gumption Gabriel, you would've insisted he see to our horses immediately, or else give us those already finished."

"But Eustacia, dearest," he said miserably, "those horses belonged to other men."

"They might have been bought."

"They might," he agreed sadly, "had I the coin to do it."

That silenced her for a moment. Gabriel asked Gregory if the blue chamber might be prepared for his wife in the south tower and he smiled lovingly at Eustacia, even though she pouted, refusing his arm again. "You'll adore the blue chamber, dearest. It is the prettiest room in the house with a breathtaking view of the grounds."

"What good will that do me, pray, when I have a head aching fit to burst and shall need the shutters closed to keep out the dratted sun?"

"I'm afraid, Master Gabriel," Gregory solemnly intoned, "the blue room is occupied."

The servants looked at Maddie and the new arrivals turned likewise to find her standing there in her fancy new gown, smiling guiltily.

Eustacia immediately forgot her headache and screamed as if she saw a ghost come to haunt her. "Why should she have it? Why is she here? I feel faint, Gabriel." She covered her eyes with limp fingers, through which she glared at her cousin with the venom of Medusa.

Madolyn apologized demurely. "It was Griff's choice that I have the blue chamber." Although she gave it her best effort, she didn't sound as sorry as she should. The fury on Eustacia's face and her insistence the room be given up for her at once made her less and less regretful. She gave no explanation for her presence, but the delight she took in saying "Griff" with that degree of familiarity, was worth the burns she received from Eustacia's scorn-filled perusal.

Gregory was steadfast. His young charge could not be moved from the coveted blue chamber. His calm, polite smile only put Eustacia in a greater state of apoplexy and this, too, made Maddie gleeful, rather than repentant, cherish the wicked spark of pleasure that came with the attention. For once she was someone special, to be treated with kid gloves. She decided it was far too easy to be seduced and corrupted by power and she chastised herself thoroughly for being swept up in it. But it was hard indeed to feel humble, with Eustacia spitting her hatred across the hall at her.

"I'm sure we can find you a comparable chamber," Gabriel tried to console his wife, but, having already extolled the virtues of the blue chamber, there was nothing he could say to convince her any other room would do. The mere suggestion that her rustic little country cousin might have a better room than hers was tantamount to treason.

Madolyn suggested she give up the room for Eustacia. "I daresay I can find another," she said somberly to Gregory. "Truly, I don't wish to be any trouble."

Immediately he assured her, "The earl wouldn't have you moved for all the world, my lady. It's more than my life's worth to put you anywhere else. Please don't fret, the earl wouldn't want you upset."

Delighting again in the mischievous, intoxicating thrill, she sighed deeply, "As you think best Gregory, of course. I'll do as I'm bid."

He gave her a sly look, knowing the rarity of such a concession from those lips. "Thank you, my lady."

Eustacia made a sound like a stuck pig and Maddie smiled at her benevolently. Much to her further amusement, they put the newcomer in the north tower. Eustacia didn't know, and her husband would surely never tell her, that these were servant's quarters and storage rooms.

* * * *

At supper, Maddie explained to Gabriel how his brother found her at Eustacia's house in London and brought her to Dorset.

"He wouldn't believe me when I told him I wasn't Eustacia."

Her cousin exclaimed sourly. "How could anyone mistake you for me?"

But Gabriel seemed amused. "And you've been here, alone with him, this many weeks?"

She felt a little too warm suddenly, as his eyes, bright with fever, gave her a sly up and down perusal. "The staff were here," she mumbled.

"Hmm." He grinned. "What has my pious brother been up to?"

There was a short silence before Eustacia never liking the conversation to stray long from herself, began to criticize the lamb on her plate, which she found too tough. "I'm certain they gave me the worst piece." Her critical gaze leapt between her own plate and her cousin's.

"You may have mine, if you want it," Maddie offered.

"I will not have your scraps!" she spat. "Lamb doesn't suit my stomach and this mint sauce is over-salted. It's given me such a thirst, I won't sleep tonight."

Gabriel blew his nose in his napkin, saying he too had no appetite. Having struggled to remain lively for much of the evening, now he was drained and limp in his chair. The poor fellow could barely raise his napkin to wipe his red nose, and his eyes watered like fountains.

"He's been like this for two entire days," Eustacia complained. "Coughing and sputtering. It has quite made *me* ill. There's nothing worse than the company of a man who constantly complains about his discomforts."

Gabriel apologized to his wife for being sick and spoiling her journey. He was also sorry her room didn't meet with her approval and promised they would leave, as soon as he shook off his fever.

Thrusting her hated lamb aside, Eustacia summoned a servant to bring the fruit platter. When it failed to arrive swiftly enough and didn't carry anything she wanted, her mouth curled into a tight snarl and she snapped at Jennet, "For pity's sake, stand still, girl. I'm rendered dizzy by your dancing about. Is this the best fruit that can be got? Gabriel, I think they must be hiding the best specimens. Surely the earl's orchards can provide better."

"It is not yet full summer, dearest."

"For sure they keep the best away from us."

As Jennet withdrew with the fruit platter, Eustacia whined to her husband. "I suppose the locals discuss me already. These people are country yokels. I can't wait to return to civilized company."

Maddie looked at her in amazement, for her cousin kept no company in London except a few paunchy, heavily-perfumed gentlemen, hardly to be described as fashionable or discriminate.

"Eustacia," she said suddenly, "is your father released yet from debtors' prison?"

She heard Jennet's stifled giggle and was certain Eustacia heard it too.

* * * *

It was late when she was roused from a dead sleep with news that Gabriel was desperately ill. Gregory feared it might be the smallpox. Apparently, he'd already consulted Eustacia, but she declared it was too much fuss to be made late at night. Morning would be soon enough to send for help.

Now, in the earl's absence, Maddie had been sought out and woken. Pleased to be of use at last, she sent Gregory for the apothecary and ran down to the cookhouse herself to supervise the making of a compress for Gabriel's fevered head and an herbal elixir for his sore throat, both recipes she'd learned from her mother.

She sat with the patient, spooning the concoction between his sad lips, promising he'd feel much better once he slept. No one expected Eustacia's help, and they made an unspoken pact to let her sleep on. When Gabriel asked for his wife, she told him they thought it best if Eustacia stayed away rather than risk contagion.

The heat of his fever could be felt even without touching his skin, but she tried not to let him see her concern. They had only two candles lit in the room, as he said the light hurt his eyes, but they burned incense, which she'd heard might help in cases of smallpox. Two years ago they'd had an outbreak in her village at home, and several folk died of it. A few others were left scarred.

She thought of those dreadful three weeks when she'd nursed her sweetheart, praying he might be saved. She'd always taken charge of him, in the same way as she did anyone she cared for. Sometimes she wondered why he'd let her boss him about, but he was a content, easy sort of person, rather like Gabriel, in fact. Once or twice she might secretly have wanted her sweetheart to stand up to her, but he never did. He took the easy route in life and would have married her, she realized, for that reason. They were of the same age, had celebrated their milestones together and people always expected they would marry. She remembered the vague feeling of being rushed down a corridor that became narrower and darker, closing in on her.

When he died, suddenly the tight corridor had opened out again into daylight and she was free. The guilt was unbearable, another layer atop the grief. But life went on and there was always another battle to fight.

As she held Gabriel's hot hand that night, he talked of his brother and their childhood together. The two men had a close bond it seemed, and as much as they were often frustrated by one another, they remained devoted brothers. Maddie understood completely.

"Master Gabriel," she said solemnly, "I must ask you not to reveal my identity to your brother."

He frowned slightly. "He doesn't know who you are?"

She shook her head.

Gabriel's brows arched high. "He didn't even ask your name?" And he chuckled. "Tsk, tsk!" But he promised to keep her secret. "Don't worry," he said thoughtfully. "My brother can solve this mystery alone. At last he has more to fret over than *my* love life."

* * * *

Griff returned to the manor in the early hours of the morning. Upon hearing of Gabriel's sickness, he came directly to his brother's chamber, but Madolyn sent him out again, worried about the risk of contagion.

"What about you?" he exclaimed fiercely.

"I don't matter," she replied, shoving him back into the corridor. "We can't have both of you dying can we? What happens to the Swafford estate then?"

He stumbled back, staring at her, but silenced.

"One of you has to survive," she added simply.

Returning to Gabriel's bedside, she thought how odd it was for the Earl of Swafford not to want children. He was such a stickler for tradition and duty, it seemed strange he didn't have at least one child with his wife, just for the future of the estate. And despite those rumors of the earl's "incapability", she knew now that was a lie.

What if something happened to him? And to Gabriel? It was too much to consider, too horrible to contemplate.

She stayed at Gabriel's bedside until the apothecary arrived, by which time his temperature had receded. There was no sign, fortunately, of the smallpox pustules. At last, assured he was no longer contagious, she gave up her vigil and let his brother take over.

* * * *

Having fallen asleep the moment her head hit the pillow, she was roused a scant few hours later by sharp fingernails digging into her shoulder, followed by a shrill hiss,

"Wake up at once, Madolyn Carver! I must know instantly everything that happened."

Much preferring the song of the marsh warbler to wake her through the window rather than this discordant screeching, she sat up and tried to peel her eyelids open. "Eustacia," she groaned, "Can we talk later? I've had no sleep."

"And how much sleep do you think I've had, with so much pressing on me?" She held a hand to her bosom. "I couldn't set my head down all night. The room they gave me is cold and dreary, little better than a dungeon. I've had nothing to comfort me, but lain fretting. I've never felt so ill."

Despite her protestations, she looked rested. Her eyes were a great deal clearer and sharper than Madolyn's felt. Of course, with her cousin's face coated in a thick, snowy powder, there was no telling if she was uncommonly pale or fraught. She always looked that way.

Madolyn considered telling her how she'd spent *her* night, but she had no chance.

"What does the Beast plan to do?" Eustacia clasped her shoulders and shook her until her teeth rattled. "I warned Gabriel we shouldn't come here yet. It's too soon, I said, the earl hasn't had time to calm his temper. Is he going to strike Gabriel out of his will?"

Aha, and here was the crux of the matter, her cousin's only true concern.

Madolyn grasped her skeletal wrists and threw those claws aside. "I should warn you cousin, I'm never in my best temper when forced awake before I'm ready, but even if I were a morning person, I must still ask what you mean by coming into my room, unannounced, unexpected and most certainly unwanted, to yell at me like a fish wife. If you don't shut up at once, I might be of a mood to beat you, as I would an old rug that needs fleas knocked out of it."

"How dare you speak to me thus?" Eustacia's skirt rustled noisily against the bed. "You get above yourself now, simply because you caught the earl's perverse attention. Truly, I'm shocked, for he is supposed to be incapable, but," her eyes flicked over Maddie like two disdainful dust rags, "some men have curious tastes. Perhaps you fulfill an eccentric fancy for coal above diamonds."

She was too tired and angry to reply.

Her cousin strolled to the window and looked out. "This view is nothing. I would rather see the bustle and life of London, than this...dull, nothingness...acres of boring fields. I cannot see what Gabriel loves about this place."

"Have you been to see your sick husband this morning? He asked for you last night."

Eustacia shuddered, arms folded. "Why do they always get sick? I must be the unluckiest woman alive. I suppose he'll die now too." She didn't like attention diverted from her, of course, and viewed Gabriel's fever as a deliberate attempt to sabotage her happiness.

Even when Maddie assured her Gabriel improved steadily, she refused to believe it. "I might have known it was too good to last," she said. "I thought this time if I chose a young man--"

"Eustacia, that is marriage, you know--in sickness and in health."

But she turned up her thin nose and sniffed. "As if you know."

Maddie shrugged, giving up.

"This house is wretchedly drafty," Eustacia continued, shivering. "And those truculent servants. Not one of them came to undress me last night. I pulled the bell chord in my room for a full five and twenty minutes before anyone came to remove the bed warmer. I'm surprised the bed didn't catch fire."

"The servants were busy tending to your sick husband."

"Then the earl should keep more staff, if there are not enough to serve his guests properly. Of course, he never keeps servants for long. His rages chase them away before they've stayed barely a month. He's a brute, I hear, and wears out so many whips he has ten made at a time."

"From whom did you hear that?"

"Oh," she waved her fingers and wandered off again around the bed, "Perhaps from Gabriel."

But surely Eustacia understood Gabriel loved his brother and the things he said were only in jest. Madolyn knew that now. The night before, as she'd sat by his bed, Gabriel spoke as if the earl was a saint, rather than the devious, conniving ogre the rest of the world painted him. Eustacia, however, preferred to believe the worst and gladly spread any nasty rumor. Maddie wondered what other canards were begun to harm the man few folk knew or had even met.

Now she sat up, shaking off her sleepiness, and asked Eustacia not to give the earl any information about her. "He thinks you put me up to it," she added, chagrined. "He suspects you of leaving me in his path as a diversion while you escaped London with his brother."

Her cousin scoffed, "You needn't worry. I certainly don't want him thinking you're any relative of mine. I'll deny any knowledge of your antics."

Relieved, Madolyn hugged her knees. "You shouldn't have left London as you did, cousin. Gabriel's brother must have worried. It wasn't right to sneak away. If you had been honest and confronted him to his face, I daresay things would be different. The earl has a right to be angry now, don't you think?" She could hardly believe this was her voice, defending the Beast.

The pearls hanging from Eustacia's ears trembled indignantly. "Who are you to lecture me? Since when have you cared for what is right?"

Maddie picked guiltily at the embroidered pattern on the coverlet. "I hope you'll treat Gabriel kindly today. Think of him for once and not yourself. If you can."

Eustacia sneered. "You have an instinct for your own survival, coz. You're no better than me." Fond of a grand exit, she swirled her way to the door. "Make the most of this. It won't last. A man with wealth like his can buy as many women as he wants and change them as often as his shirts. You'll be naught to the Earl of Swafford but a temporary plaything. There's only one thing he wants from you. It's the only thing men think of when they look at us, and once they've had it, they want it elsewhere."

Instead of hitting that snow-white face, Maddie's pillow smacked against the door as her cousin closed it. After that, she couldn't get back to sleep.

CHAPTER 26

To Maddie's surprise, the servants each came up to her at some point that morning and found a way to be kind, whether it was reaching for something too high upon the shelf, or opening a door for her when her hands were full.

"Anyone would think I'd brought Master Gabriel back from the brink of death," she exclaimed to Jennet, bemused.

Griff remained with his brother for most of the day, emerging occasionally to be sure she had not yet burned down his house, so he said. He even ate his supper in Gabriel's chamber, claiming he had much to discuss with his brother. Suspecting he avoided Eustacia, Maddie couldn't blame him for that. Eager to escape her cousin's grim complaining herself, she found entertainment in the cookhouse with the staff. By now they were accustomed to her presence and Wickes was absent, so there was no chill in the air, nothing to spoil the camaraderie. Even Gregory relinquished his last doubts when she made a mint and lavender foot potion for his aching feet. Another recipe of her mother's, it was a remedy much sought after by elderly folk at home, often hailed as a miraculous restorative.

She was explaining the recipe to Jennet, when Luke whispered in her ear, "Come with me then, missy." He put his finger to his lips and led her out to the hothouse, where he passed her a bundle of tattered, old clothes. "Put them on," he said.

"Me?"

"I'll take you to see Matthew tonight. It'll do you a service to see he bears the earl no anger. But you must wear this, or you'll stick out like a Frenchman in a nunnery."

She dressed behind the great leaves of the earl's more exotic captives, pulling on the breeches, shirt and cloak with fumbling, excitable fingers. Her hair was tucked under a hat, a few smudges of dirt wiped across her cheeks and the bridge of her nose. Luke was still not entirely satisfied, grumbling that she should keep her head down and not speak to anyone when they got there. Again he warned her Gregory would have his guts for garters if he found out.

"I'll not tell a soul," she exclaimed, caught up in the drama. "They won't beat it out of me, not even with a cat o' nine tails."

Laughing, he gestured her on ahead. A horse and cart stood ready and waiting. A few moments later they were off into the night.

* * * *

The tavern was crammed full of men who worked on the earl's land and took their ease now in the comforting glow of the warm little room. There were no women in the place, none welcomed there. These men, in worn, stained tunics and frayed hats, were tired and thirsty after a long day in the fields, and the last thing they wanted was to put any effort into polite conversation. They sprawled about with their feet up, their bellies hanging out, burping with a glad sort of carelessness into the thick air of wood smoke, earth and sweat.

When he found her lagging behind, Luke returned to drag her along by the long, loose sleeve of her shirt, muttering dour warnings of what would become of them both if she was discovered there.

Matthew waited on a bench in the corner, and she almost laughed in shock at the sight of him, for he was nothing like his brother in shape and size. Where Luke was short and square, he was tall and lean with a handsome, scrubbed face. Unlike his flaxen-haired brother, he was dark, with curls that might possibly have been brushed, but he had the same merry grin. "By all that's holy," he exclaimed when he saw her, "I thought she'd be a fine lookin' woman, not a little squirt like this 'un!" Grinning, he sent Luke for another jug of cider and gestured at her to sit. "I wonder what the earl would say to see you now here with us, little missy."

"That is of little to no account," she assured him. "I shall get straight to the point, Matthew."

He nodded, looking surprised.

"He was wrong when he accused you of stealing the Swafford pearls and he knows it now. You must come back to Starling's Roost and work for him again."

With one grimy fingernail he scratched his cheek. "And what do you know about it, little missy?"

"A very great deal," she replied firmly. "Do you want your post back?"

Matthew hesitated. "I doubt his lordship would take kindly to you interfering in the matter."

"He may have difficulties apologizing for mistakes," she agreed. "But he needs you back Matthew."

Having returned with the cider jug, Luke said, "The lady is in earnest, brother. Hear her out now she's come." He passed her a full tankard. "Take care now," he warned, "it creeps up on you."

She was pleasantly surprised he poured some for her too, but no one there would preach ladylike manners to her. Besides, she was already dressed in male clothing, not a corset in sight. What difference would one mug of scrumpy make in the vast scheme of bad behavior?

She turned to Matthew. "You do want to come back, don't you?"

He fixed her in a stern gaze, his eyes almost black. "I'd come back for his lordship, thus," he clicked his fingers, "if he wanted me. If he asked."

"I ask you on his behalf."

He sputtered, indignant. "You can do that, can you, little missy? He gave you permission to speak for him?"

"No." She frowned. "But Griff knows you didn't steal the Swafford pearls and he's forgiven you for falling in love."

"*Griff* knows does he?" He looked at Luke. "Aye, now I see what you mean, brother. She's a funny little thing."

Frustrated, she watched them laugh with one another, and then she turned her attention to the thick, syrupy amber liquid in her tankard. It couldn't be any stronger than Norfolk scrumpy surely, and she was capable of drinking the village carpenter under the table at home. The spiciness tickled her nose as she leaned over the mug and saw her face reflected there. She closed her eyes, took a breath and drank her cider straight down. It was warm and sweet, going down easily, leaving her tongue with a pleasant, tingling taste of apples. Her companions fell silent, watching in astonishment. Burping, she slammed her tankard down.

"Best pour the lady another," Matthew exclaimed. "She's dry this eve."

She burped again in agreement and Matthew perused her face, apparently struck by an even deeper curiosity than she first roused. "Where did *he* find you, missy?"

"In the river Thames," she answered solemnly, thinking back to that spring day and his kiss, taken without permission.

"You mean, *on it*."

"No. In it."

This made them hoot with laughter and Maddie, feeling the benefit of the scrumpy, laughed too. In fact, by the third tankard, she was laughing at everything anybody said. Nursing her tankard with both hands, she leaned back, bumped her head and was somewhat surprised to find the back of the settle much closer than expected.

Matthew looked at Luke. "She's not what I expected."

"Took him by surprise too, by all accounts."

"I never thought he'd find one that suited."

"They say he fell hard."

Matthew nodded. "I'm glad of it. Time he had someone to come home to."

She blinked drowsily, listening but too warm and relaxed to interrupt.

"She's an odd little thing," said Matthew.

"He's deadly keen on keeping her. Gregory said he's never seen him like it, in such a state he didn't know what to do with himself."

Matthew seemed to make his mind up. He nodded briskly. "Reckon this calls for another jug o' scrumpy."

Another cup later and she forgot silly things like time. What did it matter? Who was there to shout at her when she finally tumbled home? The earl would be with his brother still and her cousin was probably ironing out her wrinkles.

"Say you'll come back, Matthew," she begged with the peculiar depth of feeling only a drunkard possesses. "He needs you there. I think he's in danger and he needs someone to protect him."

"But he has a new man now."

"Wickes?" She shuddered. "I don't believe he has the earl's interests at heart. Griff needs you back. He needs a good man at his side."

He smiled. "Missy, I believe there are changes afoot at Starling's Roost, and good ones too. So mayhap I shall think on it."

When they left the tavern, she was obliged to lean heavily on Luke, but he made no protest. The sky was black velvet dotted with diamond chips and a kindly moon lit their path, but even as she rhapsodized on the heavenly beauty of the night, her eyes grew heavy. Luke's hands were on her waist, lifting her up, and she felt the dip as he joined her on the cart. The fresh air blew away the last remnants of tavern wood smoke, and then she was fast asleep, her head on his shoulder.

* * * *

Eustacia's voice echoed around the curiously empty chambers of her brain. "Where have you been? Are you mad? What are you…"

Maddie peeled her eyelashes apart to look up into that moonlit face. Gazing about with distant care, she found herself propped up at the foot of the staircase. Evidently Luke had been unable to prod her up the sweeping flight of stairs to her chamber, and in his own sauced mind, saw this as a fair compromise. She burped. "Good eve, Useless."

"Get up, before someone sees you like this. Drunk. Good gracious!"

"I only had two." She held up one finger. When Eustacia poked her with a bony foot, she swatted her away, laughing. "Stop that, it tickles!"

"Get up. This instant!"

It occurred to Maddie, eventually, that her cousin was fully dressed. It did not, however, strike her as odd, even at that time of night. In her current state of awareness, she would think nothing of it if Eustacia wore a pig snout.

Peering down through the oak

railings, she watched her cousin's long shadow cross the hall tiles. Momentarily snared in the wedge of moonlight through the open doorway, the thin, pewter shape slithered out of sight, leaving only the questioning hoot of an owl as the door closed quietly behind the vision.

* * * *

He found her on the stairs, on his way down to look for her, having found her bed disturbingly empty. Relief soared, but some panic remained in shards that cut into his throat, made his voice hoarse.

"Where have you been?"

"Too hot," she murmured.

"Damn you." He gathered her up and carried her to bed. "The minute my back's turned you disappear again. Yet you expect me to trust you."

Without opening her eyes, she nestled her head into the curve of his neck and shoulder. "My darling Beastie. There you are."

"Where have you been?" he repeated sternly.

"Who cares? I came back, didn't I?"

He sighed, shaking his head, feeling helpless as he laid her on the bed and watched her drift back to sleep. Yes, this time she'd come back, but eventually she wouldn't.

One day she'd leave him.

Thanks to the sweet, pungent spice of cider he had a good idea where she'd been, but not with whom. He'd find out. Couldn't encourage this bad behavior. Someone had to take this woman in hand.

But there was nothing to be done now, except lie down beside her, hold her tight and go to sleep. And while she slept, he cherished her in ways he never dared when her eyes were open and her lips capable of tender mocking.

CHAPTER 27

It was ascertained that Eustacia had bribed one of the young, new stable lads to take her as far as the north road. She left a note for Gabriel, saying she thought their marriage was a mistake and she could see she was not welcomed at Starling's Roost.

"Do you think she's gone back to London?" her husband agonized.

Maddie urged him not to worry, for Eustacia could manage by herself and would, no doubt, send him a letter within a day. With a sore head, not yet recovered from her excursion with Luke, the last thing she cared to hear was her cousin's woeful husband.

His health improved, but he moped like a sick dog, and although the servants tiptoed around as if a loud noise might cause utter collapse and shatter his fragile bones to pieces, Maddie thought Master Gabriel might benefit from one or two loud noises. At breakfast he sat with his head hanging from his shoulders, poking at his food, never putting a morsel to his down-turned lips, as if he waited for someone, like a nursemaid or a nanny--or his brother--to distract him out of his mood with toys and games. She began to feel more sympathy for the earl.

It rained heavily all day, adding to the dreary gloom, and Griff was in a bad mood, claiming everything and everyone was against him. Gabriel had kept his vow to Madolyn and told his brother he knew nothing about her. To further pinch at his temper, when Griff questioned the staff on her late night exploits at the tavern, determined to find out who was responsible for taking her there, they all claimed to have been with her. Even Jennet.

As his staff presented this united face, there was nothing he could do. He could hardly dismiss the entire staff. "Everyone," he remarked grimly to her, "is apparently on *your* side."

She stayed out of his way, waiting for the storm to pass--outdoors and in.

When she suggested Gabriel might like to play cards, he shook his head, his eyes pink-rimmed. "How can I think of entertainments with

Eustacia gone?"

Maddie was quite sure his wife would be thinking of nothing but her own entertainments, wherever she was, but Gabriel suddenly took her hand and exclaimed fervently, "I do love her, Madolyn. I know what you think. But I do love her. Perhaps she doesn't yet believe it either."

"Perhaps," she agreed, skeptical.

"Like my brother, you don't understand." When she objected, he explained gently, "Eustacia needs me. Don't you see? For once, someone needs *me*. All my life," he went on, "I was the one, protected and fretted over. When I met your cousin, she didn't treat me like a child, but looked to *me* to protect *her*."

Thus Eustacia's sudden departure brought Gabriel to a new level of consciousness, a new determination to be his own man, and now he made up his mind to go after her.

His brother would have stopped him, but Maddie politely suggested it was time the earl stopped meddling in other people's love lives, since he had no experience on the subject. He took exception to this and by the time he was done quarreling, Gabriel's horse was saddled. Maddie prepared a basket of food for his journey and made certain he was warmly clothed for travel, fussing over him as if he was her own son, much to Griff's apparent amusement.

"I know I accused you of overprotecting your brother," she said, as she came back to his side on the steps, "but I can see how it was not entirely unjustified."

Since she conceded this much, he met her half-way, admitting his brother might be old enough to make his own mistakes, occasionally. But they sent two strong bodyguards after him as a precaution.

* * * *

That afternoon the roan mare went into foal, and Griff began an anxious vigil in the stables. Madolyn went to her chamber to change into the old gray gown, planning to spend the afternoon in the cookhouse and surprise him again with her culinary skills. Struggling with the hooks of her gown, she heard the door open and thought it was Jennet come to help.

"Need a pair of hands there, eh?" Wickes slithered against the doorframe, grinning at her.

"Get out! How dare you enter my chamber?"

"You can forget those ladylike manners with me, wench." His filthy boots moved stealthily across the creaky boards. She backed around the bed, holding her gown over her shift, clutching it to her breasts. "No need to run away from ol' Wickes. You and me, we're of the same mould. We know how to survive in this world." He sniffed, looking around her chamber. "He's given you plenty o' trinkets already, eh?"

"I told you to get out."

"I don't follow *your* orders, mouthy whore." He came toward her again, grinning. "Couldn't understand where he went when he left London in the middle of the night, not even telling ol' Wickes where he was off too." He paused, licking his cracked lips. "Now I understand his haste to be alone with you. Can't blame the feller. Now you can share a little o' that with ol' Wickes and I won't tell him who you were with last night, in the tavern. Don't want to get that fool Luke in trouble, do you wench?"

She glanced at the window, but it was closed. No one was in the south corner of the house this afternoon and she was alone with Wickes. He'd chosen his moment carefully.

"You labor under a misapprehension, Wickes," she said steadily. "I'm not a whore, but even if I was one, you'd never get your hands on me."

He laughed, flinging back his greasy hair. "Aye. Not an everyday sort o' whore. Costly no doubt. Add this one to the master's bill, he'll never notice." His steps continued toward her. She made a *volte* leap up onto the bed, hoping to scramble across, out of his reach, but he caught her by the ends of her hair, pulling her off balance. She landed hard and then he was on top of her, his dank stench suffocating. He tried to pull the gown away and his rough, blackened fingernails tore a hole in the shoulder of her shift. She bucked, kneeing him hard in the groin, but this only made him angry, slapping her flat-handed, swift and hard. His boots scuffed dirt across her coverlet, his weight crushed the breath out of her as he forced her legs apart. With one hand she reached under her pillow and retrieved the knife she kept there. Her fingers closed around it, and in one burst of enraged strength, she heaved again and struck with her knee at the same time. He fell away, swearing at her, but the sound ended abruptly on a startled squeak as he felt the cool blade pressed to his windpipe.

Eyes darkened with fury, he glared at her. She pressed the knife into his skin enough to leave an indent, and held it there, jerking her shift out from under him with her free hand.

With the breath gasping in her own throat, she hadn't heard the door open again.

"Good gracious, Wickes, can you do nothing right?"

Stunned, Madolyn turned, still holding her knife in one hand, her gown in the other. A woman had entered the chamber quietly to watch their struggle. Now, slowly removing her riding gloves, she shook her head at the servant scrambling off the bed. "Want a job doing, one should do it oneself, it seems."

She wore a feathered hat with a lace veil, through which she seared Maddie with a thorough, critical perusal. The broad collar of her coat was thickly embroidered with blue and white fleur-de-lys, the Swafford colors. Her slow assessment completed, she blinked, just once. "Apparently his tastes run to peasant."

Wickes wiped his mouth on his grimy sleeve. "She's naught but a common strumpet, like I said."

The woman snapped at him to leave and he slid out, grumbling and peevish.

"Forgive me," Madolyn said coolly. "I don't know your name, madam, and I didn't expect guests."

She tossed her gloves onto the rumpled bed. "Makes two of us...on both counts."

"I don't--"

"My name, child, is Lady Isabelle Mallory."

Maddie clasped the sturdy oak post at the foot of the bed.

"You might also know me as the Countess of Swafford. His wife."

And this is my bedchamber."

She felt nauseous, slightly dizzy. This was not real. His wife couldn't be standing there in the house, looking at her.

"I suppose you're a pretty thing, if somewhat coarse and common. Perhaps that's what he finds attractive. You're disposable. I was not."

"I think you--"

She held up her hand, silencing Madolyn as if she was her servant. "Since he's out, we can talk uninterrupted. Set a few rules. I must apologize for Wickes." She bared her teeth. "He has a clumsy hand and knows nothing of subtlety."

"I can look after myself."

"So I see." The countess was expressionless, her eyes moving around the chamber, taking it in--the vases laden with flowers, the excess of candles, the silk stockings over the chair, the lapis necklace on the dresser. "I thought my husband would have this obsession out of his system by now. It is very...awkward."

She was tall, slender and elegant. Her eyes slanted upward slightly and seldom blinked. Beneath an aquiline nose, his wife's lips, wide and fleshy, opened and closed in a quick, snapping motion, each word shot out briskly, purposefully and well-aimed. It seemed this woman had no tendency to forget what she meant to say and never let her tongue run on past its point. "You're young. How old?"

"Old enough, madam."

"Apparently." Those full lips stretched over her teeth. "When I heard my husband took a mistress, I had to see for myself. The mystery, alas, only deepens. Why are you special? Surely he might find half a dozen like you in any village or whore house."

Madolyn decided, with difficulty, to say nothing further. If she did speak, she would only amuse the woman by losing her temper.

"This is the lay of the land, little girl. I'm very much a part of his life and always will be, for this marriage cannot be undone. If he must have you, so be it. We must put up with one another."

How calm she was, how prepared to share. Again, nothing like

Maddie the Merciless.

Her eyebrows moved like the widespread wings of an eagle, hovering, skimming, cold, eyes picking out her insignificant, defenseless prey. "I'm afraid you're rather a disappointment." Now she glided forward, as if she never made a clumsy step in her life. "I'd hoped for something half-way civilized."

"Why have you come here?" Ah, she couldn't hold her tongue.

The woman turned to show her profile, one hand smoothing over the front of her gown. "I came to let him know how the child progresses, of course. Oh...I see you didn't know."

She leaned back, needing the bedpost to keep her upright. "A child? But he--"

"After eighteen years of marriage he decided he wanted an heir," the countess drawled, as if confiding in an acquaintance who would share her amazement. "After eighteen years! I couldn't refuse him. What could I do? A husband's request is his wife's command."

Maddie swallowed painfully, her heart in her throat.

"It was the first thing on his mind when he returned from Spain. And you know how he is. He will not be refused. I resisted because a child is the last thing I wanted at my age, but he would have his way."

She was trying to say he'd forced her. Madolyn's belly twisted and tightened.

"He knew his brother would never change for the better. Gabriel had disappointed him once too oft. Oh," she paused, a hand to her face in feigned shock, showing off the Swafford crest on her ring, "that dreadful woman he recently married!" She shook her head, sighing. "The Beast, therefore, needs a son, another heir. Now, here I am," she continued, drawing closer still, "in this wretched state. With his child in my belly he cannot be rid of me and neither, my little barefoot harlot, can you."

Her nerves snapped, coiling. "I don't believe you."

"Ask him then." The words fell like shards of vicious glass through the air. "Although he will say it is none of your business and truly it is not. Matters between husband and wife are always private."

"I don't believe he forced you," Maddie clarified, with more calmness than she felt. "He would never do that."

The woman's eyes shone with spiteful glee. Her perfume was very strong, sweet and cloying. "Oh, my dear. I know the Beast better than you. I know the evil of which he is capable. A husband may do as he pleases with his wife. There was nothing I could do."

Maddie turned her face away rather than choke on the thick scent, but his wife's mouth was barely two inches from her ear.

"He tore off my gown and held me down on the bed, as Wickes did to you."

Moving back, she was trapped against the bed post. The woman's lips loomed closer again, her features contorted and suddenly ugly.

"His strength overpowered me. His weight on top of me, all hard muscle. He thrust his way into me. Again and again." Her fingertip brushed Maddie's cheek and slowly along her jaw. "And again." Cruel breath scorched her face. "And again."

She remembered how he'd once told her he was born of duty and hate. He was a Swafford, a stickler for tradition. Outraged by his brother's marriage, he might change his mind about needing another heir. Duty always came first. And this woman was still his wife. His pregnant wife. He refused to discuss his wife and perhaps this was why, but if it happened, it was not the way she claimed. He would never have forced himself on her.

"How long does he plan to keep you here?" the Countess inquired, her tone nonchalant.

I'll stay forever; I'll never leave him. Nothing came out.

"What is your name, girl?"

Again, nothing.

"Speak up, chit!" Her pupils shrank, her fat mouth quivered and tensed as the silence further baited her fury. "My husband clearly sets out to embarrass me by picking someone like you for his concubine, instead of any of those women he might have had from court. At least, if you were of a better class and educated, I might have had a conversation with you.

Still, I don't suppose he keeps you for conversation, does he? Your talents must lie elsewhere, and I see you're easily kept content with various..." she surveyed the rose-embroidered stockings again, "...catchpennies." Laughing quietly, she walked to the bed and retrieved her calfskin gloves. "Ridiculous creature, you are too stupid to live. If I were you I would say nothing of our visit." Her deadened eyes skimmed the rumpled bed, her lips bending stiffly. "My husband would not like to know his little whore spent the afternoon servicing his valet, but I could give a very entertaining description of how I walked in on the two of you." She paused, slapping the gloves against her open palm. "Not to mention what you've been up to with that rough-necked gardener, behind my husband's back. You don't want to get him dismissed do you?"

Having thoroughly insulted and belittled Madolyn, she now added jauntily, "I'll return shortly and I'll want my chamber back. Perhaps Gregory can find you a room with the other servants--if you're still here by then."

She was gone, leaving a thick cloud of her disgusting scent behind.

Madolyn bolted her door and sat on the bed to collect her thoughts. The terrifying memory of Wickes's attack made her blood seethe and her skin crawl, yet the words burned into her mind by the countess were far more deadly. They wanted her hurt and crushed, but she would not be. At least, she wouldn't show it. The countess had come to warn her husband's mistress of her lowly place, she understood that. But she was willing to share her husband? It was incredible. Of course, she reminded herself angrily, these were people from another world; the nobility lived by their own rules and had no real feelings. It was possible his wife wouldn't care if he shared his bed with another woman. Madolyn would care, that was the difference. She could never belong in his world.

Ridiculous creature, you are too stupid to live.

If she told Griff what had happened, he would kill Wickes, she had no doubt of it, but would he blame her too? He was such a distrusting beast and thought ill of her most of the time, even when she was completely innocent. If it was her word against Wickes and the countess, who would he believe? He'd laughed at her before when she'd expressed her suspicions. Wickes and the countess could make up any evil lie and have Luke dismissed.

And Griff's wife was with child.

Her stomach writhed. She felt hot, clammy. The room spun.

She closed her eyes and somehow she breathed.

This was no time for Maddie the Merciless to lose courage. She needed it now more than ever.

Later, Jennet came up to find her. Apparently the men were still busy with the roan mare.

Using the excuse of a bad stomach ache, Madolyn asked for a tray of supper to be brought to her room. She wanted to be alone with her thoughts and couldn't face him again, until she had it all straight and orderly in her head.

Chapter 28

The next morning, he came to her chamber door, thumping on it with his armored knuckles until she let him in.

"I heard you were indisposed with belly ache and could not get out of bed?"

It was the excuse she'd used to avoid him that morning, but it was partially true. She still didn't feel her usual brave self. Nauseous and tired, she'd lain awake most of the night, making calculations in her head, trying to count how long she'd been in Dorset, how many weeks it had been since her last courses.

He entered her room without invitation and prowled after her as she restlessly skipped out of his way and his clutches. "You look healthy enough to me," he purred throatily, reaching for her. His chestnut hair was disheveled, his shirt laces opened. Evidently he'd never been to bed or even changed out of clothes from the night before. He smelled of horse, hay, blood and worse.

And damn him, he was still irresistible.

Disgusted by this weakness, she dodged aside and scurried back to the bed, grabbing a loose robe from the chair as she passed, pulling it on over her nightshift and clasping the ruffled lace collar around her neck in a chaste manner. The gesture struck her as humorous and much too late, but it suddenly felt necessary.

"I think you'd better dismiss Wickes," she said. The new valet's quiescent evil was another cause of her sickness and deflated spirits.

His brow wrinkled. "Because you don't like the look of him?"

Clasping her ruffles tighter, she managed a tightly wound warning, "Because he means you harm." She thought of poor Luke, his post now in jeopardy because of her. If she told Griff what had happened yesterday, the countess would ensure the gardener's dismissal, or worse, if Griff believed the allegations she'd threatened. "I can't tell you how I know. You'll just have to believe..." She trailed off, realizing the futility.

Crawling away across the bed, overtaken by another surge of hapless nausea, she slid hastily under the coverlet.

"What's wrong with you?" he demanded, sounding annoyed.

"Oh I don't know," she sputtered. "What could possibly be wrong?" She hadn't meant to say anything, but it came out, as did many things that shouldn't. "It couldn't be your fault, of course, could it?"

Abruptly he sat on the bed. "You haven't had your....you know..."

"My what?"

"Your....you know..."

"*What?*"

"Your....since we first...?"

His awkward shyness was quite adorable. Pity he was an insufferable, arrogant ogre, who didn't believe in love. Pity he had a wife. And his wife was with child.

"Don't you know?" she muttered wryly. After all, they'd hardly spent a night apart.

But he still looked puzzled. Apparently no one bothered men like him with the squeamish details.

"There's no need to worry. I have the familiar pains now," she said grandly and mysteriously, fingers still gripping the lace collar to her throat.

"*That's* what ails you this morning?" His voice shook, she assumed, with relief.

"Yes." She faltered, feeling guilty for lying.

He stood again and began to pace, fingers splayed through his hair. "If we ever had a child--"

"*We* would not have one," she replied flatly. "*I* would have a child. It would be mine."

Staring down at her, he fidgeted with the filthy lace cuffs of his shirt. "You think you could keep it from me?"

"It?" Now she laughed churlishly.

He drew a sharp breath, before his words exploded on the exhale.

"My child. My son."

"Or daughter."

"One like you?" When the angry creases fell away, he looked young, almost boyish. "God help me."

"Precisely. Be thankful there is no child, despite your wanton recklessness." Under duress today she was prim, determined to be mature and composed even if it killed her. Which it might.

His eyes narrowed as he contemplated her on the bed. This time he didn't argue about who was at fault. "How do I know there is no child? You may try to keep it--the child--from me. I have a right."

"What right?"

"As the father," he blustered. "What would you know of raising a child?"

"I'm a woman."

"You're a child yourself. You have no discipline. You careen through life expecting everyone else to pick up the pieces."

"And what do *you* know of raising children?"

"I've lived fourteen years longer than you."

"That is entirely beside the point."

"It always is with you. Anything you don't agree with is beside the point."

"And everything you don't agree with is *wrong*," she screamed. "I wish I'd never let you have your wicked way with me!" She threw herself down, face first, into the pillow, feeling self-pity, but too angry for tears.

His footsteps approached the bed, hesitated.

"Go away," she bleated haplessly.

Resting one knee on the coverlet, he leaned toward her, like a tiger sniffing out its prey.

Raising her head just enough, she peered crossly at him through a tangle of black curls. "I'll bite!"

But he was, like her, not easily frightened off. Long and lithe, he stretched closer and she shrank against the bed post. "Kiss me, nameless wench."

She mewled in protest, "Go away. You stink."

Reaching for the sleeve of her shift, he trapped it in his dirty fingers. "Come see the foal. He's a beauty. I've named him Limpet."

"That's a terrible name for a horse."

For a long moment his wondering gaze searched her face.

"Stay with me?" he said. He asked this time, he didn't instruct or command. Today he treated her as a being with a right to her own choices. When it was too late, naturally.

His eyes were rich and brown this morning, no gold dazzling her. Today he was an ordinary man with whom she happened to be dreadfully, helplessly in love. A man married to another woman.

"This is eighteen years too late," she pointed out churlishly.

"Eighteen years ago…" he threw out his arms, "…you were three! Or is that beside the point now too?"

She grabbed a pillow, clutching it to her body. "What if I do have a child? What then?"

He sat on the bed, stern-faced. "I'll raise him on the estate. Make sure he gets a good education, or an apprenticeship. Noblemen keep mistresses and often raise their bastards. 'Tis nothing unusual."

"How easy for you. It won't put *you* out any, will it?" Up on her knees, she cried, "I won't have my child labeled a bastard and looked down on."

"But…" he looked befuddled, "what else did you…"

"Oh yes, I forgot." Now she was up on her feet. "I'm not supposed to expect you to have any feelings, am I?"

"*Feelings?*" he exploded.

"Well, hey ho! *I*…" she thrust a finger in her chest, "I have feelings. I'm young and alive. You're a bitter old man with no heart--only a swinging brick!"

He stared at her dancing about on the bed, as if her feet were burning, and said calmly, "What good did feelings ever do anybody?"

When she threw her pillow at him, he ducked. That was when he saw the knife she kept there. They reached for it at the same time and he got there first. "Planning to stick it in my heart one night, eh?"

"For your information, Lord Doubtful, it's for my protection and a very good thing I had it." She scrambled off the bed. Mature composure forgotten, she could barely breathe. "What good would stabbing you in the heart do me? Can't kill something that's already dead."

"Will you stop bouncing, no name wench? You're giving me a headache."

Too exasperated to argue any further, she ran out of the chamber, bare feet flying along the corridor, down the stairs and out of the house.

One sound pierced her scattered thoughts. Like a bell clapper, it knocked back and forth inside her head, until it became an authoritative man's voice, deniable no further.

"Madolyn!"

Oh, no. Not this—not *now*. Not yet.

It was her father.

* * * *

"I thought I'd find you at the bottom of a chalk pit," he exclaimed gruffly, laughing as she hugged him tight, squeezing the air out of him. "I hope you haven't been a nuisance to these good folk. No doubt you've overstayed your welcome."

That, she feared, was a severe understatement.

"Where is Grace?" she asked, deflecting the subject. "How is she? Papa, there was a man in London who--"

"Yes, she told me. Don't worry, your sister is safe at home. I took her there before I came here for you."

Suddenly she saw the earl tripping down the steps of his manor house, a sleeveless jerkin pulled on in haste over his dirty, loose shirt. Riding crop in one hand, he was already bellowing for his horse, but his eyes made a quick sweep of the gravel path and he stopped in his tracks. Another, slower sweep must have proved to his doubting eyes that it was indeed his mistress, with her arms around another man. Face dark with anger, riding crop swinging, boots crunching across the gravel, he made his approach.

"Oh," she said weakly, "Here comes the earl, Papa."

With the collision of her two worlds now inevitable, she thought herself about to die. However, it was not her heart that stopped, it was the earl. His eyes widened. *"Captain Carver?"*

"Griff?" Her father's blue eyes were laughing. Crinkled up, the white lines around them vanished. "'Tis good to see you again lad. I hope this young wench hasn't given you too much trouble. Is your master home?"

Griff? *Griff?* They knew one another?

There was a short pause. "This *is* the earl of Swafford," she muttered. "I see he has fooled you too, as is his habit."

Her father warned her loudly not to tell so many fibs. "I know this lad. He's Griff, the earl's man."

Meanwhile, Griff looked from one to the other, taking ill-concealed umbrage at the sight of an arm other than his own around her waist. She decided not to offer any explanation. Let him stew in his own juices.

"I prefer to travel incognito, captain," he managed, the words choking out in one breath.

"Ah." Her father faltered, immediately on his guard. "I see. I wish I'd known, my lord."

Belatedly remembering his manners, the earl extended a hand, the one not holding the riding crop. "Welcome to Starling's Roost, captain. Call me Griff. I don't stand on ceremony here."

She expelled a scornful chuckle, but when both men looked at her, she studied the gravel path.

Her father recovered easily. Never one to let life's many ups and downs knock him off kilter, he kept a mostly placid disposition, traveling along with a steady, plodding amble. The discovery that his friend with whom he'd shared several ales and confidences was in actual fact the Earl of Swafford caused only a small ripple soon smoothed over with good humor. "I'll have this little menace out of your hair now. We can go back to what we were, eh?"

"What we were?" Griff murmured. "And what *were* we, exactly?"

Reaching over to tweak her nose, her father laughed. "Like a bad penny, I always knew she'd turn up again. Never have daughters, Griff. They're ten times worse than sons."

The riding crop almost slipped out of his hands, and much to her wry amusement, his knees bent slightly, before they remembered how much weight they had to carry. "Daughter?" His voice cracked on the word.

Madolyn, meanwhile, caught her father suddenly assessing her flimsy apparel. His brows ruffled quizzically.

"Papa," she cried rather louder than necessary, "can we leave at once? I'm anxious to get home."

"Of course," he muttered, still considering her bare feet. "You've troubled this kind fellow long enough." Then he turned to Griff. "I daresay she drove you mad these last few weeks."

"Yesss. It has been....most interesting."

"My feet hurt and I'm cold," she interrupted, scowling hard at him. "I'll go and get dressed."

"What are you doing outdoors barefoot, in your night things?" her father asked.

"Taking the air of course," she replied, as if it was quite natural.

Griff's eyes sought hers and she saw the hot gleam of gold, tossed like a challenge to bounce at her feet.

"Aren't you going out for a ride, your lordship?" she demanded scathingly. "Don't let us keep you."

"Aye," her father agreed. "We'll not detain you. I'll get my daughter's things and we'll be on our way."

But Griff raised his hand again, this time in a halting gesture. His overheated gaze swung to her father. "There's no haste, captain. Surely you'll stay for the day and dine with me this evening? I insist, captain. Please."

He smiled broadly.

Devastatingly.

She'd never heard him say "please" before and she'd certainly never seen him smile like that.

"Will you join me for a ride over the estate, captain? I won't ask your daughter to come. There's nothing more I can show her apparently. She's not easily impressed." When she threw him a warning frown, he responded with another of those rare smiles. "No entertainments I sought to provide have been enough to satisfy."

"I hope you've not been rude to his lordship," her father muttered, eyeing her skeptically. "After he put a roof over your head these past weeks."

"And fed her appetites," Griff added slyly.

"Aye, and fed you too. I know the amount of food you can put away."

"I've been the epitome of restraint, Father." She glanced sharply at Griff. "Despite severe trial to my patience."

One eyebrow lifted, and his lips twitched. And Maddie knew whatever story she told her father, Griff would have a better one. They both knew which would be believed.

How odd the two men liked one another. Her father never cared for noblemen. In fact he often mocked and ridiculed those men who thought themselves superior just because of an accident of birth, and she would have imagined her father's manners far too casual and easy for the earl's approval. Yet, apparently they were friends.

CHAPTER 29

They returned several hours later, laughing and easy, the earl playing the part of a benevolent host--to spite her, of course. He lent her father the use of his library to write to her mother and tell her she was found safe, then he suggested Gregory prepare a chamber in the west tower.

"You must stay the night, captain, after your long journey. Please."

There it was again. *Please*. She trusted it as much as she trusted that stupid grin on his face. How adept he was at playing the part of a civil gentleman when she knew he was a savage, lusty brute, with no feelings and no heart.

"Papa," she whined, "you said we might leave now--"

"I insist you stay tonight, captain," the earl repeated, a slight inflexion of noble prerogative noticed by her, if not by her father, who eagerly agreed he was weary after his journey and would be considerably refreshed after a good night's sleep.

Griff shook his finger in her face, his eyes agleam with superior amusement. "Tsk, tsk! Captain Carver's daughter. My good friend's little daughter. And I might never have known."

It took every ounce of prim restraint not to bite that finger clean off. As her father handed his letter to Gregory, giving instructions for the delivery, she took the opportunity to whisper, "I find myself increasingly astonished, your lordship, that you've never been slapped before--as you claim."

He merely laughed as if she told some jest of great hilarity. And then he pushed his luck further still, by ruffling her hair in the indulgent manner of a fond uncle.

* * * *

"When I heard her cousin was married to your brother, I knew Maddie must have come here too. I would've fetched her before now, but had to see her sister safely home to Norfolk first."

Across the table his wayward mermaid picked at her supper,

improbably quiet, and Griff was equally sparing with his words, weighing each one carefully, having no plans to rouse the captain's suspicions. It seemed her father assumed she was there with her cousin the entire time, not realizing she'd been in Dorset alone for several weeks, unchaperoned, unguarded.

Mostly undressed.

She cast him a quick, luminous blue glance above her wine. Apparently she thought she could get away with this. Was her father intentionally blind to her antics? Did she pull the fleece over the eyes of any man with the misfortune to cross her path?

It was a balmy evening and they dined on the terrace under a full moon, surrounded by rush torches. He wanted to show off his property again, to impress the captain and that surly-faced madam who quietly complained at the number of insects feasting upon her. She scratched and itched, muttering furiously about these and many other discomforts she could not name.

The captain, unlike his daughter, was completely at ease, enjoying the relaxing effects of Gregory's special brew, chattering away to Griff more openly than ever before.

"Living a life of leisure here in this fine house, taking advantage of your good food and hospitality, it's no wonder Maddie didn't want to be sent home again. She gets blinkers on, like a plow horse."

"Your daughter *is* remarkably stubborn, captain. I've not been able to make her comply with a single command."

"She's always had a mulish spirit."

"But tell me, captain, how do you discipline such a naughty child? Is there anything that might be done to curb her defiance?" He shot her an arch grin. It was brief, quickly vanishing into his mug of ale.

Captain Carver admitted he had yet to find a reliable method, although the threat of a firm slap across the buttocks was enough to silence her cursing mouth on occasion. At this, Griff laughed again, letting his humor out for a longer gallop.

"Perhaps it is you who needs the discipline, my lord," she observed primly.

He tried to halt his laughter, clasping a kerchief to his lips.

"Don't talk to your host like that," the captain exclaimed, "or you'll feel the sting of my belt on your saucy behind."

"Father, I'm not a child," she cried. "I wish you wouldn't treat me as such." Griff found her eyes directly trained on his face. "I'm a woman now and should be treated thus."

He coughed hard at the reminder.

"Now you mention it, girl," her father mused, "you do look different. The air of Dorset must agree with you, eh? There's quite a bloom in your cheeks."

Griff studied his knuckles, the heat rising under his collar, where it suddenly rubbed uncomfortably.

The captain demanded, "Is that a new frock?" The silence that followed was broken only by the sputtering of the torches and the nervous clatter of Griff's knife against his plate. Sitting forward, her father observed her face in the flickering torchlight. "What have you been up to? What happened to you in London, under your cousin's roof, eh?"

"Naught, Papa!"

"More ale, captain?" Griff speedily gestured for Gregory to refill her father's tankard.

"Someone bought you a new frock did they?" the captain persisted.

No answer.

"I don't like it." He fell back in his chair and turned to Griff. "She's been up to no good. I know my daughter."

Jaw tight, Griff looked everywhere but at his guests.

"If I find out there's been mischief of that kind," her father continued slowly, "I'll hunt the fellow down, slice off his tackle with my blunt knife and use it for fish bait. Or throw it to my dog. He likes a good bit of flesh for his Sunday dinner."

"Papa," she protested, "How could you talk of such things and at the supper table?"

"Who was he, girl? Best save me more trouble and tell me before I beat it out of you!" When she resolutely refused to entertain his suspicions, he said to Griff, "I daresay some scoundrel bought her gifts and she's empty-headed enough to accept them without knowing what he wanted in return. My daughter is an innocent, and I fear she's been misused."

"Innocent?" Griff mumbled. "Yes, I'm sure that must be the case."

She stood swiftly. "I think I'll go to bed."

"I'll get to the root of this, girl. Don't think you can avoid the matter by skipping off to bed," the captain warned. "No man buys my unwed daughter gifts of fine clothes. What will folk think?"

"In my experience, Papa, folk will think what they wish to think, right or wrong." She aimed a meaningful look in Griff's direction, and before leaving the terrace, added, "Don't forget we leave tomorrow on a long journey, Papa, and you need a clear head."

"Just like your mother," he muttered.

They watched her walk into the house, the torchlight licking her shape, momentarily sweeping her with gold dust. Griff realized, with a fierce, shameful pang, he didn't even have a miniature portrait of her to keep. Once she was gone, he might never lay eyes on her again.

As she disappeared inside, the Captain apologized for his daughter's behavior. "Alas, she is her mother's daughter."

Griff ran a finger around the rim of his tankard. "The women in your family are troublesome, captain?"

"All but my daughter Grace. A good girl she is. Too good-hearted and gentle, in fact." He proceeded to tell of her misfortune in London, when she was led along by a gentleman called Jessop, who turned out to have a wife already. "Poor Grace was brokenhearted. She blamed her sister for sending the fellow off with a flea in his ear, but later discovered the truth, that Maddie had only acted for her good."

Griff remembered the night he'd seen Jessop confront her under the arches. Now he understood.

He knew how she liked to meddle, but it was out of kindness, it seemed, not mischief. Well, she was done meddling in his life. Tomorrow she would go home and his life could go back to what it was before, his world in tidy order. Other men who kept mistresses ended the arrangement easily and often enough. Why should he not be capable of the same?

CHAPTER 30

Candle stump in hand, she went to his door.

"With your father here in the house?" he exclaimed. Suddenly he was righteous and proper. "Have you lost your mind?" Looking nervously over her shoulder, he grabbed her sleeve and pulled her into his room, closing the door quickly behind her. "If he should see you coming here--"

"Still fretting over that disemboweling cutlass?"

He winced. "More than ever."

"I never thought the wicked Earl of Swafford would let a little thing like that worry him."

"The wicked Earl of Swafford wants to keep his parts where they are--all his parts attached exactly."

She chuckled. "Shall Gregory measure it with his notched stick to be sure it stays the same?"

He grabbed her candle, muttering she would probably drop it and set his house ablaze. "Your father might beat the truth out of you, like he said."

"He would never raise his hand to me."

"That's where he went wrong then."

He was angry with her, it seemed. His eyes wouldn't meet hers tonight and looked at her shoulder, her hand, her candle, anything but her face. Moonlight and shadow fought over the stern lines of his expression. He put distance now between them and perhaps, she thought sadly, it was for the best.

Madolyn struggled to say her goodbyes, but they died mid-way up her throat. Before she'd tapped on his door, she'd had it planned: how calm and sensible she would be, how she would thank him for their time together and wish him happiness for the future. She'd even thought she might shake his hand. Now that she stood before him, polite gestures seemed impossible. "Tomorrow I'll be gone," she blurted. "I suppose you'll miss me."

His answer was unduly terse. "I doubt it."

"We'll never meet again."

"Good thing for my sanity and my household."

Fighting tears, she tried to remember what she'd come there to say. "Take care, my lord, in your dealings with Wickes."

"This again?" he scoffed.

"I can't prove anything and I suppose you won't believe me, but I'd never forgive myself if any harm...if I hadn't warned you." She turned, walking to his door. "Thank you, sir, for giving me shelter these past weeks. I never deserved such forbearance and noble condescension." Making light of it, she kept her voice even. Understanding he could offer her nothing more than his bed, she didn't want him to think her ungrateful for the offer. She was painfully cognizant of how he'd suffered to make some room for her in his life.

Briskly she put out her hand, firm and straight. "Goodbye, my lord. And thank you."

There was a moment when it seemed he would refuse the hand she offered, but he accepted it, his expression bemused. He bowed stiffly over it, his long, cool fingers holding hers lightly. "The pleasure, madam, was mine."

Again she felt as if they acted roles in a play.

She left his chamber, slamming the door behind her, ensuring those disapproving, grim-faced Swaffords trembled in their frames along the distant gallery.

* * * *

They left early the next morning, and she caught sight of him watching from the blue chamber's window as they rode slowly away on the new horses he'd given Captain Carver.

She looked back only once, then turned her face to the gate at the end of the long, winding gravel path, painfully holding in those worthless sobs that would never do anyone any good.

Once, he'd said to her, *"Even if I wanted another life, there is nothing I can do about it. If I could walk in another man's boots, I would."*

Now she understood. For that brief time, she'd given him the chance to live another life, in that little cottage by the bay, in another world, far away from their reality.

PART IV
Fruits of Wisdom

CHAPTER 31

Sir,

Apparently your lordship has great disdain for anyone with a mind of their own. I suppose your needs and wants are the only matters of import in this world. If I were not a lady with other things to do, I would treat you to a taste of the willow switch, as I would any spoiled, cantankerous little boy. That said, I have a number of items to lay before you.

Item One.

Your brother. Gabriel is no longer a boy, yet you continue to treat him as one. Perhaps, had you been a less oppressive guardian and allowed him to make his own decisions and mistakes, he might not have fallen prey to Eustacia Shelton, whose primary appeal is likely her failure to fit into your inflexible rules. There is no arguing with love, your lordship. Sadly I know something myself of misguided caretaking and have learned no one will thank you for interfering in their love life. Better let them get on with it.

Item Two.

Captain Nathaniel Downing has been much maligned. I was once assured, by a loyal servant of yours, that you too are misunderstood and wounded by unfounded, slanderous rumor. If this is the case, you should understand Captain Downing's misfortune and urge his pardon. He is a good man, whose tongue occasionally runs away with itself. I am familiar with this unhappy trait also, for no one's tongue has tumbled so clumsily as my own.

One last item.

'Change', your lordship, is not a curse word. I appreciate that many generations of earls have perpetrated certain traditions in this house, but might I suggest adapting the rules a little could improve your servants' and your brother's life. It might even do you a world of good.

Take this advice or leave it, your lordship. It matters not to me if you continue as a bitter, miserly old *man without friends.*

> *Sincerely,*
> *An anonymous well-wisher.*

He found the letter where she'd left it, propped up against the pillow. He wanted to laugh at her officious manner, trying to tell him, a man fourteen years her senior, how to manage his life.

If I were not a lady with other things to do, I would treat you to a taste of the willow switch, as I would any spoiled, cantankerous little boy.

Then he did laugh out loud, the image of it too clear in his mind.

He ate supper alone in the hall, seated at one end of the long table, the servants fetching and carrying with quiet efficiency, the rules followed, everything in its place. But she was missing. He pictured her sitting there at one end of his table, he at the other, too far apart, but that was the way things were always done. It was tradition.

Tonight, restless, he strode the length of the table to lay his hand flat along the back of her chair, wishing she was there now.

"Are you in love with me?" she'd asked him in the hothouse, her eyes, cornflower blue, shining up at him.

Love? He'd never believed in it, but he'd never believed in mermaids either until she forced her way into his neatly ordered life.

The first moment he'd seen her, she'd changed his mind, rearranged his parts, just as she'd tried to rearrange his house. It was simple goodness she had. Unfussy, warm and sensuous, she welcomed the ridiculous challenge of loving him.

His chest hurting, he sat heavily in her chair.

"Where the devil is Wickes?" he snapped abruptly to Gregory.

"He is, I believe, in the cookhouse. Taking another nap."

The earl raised his head, eyes hot and smarting suddenly. "You don't like him either, eh? Any reason?"

"I don't know the man, my lord," Gregory equivocated. Then, suddenly, he added with a rush of boldness Griff had never before heard in is voice, "Mistress Madolyn warned me to keep an eye on him. I understand...he tried to put his hands on the young lady."

"He *what*?"

"She mentioned it to me, my lord, because she didn't want young Jennet, or any of the maids, left alone with him."

He could barely breathe. Some pagan fire roared through his veins, scorching his lungs. His hands tightened into fists. "Why didn't she tell me?"

"She said you wouldn't believe her, my lord. And Wickes threatened her if she told."

Cursing, he held his taut knuckles against the table. Did he believe her? Could he? What good would it do now? He couldn't offer her more than he had already. He was trapped.

Gregory continued quietly, "There is one thing to remember, my lord, about that vow you made to your father."

He stared at the fluttering candles, shoulders rounded, dark thoughts dripping through him like rain through a leaking roof.

"He's *dead*, my lord, along with those other Swaffords up there." Gregory turned respectful eyes to the dimly lit gallery above. "They had their life and if they made a miserable mess of it, that's no reason for you to do the same. Your father, God rest his soul, had his life. Now 'tis your turn to live."

There was no reply to that. This boldness, he concluded, was yet another result of his mermaid's presence in that house. Gregory was practically giddy with it and Griff didn't have the heart to shout at him tonight.

The steward hesitated. "Shall I snuff the candles, my lord?"

"No," he growled, "Let them burn down."

"And Wickes, my lord?"

Griff slowly ran his tongue over his teeth. "I'll deal with Wickes."

* * * *

In another fortnight they were home. Exhausted, she wanted only a bath and her old bed. Her mother was so relieved to see her safe that, luckily, she didn't force details of her adventure. Less patient than their mother, Grace followed her to bed and demanded to know what happened in Dorset.

"Please don't ask me, Grace. I've naught to tell." Maddie clasped her sister's hands and then released them, falling to the pillow. "Certainly nothing you should hear."

Grace perched on the edge of the bed. "I won't tell Papa, but I know you didn't leave with Eustacia. You were alone all that time with the Beast, weren't you? There was no chaperone."

"Hush, dear sister." Pressing a finger to her lips, Maddie squirmed her way under the quilted coverlet, nestling into her familiar old bed and falling asleep almost immediately, even before she could show Grace the shells she'd brought home for her. Only one did she mean to keep for herself--the tiny, perfect white cockleshell Griff once found. That she couldn't bear to part with.

Waking later, refreshed and hungry, she strolled out to the orchard, looking for her mother. The sun was setting over the flint stone wall and the colors changed. The dustiness of the afternoon slowly blew away, the air cooler and tranquil. The birdsong was quieter, less harried. Beneath her skirt, the grass rustled lazily. Daisies curled their heads and slept as the sun prepared to slip beyond the horizon, and dandelion clocks waited patiently for a stray breeze or a foot to knock against them and release their fluttery seeds into the evening.

She found her mother picking plums for jam. Her sleeve was warm under Maddie's fingertips and she turned in surprise at her sudden touch. Overwhelmed with emotion, Madolyn embraced her mother as she hadn't done in years, committing every sensation to memory--the comfort of a worn, much-patched old gown, the warmth of lingering sun on her shoulder, the sweet scent of lavender water in her hair.

Her mother's brow pleated with gentle lines, but her brown eyes were still clear and capable of prying out the deepest secrets. "Maddie Carver what have you been up to?"

"I tried to fix something broken,"

she replied haltingly.

"And?"

She lifted her shoulders.

Planting a quick kiss on her forehead, her mother whispered, "When shall you tend to your own life and look to your future? Fix that, my dear Maddie, and let other people worry for themselves now."

They linked arms, walking along together, bowing their heads under the plum and apple trees. Maddie felt fat teardrops trapped in her eyelashes, but if her mother noticed, she kept it to herself.

* * * *

Wickes shuffled across the room to the shutters. In the gray and purple light, the fellow was a ghostly shadow, hunched and mournful. "Should be a fine day, milord," he croaked, opening the shutters with a clatter.

Turning, he jumped to find him already up, dressed and seated on the bench at the foot of his bed. Morning light spilled through the parted shutters, falling across his outstretched legs and boots, before reaching upward to touch his face with wary fingers .

"You rise early, milord."

He hadn't slept actually, but felt no inclination to tell Wickes. "Naught to stay in bed for is there?" he spat.

"Going riding, milord?" Wickes asked, with the slightest narrowing of his weasel-like eyes.

"Yes." He caressed his whip, a slow boiling anger bubbling below the surface.

Wickes slouched to the next window, turning his back.

"Tell me, Wickes, did you truly think to get away with it?"

"Milord?"

"You tried to touch her," he spat the words through clenched teeth, syllables taut with disgust, the sound resonating around his chamber.

"Touch who, milord?" Wickes tried to shrug it off. "The little whore what was here? Is that what she told you?" His tongue rasped over his lips. "Don't believe her word over mine do you, milord? I've got a witness who--"

"It wasn't she who told me."

Wickes blanched.

"Tell me the truth and I'll be lenient."

Slowly the man scratched his cheek with a blackened nail. "That little whore wanted it. Begged for it. Don't believe her word over mine do you, milord? I told you what she was. I warned you--"

Griff was on his feet and across the room in three strides. Clasping the other man's chin, he forced it back, suddenly noticing for the first time the fresh scar on his swarthy neck. The mark left by the indent of a blade.

"She tried to get me in trouble," Wickes protested. "Wanted me dismissed. Meant to trap me--seduce me."

"And you fought her off, I suppose?"

"She wanted it. I don't know why she--"

Griff placed his thumb against the man's throat where the slender scar proved she'd wielded that knife in self-defense. And knew who he believed, who he trusted.

It was the last day he ever saw Wickes. The last day anyone ever saw Wickes.

CHAPTER 32

He knew something was wrong when he rode up the gravel path and saw Luke on the steps, face red, eyes spitting a resentful anger. Swinging down from the saddle, Griff passed his reins to the groom and looked over at the disgruntled gardener.

"What is it, Luke?"

The young man squeezed out, "The countess."

His wife was the last person he'd expected to see. She never came to Starling's Roost these days.

"She's inspecting the staff now," Luke added, his face going a darker blood red.

"And why are you--"

"She sent me out here because, in her words, my lord, I stink like horse shit."

Furious, Griff leapt the last few steps and strode into his house. Two maids were sobbing into their aprons, but the cook, in the midst of consoling them, managed to inform him the countess headed for the blue chamber with Gregory.

Her boxes were piled in the hall, her cloying fragrance--far greater insult to his nostrils than Luke's honest, earthy odor--hung in the air like a thick fog on an autumn morning. The staff were in a degree of shock, their usual tasks forgotten as they looked to him for some instruction. It was, he realized, as if death had come to the house.

Without a word to anyone, he took the stairs, three at a time, and walked quickly down the corridors. No one had slept in the blue chamber since his mermaid left and her things remained in it. He should have had them removed by now, but for some reason he'd put it off, always finding other business to tend, keeping the room exactly as she left it.

He already heard his wife, her commands shrieked out at Gregory, scoring the walls of his house. "I want these bed linens changed at once and these whorish clothes burned."

Turning the last corner, he saw the door open, a somber Gregory standing there, eyes downcast as her orders rained down on his balding head. Gregory had never liked his master's wife. In the same way the steward made no effort to conceal his fondness for that wretched, lying little chit of a captain's daughter, he was equally unsubtle in his disdain for the countess.

Of course, his wife was not a likeable person, but neither was the Earl of Swafford.

"To what do we owe this honor?" Griff growled, striding into the chamber.

The countess sat on the bed, half-way through a long list of her demands, all of which, he had no doubt, Gregory ignored.

This was the last thing he'd wanted. Faced by the woman he hated, it only reminded him more painfully of the woman he'd lost; the comparison between the two was so marked, it was impossible not to acknowledge.

Her almond-shaped eyes were clear of any conscience, or any fear she might not be welcome. They swept quickly over his long form, taking in the muddied boots. She'd often commented on his lack of fashion, mocking him for dressing "like a peasant". Today however, she held it back, quickly sliding her derision away.

"Gregory," she said in a low, sultry murmur, "you may go."

Griff laid a hand on the old man's arm and advised him, quietly and firmly, to stay. "Whatever you have to say to me, you may say before Gregory." He forced himself to face her. "I'd prefer a witness."

She must be desperate, because she made no further argument. Instead she sat tall and prim, exclaiming with false jollity, "Are you not pleased to see me, my husband?"

"I ask again…why do you favor us with your presence, madam?"

The veins in her neck strained. Her wide, plump lips spread over her teeth, but her eyes never changed, never warmed. "Oh dear, I'd hoped for a sweeter reception. Have I not given you enough time to consider?" She rose from the bed and came toward him. "Can we not begin again, as husband and wife?"

"After eighteen years?" *Of misery*, he might have added.

Still she worked her ghoulish smile, but a sharp edge of bitterness invaded the silky pretense of a peace pact. "I hear you flaunt your common little mistress in front of the servants. Even the queen knows what keeps you down here. She took great delight in telling me the last time I saw her. They must wonder why you prefer that ignorant trollop to me. How do you suppose that makes me feel?"

The shoe was uncomfortable on the other foot, it seemed, and she could ridicule him as much as she liked, but he could not return the favor.

"I am busy," he snapped. "What do you want?"

She inhaled through her teeth, a sudden rush of air drawn in and expelled with bitter rancor. "I am with child."

"*What?*"

"Regrettably. Unless you want the world to know you for a cuckold, you will recognize it as yours."

Speechless, he stepped around her, not wanting her too close, her fragrance stifling, nauseating.

"The child needs a father and you need an heir."

He should have seen it coming, should've known. Of course this was not the first time for her. Disliking children, she suffered no qualms about ridding herself of the pregnancy with "cleansing powders", but now older, with Gabriel married and on the verge of solidifying his place as heir to the Swafford estate, she must have decided to keep this one, to use it for what she could get out of her husband. She must imagine his pride would never bear the horns of a cuckold.

But he was a different man than what he'd been a few months ago. "The child is not mine, as you know."

Her gloating perusal tracked him across the room. "You would deny your own heir?" She wanted to secure her future through the child and she thought him desperate enough for an heir to let it happen.

"This is ridiculous. We've not shared a bed in--"

"Wickes will tell a different tale."

"Wickes?" He snorted. "Wickes, my dear, will not be telling any tales, not anymore."

Glancing sideways to see her reaction, he was rewarded by the sallowing of her cheeks. He hadn't suspected any collusion until she'd mentioned his manservant. Interesting.

"What have you done to him?" she demanded.

He lifted his shoulders in a lazy half-shrug.

And with that one subtle motion the balance shifted. For eighteen years she'd held power over him, knowing deep down inside he remained a fearful boy of seventeen, stifled by duty, anxious not to disgrace his dead father. It had given her a thrill to torment him, to push him as far as she could, with her lovers and her demands on his purse. But now the fear inside him was gone.

She sank back to the bed.

"Was he your lover?" he asked calmly.

"Good God no! Do you think me that desperate? You may consort with servants and stupid little whores. I have standards."

He waited a beat, wondering how she would try to extricate herself from Wickes and his crimes. Like a rat on a sinking ship, she sought a way out, looking around with those empty, glassy eyes. She thought only of herself now, her own comfort, showing no more concern for the fate of Wickes, only for what he might have confessed. What purpose, exactly, was Wickes meant to serve? He sensed from the bracing of her shoulders, the clasping of her claws in her lap, there was more to this than immediately met the eye.

"Wickes will certainly provide no juicy witness testimony to our merry revels in bed, if that was what you planned," he said slowly. "The child you carry cannot possibly be mine."

"It's too late now to be rid of it," she exclaimed suddenly. "Believe me, I wish it were not. If I were a man, it wouldn't matter. If I were *you*," she spat the word, "with a bastard child to my name, no one would think twice. I could keep as many mistresses as I wanted and plant the countryside with little bastards. Because I'm a woman, I've done wrong."

Were those tears in her eyes? How humiliating it must be for her to beg him for this mercy.

"Spare me your speeches," he groaned. "I didn't write the rules of the world."

"I want us to start again. I want you to recognize my child as your--"

"You want too much and far, far too late."

Her gaze, indignant and disbelieving, gave him ice burns. "Because of *her*? That little trollop with whom you're temporarily obsessed? Good God, how can you shame me, humiliate me in this manner?"

As much as he wanted to put his hands around her scrawny throat, he controlled himself. "For eighteen years I tried to be civil to you. For eighteen years I put up with your demands. I paid for your servants, your clothes, the food on your table, even the horses you rode. And all I received in return was scorn and false rumor spread about me. Perhaps 'tis time we were both free of this marriage, abomination that it is."

Too many words in one breath, each one loud, ringing inside his head. Surely it must do the same in hers. He couldn't stop himself today. He'd had his fill. He wouldn't suffer any longer, wouldn't swallow another ounce of frustration. No more would he stand by and accept the mortification she and her cronies heaped upon him.

"You cannot be free of it," she snapped.

"Oh yes I can!" he roared at her. "I am the Earl of Swafford and I'll do as I please for once. As *I* please!"

He had never quite lost his temper with her before, because in the back of his mind there was the possibility it was his fault. Perhaps she was right to ridicule him as impotent. After all, she was the great beauty, condescending to let him share her bed. Yet now he knew the fault was not his. A certain other lady had taught him he was capable of giving and receiving pleasure. Today, therefore, he was emboldened, his manhood no longer called into question.

"You, madam, can be hoisted on your own petard. For years you've claimed me impotent. That's grounds enough for annulment."

"You wouldn't dare!" Oh now there was life in her eyes--ugly, misshapen, grotesque emotion. "The shame of it...the scandal....you would never..."

"Wouldn't I? I've put up with the rumor for eighteen years. Why shouldn't I get use out of it?"

Those full lips flapped emptily, words deserting her, until she gathered the torn shreds of her pride, tipped her head and purred savagely, "Your father will turn in his grave."

"He might. Perhaps, after so many years, he'll welcome the change of view."

Her boy husband, the target of her ridicule and spiteful mockery, too afraid of upsetting the applecart, terrified of disappointing his father's ghost, was no more.

"You can remain at Blanchard House," he added firmly. "I'll pay you an annual pension to cover your bills and not go beyond them. When the child is born, I'll make arrangements with a good family in the country. Then you'll be free of it. You and I will not talk again, or meet again. We will communicate only by letter on matters pertaining to that child. Good day to you."

As he said this last, he put his hand under her elbow and dragged her up.

She resisted, her eyes wide. "And I am to be treated thus, cast aside, while you show preference for that whore. Are you mad? She's nothing, a nobody!" She scoffed spitefully, "Apparently you like that. Is that why you couldn't do it to me? I was not common enough?"

"You were not enough of anything, madam."

She cursed at his absent mistress with filthy words. Little drops of spittle sat upon her broad, overblown lips, put there by each strident consonant.

"For your information," he said evenly, "that woman you insult is the daughter of a respected sea captain, a good man who is also my friend."

"Daughter of a seaman?" She sneered. "Certainly not high enough for a Swafford."

"On the contrary, she is above me and beyond me. Whichever

mischievous imp dropped her in my lap, I am eternally grateful to it."

"She's a little slack-jawed slut, who couldn't string five words together when I met her."

In the process of pushing her through the door, he stopped. "You met her?" he demanded. "When?"

"Weeks ago when I came here. Did she not tell you?"

He and Gregory exchanged looks, both puzzled and annoyed. Thinking back, Griff recalled Maddie's odd behavior. Hiding herself away. Sulking.

"No," he said steadily. "She didn't tell me." There were, of course, many things she didn't tell, many secrets she kept.

Isabelle exclaimed in disgust. "She's a peasant."

"We're all equal inside, whether we dress as prince or pauper."

"She is not the same as me."

"I believe we've already ascertained that much." He paused. "Tell me one last thing. Was it Wickes's idea or yours? Sadly, I lost my patience before I got the full truth out of him."

Her proud lips parted, those cat-like eyes lengthened. "It was solely his idea. As he said, if you were dead you couldn't deny paternity, could you? Of course, I gave you the chance of sharing my bed first..."

For a split second he was confused, having questioned her about a different crime and now hearing confession to another. He stared at her, working the facts through his mind, reading it now in her malevolent stare. She continued, "If you were dead, as Wickes said, that would improve matters. A little powder slipped into your drink..."

Always aware she hated him, he'd never thought her capable of murder. He'd underestimated his wife. She'd wanted him dead before she birthed her child, which she could claim as the rightful heir to the title, the estate and the Swafford fortune.

Suddenly he remembered Madolyn the night before she left, warning him about Wickes. He thought back to that night in London, the jug of wine left in the annex, and later, the sly way Wickes glared at the wine stain and the emptied jug, trying to measure how much was wasted, how much drunk.

Madolyn had saved him that first night with her clumsiness. The very next day, he'd taken her off into Dorset, thwarting any further plan Wickes might have had to poison him. No wonder the sniveling fellow was grumpier than usual when he'd arrived at Starling's Roost with the boxes of new gowns. He must have wondered why the earl had disappeared from London with no warning.

His disgusted gaze returned to his wife's quivering lips, bile rising in his gut.

"Then you were already pregnant when you came to Whitehall. When I declined your begrudging offer to fuck me, you decided to have me poisoned--a preferable option-- so you could still claim the child as my heir. If I was dead I could hardly protest, could I?" The truth came in like a great wave, clearing out the muddled ideas and doubts. "And you have the gall to insult that woman, who may be a sailor's daughter but never meant to harm anyone or anything? Good God, you disgust me!"

She spat in his face. "I told you--it was Wickes' idea. I never gave him permission to proceed. You can never prove I had any part in it." Sadly, she was right. He couldn't prove her part in his attempted poisoning. Not with Wickes silenced forever.

Slowly he withdrew a kerchief to wipe away her spittle. "Don't ever let me hear of you within fifty miles of myself or anyone I care about, ever again." He gestured loosely at her belly. "For the sake of that child, I let you go now. The child is innocent in this. You'll remain free until the birth, but if anything happens to your child, you'll be arrested within the hour. Now get out of my house and my sight."

Instantly his shoulders felt lighter. As Gregory escorted her out and her screamed insults faded away, his spirits continued to lift until they were practically soaring. Striding to the window, he looked out on the smooth green lawns.

His breath caught, a sudden halting sound too loud in that empty chamber. With one hand, he wiped his face, quickly disposing of the hint of dampness which threatened his reputation.

"Sorry father," he muttered wryly, "but you always wanted me to be a man."

Today that's exactly what he was--his own man. Heaven and earth suddenly seemed a lighter weight to move than the burden he'd shifted at long last.

* * * *

She was feeding the pigs when a cart drew up before their gate. It had rained heavily the night before, leaving the ground boggy, the lane little better than a mud bath. Any cart and horses heaving their way slowly through it uphill certainly had a hard task ahead. The man steering the cart wore a hooded cloak, hiding his face.

"Good day, fair wench. Have you any supper scraps to spare a humble fellow? For payment I can entertain you with card tricks and juggling."

She recognized that deep, booming voice at once. Surely it was too good to be true. "Nathaniel!"

He tossed back his hood, revealing a familiar, dark, curly head and a broad grin stretching on like a lazy summer afternoon. A spark of gladness tore through her previously dour mood. Her cousin's smile was infectious, as always, and she ran to greet him. In days gone by, Nathaniel's many tales of adventure had been a bright spot on her horizon, back when she had to make do with hearing of his exploits and had none of her own. Now she felt frighteningly mature in comparison to how she was once. No more the restless, moon-eyed maiden, she tried to hide the change, for Nathaniel was extremely astute when it came to her wicked thoughts and notions. She feared he would uncover her secret love with one glance of his silver gray eyes.

"You are pardoned, then?" she asked when he set her down from a crushing embrace.

"Indeed I am!" He leaned over the side of the cart, folding back the hay-strewn blankets, revealing a veritable mountain range of casks and boxes. "And see here the gifts I bring for my family."

There were hard loaves of sugar, green ginger preserved in syrup, orange conserve, dried dates and figs, mustard imported from France, salted fish in wooden boxes, marchpane molded into miniature fruits and even rice, which they'd never had before as it was such an expense. Nathaniel merrily accepted blame for this excess, but Madolyn knew someone else was responsible, probably the same mysterious soul who'd arranged his pardon.

Proving her right, he suddenly handed her a wooden box. "For you," he whispered.

She opened it cautiously, finding inside a necklace made of silver daisies, their petals inlaid with mother-of-pearl, their yellow centers formed of amber gemstones. It was lovely.

"I don't want it," she snapped, her throat tight.

"Precisely what he said you'd say. I see thanks are in order."

Sullen, she muttered her thanks.

"Not yours, wench! Mine. I didn't quite believe him when he told me how you *persuaded* him. Now I see 'tis true."

"What did he tell you?" she demanded, closing the box before anyone else might see.

"He had no need to tell me much. It was written all over his face. And now yours."

With a sigh of exasperation, she assured him the earl was merely a slight acquaintance, nothing more than that, and she couldn't imagine why he thought such a gift appropriate.

"Maddie the Merciless." Nathaniel chuckled, one hand pressed to his heart. "I vow never to ask a thing about it, coz. To be sure, you must have your reasons for leaving the poor fellow licking his wounds and pining after you. Keep him dangling and he might send any number of gifts to satisfy your sweet tooth. Get what you can from him. I would, if I was you, coz."

Flustered, she exclaimed, "You know nothing about him, so you'd best keep your mouth shut!"

Laughing, he began unloading the cart.

Daisies, she mused, sneaking another look at the necklace. He'd remembered they were her favorites. He was indeed generous to an inconsequential scrap of a girl. Alas, she would never be able to wear it, for people would surely ask how it came into her unworthy hands, and probably assume she stole it.

What could she send him in return? She had nothing of value, and yet she should acknowledge what he'd done for her. The simple fact remained, whatever his failings, she did love the great, fat-headed oaf. She always would. And he deserved to know it.

CHAPTER 33
Midsummer 1563

It was a glorious sunny afternoon. The grass where she sat rippled lushly around her, speckled with buttercups and daisies in riotous abundance. Often in the afternoons she napped, and already her eyes closed as she lay back on her elbows, chewing a long strand of grass. Even the shouts of the dancers, recklessly flinging one another in circles, seemed a distant and leisurely lullaby. The low thunder of drums was almost soothing, the whine of the sackbut a lazy, winsome sound, like a bee drunk on malmsey.

She slyly caressed her stomach and wondered who her child would most resemble, Carver or Mallory? Poor Griff, she thought with a great surge of sorrow. Folk feared him or hated him, often only on the strength of gossip spread by people like Eustacia. His stubborn temper, his Swafford arrogance, did nothing to help improve that reputation, but Maddie, having witnessed his extreme generosity on more than one occasion, knew he was not always at fault.

He must have wondered what she meant by sending him her cockle shell on a leather string. Surely he would think it foolish, even childish. Of course, he was accustomed to finer gifts, could have any luxury he wanted.

Not that he'd ever sought luxury, she realized. Despite the title, he was a quiet man with simple tastes and no time for fancy clothes, at least not his own. If she saw him in the street, she would take him for a groom, or a farmer, or a carpenter perhaps, she thought, considering his wonderfully skilled hands and their attention to detail. She would easily mistake him for an ordinary man. As indeed, she had.

Her heart ached, missing him intolerably, but knowing there was nothing she could do to heal it, Maddie the Merciless conceded defeat.

She watched her sister dancing on the common with Nathaniel. The goodly warm scent of baked pasties drifted across the common, and once the sun set, it would mingle with the smoke of the bonfire.

Lifting her nose to the warm air, she sniffed. Lord, she was hungry, tired one moment and famished the next. She sat up, and suddenly the earth tipped and shook. Closing her eyes, she waited, thinking this simply another dizzy spell. But in the darkness, with her eyes shut, she saw the image again of the dancers on the common, and there, standing to one side, watching her...a man.

Her lashes fluttered open cautiously and she looked again.

Her heart vibrated like the wings of a captive butterfly.

It was him. The Beast. Standing there. Watching her.

Now he began a slow approach.

Oh. Her teeth hurt. He'd warned her they would, unless she curbed her appetite for sweet things.

Suddenly his imposing figure was intercepted by another and she scrambled to her feet, looking to escape.

* * * *

"Swafford!" Her father trotted over, one hand raised in greeting. "I'm glad you could visit."

"I had business in Norfolk, captain. Since I was passing, thought I'd accept your kind invite."

"We are indeed honored." Although the sentiment was warm, the captain's smile was not. In fact, he was unusually solemn. "You find us at our best today." He gestured to the dancers. "Shall you dance with one of our pretty maids? Or do you, like me, keep time like a deaf man?"

"I'm not much of a dancer," he agreed, wincing. There seemed little order to the steps, only a vast deal of falling down and laughing. It bore scant resemblance to a galliard, the one dance he'd learned.

Scanning the dancers, he found her, black hair flying as she clasped her partner's arms and he stumbled drunkenly into her. Catching Griff's eye, she instantly looked away. Several others on the common had noticed his presence and were whispering to one another, curious about the giant, ungainly stranger in all the finery. He felt ridiculously overdressed, and quietly cursed himself for the spur of whimsy which had induced him to heed Matthew's fashion advice. But what else could he have done? Having decided he should make an effort if he meant to go courting for the first time in his life and then realizing he didn't know the first thing about courtship, he'd been forced to rely on the opinion of his romantically inclined valet.

As the dance ended, the captain beckoned to his daughter and she sauntered over to where they stood, her hair loose and wild, cheeks flushed.

"You remember his lordship," her father said, nudging the surly wench with his elbow. "Curtsey, girl. Show some manners."

Saucy lips tightly pursed, she performed an extravagant curtsey, dipping low. Griff, who was unfortunately on his best behavior, had a disquieting view of a bosom even more opulent than he remembered. Pity he couldn't simply carry her off over his shoulder and have done with it.

"His lordship has a fancy to dance," said her father abruptly.

Tearing his eyes away from the woman before him, he began to protest, "But I--"

"My daughter wants a partner, Swafford."

Was that menace in the captain's tone? It was definitely new.

"As a gentleman, Swafford, you won't keep the lady waiting."

Nothing else to be done, he put out his hand, palm up. The captain, however, reckoned without his daughter's stubborn temperament.

"I've no shortage of willing dance partners, Papa," she said smugly, her blue eyes dismissive and amused. "And since I'm currently out of breath, I've no intention of dancing again yet."

He withdrew his hand and put both behind his back, squaring his shoulders. The captain glowered at his daughter.

Awkwardly, Griff fumbled for conversation, a skill he'd never acquired, having no need for it. "You are in health, Mistress Madolyn?"

* * * *

How strange it was to hear and see him attempt such politeness, as if they were phrases learned by rote. But though his words were civil, his eyes were not. Her hand moved to the nape of her neck, where she was warm and clammy. And beginning to itch. "I'm fair bursting with good health, my lord. And you?"

"I've been better."

"Oh?" She turned, lifting her gaze to his, hand still on her neck.

"'Tis but a trifling matter." He managed a tepid smile. "I will find the cure."

Her father waited for the conversation to resume, and then gave up. Complaining of a great thirst, he left them alone.

Madolyn made up her mind to make Griff speak first. It lasted approximately three seconds. "Why are you here, for pity's sake?"

His brows dipped. "Am I not permitted to go wherever I please?"

She shrugged, swinging her arms as she looked over at the dancers.

"I wanted to see where you lived." He bowed his head toward her slightly. "I wanted to see the place where such stubborn, recalcitrant women are born."

"And what do you think of us?" Looking up at him, the sun made her squint.

"I'm not yet decided."

Her arm accidentally knocked against his and she stepped away, self-conscious in her patched gown. Today he looked every bit the nobleman, from his fine leather boots to his plumed hat. Folk would speculate on his identity and why he talked to plain Maddie Carver. Wouldn't they be shocked to know the truth?

He fidgeted with his ruff, as if it was too tight. "I want you back," he said suddenly.

Shocked, she tried to calm the naughty, rebellious pixies dancing in her breast. She could not give this man an inch. Today she would be as intransigent as him. "Whatever our previous arrangement, I'm not your chattel. *That* is over."

His eyes darkened. "Because you got what you wanted? Perhaps now I want something from you."

"Your arrogance grows tiresome." She sighed. "Excuse me I--"

He grabbed her arm and she stumbled to a halt, laughing uneasily. "Folk are watching us, my lord."

Jerking away, she ran back to the dancers, leaving him there alone.

* * * *

As they readied for bed, Grace asked, "Who was that man on the common, Maddie?"

"No one," came the quick reply.

Sliding under the coverlet, Grace kicked her feet, seeking the warm patch under her sister. "Do not play the innocent with me, Madolyn Carver. What have you done to him? The poor fellow looks wretched."

"And so he should." She wriggled. "Stop it! Leave me alone."

"This is my bed too."

"There is no need to kick me."

"I didn't kick you, for pity's sake."

"Yes, you did. I'm all bruised. Ouch!"

"Hush, or you'll wake John," she warned.

Maddie turned back to study the darkening sky through the open shutters. "If you must know, his name is Lord Griffyn Mallory."

"The Earl of Swafford? Gabriel's brother? *The Beast?*"

Sighing reluctantly, she nodded. Grace poked her again with her toes and said, "He claims to be in love with you."

But he didn't believe in it. He'd told her that. "He's a damned liar!" Maddie stared hard at the purple sky, until she began to feel there were no walls around her, as if she floated in the air, like another tiny, winking star. "What...what did he say?"

"Just that. He's a man of few words, it seems. Asked if I was your sister and informed me he's in love with you. He seemed to think I might advise him on how best to rectify the matter." Grace sat up, plumping her pillow. "I told him he should cast his eyes elsewhere."

"Good," she snapped, to hide her trembling lip.

"Believe me, I said to him, my sister leaves dozens of befuddled men in her wake. Good Lord, said I, you're not the first, poor, cocksure fool to think himself in love with my sister, roll up the lane from Merryweather's with cider on his hot breath and start yelling for our Maddie."

"Thank you, sister. Now what must he think of me?"

"I did it for your own good," Grace teased. "'Tis what you always said to me when you sent my suitors on their way."

"Well, I'll leave you to your own devices from now on," Maddie vowed solemnly, flinging herself on her back.

After a brief pause Grace continued slyly, "Ask any young man hereabouts, I said to him. Many have lost their heart to Maddie, at one time or another. Who would not? What man in his right mind wouldn't love my sister?"

Maddie turned her head against the pillow. "You said that about me?"

Grace took her warm hand and squeezed it gently. "He's in love with you."

"Nonsense. He's angry because I defied him. I refused to do what he wanted. No one is allowed to defy the Beast."

After a pause, Grace said quietly. "Are you afraid to let him love you, Maddie?"

"Afraid?" she scoffed. "Why would I be?"

"Because you must always be in charge."

Flinching, Maddie tried to take her hand away, but her sister kept it.

"He's a strong man, I can tell. You met your match, Maddie. No more boys who let you take control, but a real man with a will of his own, a man who doesn't need a partner in crime, or a nurse, or a tutor."

"Ha! That's what you think."

Grace chuckled. "He wants to love you, as a deserving woman should be loved. You're no carefree, grubby-kneed urchin anymore, sister. Time to grow up and face the future. Where is your indomitable Carver courage?"

Rolling onto her side, she drew her sister's hand to her belly. "'Tis here. I'm saving my courage for her."

"Oh...Maddie!"

"Don't lecture me, Grace. I couldn't bear it."

Grace sat up, quickly practical. "Does he know?"

She shook her head. "Like most men, he never troubles himself with inconvenient matters."

"He *should* know."

Sounding much braver than she felt, she replied, "This is my babe. Mine. As if I would ever let him get his hands on my child. To raise it as he was raised? Miserable and unloved? Never. It's naught to do with him. And he's--" she broke off, unable to speak of his wife.

"Naught to do with him?" Grace exclaimed. "Do you claim an immaculate conception?"

"Stop. I will not have my condition discussed"

Grace shook her head."Such bosom-clutching dramaticals, Madolyn Carver.I see that your adventure has not changed you that much.Close the shutters.It's too cold with them open."

But Maddie was too hot with them closed, so she gave up her half of the coverlet, as long as Grace agreed to keep the shutters open. They were quiet for a while, Maddie listening to the breezy creak of the elder tree by the dairy.

"I don't know why he came here." Maddie yawned. "He won't have his wicked way with me again. From now on I'll remain celibate."

"Glad I am to hear it."

Although Maddie pretended to be asleep, her sister must have seen the blue where her eyelids were not quite closed, for then she exclaimed under her breath, "Celibate, indeed."

CHAPTER 34

After a lengthy night of celebration at the local tavern, their father rose late the next morning with a sour stomach. When their mother complained he should know better at his age, he assured her the day he listened to one of her lectures he'd be in a wooden box and why could she not hold her tongue like other wenches? She threw a ladle at his head, he pulled her into his lap for a kiss and she cursed at him, none too convincingly. Maddie exchanged a smile with her sister, for this was how their father behaved when he knew he was in their mother's bad books.

"What's so funny this morn?" their mother asked.

"Naught," Grace replied, while Maddie attempted to stifle those chuckles.

Their mother scowled. "I wish someone would share a jest with me."

Captain Carver reached for her hand. "I'll share one with you, my love."

"Oh?" she snorted. "A jest you heard at Merryweather's last night, no doubt. And not fit for the ears of children." But she let him keep her hand. "What then? Do tell."

He paused a moment, looking around the table at his greedy offspring, until his stern, blue regard settled upon Madolyn. "One of your daughters is to be married."

The fire in the hearth spat and crackled. One of the dogs scratched lazily. Outside, in the yard, the hens cackled.

"Is that not a fine jest?" he added.

Their mother turned slowly in her chair to look at Madolyn.

"Not me," she blurted. "I know nothing of it."

"What man is this?" her mother inquired.

"There is no man."

"Oh there's a man all right," said her father. "At least, he is one for now, unless I decide to castrate the bugger."

Madolyn stood swiftly. "I'll gladly do it for you."

"I thought you said there was no man." Her mother tried to follow.

"And indeed there is none." She panicked, thinking he would take her child away. He might even have her arrested for anything, she thought suddenly. Oh Lord! She was a ruined woman, a scarlet hussy bearing an illegitimate babe. And all because he'd once gazed upon her with those pitiful, sad-puppy eyes.

The entire family looked at Maddie the Merciless, she who never succumbed to any man and was never at a loss for argument--or for a cause.

Captain Carver leaned back in his chair, making it groan as he stretched. "We'll see what he has to say for himself, won't we?"

"I care not one whit. Whatever he has to say. Whoever he is."

Abruptly discarding his casual demeanor, her father sat bolt upright and roared down the table. "I'm the one who makes the decisions in this house, daughter!"

Little John burst into tears, Grace spilled the breakfast ale she was pouring and Nathaniel, who'd been half-asleep until then, woke with a start and nearly fell out of his chair.

Dropping like a stone, Madolyn sat, hands in her lap. Knowing she'd disappointed her father, fear and grief flowed like cold poison into her blood. She thought it would stop her heart completely.

"He'll be here in half an hour," he growled. "I trust the rest of you can find tasks out of the house this morn?"

Without a word, they got up from the table, even with their breakfast unfinished. Her mother lifted John from his chair and before she left the room, sent the Captain a warning message with her eyes. He nodded to her, and she slipped out silently, closing the door behind her.

"You always wanted adventure," he said, his voice lower now, his usual steadiness returned.

Madolyn looked at her hands. "And now I pay for it."

"Was it against your will?"

"No."

"Then I'll not hear another complaint from you," he muttered. "If your lot is distasteful, 'tis no fault but your own. I knew the moment I saw those gowns...didn't want to believe it of one of my daughters. I should have known you'd be the one to cause me grief sooner or later, and now he's come for you. Seems his conscience wouldn't let him rest."

She refused to believe it. He'd told her, in no uncertain terms, his world could never be changed. "He has a wife already, Papa! Even the Earl of Swafford can't have two wives."

"He tells me that marriage is to be annulled."

She clasped her hands tightly in her lap. "Annulled?" He wouldn't go to those lengths for her, surely.

"He's set on having you," her father remarked, bewildered, as if it was such a puzzle why anyone might want his most troublesome daughter.

"He'd have to get me cupshotten and drag me to the chapel door in chains. I'd rather join a nunnery! There are some still standing."

"A nunnery?" her father chortled. "Not a silent order I presume."

"I'd rather marry our goat. At least *that* beast has a heart."

"I'll bear it in mind if we get desperate, but one way or another, you'll be made an honest woman before you loosen your laces another inch for that babe."

Alarmed, she caught her breath.

"Did you think you could hide it from your mother?"

Inwardly she cursed her own stupidity.

"His Lordship Fancy Breeches came to me at Merryweather's yesterday eve--face like a smacked backside, babbling a sad tale about how he cannot bring himself to live without you. Apparently he'd thought he could and quickly found he couldn't." He sniffed disdainfully and began cracking his knuckles. "Thought he could take his pleasure from a mere sailor's daughter and pay no consequence. Like any rich man, he expects to get what he wants, but he comes up against me this time."

Crossing quickly to the fire, she sat on the old settle and closed her eyelids over scalding hot tears.

She was Madolyn the Merciless. She would survive this.

* * * *

She'd not forgotten how he filled a room with his presence. Her father was not a slight figure, but Griff exceeded his height by several inches and was forced to bend his head under the low roof beams to fit inside their house.

He avoided her gaze at first, for his attention was solely on her father.

The captain waved him into a chair. "And I thought you would never be troubled by a woman, Griff? Is that not what you once told me?"

He paled. "You make sport of me."

"Who is she then? I'm curious to hear about this wench of yours, the one you said would never exist."

"For a long time I knew her only as Limpet." He fired an accusing glance in her direction. "Now I know her as Madolyn Carver, captain. Your daughter." Falling into a chair, he sprawled there, long legs spread out, spider-like.

The memory of his strength and the glorious weight of his body over hers...it was too much and she couldn't sit still.

When she got up to leave, her father bellowed at her to fetch two mugs of cider from the pantry, adding, "You can stay put and hear what the fellow has to say, same as I must, since you got us into this mess with your jiggery pokery!"

Stomping down into the pantry, she kept one ear open, undecided whether she was most angry at him for being there or at herself for those instant lusty imps careening merrily through her womanly parts. She was indeed a dreadful sinner to think of such things now.

In the main room of the house Griff continued haltingly, "Your daughter has turned my life upside down and inside out."

She shouted from the pantry, "Of course, 'tis all my fault!"

"You stay mute, girl, until someone asks you a question," her father bellowed, "then you answer. See how it works?" When she emerged from the pantry with their cider, he was scowling, ready to snatch the tankard from her hand.

"I want her back." Griff reached for the other tankard, his fingers briefly touching hers. "I want your daughter, captain." When he looked up at her, emotions she didn't think he possessed poured out through those eyes. Before the tide swept her away, she stepped over his long limbs and hurried back to the sanctuary of the hearth, where she occupied herself stabbing at the fire with a poker.

"She put you through battle, lad." Her father sighed, suddenly genial again. "Mayhap you're better off without her."

Griff was adamant. "I want her. I don't take these matters lightly and I told her that when she first seduced me." Ignoring her indignant, horrified protests, he added, "She was a maid when I met her, captain...she's my responsibility now." When his eyes met hers again she saw the wicked glimmer. "She was mine first. She'll be mine to the last."

Her father set down his tankard, rested his large, callused hands on his knees and said gruffly, "Fine poetry, Swafford, but the fact remains-- you deflowered my daughter! Before you go around claiming ownership, an apology is in order."

Madolyn poked at the fire. "Apologize? Ha! He doesn't know the meaning of the word."

"I'm sorry, Captain Carver. I don't know what else I might do to make recompense, other than to insure your daughter's future happiness with my very life. I mistreated her and insulted you as her father. For this I do apologize."

Shocked, she looked over her shoulder. Surprisingly the great fool didn't explode into little chicken feathers, when she'd expected any confession of fault from his lips to cause no less than his immediate demise.

He added grimly, "I wouldn't blame you for taking a knife to my throat, captain."

"So I can hang for it? No. But you're lucky, Swafford. I'm an old man, not the fighter I once was, or else you'd be picking the skin of my knuckles out of your noble teeth. However," abruptly he switched again into the role of friend, "knowing my daughter, I daresay she had a little to do with it. The image of her mother, reborn and worse."

Madolyn's protests were again ignored and the two men continued discussing her fate.

"I'm to blame, captain. I should have known better, should have acted like a gentleman and not…not…" He couldn't finish his sentence.

"Should have, could have. Won't help you now will it?" Her father was pragmatic, and Maddie suspected he enjoyed himself. After all, it was not every day he got to hold a man like the Earl of Swafford at his tormenting mercy. "I remember," he said slowly, eyes agleam with mischief, "you vowed to me, not long ago, that you liked your life without a woman anywhere near it. In fact, you were so sure of your immunity, you promised me a few ales if you ever fell prey to that particular fever."

Griff nodded gloomily. "That was before I met your daughter." He looked over at her as she prodded the fire with another burst of furious energy. "Whatever it costs me. Name your price."

"As if I could sell my beloved daughter…"

"You once described her to me as a *bad penny*, captain."

"Aye, she's a mouthy girl with more spirit than sense."

"Papa!"

He continued breezily. "I can't merely give her to you." He waved his tankard. "Can't trade my daughter because you take a fancy to her. I daresay your ancestors got away with such in the past, but this is the modern world."

Apparently confused by these rapid changes in her father's attitude, Griff scratched his head. "I thought you liked me."

"Aye. Before you ruined my innocent daughter."

"You admitted it was probably as much her fault as mine!"

"I said she might have had something to do with it. *Might* have. A little something."

"She seduced me the moment we met."

"Lies!" she yelled, swinging around, brandishing the poker. "All lies! Papa, don't believe a word he says."

Her father sat tall, putting on a solemn face again. "What would my little daughter know about seduction?"

"Plenty," Griff said dryly.

"She's naught but a child!"

"She's very much a woman, captain. You speak of her as if she is a child still, and I daresay that's partly at fault for her mischief."

"And how you dealt with her is any better, is it? She left you weeping sorry tears into the malmsey, Swafford. Must not have liked your methods either."

"I made a mistake."

"Aye, you ruddy well did," her father bellowed, "*your lordship.*"

"I want her, captain. I mean to have her."

Typical arrogance, she mused. What would he do? Drag her out by the feet? Let him damn well try it. Her heat thumped with such hard and rapid force, she feared it might loosen her teeth.

"What of my daughter's wants?"

Griff swept his fingers through his hair, groaning. "In truth, I don't know what she wants." He cast her a sly glance. "I never got much sense out of her."

"Well, Maddie." Her father stood suddenly and strode to her side, finally done with his game. "What do you say? Shall you hear him out?"

She replied peevishly, "Let him speak then. I suppose I might be amused by it. But I haven't got all day. Some of us have work to do." She swung the poker in readiness. "We can't all be bone idle because we were born filthy rich."

Still in his chair, Griff shook his head slowly, hands on his broad thighs. "See, captain? Here is the danger of raising a woman to have her own opinions."

Laughing benignly, her father reached for an hourglass on the mantle and turned it. "I'll give you one hour to woo my daughter. If, at the end of that time, I find her still holding you at bay, you'll leave this house, Milord Fancy-Breeches, and never see her again. Am I understood?"

She thought Griff would leave the house in a fit of temper. It seemed doubtful anyone had ever spoken to him the way her father did and got away with it, but he stayed, battling his most persistent demons.

"And don't come to me moping and sorry if she gives you short shrift for your trouble," her father added with a sniff. "I give you a second chance, which is more than I give any other wastrel or addle-pated bugger who comes to court my daughters." He wrestled the poker from Maddie's hands, strode over to where the earl stood, slapped him hard on one shoulder and muttered dryly, "Good luck to you, Fancy-Breeches. You'll need it."

Keeping the poker, he left the house, joining the rest of the family outside in the yard, where they no doubt pretended to be occupied with chores, while secretly listening for the sound of thrown plate.

CHAPTER 35

Madolyn considered making a run for the door, but knew Griff would get there first.

"I thought I'd never forgive you for what you've done to me," he said thickly. "Alas, now you're here in front of me again, and so damnably lovely. By God, I could forgive you any sin, do anything for you, walk through fire if you wanted it."

Through the window over his shoulder, iron gray clouds bubbled, surely a fearful omen. "There's no need to get excited," she muttered, not certain he was entirely sober. If he started reciting poetry, she feared she might laugh until her knees gave out.

He suddenly reached under his collar to show what he wore around his neck--her little white shell on that leather cord. "This told me I might have a chance, Madolyn. Perhaps you forgave me."

Embarrassed by the humble gift, she looked away. "I wanted to send you a token in return for what you did for Nathaniel. It was the only thing I had."

"I've worn it since the day it arrived. It gave me courage. Now here I am."

He caught her limp hand to pull her closer, but she resisted, still not certain what to make of this. It was unsettling to have him in her world, where everything seemed cramped suddenly, plain and humble. She was aware of their stockings and petticoats hung to dry before the fire, of wooden toys scattered across the floor, her own sewing box, open and messy from her earlier hasty search of an errant pincushion. Ah, but this was her life, her family, and there was nothing shameful in it. The truth now was laid open on all sides.

Outside the window, clouds churned. The first sprinkle of drops tickled the crooked lattice panes.

"My heart aches, Madolyn," he whispered, trying to move her closer.

She was skeptical. "How can a stone ache? Are you sure 'tis your *heart* aching?"

Now his lips were tight again, the way she remembered them.

When she tried to pull her hand away, he clung to it, rendering her fingers numb, not knowing his own strength again. "Release me at once," she hissed. "I have many important things to do and...and my family waits in the rain. You embarrass me!"

"Do I? This is nothing to what I'll do if you refuse me."

"I'm sick and tired of your commands."

He wound both arms around her. "Now 'tis my turn to cling to you, eh, limpet? We'll see whose will is strongest."

"Remove your filthy, villainous paws from my person!" Alas, even as she cursed, she felt the old, impish feistiness which no amount of somber warning ever tempered. With his bastard babe already flourishing strong in her belly, she thought in despair, one would think she'd learned her lesson. It seemed not.

Rain spat harder against the windows and rattled down the chimney. She knew what her family must think—*trust Maddie to choose a rainstorm for her great moment*. All they needed now was hailstones and lightning.

"What about your wife?" she blurted. "What about the child she carries?"

He sighed, half laughing. "Why did you never tell me she'd been to the house? For pity's sake woman, I could have told you that child wasn't mine. I haven't shared a bed with her for almost eighteen years."

"Oh." Her heart slowed.

"And the marriage will be annulled, as it should have been years ago." He brought her hand to his lips, his other arm still around her waist. "Now, how shall I court you, Madolyn? What do I do?" He pressed his lips to her knuckles. "This is new to me, you see. I've never been in love before, but I'll learn, if you teach me."

* * * *

He looked down at their joined hands, marveling at how her fingers were dwarfed by his. So much of importance to him was contained in this one, compact, curvaceous package it seemed impossible she was not ten feet tall with the hands of a giant.

"You're not the only one with much to learn, Griff," she admitted ruefully.

By now he knew it was as rare for her to admit a weakness as it was for him. Hope swelled in his tentative heart. "You should have told me about Wickes."

"I thought you'd be angry with me."

Whenever he pictured Wickes sneaking into her room with foul intent, fury writhed in his gut, but it hurt even more that she imagined he would blame her. He'd been a fool, trying to prove himself impervious to love. Because of it, she could have come to harm, afraid to go to him for help.

But as he told her, this was new to him. He was learning as he went. It was like walking in the dark with wide-open eyes, waiting to stumble, yet with her hand in his they would find their way. "No more secrets," he decreed. "And never fear to tell me anything."

With a teary smile, she nodded.

"Come home with me," he whispered, "or must I steal you away on my horse again in the night?" Before she could answer, he added, "I've a few things to tell you which might sway your decision."

"Oh?"

"It may interest you to know, Matthew has come back to his post."

She smiled. "Good."

"And there is more," he said smugly.

"More?"

"I am minded to move the chairs in my bedchamber from the fireplace to the window." He paused. "Only for the summer. One change at a time. It's a start, is it not?"

Now she laughed. It was a melodious sound he'd missed these past weeks without her. "Indeed, I wouldn't want you to overdo it, sir."

Encouraged by her smile, his words flowed freely at last. "Madolyn Rose Carver will you allow me to take care of you now?"

She looked nonplussed for a moment.

He waited, trying to be patient, trembling with the effort, dreadfully conscious of his ugly size and wishing he had smooth hands to hold her instead of two great, clumsy claws.

"Griff?" she asked quickly. "What do you ask of me?"

"To marry me, of course." He felt the blood rushing out of him. "Did I not say?"

She stared. He could feel her heart thumping as she crumpled against him. "But...you need the queen's permission."

"Already granted. It gave her great pleasure. She dearly loves to win a wager." He grimaced. "She's eager to meet you. Seems to think you've improved me greatly, although I never thought I needed any improvement."

She was still breathing too hard. "And...children...you don't want..."

His arms tightened around her. "We'll have ten of 'em--a dozen even."

"I think one or two might be sufficient," she exclaimed, her tone bemused.

"As you wish. Whatever you choose, sweetheart, I'm at your disposal."

This rare humility only made her laugh, much to his chagrin.

"And when did you decide to love me after all?" she teased, lifting on tiptoe, sliding her arms around his neck. "When there was no one to quarrel with suddenly?"

His answer was somber, steady and from the heart. "There was never a moment when I didn't love you."

A fragmented breath of surprise and joy escaped her lips, before she could temper it with any ladylike decorum. She was trying, he saw, to restrain herself and keep that untamed spirit under greater control.

Dare he believe she tried to impress him? He didn't want her to change, not ever.

"Madolyn, you needn't--"

"Do you mind if they come soon, these children of ours?" she interrupted, stepping back.

"We'll begin immediately."

Taking his large hand, she laid it to her. "Good, because I'm afraid she couldn't wait. She takes after you and I."

Lips parted, he looked at his hand on her belly, and his world, which had fallen apart many times of late and been stitched back together in a new pattern, now tore apart again.

His child. Their child. Oh Christ! How did one raise a child? It seemed a formidable responsibility. He knew no one who did it without fault.

But her gaze was confident, merry, not in the least fearful. He envied her the boundless courage which let her leap where others faltered and doubted. He had much to learn from her and this child was charmed, protected by her love already, a priceless gift. His heart turned over in an odd sideways flip. *Their* child. It was almost too much to take in.

He felt a slow smile fumble across his face, unstoppable, like this woman who'd breached all his defenses and threatened to turn him into a quivering, love-struck milk-sop, if she didn't put him out of his misery. "Do you love me, Madolyn?"

She rolled her eyes. "Of course I do, for pity's sake. You've always known it. You were just too stubborn to believe." And she flung her arms around his shoulders, locking her fingers at his nape. "I'm so in love with you, I can't think of letting you go anywhere without me again."

His heart sang and he was only glad no one but he could hear the tuneless debacle. "That had better be a 'yes' to marriage then, madam."

Blushing, she rose on tiptoe to whisper in his ear. He leaned down to hear her reply, for it came in a timid voice, and then his shoulders moved, he bent his legs and lifted her off her feet, no more words necessary.

The door crashed open and her mother burst in, anxious to get out of the rain. "Honestly," she exclaimed. "Children! Both of you. To have quarreled and fought, when all you wanted was to be together. So much ado about nothing."

Behind her the rest of the family piled in, the romantic moment shattered.

No one saw that he held Maddie's hand, his finger stroking her palm. He felt more than a little proud of himself, especially when her father raised the hour glass to examine the sand, exclaiming, "Less than a quarter hour, I reckon. I underestimated you, Fancy-Breeches."

"I had to accept him," she complained, "because you were stuck out there in the rain. What else could I do?"

They all laughed, except Griff, who wasn't entirely certain she teased.

* * * *

Her mother decided she'd better put a proper distance between them. Of course, since the runaway filly had returned in foal, bolting the barn door now was too little, too late, but for the sake of propriety they were forced to behave themselves.

"Our guest shall sit at the head of the table," her mother said firmly. "And you will sit by John and keep an eye on him, if you please."

Oh, the indignity! To sit beside that five-year-old menace was almost more than Madolyn could bear. Thus she and Griff were separated by the length of a table and must be content with looking and smiling. She envied each morsel that crossed his lips. When he lifted his cup, she lifted hers. Then, watching her sip, he let his lips linger upon the rim of his cup. His eyes spoke volumes, none of them scriptures.

He loved her. The Beast, *her* beast, loved her.

She worried he might mention his wealth and title, those embarrassing matters, but he didn't mention them and was not in the least arrogant, even when John threw a piece of carrot across the table and it landed in his cider. He merely gave a pained smile, picking it out with his long fingers, listening to her mother and nodding, as if he gave her his full attention. If one didn't know any differently, one would think him quite a humble, polite, normal person, Maddie mused lovingly.

She wasn't itching anymore, she realized. He must have scratched all those itches for her.

"I daresay, Fancy-breeches," her father said, "you'll spoil my wretched daughter until she is even more intolerable." He waved his hand. "You'll pander to her every fool whim, no doubt."

"Captain, she has me utterly at her mercy."

Her father nodded, grimly reassured. "Aye. Don't say I didn't warn you."

When her mother asked how they'd met, Griff said simply, "I fished her out of the Thames."

No one in the family was the slightest bit shocked by this, although her father said he should have thrown her back in.

Maddie looked at Griff and felt her heart glow with a pleasant, comfortable warmth. She imagined him in the future, always relating that story to anyone who asked how they met. He would like to shock them no doubt.

"I fished her out of the Thames," he would say again, in that calm tone.

Many would laugh, as would their children, and most, probably, would never believe it. Unless, of course, they once knew her as Maddie the Merciless, before she became Lady Madolyn Mallory, Countess of Swafford.

It struck her then, for the first time, that she would be not only his wife, but his Countess. Suddenly she lost her appetite.

But then he caught her eye and beamed from ear to ear. It was all she needed to reassure her.

* * * *

He came upon her standing at the gate the next morning, staring at the house. Drawing close, he kissed the top of her curly head and promised she could return to visit often. She nodded. Although she would miss this place, she'd grown to love Starling's Roost too and the people in it. She would rather be with Griff and share his world, than live here without him. Her family would manage without her now.

Her new mission to love the Earl of Swafford, to protect him--and put him right, of course-- had begun.

"And my first son? How is he this morning?"

"Our *daughter* flourishes," she replied curtly. "Furthermore, I thought we might name her Eustacia, in my cousin's honor, since she's the reason we met." When she looked over her shoulder, the horror on his face was priceless. She laughed. "Oh Griff, I do love you, *ma bete*."

He smiled, relieved.

As he approached, he had his hands behind his back. Now he presented her with a rose, its stem wrapped in silk. It was one of those wild, wayward dark crimson roses that grew up the flint wall surrounding her father's property. The stems were thorny, discouraging the picking of those fragrant blooms, but Griff had never let a few sharp pricks get in his way.

"I wracked my brains to think of a wedding gift for my bride. What could I give a wench who turns up her pert nose at expensive gifts? So your father said I could take a cutting from the roses. Hopefully they will grow in Dorset soil as abundantly as they spread here, and you'll have a little of your home with you."

His thoughtfulness touched her deeply. She'd never expected a wedding gift. Until that moment, it had never occurred to her that he'd asked for no dowry. He'd accepted her as she was. She stammered awkwardly, taking the silk-wrapped rose from his hand, "I've nothing to give you in return."

"Madolyn, you're the only thing I need. You are more valuable to me, more precious, than any other gift in this world."

She wasn't certain she could handle this new and "improved" version of the man who'd once claimed she ruined his carefully ordered life. Must have had lessons before he came in search of her. She wouldn't be surprised to find a few useful phrases inked along one of his arms.

"Are you quite well, old man?" she asked politely. "You're not feverish?"

He grinned slowly, wickedly. "I'm bursting with health and vitality. As you will discover when I get you back where you belong...chattel."

Ah yes, there he was, after all; the arrogant, insatiable beast she knew and loved. But there was serenity in his face today, a happiness and hope it had never held before, and she was glad to know she had much to do with the transformation. There were a great many years of loneliness to make up for.

"I love you," he said. And when he gazed down into her eyes, she saw inside to where a new fire smoldered today. He was learning to let her in so she might tend it, finally.

Thankfully he'd not changed too much, however. Underneath that civilized, gentlemanly disguise, he was still her Beast. She wouldn't want him any other way.

ABOUT JAYNE FRESINA

I hope you enjoyed the ride with Maddie and Griff as much as I have. These characters will always have a special place in my heart, as they were some of the very first that ever slipped out of my pen. And yes, in those days, I scribbled everything by hand before I typed it up! Maddie's story has changed over the years, but those friends who read the first incarnation will recognize her and Griff immediately. Even with everything changing around them, they've remained the same. They are, possibly, two of the most stubborn characters I've ever met, although Maddie's little brother, John Sydney Carver, can give her a run for her money -- as you will see in *Once A Rogue*, the next book in this series. As for Maddie's daughter, Cate -- well, perhaps the less said about her the better. I'll let you read for yourself in *The Savage and the Stiff Upper Lip*. Suffice to say, Will Shakespeare had to get his inspiration for *The Taming of the Shrew* somewhere, didn't he? I'd love to hear what you think of Maddie's story, so please contact me through my website at www.jaynefresina.com. Thank you!

Jayne's Website:
www.jaynefresina.com
Reader eMail:
jaynefresina@gmail.com

WHERE REALITY AND FANTASY COLLIDE

Discover the convenience of Ebooks
Just click, buy and download - it's that easy!

From PDF to ePub, Lyrical offers
the latest formats in digital reading

YOUR NEW FAVORITE AUTHOR
IS ONLY A CLICK AWAY!

LYRICAL PRESS INCORPORATED
WWW.LYRICALPRESS.COM

Shop securely at www.onceuponabookstore.com

CPSIA information can be obtained at www.ICGtesting.com
Printed in the USA
BVOW071218120613

323114BV00002B/63/P